THE HAVANA FILE

A JACOB HUNTER THRILLER

DAVID ARCHER

DAMIEN WILD

The characters and events portrayed in this ebook are fictitious. Any similarity to real persons, living or dead, is coincidental and not intended by the author.

ISBN-13: 978-1-63696-469-0

ISBN-10: 1-63696-469-9

Printed in the United States of America

www.righthouse.com

www.instagram.com/righthousebooks

www.facebook.com/righthousebooks

twitter.com/righthousebooks

JACOB HUNTER THRILLER

The Kyiv File (Book 1)
The Bogotá File (Book 2)
The Havana File (Book 3)
The Amsterdam File (Book 4)
The Saint Petersburg File (Book 5)

PROLOGUE

HAVANA, CUBA

THE RUMBLE OF AN APPROACHING STORM ECHOED across the expanses of the Straits of Florida, a buffeting wind creating a mass of white-caps in the waters of Havana Port. A crack of thunder boomed, reverberating through the claustrophobic streets of the historic downtown district. He pulled up the coat collar to cover his neck from the slanting rain as he wound his way through the labyrinth of streets, then felt the reassuring hard steel of the Makarov pistol tucked into his belt. This was a mission too important to be delayed by inclement weather. He quickened his step.

THE DILAPIDATED BAR was tucked away in a gloomy alley, a flickering neon sign swaying above the doorframe. Inside was the rhythmic clink of glasses and murmured conversations, clouds of pungent cigar smoke and softly playing rhumba music. Despite the chic ambience, an air of growing unease hung over two men sitting at a corner table, hunched over their glasses of over-proof rum. The dim light struggled to cut through the thick smoke that hovered in a haze around them.

One of the men, Cristian Passo, once a respected Cuban intelligence officer, now a man-for-hire and occasional CIA informer, wiped his brow and glanced at his timepiece, a sturdy and reliable Russian-made Vostok amphibian diver watch. His contact was ten minutes late. But that was the least of his worries. Passo knew he was sitting on information that could tear apart Cuba's delicate relationship with its foreign allies and maybe bring him a windfall—or a bullet. It all hinged on whether or not the contact coming tonight would be willing to talk to the American.

Across from Passo, a man in a brightly colored Hawaiian shirt fidgeted with his drink, his eyes darting nervously toward the door every few seconds. Frank Cain, a journalist with a nice, safe life in Washington DC, was more than just uneasy. He was terrified. And with good reason. He had come to Cuba chasing the story of a lifetime—an audacious military operation designed to make the United States look like the worst bad guy among nations. Breaking this one would make him a modern-day Carl Bernstein, the man who blew the lid on Watergate.

Cain had a long list of contacts in the intelligence world who had pointed him to Havana. They'd whispered of a dangerous man embedded within the Cuban government, passing information to America's enemies for decades. He even posed a risk to his own regime. One of those contacts connected him with Passo, who claimed this dangerous man was working with China, perhaps Russia too, to stage an operation so bold it would throw the world into chaos. If Cain could expose it, his name would be on every headline from New York to Sydney. But first, he had to survive the night.

Passo leaned forward, his voice low, his English flawless and only lightly accented. "The man you're looking for, he's not just anyone. His name is Miguel Domínguez. A big shot in the government, very close to the top, but a traitor to his own country. He's the key." Passo tapped the table with talon-like fingernails. "For years he's been feeding intel to both the Chinese and the Russians for money. And now, together they're planning something bigger than anyone realizes. A false-flag operation—Bay of Pigs all over again. And of course, they want the world to think it's America pulling the strings. You follow?"

"Yes, I follow," Cain said impatiently. He then corrected his tone, which he realized had been sharpened by his anxiety. "It was us, after all, who tried and failed the first time back in the 1960s. And with this new president about to be inaugurated...man...this is huge." Cain's heart raced, but he forced himself to stay calm. Hand wrapped tightly around his glass, knuckles white, he asked, "And you're sure it's him? Domínguez?"

"I have no doubt. His father was of a hawkish disposition too, back in the Cold War. It runs in the family." Passo shifted in his seat, his gaze flicking nervously to the entrance. "But listen to me, Cain, you need to understand. You're playing a dangerous game. These people—they don't leave loose ends."

For a second, Cain pondered the wisdom of his decision. Then all doubts vanished: the fame and glory were worth it.

"There's a man coming tonight who can confirm what I say," Passo continued. "He will provide you with incontrovertible evidence. You must talk to him." He rubbed his thumb against his index and middle fingers. "And you will pay me for this tip-off as we agreed, *correcto*?"

Cain nodded, opening his mouth to reply, but before he could speak, the door to the bar creaked open, letting in a gust of humid, rain-soaked air. A figure stepped inside, silhouetted against the storm, water dripping off his long coat.

"That is not the man we are expecting." Passo stiffened. "We need to go. Now."

But it was already too late.

The newcomer crossed the bar with deliberate, slow steps. A lean and tall figure, he approached their table; water droplets flew as he ruffled his mane of dark, curly hair. A pair of cold eyes swept the room before landing on the two men. A glint of white teeth as the man smiled with satisfaction. Passo muttered a blasphemous curse and reached for the gun tucked under his jacket. Cain's pulse hammered in his ears as he struggled to figure out what the hell was going on.

"Cristian," the man said, his voice a predatory growl. "You been talking too much, *coño*. And to the wrong people." The man nodded at a stunned Cain, only now realizing that, apart from the profanity, the man was speaking in English. Which meant he probably knew who Cain was. Or at least where he was from. Not good. Not good at all.

Passo's hand was halfway to his gun when the man moved in a flash, faster than Cain could follow. A muffled shot echoed through the bar—a suppressed pistol. Passo slumped back in his chair, a dark red stain blossoming across his chest. His eyes, wide with shock, locked on to Cain's for a split second before going glassy and closing.

Cain leapt from his chair, panic flooding his veins. His mind screamed at him to run, but his feet remained glued to the floor. The gunman, calm as a lion sizing up its next meal, stepped closer. Cain could feel the walls closing in, the air too thick to breathe.

"You should have left this alone, *gringo estúpido*," the man said, raising the gun to eye level.

Cain instinctively ducked and turned, grabbed the chair he'd been sitting on, and flung it at the man. The spine of the chair struck the stranger in the left shoulder, momentarily throwing him off balance. Cain seized the opportunity to bolt.

His feet slammed against the uneven flagstone floor as he shoved his way through the crowded bar, muted gunfire behind him, the *thwut-thwut* sound of bullets ripping holes in plaster walls. He barely registered the shouts of protest from the bar's regulars as he crashed into tables and chairs, forging his way toward the back exit. Rain lashed his face as he burst into the pitch-black alley. His heart pounded so hard, he feared it would burst out of his chest.

He ran toward a light, not knowing where he was headed—only that if he stopped, he'd certainly die.

The narrow streets of the rotting neighborhood blurred around him. He darted between dilapidated buildings, his shoes slipping on the rain-slicked pavement. Even above the noise of the growing storm, he could hear heavy footsteps pounding behind him. Too close, too damned close. He needed to shake the man, but where could he go? Havana was an alien city. He was a recently landed foreigner with no idea where he could hide, his hotel miles away.

Up ahead, the street opened into an empty square. Cain spotted a small church looming in the distance. He sprinted in a straight line with a speed he never thought possible, then, with the robotic footsteps persistent behind him, ducked down another alleyway. Maybe he could hide in an alcove or a dumpster, then try the church? For a second, the world fell silent, no more pounding footsteps. He would escape. Yes, he was certain of it now.

But just as he was about to round a tight corner, a *pfft* sound, then an agonizing pain tore through his side.

Cain gasped and fell to the ground. He crashed against hard, wet cobblestones, a grunt escaping his lips. Instinctively, his hand pawed at his side. He looked wide-eyed at his shaking hand, slick with blood. He'd taken a bullet. He clawed his way up the bricks in the wall, each breath like a punch in the guts. No good. He collapsed again, the world spinning around him. This was the end of the road. He was going to expire here, alone in the deserted streets of Havana, with the truth eluding him, his quest unfulfilled.

The footsteps became audible once more, louder by the second. He glanced up, the shadow of his relentless pursuer loomed over him.

"This was none of your business, *gringo*," the man snarled. He aimed the gleaming pistol at the middle of Cain's nose. Just before he could pull the trigger, a distant shout interrupted the moment. The gunman hesitated, glancing over his shoulder.

A chance.

Ignoring the excruciating pain coursing along every nerve fiber, Cain summoned the last of his strength. He unleashed a side kick, striking the man in the patella and knocking him off balance. Cain again scrambled to his feet, a new boost of adrenaline giving him a surge of energy as he stumbled back into the broader alleyway. Blood poured from his gunshot wound and his vision blurred, but he plowed on. God—or fate—had sent him a lifeline.

Ahead, approaching headlights cut through the rain, getting heavier by the minute. As it passed under a dim headlight, he made out a big, clunky Buick. Gaudy yellow.

Cain waved his arms frantically, praying for another miracle. The car screeched to a halt, and the door flew open. A figure inside yelled in urgent, staccato Spanish, "*Rápido, súbete al maldito carro!*" but Cain only understood the first word. *Quickly*. It was enough.

He yanked open the door and flopped into the back seat, barely conscious, as the car sped away into the night.

The last thing Cain saw out the window before he slipped into unconsciousness was the gunman, bent over double and furiously rubbing his knee.

ONE

Fletcher's Tribeca converted warehouse was enveloped in a shroud of silence. Not an uncomfortable one: Skia director Grant Fletcher and his number-one agent, Jacob Hunter, didn't need words to fill the space. They were men cut from old-fashioned cloth, comfortable in their roles.

Fletcher's raspy voice finally broke the quiet. "Have a shot of liquor and relax. Should be a CIA job, but their Deputy Director Joel McDonald doesn't want to touch it with a ten-foot pole. He's flicked it to us. And by us, I mean you."

Jacob rolled his eyes and sighed at the '*I mean you*' cliché the boss busted out ahead of every assignment.

"This is a big mission, son." Fletcher offered a look of sympathy mixed with encouragement.

"Aren't they all big missions, Grant?" Jacob grinned, pouring himself a measure of Hennessy XO into a crystal glass. He didn't drink much; only with Fletcher, and when a mission demanded it. "Not sure I'm ready for this briefing. I'm still processing Zerina's death."

"Come off it, Jacob." Fletcher clipped the end off a stogie, lighting it with a silver Zippo. Through the smoke, he added,

"You're surrounded by death every time we send you out into the wild."

Jacob leaned back, eyes drifting to the stash of cigars. Without being offered, he plucked one from the wooden box. Fletcher passed him the lighter. With both puffing away, Jacob circled back to Zerina. "Will there be a funeral?"

"Yes. Three days' time," Fletcher replied, tapping ash into a glass ashtray. "But you won't be able to make it. Unless you pull off a miracle and wrap this mission up before they lower her into the ground."

"I'll do my damndest." Jacob shook his head. Zerina Mills had meant a lot to him, and she was a good friend to Irina. The woman had been a brilliant young agent, cut down in her prime by a relentless and incurable illness. Jacob's grief was real, but years of training kept his emotions in check. Irina, though? She'd cried for days after hearing the news.

Fletcher rubbed his prominent chin. "We'll have a private memorial when you get back. How's that sound?"

"Better than nothing, I guess." That was the eternal caveat.

Fletcher nodded sympathetically. "This one's going to take every ounce of skill you've got. And then some." He blew out a perfectly formed smoke ring. "Tomorrow evening, you're heading to where these delicious tubes of tobacco come from. Cuba. There's serious trouble brewing."

"What kind of trouble?"

Fletcher rocked back and barked a laugh. "That's the problem. We don't know exactly. We suspect it involves the Russians and the Chinese. The smart money is on a plot to bring down the US government, turn the world against us. More than it already is. They believe if it is to happen, it will be soon."

"How soon?"

"On or before Hannah McIvor's inauguration as this country's new president."

Jacob grimaced. "What's this prognosis based on?"

Fletcher leaned forward. "The murder of a man called Cristian Passo. He'd been drip-feeding information about this big operation to a CIA agent in Havana. Our officers over there took his claims with a grain of salt. Too far-fetched, they thought. Now he's been assassinated in such a clinical fashion, they're suddenly inclined to believe he was telling the truth."

Jacob's nostrils flared. "I know who Passo is. I remember seeing his name high up on a list of our most valuable assets in the Caribbean. A Cuban intelligence officer, right?"

"You remember correctly."

"He's supposed to have had a lot of pull with decision-makers in the *Dirección de Inteligencia*, or DI."

Fletcher shook his head. "Must have been a while ago you saw that list. You're thinking of the old Cristian Passo. He's now an ex-intelligence officer. A traffic accident last year took him out of the game. Spinal injuries. The state was supposed to look after him generously, but instead, they tossed him on the scrap heap. He's been living on a pitiful pension in a bolt-hole outside Havana. Plus the odd bit of chump change the CIA put his way."

"You're kidding." Jacob drained his glass and wandered over to the giant aquarium, watching the fish swim lazily. "He must have pissed someone off to be treated like that. I hope I'm better looked after when I'm retired from the game."

Fletcher smirked, admiring a chain of perfect smoke rings. "You don't need a pension. You've made enough money with Skia to buy your own third-world country."

"You don't know if I've lost it gambling." Jacob cracked a wry smile. "In fact, tear up my contract now, burn it in the ashtray. I'm ready to retire."

Fletcher laughed. "I don't need to remind you of the deal, do I? No get-out clause until..."

"Until I'm 55, get fired, or disappear." Jacob resumed his seat. "There's little I forget."

"That's why we hired you. Also pattern recognition. Your knack for languages, too. You're perfect in Russian and Spanish. How's the Chinese?"

Jacob groaned. "Not great. If I'm talking to a Chinese child, maybe I can order takeout."

"Luckily, you won't need it. The language, that is; not sure about the takeout. Seriously though, the Chinese diplomats and spies embedded in Cuba will have excellent Spanish. English and Russian, too, probably."

"Still, not knowing Mandarin is a big gap in my skill set."

"Chinese is a pain in the ass to learn, I'll give you that," Fletcher said. "But let's scratch it from your list for now."

"No, I'm going to learn it properly." Last year, Jacob had quickly reached fluency in modern standard Arabic. Surely, Chinese wasn't out of reach.

Fletcher nodded. "Might not need it now, but it'd be a good addition. You're the best we have. We could fire half the China desk and replace them with you."

"Stop it, Grant. You're embarrassing me."

Fletcher clapped him on the shoulder. "I enjoy embarrassing you. One of the perks of the job." He shifted his attention to a manila folder on the glass-topped table. "Let's get to it. Yesterday, a journalist named Frank Cain witnessed Cristian Passo's murder in a dingy bar in Havana. Cain miraculously escaped after Passo was shot at close range. The killer was gunning for him too, but he got away, picked up by a man in a Buick. Cain's description of the man driving the vehicle fits Raúl Espinosa, another deep-cover CIA agent. Unfortunately, Espinosa has gone to ground. Cain's being flown out under government protection as soon as he's fit to travel, but not before you've spoken to him. We've squared that away with the State Department." Fletcher paused for a beat, then said, "Cain's psychologically scarred by what he witnessed, so you'll have to tread carefully with him."

Jacob scanned the dossier, stopping at Cain's bio. "This guy writes pieces for the *New York Times*. Syndicated to a bunch of other outlets. I've read his stuff. Sharp, knows his way around diplomacy. If he says he was targeted for assassination, I'm inclined to believe him."

"Believe him after you've grilled him."

"Fair call." Jacob nodded. "Mind if I read the file a little more thoroughly first?"

Fletcher sighed, standing. "Go ahead. Nature calls."

With Fletcher out of the room, Jacob focused on the file. Clearly, finding Espinosa was paramount. Raúl Espinosa was a former military intelligence officer turned baker, a trade he learned from his late mother. The man had also been feeding the CIA low-grade intel for fifteen years. Now, apparently, he had something big to sell. The question was: why was he bypassing the CIA and using a journalist? In Jacob's mind, the answer was simple—money.

Fletcher returned, looking relieved. Jacob said, "So we're talking about a classic false-flag operation. Bay of Pigs II?"

"That's McDonald's take. To be certain, we really need to talk to Espinosa. More precisely, *you* need to talk to him. He's been refusing to spill the details or name names to his CIA handler. It's now clear he knew as much as Passo, but we're hazy on what the connection is. Looks like he must have known Passo, who in turn lured Cain into the vortex." He poured himself a glass of fresh water. "Like I said, Passo's intel was previously dismissed as fanciful. Now it seems he was too close to something. Based on what he'd already revealed, we believe the Chinese and Russians are involved in the plot. And someone inside the Cuban government is pulling the strings."

Jacob's brain processed the web of details as he glanced over the file again. The facts blurred momentarily, subconsciously pulling him back to a different puzzle—Sally-Anne Vincent. His high-school sweetheart. A loner like him. She had been too young, too innocent to die. Twenty years had passed since her murder, and still, no answers. A wound that refused to heal, a mystery that taunted him.

"Earth to Jacob Hunter." Fletcher clicked his fingers. "You good?"

Jacob blinked. "Yeah, just old memories creeping in." He poured another half-measure of cognac.

"Irina or Sally-Anne?"

A faint smile touched Jacob's lips. Irina, the IT genius he'd saved in Moscow two years ago, was as brilliant with code as he was with languages. They were fiercely passionate and surprisingly balanced, like two pieces of a puzzle that fit perfectly. She'd even come to understand his connection to Sally-Anne, the dead girl from his past. Now she was helping him look for Sally-Anne's killer.

"Both, in a way," Jacob admitted. "What's the timeline on this thing?"

"Unknown." Fletcher folded his hands together. "But we have to move fast. If there's a loose cannon in the Cuban cabinet, the situation for us is critical. McDonald's received reports that the Ministry of the Revolutionary Armed Forces, aka MINFAR, is at the heart of this."

"That's a worry. If something's cooking, that's a good place to hide it."

"Damn straight." Fletcher nodded as his cell phone buzzed. He scanned it for a moment, then handed it to Jacob. "From Langley."

Jacob squinted at the blurry image. "This is what they call grainy."

"Yes. But read the text."

Jacob read aloud. "Deputy Minister Miguel Domínguez snorting something off a prostitute's breasts in Budapest." He looked up, smirking. "This photo could be of anyone."

"It's worth investigating. Domínguez was seen the next morning talking to a Russian businessman—Vitaly Botvinnik. The Russian has a track record of arms deals with some nasty regimes, terrorist groups. He ain't too fussy about where he gets his money from."

Jacob tapped the screen. "Okay, now we're talking. And if

Domínguez is tied up in this, why hasn't the Cuban president fired him?"

"Kompromat, maybe," Fletcher said. "Or maybe he's got dirt on the president himself." He narrowed his eyes.

"Then why not eliminate Domínguez altogether? I imagine the leader of an authoritarian country could do what he liked with impunity."

"Good question. One I'm sending you to find out the answer to."

Jacob leaned back, a smile tugging at the corners of his mouth. "Your gut is not only slightly protrusive, Grant, but sometimes right. Think Domínguez is the key?"

"I believe so. He's linked to the old guard. His father was one of Fidel's foot soldiers. If this is a major false-flag operation and it goes forward, Domínguez will play a major role. By the way, I'm filing away that 'protrusive gut' remark to be dealt with at a later date."

Jacob grinned, his mind already creating scenarios of what might await him once he landed in Havana. "Anything else?"

Fletcher chuckled. "Of course. Your legend. It's one that's been nurtured for a number of years. You'll be undercover as a freelance Argentinian journalist called Manuel Vargas. Backstops are all organized, including a shit-ton of web pages going back a decade, photos, even some lifelike AI videos, a portfolio of articles you've written on a range of subjects." He handed Jacob an Argentinian passport. Well-worn with a number of stamps and a press visa.

Jacob flicked through the pages and snorted. "Perfect. Easy to pull off. *Yeah, right.*" His command of Spanish had gotten him through tricky situations on his last mission in Colombia and Mexico, but Cuba...that was like another planet.

"The visa in there is actually a real one. Proving your legend will hold up to the highest scrutiny."

"Comforting."

"It should be. It was issued by the Cuban embassy in Buenos

Aires. We had to pay for fast-tracking since the process takes weeks, usually. The forged papers used in the application did the job perfectly. You'll find it a lot easier to get access to Domínguez and others with that visa. Hopefully."

"A lot of effort's gone into this, Grant."

"For good reason. McDonald's worried this could blow up like 1961, only much worse. He wants the CIA kept out of it as much as possible. Their track record in the region is..." Fletcher trailed off.

"Terrible?"

"Exactly. So it's up to us."

"Of course. Because we don't exist, and if we screw up, there's no one to blame."

"That's the spirit, Jacob."

Jacob's stomach churned at the thought of another Bay of Pigs happening, only this time with Russian and Chinese involvement. It wasn't just dangerous—it was catastrophic. A misstep by him, failure to nip it in the bud, could reshape global alliances in a way the US wouldn't recover from. Allies would rip up long-standing defense treaties, pointing the finger at America as the 'aggressor' state.

"You'll start by tracking down Espinosa," Fletcher said. "I'm sure he knows more than what's in that file."

"Who's looking after me when I arrive?"

Fletcher squinted. "Looking after you?"

"Yeah. There's usually someone on the ground to pick me up, or at least show me around the place. I've never been to Cuba. Be nice to have a welcoming face at the airport."

Fletcher shook his head. "You're going to have to play detective for a while."

"The file says Espinosa's a baker. Surely there's details on his employment after he left the intelligence agency. Hang on a second." He thumbed through the pages and found an address. His bottom lip jutted out in a frown. "No record of him working as a baker anywhere. It's just taken as a given that he was because that's what he told the handler." Jacob cursed quietly. "Sloppy work."

"Talk to the journalist Cain. Get him to take you to the bar where Passo was killed."

"Doesn't he know the name of it?"

Fletcher shook his head. "Passo picked him up in a taxi they hailed on the street. It was dark, stormy. Cain doesn't speak Spanish, and he can't remember what it was called. He..."

"A dark and stormy night? Spare me the clichés."

Fletcher ignored the remark. "I'm sure with a bit of driving around, he'll remember something."

"Definitely worth a shot." Jacob nodded, his mind sorting through the web of connections. Cain, Passo, Domínguez. It would make a lot more sense once he was there. "I get the feeling I'll be chasing a bunch of Cold War ghosts."

Fletcher gave a nod. "History's got a funny way of repeating itself."

"I damn well hope not." Jacob closed the file, his mind shifting into high gear. Every mission had its risks, but this one felt different. "What about Irina? Are you giving her clearance to know about this case?"

"You bet. Use her skills however you need to. She's proven herself in terms of ability, discretion, and loyalty."

"She knows the drill." Jacob stood, sliding the folder into his jacket and tucking the expandable file under his arm. "She worries when I'm away, but she understands."

Fletcher chuckled, moving back toward the aquarium. "You two are a good match. She keeps you sharp."

"She does more than that." Jacob grinned. "But I'll keep those details to myself."

The moment of levity faded as Fletcher's expression turned serious. "This one's going to be rough, Jacob. There's a lot riding on it."

"I know. I've never set foot on Cuban soil. I've got a lot of reading to do."

Concern crinkled the corners of Fletcher's eyes. "If you get even the slightest sense this thing's about to blow—back off. No one's coming to save your ass if it all goes sideways."

Jacob nodded. "I'll keep that comforting thought in mind."

As he made his way back to his apartment, the lights of Manhattan reflected off the inky-black waters of the Hudson. The mission ahead lay out like a chessboard in his mind, but his thoughts drifted, as they often did, to Sally-Anne. The one puzzle he hadn't solved. Twenty years of searching, no answers. And now, another puzzle waited in Cuba—one that, if left unsolved, could blow up in his face. And the world's.

When he reached the front door, his phone chirped in his pocket. A message from Irina: *Feel like a late-night visitor?*

He grinned as he tapped. *If it's you, always.*

TWO

Jacob Hunter glided across the polished concrete floor like he owned the place. Producing the Argentinian passport earned a quick exchange in Spanish with the customs official. Was that easy, amiable encounter a good omen for what lay ahead? He could only hope.

Negotiating the packed halls of JFK Airport, his stride slow and steady, Jacob wondered whether the orchestrators of mischief in Havana would be easy to pin down. Fletcher's early-morning SMS flashed in his brain: *Find out who's behind it and what's planned, that's all you need to do. Do not engage in anything dangerous if at all possible.*

Always the same. Learn the details, pass on the information, let the other agencies do the wet work. He swore under his breath as he read the giant notice board to check the gate—changed at the last minute.

He spun around, dragging his carry-on suitcase behind him. Luckily, the gate change didn't require him to traverse the entire terminal—just a hundred yards or so. The final boarding call rang out. The stop in Canada was a pain, but there was no way around it. There were plenty of direct flights from major cities to Havana. Jacob wanted to fly via Miami—it only took an hour and 15 minutes—but Fletcher had canned the idea. Wanted to keep an extra degree of separation. *Then why not fly me to Buenos Aires, and from there to Cuba?* Jacob had asked. *I'm supposed to be an Argentinian reporter*. Fletcher said it would take too long. A fair point, and Jacob reluctantly agreed to the plan.

Fletcher's secretary, Susan Stonehouse, had come through for once. Almost. She'd managed to book a business-class seat on a direct flight from Toronto to Havana. But, as usual, there was a wrinkle: economy out of JFK to Toronto. It was only an hour and 50 minutes, so he'd grit his teeth and bear it.

Shuffling toward the gate in a long line of passengers, there was an insistent buzz in his pocket. He pulled out the cell phone —purchased in Argentina with an Argentinian SIM card, a ton of fake calls and texts in its memory—and smiled. He read the message in preview mode. The message: *Recoge leche de camino a casa*. Pick up milk on the way home. Which meant it was Irina. She'd changed her name to Irene Frobisher to blend into American society, but to Jacob, she would always be Irina Frolova. Sometimes Ira or Irochka, but never Irene. A 5-foot-4 ball of energy, she was a tech whiz trained at Moscow State University and had briefly worked at the Russian Ministry of Finance. A hacker's pedigree made in heaven. But Irina was more than that—she was his partner, both in the field and in the 'civilian' world. He found an empty row of seats next to the line of passengers crawling toward the boarding gate.

The coded message meant she wanted him to call from a pay phone. There wasn't one, so he pressed the calculator icon which brought up Skia's proprietary app that functioned like Signal or WhatsApp.

"Hi," he said, leaning into the back of the seat. His eyes constantly scanned the people around him. You never knew. "No payphones anywhere. They're becoming as rare as rocking horse shit. Everything good?"

"*Da, zaichik.* Yes, darling." Irina's soft voice reminded him of a tiny, vulnerable bird. It belied the fiery temper that simmered beneath. A hint of concern elevated her tone a fraction. "You know I worry about you when Grant sends you on these crazy missions."

"This one's more like a research trip," he soothed. "My job is to discover what's being plotted and by whom. Then report back with my findings."

"Every other time the same!" she snapped, switching from Russian to English. Her grammatical stumble made him grin. She only made errors when emotions got the better of her. "And like every time, again, bad guys will be—how do you say—gunning for your ass!"

He held the phone a couple of inches from his ear. A middle-aged man in the slow-moving line shared a look of understanding with Jacob. *My wife's a ball breaker too.* Jacob offered a thin-lipped smile and nod, then returned to the call. "I never take unnecessary risks, you know that. Everything will be fine, I promise."

Switching back to Russian, Irina said, "*Da, konechno.* Yes, of course." Then, lowering her voice, she added, "There's something I need to tell you before you arrive in Havana. It's important."

Jacob's mind jumped into high gear. "*Davai.* I'm all ears."

"I've been looking into Havana's surveillance setup. It's more sophisticated than we thought." He could hear her take a sip of something. "Cuban intelligence have beefed up their operations recently. With help from China."

"How do you know it's not Russia? They're the masters of surveillance."

"It's straight out of the Communist China playbook—super-advanced real-time tracking systems."

He shook his head, whispering, "How are they going to track me if I have an Argentinian SIM card? Or if I buy a couple of SIMs in Cuba to use in the cheap burner phones I've brought with me?"

"My recommendation—don't make international calls unless it's a life-or-death situation. If calling locally, use multiple SIMs, phones too. Use them only once if needed, then dispose of them. Better yet, use someone else's phone. With your memory, you don't need stored contacts." She paused. "Actually, ditch those burners when you can. Leave them at the airport. If you're selected for a random search in Havana airport, all those phones will arouse suspicion."

"Come on, Irochka. I'm an Argentinian journalist. I'd have a legitimate reason to have them. If the batteries die, where am I gonna get them in Cuba? Their shops are empty and—"

"There will be a black market for goods like batteries. If you have US dollars, you can buy stuff the locals can't. I was a baby at the end of the Soviet Union, but my parents told me lots of stories. Cuba today looks like a tropical version of the USSR."

"Tell me why I shouldn't use this phone. It's got the best encryption software on the planet installed."

"Doesn't matter. Yes, you've got end-to-end encryption with Şkia's messaging app, but it's not foolproof. Trust me, this is my area. Heard of IMSI catchers? Rogue towers? They can get into any phone from any country. And don't get me started on the facial recognition. Keep a low profile, especially when you first enter the country. It won't be easy to move around undetected."

Jacob frowned, glancing over his shoulder at the bustling crowds. "What kind of scale are we talking about?"

"Surveillance points at all key locations—airports, seaports, government buildings, tourist hotspots. You're tall and blond and—"

"Not anymore. Well, still tall, but I shaved my head this morning after you left."

"Hmm, I remember you doing that in Milan. It suits you. I was sorry you let it grow back." She paused a moment. "And wear a hat when you can. And sunglasses."

"I have been doing this a while, you know."

"*Da. Izvini*. Yes, sorry. And remember—keep communication to a minimum. Only call or text if absolutely necessary. Burners or not. Email from your laptop is safest."

He sighed, running a hand over his bald head. "I love that you worry about me. Don't. I'm a big boy, I know how to take care of myself. Anything else?"

"Just...be damned careful, Yakov," she said, using her preferred Russian version of his name. "You have no idea what you're walking into. And you're stuck on an island."

"I'm a good swimmer," he replied with a smirk. He decided to switch topics; anything to stop her worrying about him. Her son, Vova, had struggled emotionally since moving to America. Now there was some hope things were improving. "Vova's doing better, right?"

Irina exhaled loudly. "Much. Since you taught him those self-defense moves, the bullies have backed off. His grades are improving, and he's making new friends."

"The kid's got plenty of spunk. I'm sure he would've handled it, one way or another."

"I'm keeping a close eye on him. One of the bullies gives me the creeps. I wouldn't be surprised if he's planning something."

"I doubt it," said Jacob in his best reassuring voice. "Bullies are cowards. Once they're put in their place, they tend to stay there. If anything does happen, we'll move upstate together. Keuka Lake—three-bedroom, three-bathroom, five acres of land, views to die for."

"You know I can't agree to that right now," she protested. "I just got promoted, remember? Maybe in a couple of years..."

"Is it you or him that's the roadblock to moving?"

"Mainly me, but Vova too. He's a city boy; raised in Moscow and now getting used to life in Manhattan. I think he'd go crazy out in the wilderness."

Jacob scratched his head. "Maybe you'll both warm to the idea later."

"I hope so," she replied, though her frustration with the intractable situation was clear. "We'll see."

"Let's figure it out when I get back. You watch out for Vova. I'll handle Havana."

"Oh, Yakov," she sighed. "I hate to repeat myself, but please be careful in Cuba. If you let your guard down for even one second..."

The line at the gate was moving fast now. "I'll call you from Toronto. *Lublyu tebya*. I love you."

Jacob slipped his phone back into his jacket and double-checked that he had his travel documents ready and laptop charged for serious homework at 30,000 feet.

He was the last to board the plane, receiving a narrow-eyed, wordless scolding from the middle-aged flight attendant. He offered her a smile of contrition, which brought a reciprocal nod of understanding, her stiff hairdo unmoved. Inside the aircraft, he found a tight space in the overhead locker. Moving items fractionally left and right, he somehow squeezed in his bag. He grunted a greeting to a man with an unruly beard and a large stomach, then dropped into his window seat.

The flight to Toronto wasn't long—just over an hour and a half—but it would give him a block of time to study the files Irina had sent the night before. At maximum altitude, with his neighbor mesmerized by a cartoon movie playing on an iPad, Jacob opened his laptop. He'd already digested screeds of data on Cuban history and politics, but you could never know too much. Now he devoured even more information. Turned out Cuban politics was a maze of cronyism, corruption, and inefficiency. To be fair, Jacob mused, that was pretty much the model for most countries. It was only the extent that varied.

The operation he was tasked with uncovering would be military in nature. The search for the ringleaders would begin there. General Alejandro Muñoz Sierra, a man with an uncanny likeness to the late Saddam Hussein, commanded the Revolutionary Armed Forces. Perhaps Sierra, and not Domínguez, was behind it all. Would it be worth trying to get access to him? A day or two on the ground in Havana, along with insights from informers, would help him make that decision. Maybe journalist Frank Cain would have some ideas. Reporters were right up there with spies when it came to nurturing confidential sources.

But Jacob's eyes were naturally drawn to the rap sheet of General Miguel Domínguez. Retired from the military since 2005 but still using his rank as a title, Domínguez had attained the position of Deputy Minister of MINFAR largely by currying favor with the ruling elite. His father had been a close friend of Fidel Castro, a boon to his rise up the ladder. Today, Domínguez junior was within arm's reach of becoming one of those elites himself. A dogged and loyal believer in the Marxist-Leninist creed—at least outwardly—his motivations weren't entirely clear. If he was involved in the planned false-flag operation, and the shit hit the fan, his life would be over.

As the flight attendants trundled the drinks cart up the narrow aisle, Jacob waved away the offer of refreshments. An interesting detail had caught his eye. Irina had highlighted the fact that Domínguez had a relative in Venezuela, a niece, the director of an import-export business and a major figure in that country's oil industry. She was among the wealthiest citizens in a land of abject poverty. The file on Lourdes Domínguez made for fascinating reading. Fifteen minutes later, Jacob believed there could be a vital connection between this woman and the suspected Bay of Pigs II operation. Irina must have thought the same, as there was a note at the end. *I will follow this up in more detail. Your boss authorized me to contact the US Treasury Office on Terrorism and Financial Intelligence (OTFI) to see if they have anything on this woman. As soon as I get a reply, I will send you an encrypted email.*

A slurred voice jolted Jacob back to the here and now. He slammed closed the lid of his laptop, stuffed it back in its soft case, and placed it under the seat in front of him. It was highly unlikely his neighbor had a clue about what was on the screen, but there was no point taking a chance.

"Hey, man. This your first trip to Canada?" The scent of several days' worth of beer consumption topped up by a couple more on this flight wafted into Jacob's face.

"*No hablo inglés,*" Jacob replied, flashing the man a hangdog look of apology. Now was as good a time as any to slip into the role of Manuel Vargas.

"I'm in and out of the place constantly." The man continued waffling, oblivious to Jacob's apparent inability to converse in English. "Especially at this time of year. I'm a hockey junkie, can't get enough. Tonight I'm going to see the Maple Leafs and the Rangers. You like hockey?"

Jacob smiled grimly and shook his head and shrugged. In a loud voice he said, "No speak good English. Sorry!"

The man got the message, grumbled something under his beery breath, and fastened the seatbelt across his expansive girth. The captain announced that the plane was about to land, and Jacob gave a sigh of relief. He glanced out the window; below were snowy fields bisected by black ribbons of sealed road. You had to hand it to the Canadians, they knew how to do winter weather better than anyone. It was going to be hotter in Havana. Much hotter.

TORONTO PEARSON INTERNATIONAL AIRPORT, all shiny glass and steel, was considered a testament to modern architecture and transportation efficiency, but it left no impression on Jacob. To him, it was just another painful transit stop. Inside the busy terminal, he found a semi-deserted café. Its slim pickings on the menu and slack-jawed staff did nothing to attract customers, which was fine by Jacob. He ordered an espresso and a croissant, sat in a booth at the back, and opened his laptop again. The coffee and pastry were surprisingly excellent.

Irina had done her part and more. The files she'd compiled on Domínguez and the Cuban power structures were dense, but Jacob had a knack for sorting through the noise. He drilled down. Social interactions over the course of the last year between Domínguez and Vitaly Botvinnik, the man in the photos with

Domínguez in Budapest. CIA watchers believed Botvinnik was behind supplying illegal arms shipments to Domínguez, but so far, there was no proof. Except for photos of the two of them partying hard in Europe and the Caribbean.

Jacob chewed his bottom lip. Botvinnik was notorious for moving weapons into conflict zones under the radar. The connection between him and Domínguez needed fleshing out. His gut told him Irina was going to dig up something juicy on Lourdes Domínguez in Venezuela. As a businesswoman with 'explainable' wealth, she would be well placed as a conduit of dirty money going into Botvinnik's pockets and those of her uncle.

He closed the laptop. The flight to Havana was boarding in fifteen minutes. He called Irina one more time and told her to look at every conceivable angle. Had Domínguez traveled to Caracas recently? Had Lourdes visited her uncle on his home soil? Had Botvinnik been to either country and, if so, whom did he meet and what the hell had he been up to? She agreed to spend as much time on the task as she could. Which might not be a lot: she'd developed her own search engine that looked for content not just when you clicked a button but toiled away like a fishing trawler working 24/7. Any hits on keywords and phrases were converted into summaries and included in periodic reports. Jacob's brain was capable of a lot of things, but Irina worked on a different frequency altogether. At the end of the conversation, she again implored him to watch his back. Again, he promised not to take unnecessary risks.

The four-hour journey from Toronto to Havana gave Jacob time to meditate and mentally prepare for what lay ahead. A truckload of unknowns.

As the plane began its descent into José Martí International Airport, Jacob felt the old butterflies running riot in his stomach. A glance out the window: Havana sprawled out below, its pastel-colored colonial buildings disintegrating after decades of neglect.

After the cold of North America, the warm, humid blanket of air that embraced him as he stepped onto the bright-red skybridge came as a shock. Although the corridors were busy with passengers and there were no security measures in place different than those you would encounter in any airport, his senses were on high alert. Cuban intelligence was watching.

He waited his turn at the customs window as the officer processed a family of three. The formality was over quickly, and the man waved him to approach. Jacob handed over his Argentinian passport with as blank an expression as he could muster. The officer, a young man with sparse stubble and sharp eyes, gave it a once-over, looking up three times to make sure Jacob was the same person as that on the photo. "You are a journalist?" he said, more a statement than a question.

"*Sí.*" Never give more information than required.

"Here for the boxing tournament?"

Jacob shrugged. "I hadn't heard about it. Would it be worth my while attending?"

"*Por supuesto!* Absolutely! It's going to be awesome." The man grinned affably. "You should definitely try to go and then write a story about it." He looked both ways as if checking the coast was clear. "My cousin Manny, Manuel—same first name as you—is fighting in the welterweight division. He's going to KO the Russian *cabrón* into next week."

"I'll think about it."

"*Bienvenido a Cuba*. Welcome to Cuba," he said, still smiling. He slid the passport back under the partition.

THREE

He tapped on the passenger window of a parked orange taxi. The driver gave a nod and popped open the trunk from the inside. Jacob walked to the rear of the cab, closed the lid of the trunk, opened the rear passenger door, and placed his carry-on bag on the seat next to him.

The driver, wearing a pair of stylish eyeglasses, glanced at him in the rearview mirror, a friendly twinkle in his eye. The engine groaned as the car lurched forward, heading toward the heart of the city.

"What make of car is this?" Jacob asked from the back seat. "Never seen it before."

"*La mierda china, hermano.* Chinese shit, brother."

"Is that the actual name?" Jacob joked. "Chinese shit?"

The driver burst into raucous laughter. "Good one! No, it's called a Geely Emgrand, if you can believe it. What a stupid name! If you don't mind me saying, I'm concerned about the influence of China in my country. The Russians—bad. Chinese—worse." He laughed sarcastically, flicked on the turn signal, and moved onto the main highway. "By the way, where to?"

Jacob recited the name of the hotel, the Meliá Cohiba, located in the Vedado district.

"A swanky hotel. That's the wealthy part of town. You must be a celebrity. A boxing coach or official or something like that, right?"

Jacob laughed. "Nothing like that. I'm a journalist."

Pepe thumped the steering wheel. "I should have guessed!"

"You know, I've spoken to two people since I arrived just minutes ago, and you both mentioned boxing."

"*Sí, señor.* There's a big championship next week. We love boxing here in Cuba. Nearly as much as baseball and soccer. Our fighters have only recently been allowed to compete as professionals again. And they are winning in many weight divisions."

The man droned on for a couple of minutes about the country's love affair with pugilism. As they passed a line of old warehouses, windows broken and covered in graffiti masked by creeping vines, Jacob yawned involuntarily.

"Am I boring you?" asked the driver. "I apologize."

"No. It's fine." A thought suddenly occurred to Jacob. He was about to verbalize his idea when Irina's words of warning flashed like a neon sign in his mind. This super courteous and friendly taxi driver could be part of the surveillance. There were no obvious cameras in the vehicle, but that didn't mean they weren't there.

"You think that car behind me is a little too close?" said the driver. Without waiting for an answer, he added, "Could you turn around and give that *cabrón* the middle finger?"

The back of the driver's head grew brighter as the driver of the following vehicle flashed its high beam. Jacob's heart thundered in his chest as the headlights dipped and flashed high in quick succession. Then came the blast of a *woop-woop* siren, a blue light flashing atop the roof of the other car. Shit.

"*Momentito, señor.* It's the police."

Ten minutes later, they were on their way again. Jacob once again got the friendly and deferential treatment, while the driver was reprimanded for having a blown bulb in a tail-light. He promised to get it replaced first thing tomorrow, the answer earning him a handshake from one of the cops. Jacob's heart rate back to normal, he decided to throw caution to the wind. He had no idea why, but the man behind the wheel seemed like someone Jacob could trust—not with classified information, but at least to be discreet. He'd previously made good use of a cabbie and his connections in Mexico. Why not here, too? "Listen, *hermano*. I'm looking for a driver to show me the sights. On call for the next couple of days. Does that sound like something you might be interested in?"

The whites of the driver's eyes glowed brightly in the rearview mirror as he caught a glimpse of the wallet in Jacob's hand, pulled apart to reveal a sheath of greenbacks.

The driver pulled over and parked under a tree, spun around, and thrust out his hand, which Jacob shook firmly. "My name is Pepe Feliciano, and it would be my pleasure to be your driver."

"Here's a downpayment, Señor Feliciano."

"Pepe, please." He quickly made the two Ben Franklins disappear into the pocket of his shorts. Tears of gratitude welled in the corners of the man's big, brown eyes.

"If you can help me get a scoop, there'll be plenty more where that came from."

"I will do whatever I can, señor."

"Please, call me Manny."

FOUR

"What did you say? I'm not sure I heard you correctly."

"I said my knee will require treatment. I'm having trouble walking."

Miguel Domínguez's fingers twitched, the muscles in his neck tightening. Without warning, he hauled back and struck the man a fearsome slap across the face with an open palm. The blow landed with a sickening crack. The man's head rocked violently to the right, his neck snapping under the force. He couldn't shield himself—the gorillas, two hulking figures who smelled of sweat and moldy cheese, had a death grip on his arms, pinning him to the chair.

"Wrong, asshole!" Domínguez's voice rose, an ugly squeal. "Your knee will receive no treatment. You've already failed the first test, Simón. The mission was simple. *Too* simple, and you screwed it up."

Domínguez stepped back, wiping the blood from his palm onto a small towel, the fabric clinging to his shaking fingers. His thoughts raced in furious circles—everything had been set. The job was an easy one. *But Simón,* this fool who'd let arrogance cloud his judgment, had managed to turn everything upside down.

Domínguez barked a humorless laugh. "I'll give you this: you got half of it right. Passo had to die. But the real mission, Simón, was the American. *Him.* Your task was to take him out first. That was the deal. What the hell happened?"

Simón's lips trembled. "I don't know how it happened. Let me make amends. I can—"

"Tie him up!"

The gorillas worked quickly, using thick cable ties to secure Simón to the chair. His limbs were immobilized, the silence that followed heavy with anticipation.

"You two," Domínguez commanded, his tone cold and precise. "Go find out what happened to that damned nosy journalist."

The men nodded and shuffled out, their heavy boots echoing in the hall. Domínguez didn't watch them go. His attention was already on the third—a giant of a man, his leather gloves creaking as he slowly approached Simón. Each step measured. Purposeful. He slapped his hands together like a power lifter: once, twice.

"How far should I go?" he asked in a low rumble.

Domínguez slouched against the wall under a grimy translucent window. His eyes locked on Simón, and the words came without hesitation.

"Until I tell you to stop."

Simón, already battered and bloodied, tilted his chin upward and closed his eyes. There was no fear in his expression—merely acceptance. The kind that comes from a man who knows, deep down, he will pay the ultimate price for his grave mistake.

Twenty-seven minutes later, the door opened with a quiet creak; a petite woman in a white coat stepped inside. She froze at the sight of Simón's face—disfigured beyond recognition. Her breath caught in her throat; she quickly side-stepped around pools of blood and an assortment of teeth scattered across the floor. She bent over him, her hand tentative as she took his limp arm, fingers searching for a pulse that wasn't there. She glanced at Domínguez, her eyes wide with disbelief.

"A pity," Domínguez said. "He was one of our best." His gaze flicked upward, catching the twinkle of the naked bulb hanging from the ceiling, casting eerie shadows across the blood-slick floor. "Make the arrangements to have him taken to the morgue. We'll tell his wife it was a car accident."

She bowed her head, her hands trembling as she murmured, "*Sí, Señor General.*"

When she was gone, Domínguez remained to gather his thoughts, staring at Simón's lifeless body. Anger churned deep in his gut, but there was no time to wallow in failure. Not now. Not after everything that had been set in motion. The money had been transferred to the right accounts. The arms shipments had arrived from Venezuela. The men were trained, eager, ready to do whatever was necessary. A couple of details to tie up with Botvinnik and Zhou, then they'd be ready to roll.

And yet, like Simón, they were all blind to one fatal truth. They were all expendable.

But not Domínguez. Not him. He would rise above all of this. He would reach the top. The government would appoint him *el presidente.*

He rinsed his hands in the corner sink, the water running crimson for a moment before clearing. His phone vibrated in his pocket, and without a second thought, he pulled it out. A reminder in his calendar. Call the number that would kick everything into motion. Zhou was the key to ensuring the plan *would* succeed. Lourdes would organize a new account for him, then the last payment. No more mistakes.

FIVE

Jacob memorized Pepe's cell phone and landline numbers, tore the piece of paper into tiny pieces, and flushed them down the toilet. He moved to the huge window overlooking the Malecón, the road that ran for five miles along the northern coast of Cuba. He'd seen it in pictures; in real life the Avenida de Maceo, as it was officially known, was breathtaking in its grandeur and scale.

After unpacking his supply of clothes, folded with origami precision to fit the maximum possible into the small hard-shell suitcase, he took a hot shower. Toweled and dressed, he made himself a strong coffee using the state-of-the-art machine—a machine most Cubans could only dream of owning. It was getting on for 10 p.m.; he needed the caffeine hit for the next stage of the operation.

Sitting at an expansive round dining table, the light from his laptop screen flickered. He inserted the 2-terabyte USB drive. His laptop contained oceans of information pertinent to the mission, dug up, sorted, prioritized, and analyzed by Fletcher, Irina, and a faceless team of backroom researchers. Savant that he was, even Jacob couldn't digest all of it. Nevertheless, he highlighted all the folders, copied them across to the flash drive, tucked them away in an obscure subdirectory, then hid them through the properties function. Findable by a first-year IT student but not your average spy. He hoped. He slipped the cap back on the device—disguised to look like a pack of Wrigley's Doublemint gum—and stowed it in his toiletries bag. He'd refer to the material if required, but Jacob's gut told him the key information he needed was waiting to be unearthed here, on the ground, in Havana.

A quick call to Pepe confirmed the cabbie was parked and waiting for Jacob. It was clearly too late to visit the embassy, where Frank Cain was probably holed up. If he'd had more time to be certain he could trust Pepe, a drive there might have been on the cards. But not yet. Besides, Fletcher had assured Jacob the journalist wouldn't be allowed to leave the country until Jacob had the chance to talk to him. The man was probably stewing in his own juices, but even if he was available, there was no point trying to interview him at this late hour.

Pepe stood leaning against his cab in a side street 350 yards from the hotel. He crushed a cigarette under a well-worn sneaker and gave a wave as he saw Jacob approaching. "Why don't you want me to fetch you at the front gates of the Meliá Cohiba? Got a wife trying to catch you out?"

"Ah, no." Jacob laughed politely. "I like to stretch my legs before jumping straight in a car," he lied.

Pepe shrugged, as if the answer wasn't entirely satisfactory but he'd settle for it. "*Adonde, mi amigo?* Where to, my friend?"

"Do you think you and *la mierda china* could show me around some interesting bars in Havana?"

"*No hay problema*. No problem."

"I want to get some atmosphere to describe my first night in the city. You must have a clue about where the most authentic local action is?"

"*Sí*, Manny. There are many to choose from. You want where there are local people or tourists?"

"Locals, mainly."

"Or maybe you're looking for a pretty *jinetera*?"

Jacob hadn't heard this word before but had a good idea what it meant. "A hooker, right?"

"*Correcto.*"

"No thanks. I have a girlfriend at home, and I make it a policy never to pay for sex."

"Our girls are very special. You might regret such a decision." The advice came with a wink.

Jacob chuckled. "One might be forgiven for thinking you've got a stake in the business." A short pause. "A cousin living off immoral earnings with you getting a referral fee?"

"Ha ha, of course not." Pepe's voice elevated a fraction. "I thought maybe you were looking for a special angle for your story."

"I wasn't. But now that you mention it, perhaps an article about sex tourism would interest our readers."

"Hey, that's your decision to make. Me, I'm just a patriot who believes our women are the most beautiful in the world. You make no mind about what I say. I tend to ramble on about things. Open my mouth and things come out without me having thought it through too much. *Entiendes?* Understand?"

"*Sí.*" Jacob had been prone to the same fault most of his life. Skia had mostly trained it out of him. On a subliminal level, and depending on the setting, he weighed his words before he spoke. In some situations—in bed with Irina, for example—spontaneity ruled. He was only human, after all.

They continued to drive along dark, narrow streets, past clusters of locals and tourists enjoying the warm evening. Jacob glanced left and right, not sure what to look for. Cain, preoccupied with the information he was about to receive from his contact, had paid less attention to his surroundings than he should have.

Havana's humid, tropical air drifted through the open windows, the sensation pleasant against Jacob's face.

Pepe, hands resting comfortably on the wheel, glanced back at him. "Señor, if you want I can take you to the area where many—

how can I describe it politely?—downscale bars are located. It's called Cayo Hueso. Let me know when you see something you like, and I'll drop you off. I can wait outside or pick you up at an agreed time."

He ran a hand over his freshly shaven head, the sensation taking him back to a previous mission. He hadn't given Pepe much to go on. Jacob had learned the hard way that caution wasn't a burden—it was survival. He was warming to the guy, though, and chanced a long shot. "I heard there was a man killed in a bar a couple nights ago. You hear anything about that?"

An unsure voice drifted around the headrest. "Where did you hear that?"

"On the Internet," he laughed. "Where else? Some forum or other, I can't remember right now."

Pepe's shoulders rose and fell in a shrug. "The Internet isn't something I take much interest in. The service is shit here in Cuba. We only see what the government lets us. I guess that includes saying nothing about people getting killed in bars." He let loose a sarcastic snort. "We're officially classified as a 'small island developing state,' can you believe it? Once the richest nation in the Caribbean, now we're all driving *la mierda china*. The ones who can afford them, at least. And that isn't many." He shook his head vigorously. "We're a third-world country in many respects, señor. And that's the truth." He fingered his closely cropped beard.

"But you do know something about what happened in the bar." Jacob's heart began to pump a little faster. "I can tell by your tone."

Pepe turned around for a second, heard a honk, and refocused on the road. "We taxi drivers get to hear a lot. Whether it's true or not..." He let his voice trail off into non-committal silence. "Why would you want to go to a dangerous bar where people get shot?"

"I never said the victim was shot." Jacob leaned forward in his seat. "You *have* heard the story. Take me to that place."

"I don't know which one it is, Manny. How would I know that? It's just a rumor."

Jacob scratched his head. "Listen. What if it's true? This could be a scoop for me. People think Cuba is a country where violent crime doesn't happen. I could show the world the truth. From the way you were talking just now, I get the feeling you aren't the biggest fan of the government. *Verdad?* Am I right?"

"You sure you're not setting me up? Maybe recording me on your fancy reporter's hidden microphone?"

"I'm only asking you to take me to a bar, not to denounce your president." He pulled out a note bearing the portrait of Andrew Jackson, waved it beside Pepe's right ear. "Besides, no offense, but unless you're involved in illegal activities—apart from petty stuff like working off the books—I'm sure you're of little interest to the authorities."

Pepe gently took the twenty-dollar note between thumb and forefinger and stuffed it into the console, then, as an afterthought, covered it with loose papers. "*Hostia!* Dammit! No more bribes. You already paid me a shitload."

Jacob made a come-on gesture. "Give it back then."

"Don't be so hasty." Pepe slowed to negotiate a dogleg bend in the road. "I have an idea where you might find out something." He crossed himself. "Honestly, Manny, I do not know the exact bar where this killing happened. But I hope you've got more dollars stashed away in your pocket. The people who go to the dive I'm taking you to, you can only loosen their tongues by flashing some *baro* around." Jacob had heard the same slang term for money in Mexico. "I wouldn't make a big show of it, though. Someone sees you with a stash, they might jump you in the bathroom and steal it." He swallowed hard. "Or worse."

"Thanks for the advice. Now just take me there and let me do the worrying, OK?"

"*De acuerdo*. Gotcha."

They drove in silence for a while, winding through the city's connector arteries, deeper into its older districts. Pepe spat out the window, the glob of spit soon followed by the glowing end of his cigarette.

"You totally sure about this?" Pepe asked as they pulled up to a darkened doorway. The building looked deserted except for a rectangle of yellow light spilling out under the door. In the mirror, the cabbie shot Jacob a look of caution.

Jacob shrugged. "It's my job to go to dangerous places. I know how to handle myself."

"You're sure to stand out with that Argentinian accent, superior attitude, and new clothes, but if you mind your manners, no one will care who you are. We like foreign writers in Cuba."

"Even journalists?

"Not sure about that."

Jacob smiled. "I always fancied myself as a modern-day Hemingway." He stepped out of the car and walked around to the driver's side. "I could be a while. Over an hour. You prepared to wait?"

"All night if I have to." He gestured toward a corner. "I'll park around there under the first streetlight. Call me on my cell if you need anything."

Jacob strode toward the bar, his footsteps echoing eerily in the deserted street.

SIX

JACOB STEPPED INSIDE, DIM LIGHTS CASTING ERRATIC shadows across the cracked, grimy tiles. The air was thick with the smell of stale sweat, tobacco smoke, and alcohol. The bartender, a wiry bald man in his early sixties, didn't even bother to look up, his focus trained on wiping down glasses with a threadbare rag. Locals huddled around tables with glasses of rum and beer in front of them, their murmured conversations blending with the soft clunk of an ancient ceiling fan.

In a far corner, two ancient Afro-Cubans, their crepe skin the color of dark mahogany, were absorbed in a game of backgammon. Across the room, two women, just as old, sat at a small table near the wall, their conversation punctuated with wild hand gestures.

He strode to the bar, his movements deliberate, trying to strike a balance between casual and observant. He leaned against the worn wooden counter. No one seemed interested in his presence, at least not overtly. But he knew never to let down his guard. In places like this, curiosity worked in silence, eyes closely studying newcomers when they thought no one was watching.

"I'll take a rum," he said, his voice friendly yet assured.

From a high shelf, the bartender pulled down a bottle of

Cuban Club smoky dark rum. The shot cost Jacob 25 Cuban pesos, a mere dollar. He tossed his money on the counter, took the glass, and knocked back the first sip. It burned its way down his throat, the fire spreading through his chest. By the second sip, the burn had lessened, leaving only a warmth that settled in his gut. He wiped his mouth with the back of his hand, savoring the taste of something authentic, raw, and real.

He ordered a small Guantanamera cigar next. Another dollar. The bartender handed it to him without comment, moving on to wipe more glasses. Jacob lit the cigar and inhaled the first puff; the rich tobacco smoke filled his lungs. He could see how a man could lose himself in a place like Havana, where everything felt surreal.

Jacob scanned the room again, this time more intently. The exit routes caught his eye first. The front door and a window were off to the left, its glass dirty and cracked. Thin enough to crash through. A curtain behind the bar, possibly leading to another way out—hard to tell from where he stood.

"Like that cigar you're smoking?" The bartender's voice snapped him back to the present.

Jacob turned to him with a relaxed grin. "I sure do. Well worth the small expense."

"They got cigars like that in Argentina?" The bartender's tone was casual, but there was curiosity in his eyes. The kind that came from a man who had seen his fair share of tourists brave enough to leave the well-beaten track but knew how to size up a stranger.

Jacob gave a mental nod of approval—his Argentinian cover was holding up. "That obvious?"

"Uh-huh." The bartender didn't look away, waiting for Jacob to expand.

"These cigars cost a lot more back home than what you're charging."

"It's criminal to pay more than a couple pesos for these. They're machine-rolled, not hand-made. Cheap stuff." He squinted, as if assessing Jacob more closely. "Why're you drinking in this dump, amigo? We don't get too many foreigners. You looking for a *chica*?"

Jacob chuckled lightly, feigning amusement. "I thought they were called *jineteras*?"

The bartender erupted into laughter. "This isn't Old Havana. You want *jineteras*, you head to the tourist traps. Not here."

Leaning in, Jacob lowered his voice. "I'm wondering if you've heard anything about an... incident... around here a couple of nights ago?"

The bartender's face darkened. "Odd question," he said carefully. "What kind of incident?"

Jacob let his hand slip a fifty-dollar bill across the bar, covering it with his fingers. Just enough of it peeked out for the bartender to notice. "The kind that doesn't make the newspapers," Jacob murmured. "Or the television. You know what I mean."

The bartender's eyes darted down to the money, then back up to Jacob's face. Suspicion flickered, but so did temptation. The man's fingers inched toward the cash but hesitated. It wasn't an outright refusal, but caution was etched into every line on his wrinkled face.

"I'm not here to cause trouble," Jacob assured him, lowering his voice even further. "I'm a journalist, looking for a story. I heard whispers, and I'm willing to pay for information."

The bartender eyed him for a long moment, the muscles in his jaw working. Then, with a resigned sigh, he took the bill and stuffed it into his apron pocket. He leaned forward, his voice now a hushed whisper.

"You must look for El Gato Negro."

Jacob furrowed his brow. "What the hell is that? Another bar?"

The bartender shook his head. "It's... something else. Maybe a place. Maybe a person. You are not a stupid man. Use your intuition."

Jacob's frustration bubbled under the surface, but he forced a neutral expression. "I don't buy that. You know more than you're saying."

The bartender stiffened. "I gave you what you asked for. Now please get out before you start trouble."

Jacob tensed, debating whether to press further. He was about to ask another question when the bartender suddenly barked, "*Jesusito! Ven aquí ya mismo!* Come here, right now!" A moment later, the black curtain behind the bar swished aside, and a towering figure stepped into view.

The man stood around six feet six inches, muscles so thick they strained the material of his singlet. Arms crossed over his barrel chest, his expression was stone-cold.

"You'd best be on your way," the bartender sneered, his tone shifting now that backup had arrived. "I told you what I know. Be grateful."

"Sí," the giant growled. "Grateful."

Jacob stood for a moment, weighing his options. He could probably take them both down if he needed to, but that would draw too much attention, and right now, more attention was the last thing he wanted. So he smiled, a tight, polite smile, and slid a few pesos onto the bar.

"I'm leaving," he said calmly, making his way toward the door.

At the threshold, he paused, glancing back at the bartender, whose eyes glinted with something unreadable. Then Jacob nodded politely and wished everyone a good night.

SEVEN

"El Gato Negro? The Black Cat?" Pepe repeated as Jacob climbed into the back seat of his taxi.

"Yeah. Does it mean anything to you? Is it another bar?"

Pepe's brow furrowed as he started the engine. "Not a bar that I know of."

Jacob sighed and slumped back in his seat. "Fantastic. Total waste of time. Let's go back to the hotel."

Pepe's lips twitched into a slight grin. "I didn't say it wasn't important, though."

Jacob straightened. "What do you mean?"

Pepe pulled out into the street, weaving through Havana's narrow lanes with practiced ease. "I've heard something about el Gato Negro. Only it's not a bar. It's something else."

Jacob leaned forward. "What?"

Pepe chuckled softly, his eyes glinting mischievously in the rearview mirror. "Rumor has it, el Gato Negro is a criminal gang. Small-time, but they deal in... a lot of things. Drugs, girls, whatever makes them money."

Jacob pondered a new possibility. Could this gang have something to do with Passo's murder?

Pepe's voice broke through his thoughts. "If you ask me, I'd say a gang like that would kill to protect its secrets."

They drove in silence for a while, Jacob deep in thought. Finally, Pepe lit a cigarette, the noxious smoke curling through the open window. "I remember something else I heard about el Gato Negro," he said.

Jacob perked up. "What?"

"They deal in weapons. Smuggled into the country right under the government's nose. Or maybe with the government's blessing. Who knows?"

"Bullshit." Jacob scoffed. "Gun crime is not an issue in Cuba."

Pepe chuckled darkly. "That's what they want you to think. Guns are rare, true. But they're here. And expensive. Only the desperate or the very wealthy can afford them."

Jacob mulled that over. If this gang was smuggling weapons—perhaps under the direction of Domínguez—it could change the direction of his inquiries. It could tie directly into Passo's assassination.

Pepe glanced at him in the mirror. "If you can find them, you'd have one hell of a story."

Jacob grinned. "And how exactly do you expect me to find a shadowy gang in the middle of Havana?"

Pepe's eyes twinkled with mischief. "Because you have me."

They drove on, the city's lights reflecting in the cab's windshield. After a few minutes, Jacob pointed to a flickering neon sign. "Stop the car!"

Pepe swerved to a halt. "What is it?"

Jacob pointed to a black cat, curled up asleep on a windowsill above a door marked La Taberna del Marinero. The Sailor's Inn. "El gato negro is that damned cat," Jacob muttered. "Maybe that cartel story you spun is nothing more than a legend."

Pepe sighed. "It sure sounded good, though, didn't it?"

Jacob grunted under his breath then pointed up the road.

"Wait a hundred meters away. If I'm not back in thirty minutes, leave."

"You sure?"

Five minutes later, Jacob marched back to the cab. "Go."

"Was that the place?"

"I'm not sure."

"But it could be?"

"If it is, I don't want to go back. I got a very unfriendly vibe from the staff and the patrons."

He would return tomorrow but with Frank Cain and without Pepe. This was where Passo had been assassinated. There were marks in the walls that looked suspiciously like bullet holes. And no one had even bothered to clean up the blood stains.

EIGHT

THE WATER IN THE HOTEL SHOWER GUSHED OUT HOT, steam billowing up as the high-pressure jets massaged Jacob's neck and shoulders. His muscles, still humming from the punishing session in the gym, slowly began to loosen. After hitting the free weights, pounding the heavy bag, and clocking twenty laps in the pool, his blood surged, and his mind was locked in. The physical strain had brought him to this moment of calm—a necessary precursor to what came next. Today, Frank Cain would speak, whether he wanted to or not.

Fear. It had to be fear that kept the journalist from spilling everything. Jacob had seen it before—people forget under pressure, their minds willingly shut down. Maybe Cain had been threatened, maybe he was simply too scared to remember. But Jacob knew how to ignite those lost memories, how to make a man's mind unlock, whether through persuasion or subtle pressure. Cain would remember the details; Jacob would make sure of it.

One last task before heading to the embassy. He could've had housekeeping handle it, but the ritual calmed him, let his thoughts settle. The iron glided smoothly over his shirt, steam rising as he worked out the wrinkles. First the front, around the buttons, then the sleeves and the cuffs, finishing with the collar. The fabric was crisp, immaculate. Jacob held it up to the light, satisfied. The process was meditative, a chance to rehearse the mental maneuvers for the day ahead.

Frank Cain wouldn't know what hit him.

He set the iron aside, flipped open his laptop, and connected to the hotel's Wi-Fi. His fingers danced over the keyboard as he opened the secure VPN. He composed a short, encrypted message to Elijah Dundas, the CIA station chief waiting for his contact.

"Manuel Vargas has arrived. Will debrief Cain prior to extraction. Preparing for transfer."

Jacob hit send. The message vanished into the ether, carried by encrypted tunnels that would make it nearly impossible to trace. If Cuban surveillance was watching, they would see nothing more than routine correspondence between two parties. Jacob shut the laptop and packed it away.

The embassy was a little over a mile away—close enough to walk. The morning was clear, the sky a pale blue after days of stormy weather. The Malecón stretched ahead, the sea breeze promising a respite from the heat. Temperatures in the high seventies. No need for a cab. Pepe could rest easy this morning. Jacob would enjoy the sights and sounds of the city waking up.

Taking the route he'd memorized, he headed down an alley that ran behind a nondescript four-floor apartment building three blocks from the embassy. The two delivery trucks were parked exactly as they were supposed to be, nose to tail with barely an inch between them. He turned his back on an approaching woman walking a dog, pretending to be engaged in an animated phone conversation complete with flailing arms. When she rounded the corner, he tapped on the passenger-side door of the first truck. Seconds later, the driver with ropy arm muscles and a face like granite was beside Jacob on the sidewalk. The men exchanged codewords before the driver quickly untied a tarpaulin flap, Jacob clambered inside the van, and the tarp was tied down in place again.

He sat on a metal bench welded to the wall of the truck, hearing the rumble of the engine. Two minutes later, he heard some words exchanged between the driver and another man, the clanging of an automatic steel gate opening. Then the truck inclined forward as it descended the short distance into an underground parking garage.

Three honks of the horn and the tarp lifted. An attractive woman in her early forties, jet-black hair pulled back into a severe bun, look up at him. Next to her was a goon built like a refrigerator and with a crew cut straight out of Hollywood casting. "Señor Vargas?" she said with an alluring smile.

"Sí."

"May I see your passport?"

She examined the document and handed it back. She smoothed down her black pencil skirt and said, "Please come with me. The chief of station is waiting for you."

He clambered down from the truck and slipped into stride behind the woman. Her plump butt jiggled in a way that would have had the single Jacob Hunter's heart racing. These days, it made him smile but nothing more.

Today his attention would be on assessing the key players at Havana Station and then Frank Cain. A man who had buried his memories deep—as a civilian who had recently witnessed an assassination might—but Jacob understood the art of excavation. Today, Cain would remember.

NINE

Jacob extended his hand to a smiling Elijah Dundas, who bore the official title of political counselor. The spy boss rose from his leather swivel chair with an air of calculated grace and strode toward his guest. Channeling his inner Argentinian, Jacob said, "Hola, Señor Dundas. I'm glad to finally meet you."

The well-toned CIA man moved back to his seat with rolling hips, gesturing for Jacob to take the chair opposite his desk. At moments like this, Jacob always felt like he was being interviewed for a job. Dundas's office had the cold, impersonal feel of a pen-pushing bureaucrat's den. Diplomas framed in heavy wood adorned the walls, alongside neatly arranged bookshelves with titles no one had touched in years and a portrait of soon-to-be ex-President Claxton.

"I was kind of hoping to see you yesterday evening," Dundas said in a well-modulated voice, like a radio announcer warming up to his audience. "Mr. Cain is getting antsy. Wants to go home."

Jacob steepled his fingers, letting the silence linger for a moment before replying. "*Sí,* I understand. But the connector flights were too... how do you say... disconnected. Ha, ha! I mean, there was a long stopover in Toronto after meeting with the State Department bigwigs in Washington."

Dundas scratched his prominent cobalt-blue chin, his Rolex catching the light. "I'm curious as to why State saw fit to send someone from Argentina. We've got our own agents who are more than capable of sorting out this mess."

Jacob wobbled his head from side to side, feigning thoughtfulness. "It's not the first time I've done this kind of work as a foreign contractor," he lied smoothly. "Only last year I carried out covert special ops in Russia on behalf of the United States when they wanted to, how do you say, keep things at arm's length. The mission was so successful it thwarted an attempt by the Russians to bring down the US government." The second part was a hundred percent true. "As to your other observation, I beg to differ. Your own agents cannot sort out this mess. They are not able to operate here in a truly covert manner. Their embassy 'jobs' have them squarely in the cross-hairs of local intelligence."

Dundas paused, adopted a pensive expression, then scratched his chin again. "Well, the authorization came from the very top, the Secretary of State himself, so I couldn't argue with the choice even if I wanted to."

Jacob leaned forward slightly. "How is Señor Cain? I mean, psychologically?"

Dundas shook his head just a fraction, and a hint of empathy softened the lines around his eyes. "Good question. To me, he's shell-shocked. We've had one of our in-house psychologists speak with him. She thinks he's headed for serious PTSD. Recommended regular follow-up treatment once he's back home."

"I agree," Jacob said, his voice calm, playing along.

Dundas sighed. "He's anxious to get home, but my instructions were clear. I've been told to hold him here until you arrived and spoke with him." He hesitated, then added, "I'm not thrilled about it. Feels like I'm holding an innocent man prisoner."

"Does he understand why it's necessary?" Jacob asked.

"He does." Dundas nodded. "Still, the sooner we get this sorted out, the better for everyone."

Dundas ran a hand through his wavy hair, flashing the chunky Rolex again. Jacob had seen more expensive watches in his life, but the station chief wore his as if it were an extension of his ego. "You wanna know what I think?" Dundas said, leaning back slightly.

"Sure," Jacob replied, already preparing himself for the inevitable lecture.

"I think you'd better be damned careful." Dundas's voice dropped. "If the Cubans had already sniffed out Frank Cain before he's even published a word, then eyes are everywhere." There was a slight sheen of sweat forming on Dundas's forehead. "More than they usually are. Especially with the Chinese supposedly in on the act, creating sophisticated surveillance systems for them."

Jacob gave a measured nod. "I'm planning on taking him back to the scene of the crime."

Dundas's hand, mid-sip on his glass of water, froze. "What the hell for?"

"To make sure it really is the scene of the crime. I'm going on a hunch."

Dundas's nostrils dilated with frustration. "What difference does it make if that's where it happened or not?"

Jacob smiled thinly. "It means I won't be wasting my time when I go there alone later, trying to figure out where to find Señor Espinosa."

Dundas slammed his hand on the desk, the sound echoing in the room, causing a glass paperweight to wobble. "Damn that man to hell and back. We had Espinosa on a tight leash. And Passo..." He put his head in his hands. "He was another of our informers. Like Espinosa, ex-Cuban intelligence. Often acting solo, not reporting on schedule. Still, occasionally he produced gold for us. His death is...unfortunate."

Jacob nodded. "Yes, very sad. Now our priority is finding Espinosa. Who was his handler?"

"Our best man. Wilfred Arnold."

Jacob's eyes narrowed slightly. "Is he in the building?"

"Yes."

Jacob leaned back, his fingers tapping lightly on the arm of the chair. "Have him on stand-by to talk to me when I'm done with Cain."

Dundas's eyes flashed with irritation. "Hang on a second. I'm not liking your bossy tone."

Jacob forced a conciliatory smile. He'd dealt with enough station chiefs over the years to know their egos were often their biggest weakness. This one was no different. "I apologize, Señor Dundas." He paused for effect, allowing the awkwardness to dissipate. "I know you've been instructed to afford me all courtesies. I don't mean to tread on anyone's toes, but you must trust me. I will listen to your advice and take note of everything Señor Arnold has to say. All with the utmost respect." He bowed his head slightly in a gesture of humility before straightening up. "I would respectfully ask for access to the embassy's armory. My needs are simple: one pistol and maybe six magazines. I'm not fussy about the make."

Dundas's eyes widened like dinner plates. "Only the regional security officer has access. You can't be serious."

"I'm as serious as..." Jacob paused, pretending to be searching for the phrase, "...as a heart attack. If you cannot grant me access, then the RSO can bring me the weapon and ammunition himself. *Entiendes?* But before he gives me the means to protect myself out there"—he gestured toward the wall—"which is only reasonable, I would very much like to meet with Frank Cain."

Dundas, face flushed crimson, stared at Jacob for a beat longer, clearly weighing his next move, before rising from his chair. The tension in the room hung like a curtain, neither man quite willing to drop it, but the station chief knew he must not obstruct the operation. He smoothed his tie, grabbed a file off the desk, and gestured for Jacob to follow him down the corridor toward the secure rooms where Frank Cain waited.

As they walked, the sound of their shoes against the polished floor echoed faintly through the stark hallway. The embassy was a fortress, its reinforced walls a testament to the strained relationship between Cuba and the United States.

The thick steel doors ahead opened with a buzz. Jacob and Dundas entered a small room furnished with little more than a steel table, a couple of chairs, and a solitary lamp casting a dull glow over the space. In the corner on an additional piece of furniture, a soft sofa, huddled Frank Cain.

TEN

Jacob could feel the reporter squirming in the seat next to him. Cain had pulled his hat down low, reflector sunglasses masking his eyes, as if he could somehow block out the reality of where they were by avoiding even a glance out the window.

Pepe drove at a steady pace, the midday streets buzzing with life. People lounged on the steps of old buildings, while the smooth rhythm of salsa music poured out of battered boomboxes. Locals chatted animatedly, their arms and hands moving in perfect time to the music, almost as if their conversations were part of the dance. Jacob took in the scene, noting that the demographics of Cayo Hueso leaned heavily toward the Afro-Cuban community.

They passed lines of people waiting outside small counters and makeshift shops, some hoping to get their hands on scarce essentials. One line stood outside a bakery, a place where bread was sometimes exchanged for government-issued coupons rather than money. Jacob glanced at the storefront, for a moment hopeful it might be a lead. Espinosa was supposed to be a baker, but reality quickly set in. If Espinosa had truly gone off the grid, there was no way he'd be working in a place this visible. Too risky.

Especially for a white man in this part of town—he'd stand out immediately.

The silence in the car was suffocating, so Jacob broke it with a direct question, still watching the streets blur past. "Señor Cain, one thing doesn't add up. Why didn't you take your cell phone with you when you met this mystery man? We could've retraced your steps using geo-tracking."

"Passo told me to leave it behind," Cain mumbled, fidgeting with his hands. "Said it was better if I had nothing on me that could identify me. In case things went bad."

Jacob felt a jolt of irritation but held it back. Cain was still fragile, haunted by what he'd seen. Jacob had to tread lightly. "Hmmm. Maybe he was trying to cover his own tracks, just in case. Not that it helped him in the end."

Cain shifted, his voice trembling slightly. "Can we hurry this up? This place gives me the creeps."

They were less than 100 yards from La Taberna del Marinero, the bar with the black cat. Jacob had seen the bloodstains there the night before, but Cain's confirmation would seal it. He needed to know for sure that this was the spot where everything had gone down.

"There's no one out there," Jacob said gently, leaning closer. "Look up. Just for a second. See if anything rings a bell. We're close."

Still, Cain refused to move.

Pepe brought the taxi to a slow stop, directly opposite the bar's entrance. "We're here now, Frank. You have to help us sort this mess out. The sooner it's done, the sooner you get to go home. Now please look," Jacob instructed softly.

Next to him, Cain hesitated, then slowly raised his head, peeking over the edge of his sunglasses. He drew a sharp breath. "Yes. This is it."

Jacob squinted at the man. "That was quick. Before you had no idea about anything. Are you sure you're not just telling me what I want to hear so we can get out of here faster?"

"No, no." Cain's voice had an edge of excitement now, as if some buried memory was finally surfacing. "It's the name of the place—La Taberna del Marinero. I'd forgotten, but now it's coming back to me. My Spanish is terrible, but I know that line from the old song 'La Bamba': '*Yo no soy marinero*—I'm not a sailor.' That's why I can recall the name."

Jacob nodded slowly, his mind whirring. He knew all too well about repressed memories. After suffering a brain injury in college football, he had regained his knowledge of Russian—something he'd learned as a toddler but had forgotten for years. It had come back in fragmented bursts, like a fog lifting, revealing something that had always been there. It made sense that Cain, rattled by trauma, might experience the same kind of delayed recall.

"Well done," Jacob said, patting Cain's shoulder in reassurance. Then, turning to Pepe, he said, "I've got what I needed. Let's go."

ENSCONCED IN HIS HOTEL ROOM, Jacob spread out the printed report compiled by the CIA officer who had originally interrogated Cain over several hours. At Jacob's own request, no electronic copy had been provided, although he did watch the ten-minute video recording of the interview back at the embassy. Once he finished with it, the paper document would be destroyed.

The CIA man—anonymous and unseen in the video version—had asked all the right questions, but the answers had been frustratingly thin. Cain's memory seemed fractured, incomplete. Either he was subconsciously protecting himself, or worse, he was lying. Jacob toyed with the idea that Cain was deliberately holding back, but the man didn't seem capable of it. Physically, Cain was slight, nervous—he wouldn't last long under serious pressure. The idea that he was faking ignorance felt increasingly unlikely.

Still, Cain's story was sketchy. He'd soon be airlifted out of Cuba, out of Jacob's reach, and there wasn't enough time to push him further. Even if Jacob wanted to, there were limits. Lines he wouldn't cross, methods he wouldn't use on US citizens. But if Cain were an enemy agent, someone on the other side, the situation might have been different.

Jacob leaned forward, reading the key questions again.

How did you first hear of Cristian Passo?

"An anonymous call in Washington."

Could it have been Passo himself?

"Maybe. The line was poor, distorted."

Who were you supposed to meet at the bar in Cayo Hueso?

"An informer."

Did Passo tell you what the informer was bringing to the table?

"I think he was going to confirm a big false-flag operation, when it was going to happen and who was behind it. Maybe some more details."

Documentary evidence?

No idea.

Did Passo tell you the informer's name, and you've just forgotten?

"No. I mean, I don't know. I can't remember."

Could you tell me the name of the person Passo believed was orchestrating the false-flag operation?

"Someone high up in the Cuban government. I think it starts with 'D.'"

Domínguez? The Deputy Minister of the Revolutionary Armed Forces?

"I think so, yes."

The interviewer noted in the margins of the transcript Cain's distressed body language, which he believed wasn't an act. He then asked Cain to describe the assassination and his miraculous rescue. Cain broke down, sobbing. After a couple of minutes, he recovered and stated he could only remember that the killer was a big man. The actions that led to his escape were pure instinct. Cain studied a few photographs of potential rescuers and stated that, in all probability, one of the men in the pictures was the person who saved him and dropped him off a street away from the embassy. He couldn't provide a good description of the vehicle, apart from the fact that it was an old American relic from the 1950s or so, painted a bright color.

Did the driver say anything to you, or you to him?

"I remember he said something like, 'Lie down on the seat and don't get up until I tell you it's time to get out.' Or words to that effect. After a while, he pulled over somewhere, opened my door, and gave me directions to the embassy. It must have been close by, because the next thing I knew, I was lying on a bed in a small room, shivering."

No offense, but your reporter's instinct of getting the story at all costs seems to have abandoned you. You took a lot of risks to attend this meeting. And now all you want to do is go home. How would you respond to that observation?

"I don't know. I need to be with my family. When can I speak to my wife?"

Soon.

At that point, Cain said he was totally drained and asked to end the interview. The interviewer asked if he would like something to calm his nerves, help him sleep. Cain replied affirmatively. A staff nurse administered a sedative intravenously.

It was like pulling teeth, Jacob thought bitterly as he set the report to one side. The man's memory seemed to be a sieve, everything leaking through. He wondered how much of this was trauma and how much was Cain's mind trying to protect him from whatever deeper truths lay beneath.

Jacob sighed, letting his gaze drift out the window. From here, he had an unobstructed view of the Malecón. Waves crashed relentlessly against the seawall, as they had for decades.

Unless the machine had eliminated him—which was a possibility—Espinosa was out there somewhere. If not in Havana, then somewhere else on the island. If it was the latter, the task would be that much harder.

The starting point would be a return visit to La Taberna del Marinero.

Worst of all, there was no clear timeline for Bay of Pigs II. Fletcher assumed it would happen on or before Hannah McIvor's inauguration. Hell, that could be tomorrow or nearly two months from now.

The room felt too quiet, so he turned on the radio. Pulsating Spanish-language hip-hop filled the space. The infectious beat had Jacob's body involuntarily jerking along. He stood, stretched, drank two glasses of cold water, and turned back to the report. He speed-read it again, in case there was something between the lines he'd missed. There wasn't.

He used the edge of a local phone directory like a ruler, tearing the pages of the report into thin strips and flushing them carefully down the toilet. Jacob tapped the pistol under his jacket. A Smith & Wesson M&P 22 Compact. Slim, light, and perfect for deep concealment. It came with a dedicated micro suppressor and a couple of spare 10-round clips. A few practice rounds at the embassy's range had instilled a ton of confidence. The shots were as quiet as a snake's hiss. *Please, God, don't make me have to use it.*

If getting information out of Cain had been like pulling teeth, obtaining the weapon was an even bigger pain in the ass. The RSO initially didn't believe Jacob had the authority to take anything from the armory and flatly refused his request. He only relented when Dundas showed him an email from the Secretary of State, countersigned by the Secretary of Defense, overriding the usual protocols for Señor Manuel Vargas, on special assignment from Argentina's Secretaría de Inteligencia del Estado.

Outside, the sun was sinking, casting a ribbon of golden light across the Straits of Florida. Somewhere in the city, the pieces were out there, waiting to be found. Even if he wanted to, Jacob couldn't leave Havana without fitting them together.

He called Pepe. "Take me to see *el gato negro.*"

ELEVEN

"Have you managed to get that small problem with your car solved?" asked Domínguez, tapping a finger on the edge of his small desk that wasn't much bigger than the one he remembered from grade school. His office in the MINFAR building was being renovated—something to do with electrical upgrades. The work was supposedly essential; the engineer said the wiring was a fire waiting to happen, but it was damned inconvenient. Worse still, he had to make do with a tiny office space that was barely the size of a broom closet. Not exactly befitting his status, but he'd have to make do for now.

"Getting closer," replied the Russian, his heavily accented Spanish rumbling through the line. "Once the mechanic sources the spare parts I need, I can foresee it being fixed very soon. Maybe as early as Christmas Eve."

Domínguez let out a low chuckle. The subject of the conversation was an Osa-class missile boat. Built in 1973 and, not surprisingly, prone to mechanical and other issues. "Then congratulations may be in order. I know how important it is for that car of yours to be running smoothly, especially considering the rough roads you have to drive on." A practicing Catholic, Domínguez had no issue with choosing Christmas Eve for the false-flag event. After all, the more festive the backdrop, the less people would expect what was coming. But beyond that, he didn't mind speaking in circles—especially over this phone line. It was no secret the DI would be listening in. In fact, he counted on it. Every high-ranking official in Cuba was closely monitored for any signs of disloyalty. And although Botvinnik was a trusted 'friend' of both the president and the head of the DI, it only took one overeager agent to expose Domínguez and what was really in the works.

The government wouldn't see his motivations as patriotic; they would see them as treasonous, a betrayal of the state. But to Domínguez, snuggling up to the Americans now after all these years of being treated like shit, that was the real treachery. His own government, in his view, was bending over backwards to undo Fidel Castro's legacy. All this new 'cooperation' and 'diplomatic accords' made him sick to the stomach. The foreign minister, in particular, was a traitorous dog he wouldn't hesitate to put down with a bullet given half a chance. Domínguez's father, who had also held high rank in the government, would be rolling in his grave if he could see the direction his beloved country was going. Well, these new policies were not going to continue—not on his watch. "I believe the Christmas season could be the perfect time for the theater."

"Speaking of theater," said Botvinnik, "when is that Chinese cultural show having its official opening?"

"I'm meeting with the director tomorrow at lunchtime to discuss the technical aspects of the spectacle. We'll be going over what props we'll need and the logistics. There's going to be a dress rehearsal in a couple of days. Honestly, if everything goes smoothly, we could actually move things with the big production forward—possibly as soon as the end of November."

Domínguez could hear the flick of a lighter on the other end of the line, followed by the sound of a deep, satisfied draw on a cigarette. "*Perfecto*," the Russian murmured, the word drawn out as he exhaled smoke. "We Russians love a good show."

Domínguez smirked. The threat of surveillance meant the cloak-and-dagger routine was still part of his daily life. Speaking in these coded phrases and double entendres had become second nature, but it didn't stop him from feeling the weight of the DI's ever-watchful eye. He had to remind himself that as long as he stayed sharp, Botvinnik, too, would keep out of the crosshairs. They were both seen as too valuable to the regime to be cast aside. Still, there was always the possibility that one ambitious, overly cautious officer might decide to make a name for themselves by turning over a high-ranking official like Domínguez. And for that reason, extreme caution would continue to be exercised.

The irony wasn't lost on him that Cuba had once been the best of friends with the Russians, comrades in arms against the evil West, and now they were dancing a fine line of half-trust and half-necessity. The same was happening with the Chinese, slowly embedding themselves into Cuban affairs. Domínguez had no delusions about what this cultural show really was—another layer in Beijing's subtle but expanding influence over Havana. And he wasn't entirely opposed. He believed in fostering strategic alliances to strengthen Cuba's position. Especially with ideologically aligned nations, of which there were few in the modern world. But what he didn't believe in, and what gnawed at him every day, was the way his own government was selling out Castro's honorable legacy for tiny fragments of influence in the new world order.

He ran a hand over his mustache, thinking about the coming weeks. The false-flag event, which he had dubbed Operation Restore Dignity—had to go off without a hitch. His team was ready; everything was falling into place. This wasn't just about him attaining the highest power in the land—it was about Cuba's future. "By the way," he said, shifting the subject back to the boat, "I trust the mechanic will ensure your car is running at full capacity?"

"Of course," Botvinnik said, his voice muffled for a moment

as he took another drag on his cigarette. "And when the car is back on the road, it won't miss a beat."

Domínguez smiled. "Excellent. You can't afford breakdowns now, especially considering the investment you've made in that vehicle."

Botvinnik gave a low, knowing chuckle. "No breakdowns, Miguel. Only smooth roads ahead."

Domínguez glanced at the scattered papers on his temporary desk. The renovations to his office couldn't be finished fast enough.

Shifting the conversation, Domínguez brought up a legitimate deal for the Cuban military, keeping up appearances for potential eavesdroppers. "About that other hardware?"

"I'll have another chat with my contacts at Rosoboronexport," Botvinnik said. "They're warming to the idea of selling you some new fighter jets and tanks."

"*Gracias,* Vitaly. I hope you can negotiate a discount for us."

"Hmm, that might be tricky. Sanctions are hurting our economy, and I'm not sure President Putin will approve lowering the prices."

"I understand," Domínguez said, glancing over the military procurement papers on his desk. No major weapons purchases from Russia had been made since 2004, and Cuba's budget was stretched thin. But they had to keep up the ruse. The truth was that neither Cuba nor Russia had the financial bandwidth for trade in new weapons. Russia's resources were tied up fighting Ukraine and conducting other local shit-fights; Cuba was struggling to maintain and repair even its outdated equipment. The brutal reality could not be denied: China was the real backbone of the operation.

When the call ended, Domínguez sat back in his chair, staring at the wall for a moment, considering the elaborate web of deceit he was weaving. With Christmas approaching and the key pieces in place, their operation was nearing a pivotal moment.

Yes, there was the unfortunate hiccup with Cain getting away, and Domínguez hated having to take out Simón for his error. On the plus side, loose lips in the US embassy were responsible for a rumor making it all the way to Caracas, and from there back to Domínguez: the reporter was so mentally scarred after witnessing Passo's execution that he'd become almost catatonic. In fact, he was being shipped back home. The mole's guess? Cain was of zero value to the Americans now.

Before heading home to his family, he had one more call to make. He dialed the number. "Mr. Zhou? Still on for that lunch meeting tomorrow?"

"Yes, indeed. I'm looking forward to it," the diplomat enthused.

"See you then." A few more pleasantries were exchanged before he ended the brief call, feeling a renewed sense of confidence. His allies would not let him down. The theater was set, and the performance would be staged soon. With the weight of his decisions heavy on his shoulders, he glanced out of the window at the fading light.

There was no turning back.

TWELVE

Dundas stood at the shoulder of Wilfred Arnold. Close. As if Arnold was a prize fighter at a press conference and Dundas was his manager, poised to protect him from nasty trick questions. His posture was rigid, hands clasped behind his back. Jacob knew it well—Dundas had that air about him. The type of person who could talk you out of your own conviction, no matter how right you felt.

Jacob was having none of it.

"Por favor, Señor Dundas. I would prefer to speak to Wilfred alone." He gestured toward the door of the anteroom that led back to the chief of station's office.

Dundas didn't budge. His eyes burned, like a bull ready to charge.

"And please close the door to give us privacy. Are you also able to lock the anteroom door? I don't want any interruptions."

Dundas grumbled but moved to turn the latch, making sure no one could enter from the corridor. The metal scraped against the lock. He muttered something under his breath about respect and the value of transparency, but Jacob didn't bother to listen. His focus was entirely on Arnold.

"Excluding me from the process is not only rude, but counterproductive," Dundas said, his voice carrying a hint of condescension. "You know I'm going to debrief my man after you've chatted with him, don't you?"

Jacob nodded slowly. "Of course. I wouldn't expect otherwise. I don't mean to be rude," he continued, turning back to Arnold but still addressing Dundas, "but I prefer privacy when I'm talking to someone like this. It's more for his benefit than mine."

As Dundas retreated into his own office, Jacob could picture steam coming out of the man's ears. The pressure in the room shifted instantly, now that they were alone. Jacob knew he'd been careful in choosing his words, but the tension between him and Dundas wasn't something that could be resolved with simple pleasantries. Dundas rubbed him the wrong way. Too tight-lipped, too interested in power, too used to pulling the strings.

Jacob kept his voice low, even though there was no need to. "Please, take a seat, Señor Arnold."

He gestured to the white tufted sofa that sat awkwardly against the wall. It seemed like a prop, never truly used except to make the room look more inviting. Jacob remained standing next to a water cooler, pretending not to notice Arnold's intense stare. Jacob studied the room, scanning the walls and the ceiling, in particular the corners. No obvious cameras or recording devices. But that didn't mean they weren't there.

"How can I help you?" Arnold's tone conveyed a cooperative attitude.

"Where can I find Raúl Espinosa?"

Arnold blinked, expression unreadable for the briefest moment before his lips formed a slow, disarming smile. "You like to get straight to the point, don't you?"

Jacob nodded. "Time is not our friend."

"Why do you need to find him? Is it to do with the big terrorist event Passo said was about to go down?" Arnold shook his head as though the thought itself disgusted him, and then lowered his voice to a near whisper. "I told Dundas there was some credence to the claims. But, oh, no. It was too preposterous, he said."

Jacob waved a dismissive hand, keeping his face neutral. "Let's not speculate on any of that right now. I'm sorry I can't go into the details with you. All you need to know is that we need to get our hands on Espinosa—fast. So where could he be?"

"No idea. I wish I knew. Raúl has been valuable to us with some useful intel. From what I hear, the State Department has been happy with his service." Arnold pulled out a stick of gum, offering a piece to Jacob, who declined with a slight shake of the head. Arnold unwrapped the gum and popped it into his mouth, visibly trying to calm his nerves. "I actually like the guy on a personal level," he continued, crossing his arms over his chest. "We had some good conversations, shared a few laughs. I'm sure he'll turn up. If he was the guy who dropped Cain off, I'd say he's just waiting for the heat to die down, as they say in the movies."

Jacob's brows pinched, his thoughts spinning. A man who'd disappeared after dropping off Cain—this wasn't a run-of-the-mill informant. Jacob's lips curled up into a sardonic smile. "Maybe he also liked you, Señor Arnold, on a personal level?"

"I'd say he did." Arnold's grin returned, but it wasn't entirely without tension. "Our brief meetings were always...cordial."

"Where did you meet him?"

"Never the same place twice. Though the Cayo Hueso quarter was used on multiple occasions. Parks, small cafés, a library."

"Why that district more than others?"

"Easier for a Black man like me to blend in," Arnold said with a grin that didn't quite reach his eyes. "Plus, surveillance there is a lot less of a problem. No cameras. No one's interested in what happens in the poor parts of town."

"Ever meet him away from the capital?"

"No. It's best not to roam around too much in this country. Meeting him, an ex-intelligence officer, involved using all the tools of tradecraft to avoid detection. On my part and his."

Jacob gave a short nod. "Did he share information about himself, reveal his personality to you?"

Arnold's gaze flickered for a moment, the slightest hesitation before he spoke. "A little, but only on a superficial level. He's a sports nut. Like many Cubans, he loves baseball, boxing. So we had some common ground there."

"Boxing, huh?" Jacob mused. "There's a big international tournament happening in Havana. Might be worth staking out to see if he turns up."

"That's not for another week," Arnold replied.

"*Mierda*. Shit." Jacob walked to the cooler and filled a cup with cold water. He leaned against the wall, tugging at his lower lip. "The file tells me the man is trained as a professional baker."

"Not formally. His mother was a baker. He learned the trade from her. At least that's what he told me."

Jacob's eyes focused sharply. "And where was the last place he worked in that capacity? I take it there are few, if any, privately owned bakeries in this country."

"He... uh... I'm sure it's in the file," Arnold said, his voice wavering slightly.

"That's what's curious," Jacob pressed on. "Yes, it's in the file that he has this qualification, but there's nothing on record of him actually working as a baker anywhere. The detail was added to the file by *you*, and only based on your conversations with the man."

Arnold struggled to look Jacob in the eye. "I guess so. But why would he lie?" He took a couple of breaths, preparing to go on the defensive. "Where else am I going to get the information from, except straight from the horse's mouth? This is Cuba, man, not Germany or Sweden or somewhere nice and open and free like that. You can't just hop online and check out LinkedIn, see where a Cuban has left a timeline of his whole working life." He gritted his teeth and swore gently under his breath. "Everything's a secret here. Communications are primitive. We've got our backs against the wall. So, yeah, Espinosa struck me as a genuine sort of guy, and I took it on face value."

Jacob remained silent for a moment, weighing Arnold's words carefully. It was obvious that Arnold had placed a lot of trust in Espinosa. The kind of trust that could be dangerous if misplaced.

"Anyone check his registered address?" Jacob asked.

"Of course. No sign of life for a couple days."

"What are his living arrangements? Write his address down for me."

Arnold scribbled the information. "No kids. Divorced his wife a long time ago. He lives alone in a fairly decent apartment in the south-west of the city."

"Didn't you ever wonder how a so-called baker could afford a nice apartment?" Jacob pressed.

"We pay him a modest retainer." Arnold shrugged. "And maybe he got looked after by the government after he left the intelligence service."

"Passo was ex-intelligence. He didn't get looked after. He was abandoned." Jacob flicked the cup with a fingernail. He paused for a second, a thought forming in his mind. "How's this for a hypothesis? Espinosa never left the DI. Apart from this so-called bakery angle, I can't see any other sources of local income that would satisfy the government."

"You don't think we considered he might be a double agent? Of course we did," Arnold replied, but Jacob could tell the doubt still lingered in his voice. "He's been on our books for the last ten years; so far he's never led us down the garden path. No one's been compromised or hurt."

"Until your other informer, Passo, got himself killed and Cain nearly joined him in the afterlife. You were also Passo's handler. It's only fair to assume the two men knew each other. Perhaps Espinosa was the man who offed Passo, then rescued Cain to make himself out to be the hero before he mysteriously vanished?"

Arnold's jaw clenched. "Yes, I was Passo's handler, and yes, they knew each other," he said quietly. "Do you really believe these wild theories you're tossing about?"

Jacob shrugged, his eyes squinting as he observed Arnold's every move. "This is your territory, Señor Arnold. It's my first time in Cuba. You should have a better feel for the place than I do. And it's scenarios that I'm 'tossing about,' not theories. At this point, I don't believe or disbelieve anything."

Arnold squeezed the sides of his plastic cup as if it would give him clarity. "My opinion, for what it's worth," he said slowly, "is that something's spooked Espinosa after he dropped off Cain. I've got two numbers to contact him on; neither are answering. Like I said before, he's either waiting for the heat to die down or—"

"Or he's dead." Jacob frowned, his words almost a whisper. "Thanks for your time, Señor Arnold. Please, keep trying to contact Espinosa while I do my own digging. If you have any luck, contact me immediately on this secure email." He handed Arnold a slip of paper with an encrypted address and a phone number. "If you call me on my cell, try to make it from a payphone. Not close to the embassy or your residence."

"Understood," Arnold said, pocketing the paper.

The men shook hands, Jacob in awe of Arnold's massive hands and the strength of his grip. As Arnold turned to leave, he glanced over his shoulder and offered a tight smile.

"If all this shit gets sorted out within a week, you wanna catch some of that boxing?"

Jacob smirked, his mind already a million miles away from the offer. "Sure," he replied. The first thing Jacob would do after resolving this case would be scrambling out of Cuba in one hell of a hurry.

His knuckles rapped on the door of Dundas's office. It opened after a couple of seconds, as though Dundas had been waiting on the other side, ear pressed to the door.

"Yes?" he asked, his eyes blinking rapidly.

"That man, Arnold. How long has he been handling Passo and Espinosa?"

"Since he was posted here. Four years ago," Dundas replied. "He's got one more year before the powers that be will want to move him on."

"Five years is over the odds for an operative in an overseas posting. Why so long?" Jacob asked, glancing sideways.

"Wilfred's a rare bird," Dundas laughed. "Actually likes it here. Plus, he's got perfect Spanish and street smarts that help him blend into the landscape. Better than most."

Jacob thought for a second, then pressed on. "He just told me Espinosa had been on the payroll as an informer for ten years. Who handled him before that?"

"I've only been chief of station for three years myself," Dundas said with a shrug. "I'd have to look it up."

"Please do. I'll wait."

Before leaving the embassy, Jacob had the names of two other spooks who used to work with Passo and Espinosa. One, an overweight man in his 60s, had died of a heart attack while banging a Thai hooker; the other was still active for Langley. Seb Goulding, currently posted in Caracas, Venezuela. An operative with a background in financial forensics.

Jacob's ride from the embassy was in the rear seat of a 4x4 with opaque, bullet-proof windows. At the drop-off point, he called Pepe to take him back to the hotel. At his desk, he composed a message to Irina. *Look into a man called Seb Goulding* was the thrust of it. Plus, *check for any whiff of a connection between him and Lourdes Domínguez and, by extension, her uncle Miguel.*

Could it be possible the old handler was still having an impact on what was happening in Havana? If so, it might just explain how Passo's killer knew where his victim would be.

THIRTEEN

THE BLOODSTAIN HAD BEEN WIPED AWAY. THEY MUST have used bleach because the patch on the wall was now white instead of dull maroon, and the place reeked of the substance. The pockmarked walls had also been puttied up to hide the evidence of what had gone down just days before.

"*Buenas noches, guapo*. Good evening, handsome," said a woman behind the bar. "You were here last night but didn't stay for a drink. I hope I can tempt you this time."

Under a bright fluorescent light that hung above the counter, her teeth sparkled and her eyes shone. "I don't forget a handsome man like you in a hurry," she added with a wink. "I've got a weakness for tall, bald, white men." She placed a hand on her hip, giving her torso a tilt. "Like a drink, or you gonna stand there staring at my tits all night?"

Jacob couldn't deny that it was hard to look away from her heaving bosom, nearly bursting out of her tiny blouse, its bottom corners tied into a knot at her waist. "I'll take a beer."

"You sound like a South American. Colombia?" she asked, sliding him a cold Cristal beer.

"Argentina, actually."

"What brings you to this part of town? I don't remember a tourist visiting our humble establishment for some time."

"Really?" He leaned in closer, keeping his eyes above her neckline, ignoring the noisy distractions of the dominoes game across the room. Two men were getting heated, accusing each other of cheating. "Why is that?" he asked.

She shrugged. "Sometimes, things get a little out of control."

As if on cue, one of the domino players erupted in anger. Jacob turned just in time to see him hurl the domino board at his opponent. The other man dodged the flying board, but a stray tile struck him in the eye. They both jumped to their feet, throwing wild punches, attracting the attention of a third man, who quickly intervened, pulling them apart.

Jacob's heart raced for a moment, but the barmaid remained unfazed. "Don't worry," she said behind him. "Those two are always fighting."

Once the scuffle subsided and the game resumed, Jacob turned back to the woman. She was now scolding an elderly man fumbling with a small bag of coins. "*Abuelo*, stop wasting your last pesos on booze," she snapped. The old man growled something unintelligible, grabbed his rum, and shot a glance at Jacob before limping away to a stool by the window.

"You said you don't get tourists in here," Jacob noted, resting his beer on the damp bar runner. "I know for a fact that's not strictly true." He lowered his voice just enough to blend in with the room's ambiance. "I know an American was here a couple nights ago. Witnessed something that would have had this place shut down for a week if it were in Buenos Aires. Crime scene tape all over the place. But I guess the authorities handle things differently here, huh?"

A flicker of fear passed through her eyes, a telltale sign that Jacob had hit a nerve. She glanced nervously around the room.

"Who the hell are you?"

Jacob held up his hands in a calming gesture. "I'm not here to cause trouble for you."

"I wasn't even here!" she hissed. "I saw nothing, and I know nothing. *Entiendes?* I need this damn job."

"And I need mine." He stopped, allowing her to serve another customer, a bearded man in a navy-blue baseball cap who appeared from behind and slapped a few crumpled pesos onto the bar. When the man disappeared into a dark corner, Jacob turned back to her and said, "Let me repeat: I'm not here to cause trouble. I'm a reporter from Argentina. I'm just trying to track down a man who might have been in this bar, nothing more."

She stared at him, skeptical, her lips tight. "I don't care who you are. I want you out of here."

Jacob reached into his pocket, pulling out a small wad of cash. The instant the banknotes hit the counter, her breath caught in her throat. Two hundred dollars. More than half a year's salary. Her eyes darted from the money to the customers around them. Jacob quickly placed his hand over the notes, preventing her from grabbing them too soon.

"You know the guy I'm talking about," he said softly. "Just tell me what you know, and this is yours."

Her fingers fidgeted at her sides, her mind weighing up the options. After a long moment, she exhaled sharply and nodded, her voice suddenly quieter, more cooperative. "Describe him."

Jacob smirked. "I can do better than that." He took out his phone and scrolled through a few images before landing on one of Raúl Espinosa. He held it up to her.

"*Dios mío!*" she gasped. Her hand flew to her mouth. "Oh my God."

"You know him?"

Her eyes expanded, filled with a mix of fear and recognition. "No," she pouted. "I never saw him before... until two minutes ago."

Jacob raised an eyebrow. "What?"

She leaned in, her voice barely a whisper. "He's sitting around the corner. He's the guy in the blue cap who bought a rum from me just now. He doesn't have the beard in the photo, but the eyes, nose... Yes, it's him."

"You sure?"

"Positive."

"He been here before?"

She shook her head, eyes darting toward the door. "The manager's back," she whispered. "I can't talk anymore. Pay me!"

Jacob nodded, slipped her the money, and moved toward the back corner.

FOURTEEN

The alcove was dark, but Jacob could make out the figure of the man he had come to track down. In the end, he didn't have to try very hard. The mountain had come to Muhammad. A weathered face, thick beard. Forty-seven years old, extremely fit and strong, judging by the upper body development. Raúl Espinosa, enveloped in a cloud of cigar smoke, nursed a large rum and stared blankly at the screen of his cell phone.

Jacob approached slowly, his mind already calculating the next steps. "Señor Espinosa?"

The man reflexively stashed the cell in his pocket and looked up, his eyes tightening in suspicion. He clearly wasn't expecting to see anyone, especially not a stranger who knew his name. One hand sneaked below the table; perhaps he had a gun sitting on his thigh. Jacob had to play it cool. He had the S&W tucked under his belt, an insurance policy he didn't want to use.

"Who's asking?" The voice was gravelly, guarded.

"You seriously don't know who I am?" Jacob took the seat across from him without waiting for an invitation.

"No. Why should I?"

"It's just strange that I've come to this bar to start searching for you, and here you are!" Jacob rested his elbows on the table. "You weren't following me?"

"I don't follow people I've never even heard of." He shrugged. "And there's nothing strange about me being here. I come here now and again. The rum's cheap, and there's no nosy questions." He glared at Jacob. "Usually."

"The barmaid said this is the first time she's ever seen you here."

"Larisa?" He leered. "She's a good actress, that one. And a tiger between the sheets. I've slept more than one night with my weary head resting on those big breasts of hers." He tipped his glass up, then let it down with a knocking sound on the hard wooden table.

"Larisa?" Jacob rubbed his chin. "That's more like a Russian name."

"What can I say? Her parents must be good communists." He laughed without humor. "You said you were searching for me. Well, you've found me. Please, state your business or fuck off. In fact, if I don't like what your business is, you can fuck off anyway."

"Manuel Vargas," Jacob said smoothly. "I'm an Argentinian reporter, and I'm here to ask you a couple of questions about Deputy Minister General Miguel Domínguez." He showed Espinosa a laminated press card. It may not have convinced an experienced spook like Espinosa, but still, he gave a nod as if the ID was satisfactory. "I'd like to talk to you about some other matters too. Things I might be able to help you with." He pulled out a small notepad and pen as props, despite the fact he would remember everything Espinosa said. He nodded at the pad. "Do you mind?"

"You've sparked my curiosity." He pointed at the pad and pen. "But put them away. Nothing on the record. And hand over your phone while you're at it."

Jacob gladly did as he was asked. Espinosa was about to talk.

Espinosa's jaw tightened as he ignited a small cigar. "What do you want to know about Miguel Domínguez?"

"His plans." Jacob leaned forward. "I know you were once close to him, from when you served in the military together and later on, but things have changed. I know about the Bay of Pigs II operation."

Espinosa's eyes flickered with surprise, but he didn't deny it. He took a slow sip of his rum, studying Jacob carefully. "You seem to know a lot already."

Jacob smiled faintly. "It's my job to know things. I'll let you in on a little secret. I work for Argentina's spy agency, the Secretaría de Inteligencia del Estado. But here in Havana, I'm helping the Americans."

"They've got more than enough of their own people to do their spying." He let loose a cloud of smoke. "That's the most ridiculous thing I've ever heard."

"Maybe it sounds crazy to you. But it's the truth. How do you think I know so much about you?" Without waiting for an answer, he continued, "I'm here to try and stop Domínguez from destroying Cuba with this insane plot. Or at least to expose his plan with proper evidence. If we can do that, the exercise won't go ahead. But to do those things, I need your help."

Espinosa laughed bitterly. "My help? You're crazy, Vargas. I don't even know who the hell you are."

"I've told you who I am," Jacob insisted. "I know in your gut you believe me. And I can already tell you're not on board with Domínguez's vision. That's why I'm here. You know it's treachery, what he's planning. You don't want to see your country destroyed."

Espinosa's gaze hardened before he stared at scratched initials on the table. "You don't know a damn thing about what I want." He looked up suddenly. "Tell me where you got your information from. It sure as hell wasn't from me. I've said nothing to anyone."

"But you were going to. You were going to confirm everything I've claimed to Frank Cain, an American journalist. We know this because of intel from a guy called Cristian Passo. The CIA was unwilling to believe him—he was acting irrationally. But you had agreed to confirm all of this to Cain because you are closer to the action than Passo was. I know this because you"—he jabbed a finger at Espinosa—"just happened to show up at this shit-hole of a bar before Cain met his maker, rescued him, and dropped him near the embassy. You then went off the radar, unable to be contacted by Wilfred Arnold."

That was the clincher. Naming his handler. The hardness around Espinosa's eyes softened like butter. He expelled a quart of air mixed with smoke as he sighed.

"My theory?" Jacob continued. "You got nervous after Passo's death and decided to clam up."

"Speculation." There was no conviction behind the objection.

Jacob took a breath, shifting gears. "Let's start with what I do know." The accurate retelling brought nods from Espinosa. "And now, here's me actually speculating. Cain was waiting for you, but you were simply late, and this may have saved your life. Somehow, Domínguez got wind of this meeting—I've got a theory about that, but that's for later—and sent an assassin. I think both you and Passo stood to gain financially from spilling the beans to Cain. Moreover you believed that Cain revealing it to the world was a better option than banging your head against a brick wall with all the Doubting Thomases at Havana Station. How am I doing so far?"

A toothpick found its way between Espinosa's front teeth, and he gave it a chew, rolling it around with his tongue. "You are smarter than you look, pelón."

Jacob smiled at the epithet, 'baldie,' then said, "And the craziest part? You returned here, to the scene of the murder, because you thought you might find a clue leading to Passo's killer. You and him weren't good friends, but the 'professional' side of your nature wants to know the truth. And you feel safe coming here because Domínguez would've called in a favor with the cops, told them any reports of murders committed in the bar were not to be investigated. To round it all off, the general thinks you are still on his side. Am I right?"

Another nod. "You're good, *hermano*." He tapped the tabletop with fingernails long enough to play classical guitar. "You and I are going to stop this madman. As you say, I'm in the good books with Domínguez—for now—but I don't fully trust that Larisa. She might be a part-time whore with a heart of gold, but you probably rattled her with your questions. We should go. You wait a minute after I've gone, then you leave. Turn left, walk two blocks, then another left. I'll be sitting behind the wheel of a dirty white Lada." He rattled off the license plate number.

"Don't leave without me," said Jacob.

"I wouldn't dream of it." Espinosa crushed out his cigar and walked away.

FIFTEEN

Espinosa put the Soviet-made clunker into first gear and glanced at Jacob riding shotgun. "Keep that baseball cap pulled low over your eyes, and maybe shield the side of your face with your elbow and hand. Try not to look out the window."

"That sounds a little desperate." Jacob nevertheless did as he was told. It was Espinosa's turf—he knew best.

"Every small action counts. The Chinese have given the government lots of security cameras—facial recognition, LPR cameras. I've put a piece of tape over two of the license plate letters to disguise them, but if a zealous cop pulls us over, it could be game over. So yeah, I want to take all the precautions, even the little ones." He wound down his window and lit a cigarette. "It's unlikely there are cameras in this neighborhood, but I have no doubt they'll be planted somewhere along the way. They're mounted discreetly, and no one can be sure where they are."

The car groaned as they rolled away from the curb, heading west. Five minutes later, Espinosa's eyes flicked to the rearview mirror—barely noticeable, but Jacob caught it. They were being followed. As instructed, he kept his head down despite the temptation to turn around in his seat. "What is it?"

"A motorcycle, maybe thirty meters back. Been with us for a while, but he's getting closer."

Jacob's hand drifted to the gun tucked under his jacket. "A tail?"

Espinosa didn't reply immediately. His expression was grim, but his voice stayed flat. "Not sure. Could be nothing, could be Domínguez's people. He sometimes likes to remind me I'm never out of his sight."

The Lada rattled as they headed away from the denser parts of the city. The buildings shrank in stature, their decay more pronounced. As they moved toward the edges of the Vedado precinct, the streets widened and the air cleared a little. Traffic thinned out.

"We can't lose him here," Espinosa muttered. "I'm taking a detour." He turned onto a side street, weaving through the maze of aging apartment blocks and half-abandoned alleys. They passed worn-down markets and clusters of kids playing soccer in the streets, their voices fading as the car rolled farther from the city's heartbeat. Espinosa drove like a man who'd clocked thousands of hours in this car—steady, never drawing attention.

But the motorcycle was still there. Jacob could hear it.

The Lada's engine grumbled, a low constant noise that seemed too loud in the quiet of the dusty streets. Espinosa took another turn, then another. "We're going to the La Lisa district," he said. "There's a huge park there."

A few minutes later, they pulled into a small parking lot abutting the Parque Metropolitano de La Habana. No sound of any motorcycles. "We wait," said Espinosa.

The two men sat without speaking for a full five minutes. Espinosa smoked, and Jacob wondered what the hell was going to happen next. His neck, tired from being held turned away from the window, began to ache. He chanced a glance to the right, quickly scanning the tree line, benches, an area with play equipment. There was no one around except for an old man fifty yards away. Carrying a string shopping bag, he shuffled along as if he'd been walking the park's pathways for decades.

"Someone's definitely watching us," Espinosa muttered.

"Not the old man, surely?" said Jacob.

"No. Someone else. I can feel it. I'm gonna need your help scoping the place out. If you feel your life is in danger, get the hell out of here." He opened his door slowly, and Jacob followed suit, slipping out of the Lada and keeping his movements fluid and natural. He looked up and down the street. A light breeze from the north hit the sweat under his shirt, cooling him.

"The motorcycle's gone," said Jacob quietly. "I think we're OK."

"Doesn't matter," countered Espinosa.

Jacob's eyes swept the park again, left to right, then back again. That's when he spotted him. A man standing by a tree, partially hidden in the shadows. "See him?"

"*Sí*. Asian, maybe early thirties. I think it's the rider; ditched his helmet and jacket somewhere. The pants are the same color. Yes. I swear, it's him."

"I agree. He looks out of place in this setting."

"Totally."

"What do we do?" Jacob asked under his breath.

"Ambush the *cabrón*. You go round the back, I'll distract him from here."

Jacob moved slowly at first, reached a screening hedge, then picked up the pace. He circled around a stand of flowering hibiscus to observe the man from another angle while Espinosa made a show of reading the park's map board. The man lurking under the big tree stood still as a statue; Jacob thought he could make out the bulge of something under his untucked shirt. A gun. Jacob walked a couple of connecting paths to make sure the watcher didn't have company. Finding a motorcycle lying on its side behind a public restroom, but no other goons, it was time to confront the watcher.

Jacob approached the man with a loping gait, holding out a

well-worn map and a pen he'd found in Espinosa's glove compartment. The man didn't flinch; Jacob's eyes were drawn to the unmistakable outline of the pistol under his loose shirt. In English, Jacob said, "Excuse me, sir. I'm totally lost." He offered his goofiest laugh. "Can you help me find my way out of here?"

The man sneered. "No speak English," he said forcefully, waving Jacob away. The man frowned as Jacob asked the same question in Spanish. "*No hablo español!*" he said.

By now Jacob was right up in the man's face, where he could smell something foul on his breath, a combination of onion and garlic. He smiled genially and locked eyes with the Chinese man, opened his mouth as if to speak, and suddenly brought his right knee up, hard, into the man's groin. The man's face contorted in agony, his hands instinctively dropping to the injured area. His groaning was cut short as Jacob unleashed a brachial stun neck chop to the throat. The unconscious man crumpled like an old accordion and crashed onto the grass.

Espinosa was there in seconds, a pair of blue rubber gloves on, rifling through the man's pockets with the efficiency of a customs official looking for contraband. A cell phone, scraps of paper with indecipherable Chinese writing on them, a pistol. "We're keeping all of this stuff. I'm going to get someone to translate the writing," said Espinosa. He looked at the gun from various angles. "The gun's a Norinco QSZ-92."

"I've never seen one of those."

"Chinese make. I've seen plenty." From his kneeling position, he looked up and added, "This man is PLA or an MSS employee from their embassy. Maybe simply hired muscle on vacation. Whatever, where there's one, there could be more."

As Espinosa spoke, Jacob was already pulling the man farther into the undergrowth, out of sight. Before he could object, Espinosa produced a weapon of his own—looked to be a Makarov—screwed a silencer into the end, crawled into the bushes, and calmly fired three shots into the unconscious man's skull. Espinosa scrambled to his feet and grabbed the dead man's personal items as Jacob said a silent prayer for the fallen adversary.

Espinosa gestured toward one of the park's entrances, where a small crowd of teenagers in school uniforms was forming. "People are starting to come into the park. Someone will find the body eventually, maybe soon. We have to get out of here."

Back in the car and on the open road, Espinosa was sweating profusely. His fingers trembled, knuckles white, resting on the steering wheel. "You OK?" said Jacob, wondering if the guy was on drugs.

"*Sí. Todo está bien*. All good." He wiped his brow with the back of his wrist. "I had to waste him. I didn't get any joy out of it...he would have reported seeing us together."

"He might have already done that by the time you shot him. In fact, I'd bet on it." Jacob pressed the on button of the dead man's cell. PIN required. Naturally. "They'll be able to track this." He wound down the window and tossed the device into a water-filled ditch by the side of the road that stank of raw sewage.

Espinosa swore under his breath. "What else could I have done?"

"Ah...not killed him?" Jacob stared at him with exaggerated bug eyes. "Think about that?"

"What the hell do you care? He was a dirty rotten Chinese operative. Those guys would kill their own mothers if they were told to."

"You don't think killing him will piss off his masters even more? If they've gotten wind that you're in the company of a tall stranger, their alarm bells will be going off. Think about it. You told me about all the surveillance upgrades—which I already knew about. They would have filmed me at the airport on arrival, maybe had me marked for observation as a person of interest. If this dude managed to snap off a long-distance photo on his phone and sent it off, we could be royally screwed."

"Still had to kill him," grumbled Espinosa. "Now shut up for a while. You're starting to give me the shits."

"Where are we going?"

"What part of 'shut up' don't you understand? Just trust me, OK?"

Continuing the conversation would be a bad idea with Espinosa in this mood. Besides, what was done was done.

The 12-mile westward journey from the park to the town of Bauta—some of it necessarily via the heavily monitored Carretera Central, the national highway that bisected Cuba from east to west—took them just over thirty minutes. Twelve minutes into the trip, Espinosa suddenly lost his foul mood and got all friendly again. He told Jacob he was taking them to an old abandoned house. It was on an old army training ground that had been abandoned many years ago. They would lie low there for a while. "An old navy buddy of mine used to run a state-owned melon farm a couple of kilometers from there." Espinosa explained to Jacob how the guy had grown tired of working his ass off for little reward and moved to the city. After he left, no one wanted to take on the role of farm manager, so the place was left to rot. This buddy was now driving taxis for a living—part time—and earning a lot more money. Jacob asked half-heartedly if Espinosa ever thought of doing likewise. He had, but he wasn't capable of being nice to people all day long. Jacob nodded understandingly. He wasn't a 'people person' either.

Open fields soon gave way to small farms, then houses bunched closer together until they reached a wooden sign welcoming them to Bauta. They drove on through the town, due west, back into rustic territory again. Espinosa took a red-dirt road tracking north, a couple more turns, then onto a corrugated section with vegetation growing wild, from both edges into the middle of the road. No one had driven here for months. The brave Lada was no 4x4, but it handled the rough terrain with only minimal whines and rattles from under the hood.

Jacob memorized the route as they went, making note of landmarks and converting the turns into opposite directions in case he needed to make the return journey alone. At last, they reached the abandoned house, sitting atop a hill and surrounded by thick scrub. Long grass lined either side of what remained of a gravel driveway. Espinosa's earlier signs of distress were all but gone, the sweat had dried in his pores, and his hands had stopped shaking. "Thank God, we've arrived in one piece and with no one following us."

"Why did you bring me all the way out here?" said Jacob as they strode up a short set of stairs. Weeds poked through between rotting planks that were barely holding together.

"To talk." Espinosa gestured to the long bench-seat on the front deck of the main house. Jacob brushed away flakes of decades-old paint, exoskeletons of an array of insects, and sawdust from woodborers and sat on one end of the bench. The Cuban remained standing, blinking hard as he shooed a couple of flies from his face.

"Not to kill me like you did the *chino*?"

"Don't be an idiot." Espinosa extended a crumpled packet of cigarettes.

Jacob shook his head. "I only smoke cigars. And those only rarely."

"Fair enough." He grinned. "More for me."

"Why are we all the way out here, in the middle of nowhere? You're making me nervous."

"Cut the crap. I can tell not much makes you nervous. I simply wanted to ensure we had complete privacy. We can talk here undisturbed, without looking over our shoulders every five seconds. Something tells me this is your first time in Cuba, no?"

"*Sí.* Hopefully my last."

"Then you should see a bit more than just the capital, to appreciate the beauty of this country."

Jacob nodded. "Got it." He reached out, fingers beckoning. "On second thoughts, give me one of those smokes."

While Jacob lit up, Espinosa trotted down the stairs, opened the Lada's trunk, and carried back a foam cooler. He placed it on the floor, unzipped it, and pulled out two bottles of beer.

Droplets of condensation rolled down the glass. "I find a small amount of alcohol can help people overcome their inhibitions and, well"—he shrugged—"...get along better."

"Couldn't agree more." Jacob tilted back the bottle, savoring the beer's refreshing hoppy flavor. The sun glimmered faintly through the trees running along the boundary of the property to the west. A couple of flies buzzed around his face until he caught them in mid-air and squashed them between his fingers.

"Nice ninja skills," said Espinosa with a trace of real admiration. "I can never catch the bastards."

"Nothing to it, really," said Jacob. "We've got faster flies to practice on in Argentina."

Espinosa chuckled, and they clinked the necks of the bottles together. "You're all right for a foreigner." The sun would be setting in about twenty minutes. On any other day, sharing a beer with a fellow spook while soaking up the rural ambiance would have constituted a good time. And, in a way, it was.

"I'm ready," said Espinosa. "Let's you and I talk about that asshole Domínguez, hey?"

SIXTEEN

Swarms of mosquitoes outside were attacking fiercely and without respite—mainly homing in on Jacob's pale and unprotected skin—and the men decided to take the meeting indoors. His mood lifted immediately when Espinosa hoisted two more beers out of the cooler.

A crescent of light was all that remained from the setting sun, shadows growing longer from one end of the room to the other. In the dying light, Espinosa grabbed a couple of long white candles from a kitchen drawer, lighting them with his cigarette lighter.

"You knew exactly where to look for those candles," said Jacob.

"*Sí*. And I could rustle us up a can of beans if you get hungry. But you'd have to eat them cold. The only downside to this place—no power connected. There is a generator in a shed out back, but I think it's run out of fuel. It was the last time I came, and as far as I know, I'm the only person who's been coming here the last couple of years or so." He gave a low chuckle. "Back when I was working for the DI, I'd sometimes bring 'enemies of the state' for a visit. They didn't always leave...alive."

Jacob was grateful for the man's honesty but on guard. He

was a little too casual when talking about killing. When Jacob had to do it, there was always a heavy weight on his conscience, even when dispatching the most evil of people.

"You sure no else comes here?"

"Of course not. It is always a possibility. Maybe people do stumble across the place and have a poke around, who knows? But if they have, no one has ever left evidence of their presence. Not that I've been able to find anyway."

"There a flushing toilet somewhere?" said Jacob, more in hope than expectation.

Espinosa laughed. "No. Long drop in the back yard."

A couple minutes later, fumbling around in the gloom with only the flashlight on his cell for guidance, Jacob was back, ready to hash it all out.

"Let's have all cards on the table," said Jacob. "Who wants to go first?"

The Cuban scratched his bearded chin. "I'll toss you for it. You call." He pulled out a three-peso coin, flipping it high.

"Heads," said Jacob. The coin struck one of the old wooden beams that hung in the kitchen and ricocheted off into a corner. "That's a foul toss. I'm disqualified."

"In that case, let me tell you, in as much detail as I can, all I know." Jacob began, like a return journey, from the newest intel he had gathered working his way back to the oldest.

"Seb Goulding. The CIA man who handled Cristian Passo before Arnold came along. So far, all I know about the guy is the name and that he's now based in Caracas. The fact he's working there sparked something in my brain, because I also know about Lourdes Domínguez living and working in Venezuela."

Espinosa wriggled in his seat, itching to add his two cents' worth. "Can I say—"

"Please, let me finish, and then you can have your turn, ask questions, whatever. Interrupt, and I lose focus. *Bien?*"

Espinosa's eyes blazed, and his nostrils flared for a moment. "*Bien.*" He leaned forward, elbows resting on his knees. "Keep going then and hurry up about it. I gotta get home and feed my cat."

"I have a specialist looking into the activities of the deputy minister's niece. This person is cooperating with the Americans at the highest level, following money trails. If there's a link to Lourdes making or channeling transactions to finance this operation, they will find it.

"I'm also aware of the relationship between Domínguez and the Russian arms dealer, Vitaly Botvinnik. We have photos of the two of them partying hard in Europe."

He held up a finger; Espinosa was busting a gut to chip in again. "Please." He paused a second then added, "We know there could be legitimate reasons for these men to liaise about Cuban defense matters. However, the fact that Russia hasn't sold your country any serious military equipment for 20 years rings alarm bells, at least for me. Documented evidence of collusion between these two could be the clincher."

Jacob observed how Espinosa sucked his lips between his teeth, again wanting to butt in. To his credit, he remained silent.

"Which brings me to Passo and Cain. First, Passo. He believed you had the dirt on Domínguez and you were coming to deliver. Nod if I'm right."

Espinosa nodded.

"And Cain intended to pay Passo for bringing you to him with the information he wanted for his scoop."

A slower nod this time.

"With a little tip for you."

A shake of the head accompanied by pursed lips.

The fact surprised Jacob. "OK, you can elaborate on that when it's your turn." He glanced at his wristwatch. 21:37. He grinned in the flickering light. "Which is now."

After a long pause, Espinosa puffed out his cheeks and began to talk.

"Let me start with Seb Goulding, like you did. He was Passo's most recent handler, as you rightly pointed out. Not mine, initially. I had a guy who was more interested in *jineteras* and getting drunk than anything I had to say. That guy, Jim Cryer, was sent home in disgrace after getting caught with a hooker by Thai police. After that, Goulding became my handler, too. I would not be surprised if Passo still had contact with him. I never fully trusted Goulding; I was careful about revealing too much to him. Passo, on the other hand, thought the guy was 'cool.'" Espinosa shook his head slowly, then tapped the top of the old table. "If you can get surveillance on Goulding in Caracas, do it."

He opened the last of the beers and handed one to Jacob.

"Which bring us to Lourdes. Everything you say about her is true, as far as I know. Domínguez still thinks I'm loyal, so he sometimes lets things slip. Like how influential and important his precious niece is in Caracas. You know, the woman wrangled her way inside, got close to the inner government elites, by marrying a friend of the loco Venezuelan president?"

"Impressive."

"Gold-digging bitch. Turns out, she had more business acumen than her dopey husband, who is a pathetic hen-pecked weakling. The board of directors of her company appointed her financial director."

"*Importaciones y Exportaciones de Calidad Venezolana, SA.* I've heard—'

"Don't interrupt me," chided Espinosa. "I afforded you the courtesy. Do the same."

Jacob nodded a little sheepishly, caught out by his own rule. "Sorry. Go on."

"Domínguez has been visiting Caracas more frequently than ever. Going there with that Russian asshole, Botvinnik. I heard them talking on the phone once. In Russian—even though I know for sure Botvinnik speaks fluent Spanish. Like I said, Domínguez trusts me, but the fact he shielded me from this conversation tells me the Russian has a huge role in this.

"One thing you didn't mention—I guess because you know nothing about it—is the Chinese involvement. I can only go on my gut. Domínguez has been meeting with a man called Zhou Jianyu. His title is deputy director of cultural and strategic affairs, but he's most likely the equivalent of Elijah Dundas. I suspect Zhou set the tail on me."

"Can the bullets you fired be traced back to you?"

"No. Generic 9mm Luger ammo fired from a ghost gun. I purchased this one on the black market. No record of the weapon existing."

"Still, if this Zhou and Domínguez are cozy, as you say, the death of that goon could spell bad news for you."

Espinosa shook his head. "I don't think so. Zhou wouldn't like to admit he's got tooled-up spies running around Cuba. As for Operation Restore Dignity, my feeling is the Chinese role will boil down to technical assistance and advice, no on-the-ground personnel or inventory."

"Sounds logical."

"Which brings me to the operation itself." He waved his hands around dismissively. "You're missing one point in this entire discussion. I *know* it's going to happen. You don't really need proof to tell the world about it." He tilted his head to the side and added, "You know how you've been calling it Bay of Pigs II? I kinda like that name." He stood and paced the room, his profile a silhouette in the candle light. "But—it's way more audacious than that. There are boats waiting on the Isla de la Juventud, a small armada that will sail into Havana Harbor with a massive landing force of men. The plan makes special allowance for some of the 'invaders' to be sacrificed as Domínguez's special forces suddenly come out to crush them like insects."

"*Hostia!* Jesus! There'll be war on the streets of Havana."

Espinosa nodded. "Something any reasonable person would want to avoid. By the way, you're butting in again. But you know what? I don't care. You have my permission to interrupt whenever you like, *argentino*. Your rules suck. I prefer a normal conversation with some back and forth."

"As you like." Jacob smiled his agreement to the new terms.

"One of the biggest questions for me is: how are they going to pin this on the Americans?"

"Good question. I've got a couple of theories."

"Explain."

"American IDs for the soldiers to be slaughtered, for starters. The Chinese are going to use their AI programs for a lot of this kind of stuff." For the next five minutes, Espinosa rattled off a number of other totally plausible scenarios to make the operation seem like the United States was behind it—fake leaked communications; American-made military equipment and arms obtained and supplied by Botvinnik; a phony anti-Cuban resistance cell. He enumerated half a dozen more tactics in the area of psy-ops on a global scale, carefully crafted to manipulate world opinion.

As Espinosa spoke, it was like a switch had flipped in the man's head; the Cuban had morphed from ground-level grunt to insightful intelligence analyst. Jacob listened, at once enthralled and impressed. He committed all the details to memory, to be included in a report he would send to Fletcher later tonight.

Assuming they got back in one piece.

"Thanks for that. But let me return to something you said a moment ago. *We don't need proof.*" Jacob shook his head. "I'm afraid we do need it. Your word is not good enough."

"Even with my proximity to Domínguez?"

"That could be easily explained away. You're making up bullshit because you have a grudge against him, want to set him up."

"Yeah? And what about Passo getting killed in the presence of Frank Cain?"

"I assumed they were waiting in the bar for you to bring them the proof I'm talking about. Do you actually have any at all?"

"That proof was my fucking testimony. I've got enough information in my head to blow the whole scheme apart."

Jacob frowned. "It's what the legal people call hearsay. We need documents, recordings, things like that. Can you get that?"

"Are you kidding me? You gotta pass through an x-ray to get into the Ministry, then get frisked by some goons. There's cameras all over the place. If I had a wire they would find it; if I tried to take some sneaky photos, they'd see me. It's impossible."

"What about off-site? Away from the Ministry?"

"No go. He sees value in having me as a key soldier in the operation, but he'd never mix with me in a social setting. He pretends to be a friend, but it's all bullshit. Which is fine by me because a monster like him could never be my friend. He's changed in ways you can't imagine since his days in the military, when he was more or less a normal guy."

"Then I'm gonna need you to help me get inside the palace, so to speak. I want to interview Miguel Domínguez. Get him to confess to what he's up to. Or at least for me to find the proof you seem too chicken to want to get your hands on."

"*Estás loco!* You're crazy!"

"Maybe, but it's the only way forward I can see."

"And how the hell are you going to get access to him?"

"You are going to introduce me."

"And how do I know you? I'm an ex-intelligence guy making a living by repairing old appliances. That ain't gonna work. You're gonna have to come up with a better plan than that."

"Appliances?" Jacob guffawed. "First I've heard of that."

Espinosa shrugged. "You never asked."

"True." He waited a second, watching a line of wax drip down a candle. "You know, there was a theory floated at Havana Station that maybe you're still in the employ of the DI." Jacob neglected to mention that it was also *his* theory. "You told your handlers you became a baker after you left your other job. But you've never worked as a baker."

He shook his head. "I have. At a bakery three blocks from my apartment."

"For how long?"

"A month. I hated it." He stood, leaning over Jacob. "Listen, Señor Vargas, if that's even your real name, I'm not here to be interrogated, *entiendes?*" He sat, lit a cigarette, and exhaled a haze of smoke almost violently. "We are here to cooperate. Yes, I repair appliances for pennies, and I receive a pension from the DI and also cash payments from Wilfred Arnold. But you know what? Money is not my prime motivator, as I am sure it's not yours." A heavy drag on the cigarette, deep into his lungs. "I was never promised money from Cain either, and I didn't expect any. I just want Domínguez stopped in his tracks."

Jacob nodded. Although Skia paid him an absolute fortune, he wasn't driven by the money either. A sense of duty, right and wrong. It was as simple as that. He sometimes joked with Fletcher about getting furloughed out of the job because it was too dangerous, but cliché as it sounded, it was an honor to serve.

Jacob scratched the side of his neck, a mosquito bite starting to irritate. "On the drive back to Havana we'll figure out a way for me to get an audience with Domínguez." He leaned back, the spine of the old wooden chair creaking. "What I'm curious about is this: how the hell did Passo decide to contact Frank Cain?"

"I was also curious about that. Cristian refused to tell me. I didn't push him on it. Now he's dead, we'll never know."

Jacob stood and stretched his arms and legs, pacing for a few moments to walk off pins and needles. "In his interview with a CIA officer, Cain claimed he got an anonymous tip-off. A phone call in Washington. You think Passo made that call?"

A shrug. "He could have. His English was excellent, better than mine. Although I can speak it and understand it good enough. Cristian liked to read political stories from America. So yes, he might have made direct contact with Cain."

Jacob sat back down on the wobbly chair with a sigh. "I tend to agree with you." He took a cigarette from the packet in the middle of the table. No more after this one. "Tell me what you know about the operational details. So we know what we're dealing with if we can't stop it."

"It's getting late. Let me entertain you with that fun stuff on the drive back to the city. I've satisfied my number one goal while we've been talking."

"And what's that?"

"Deciding whether or not to trust you."

"And do you?"

"Ninety-five percent."

Jacob stood and clapped the man on the shoulder. "That's about the highest trust rating I ever scored."

Espinosa switched on the flashlight in his cell phone, bent low, and blew out the candles like it was somebody's birthday. "Let's move. And be careful on those rickety stairs."

SEVENTEEN

THE LADA LURCHED AND JUDDERED ON THE WAY BACK down the track. It had struggled on the way up, but on the descent, the effect was amplified. Jacob attributed it to the fact that Espinosa was driving in the dark. But he cut him some slack. The Russian vehicle's high beam was barely brighter than the candles they'd burned in the kitchen.

Bones rattled and muscles pounded, Jacob breathed a sigh of relief as they left the dirt road and hit the highway. "You going to start spilling the beans on the details?"

Espinosa turned his head sharply, his almost maniacal grin illuminated by the dashboard lights. "Want the best part first?"

"Why not?"

"Domínguez thinks I'll be leading a platoon." He tilted his head back and let rip with a belly laugh. "Driving one of the landing craft."

"You must be kidding."

"Not at all. I've agreed to do it. I've attended briefings, met with other commanding officers. Pretended that joining his cabal was the greatest honor of my miserable life."

"How are you accepted by the other officers? Like you said, you're an appliance repair man."

"Sure. But they know my unblemished navy background. I attained the rank of *capitán de fragata*. Besides, they're not all full-time professionals either. There's diversity in the ranks. Some Russians. Even, believe it or not, one real American. A stupid sympathizer."

"Wait a second. Surely you must have been given something in writing? Instructions? Maps? Something I can take to my boss to prove the existence of the plan?"

A fierce shake of the head. "If this was a normal military exercise, perhaps. But Domínguez wants to leave no paper trail. Minimal digital trail, too. So no emails. Just phone calls and texts, and then only to notify participants of briefings."

"You mean to tell me he's relying on people remembering stuff?"

Jacob watched Espinosa's larynx rise and fall as he swerved to the left. "Big pothole." He offered a half-smile of apology. "To be honest, there's not much to remember. Turn up when required, do as commanded on the day of the mission. It's mainly pep talks, ideology."

Jacob muttered to himself. General Domínguez was taking no chances with potential leaks.

"How about training? Exercises?"

"None. He's recruited soldiers who can handle any weapon you put in their hands, ready to do anything required on the day. More important, they are pre-qualified as obedient and ideologically sound."

"Then how did *you* get the call up?" Jacob couldn't hide the irony in his voice.

"Because I am all of those things. At least in Domínguez's eyes. He sees me as one of his greatest assets. And he confided in me that my boat will be landing far from the main theater of action, where the invaders will get their asses kicked."

They drove in silence for a while. Jacob could feel nervous and physical exhaustion approaching. He sensed Espinosa was getting to the same stage. He took the opportunity to flick a text to Pepe.

Discretion required: could he suggest a pick-up point? The answer came in under a minute. Jacob confirmed the location with Espinosa, who nodded in appreciation. "Perfect. Your driver is a smart guy."

"I got lucky, I guess." Jacob scratched the side of his head where a mosquito had left a particularly annoying bite. "You said Domínguez was willing to sacrifice men. But not you?"

Espinosa ran a hand through his hair. "Not me. I'm to be spared. That's if you can believe a word coming out of that snake's mouth. He's promised if everything goes smoothly, there's a top position in the government waiting for me."

"Why hasn't he offered you something like that already?"

The Cuban laughed, his body rocking back and forth in his seat. "He has. More than once. But I've always refused. Which, to him, is a positive trait—it means I'm happy to remain a proletarian in this communist utopia. And that makes me 'ideologically sound.'"

Another anomaly occurred to Jacob. One that suddenly had him questioning Espinosa's honesty. "If you are to be spared, then why not put you on the other side? The side that crushes the invasion force?"

"A very good question, and one I asked him."

"And?"

"For some reason, he's decided the defenders can only be comprised of real, active soldiers from the Revolutionary Armed Forces. He's got an ally near the top of FAR; one of them's going to take control of the defense with an iron fist and become an overnight national hero. Once the 'uprising' is quelled, my theory is that Domínguez will step in, declare a state of emergency, call for a vote of no confidence in the current leader, and demand *he* be appointed president."

Jacob's head spun with these revelations. Out of sheer curiosity, he said, "What kind of boat are you supposed to be commanding?"

"An Osa-class missile boat. Old, but it's been modified. Something I could handle no problem. Some Russian weapons on board: AK-630 cannons, .50-caliber heavy machine guns."

"Where's that boat now?"

"Docked at the Isla de la Juventud." Jacob pictured the island, to the south of Cuba proper. "Me and the other platoon leaders are supposed to travel there on the quiet where the soldiers are already encamped. There are a number of other boats like the one I'm commanding. The weapons on them differ a little, but basically they're the same."

A thought occurred to Jacob. "You said before the plan was to use fake US IDs and equipment. If America was really planning this, do you think they'd make it obvious by using their own gear? They'd do everything in their power to avoid that."

"The original Bay of Pigs was carried out by the USA, correct?"

"Yes."

"And they wanted the world to believe it was the Cubans themselves, correct?"

"Correct."

"And how did that work out for them?"

Jacob blinked hard twice. "Not so good."

"So—and this is just my gut talking, not my brain—Domínguez is probably aiming for a similar ratio of American and non-American gear again. It worked before, it can work again. What the real ratio is, I have no idea." He shrugged. "Like I said, I'm just driving one boat."

"Who are his commanders?"

Espinosa turned and gave a slight shake of the head. "His 2IC is a man called Rafael Varona." He reeled off the names of five other men, all high-ranking military officers. The muscles in his jaw twitched as he reapplied his grip on the steering wheel. Jacob took this as a sign the conversation had run its course.

As they drew closer to the heart of Havana, the buildings

getting taller, the streets more crowded, Jacob stared at the man's unflinching profile. Time to ask more questions. "Do you know how many men will be involved in the invasion force?"

"Double the number from 1961. Probably in the order of 3,000 men, maybe up to 4,000. Domínguez is setting the stage for something catastrophic. Casualties will be enormous. Plus, because of the urban setting, there are going to be civilian casualties galore." He turned to Jacob, fire in his eyes. "You can see why this is going to be, as the Americans call it, a clusterfuck?"

"What about from the air?" Jacob felt a chill run down his spine even as he put the question. The original Bay of Pigs saw eight CIA-supplied B-26 bombers carry out attacks on Cuban airfields two days before the invasion. Modern planes could do a lot of serious damage.

"I don't know," said Espinosa through gritted teeth. "If he plans on dropping bombs, then it better be well way from the city." He sucked in a big breath. "There's a special place in hell for pricks like him."

The man's pessimism had to be turned around. "You make it sound like this is definitely gonna happen. It damn well isn't. We'll make sure it doesn't." Jacob leaned back, thinking through the implications if they couldn't stop it. "Do you have any idea of the timeline?"

Espinosa shrugged. "Deep down, Domínguez is paranoid. He's waiting for final confirmation from all his backers: in Havana, Beijing, and Moscow. Venezuela, too, if your theory about his niece is correct. He won't move until he's sure everything's in place. Could be days, could be weeks. He's keeping that part tight."

Jacob clenched his fists in his lap, his mind working overtime. "You're going to keep playing along," he said coldly. "Stay close. If you get a chance to visit the Ministry in the next day or so, swipe an incriminating paper from his desk—'

"I told you. That's impossible!"

"You're a goddamn spy, Raúl. Don't you have a bug-sweeping device?"

"You didn't listen the first time, did you? They frisk people at the door, make you walk through an x-ray machine. Even people who work there. Even fucking Domínguez. How do I get a damn device of any kind in there, huh?"

"OK, OK. I get it." Jacob chewed his lip.

"Man, he could call us all tonight and put us on stand-by." Espinosa gestured to the pack of cigarettes in the console. Jacob pulled one out and handed it over.

"Stay calm, amigo."

"Easy for you to say." Espinosa drew on the cigarette, then muttered something incomprehensible under his breath. The closer they got to central Havana, the more his previous confidence and bravado seemed to fade away. His fingers began to shake like they had earlier in the day.

They pulled up at an old dry dock in the Regla district, rusty hulks of decommissioned vessels looming like zombies in the dark.

"What's your plan then? You said we were going to come up with a way to get *you* inside the Ministry to interview Domínguez. Somehow, we forgot about that." He flashed his headlights twice. Another vehicle flashed twice in return.

"That's my ride."

"You didn't answer my question."

"Let me handle it. I need to talk to a colleague. Someone who's good at finding answers to intractable problems."

"When and how do I contact you again?"

Jacob's eyes hardened. "This morning you didn't even know I existed. Now you can't get enough of me."

"I'm not that way inclined," said Espinosa, a smile taking the edge off the tension. "But there's something I like about you."

"Yeah, what?"

"You give me hope."

Jacob handed over Pepe's card. "Call this number tomorrow at 8 a.m. I might have something figured out."

"Will do." He flipped the card between his fingers, wound down the window, and drove away.

"Good day?" said Pepe as Jacob climbed into the back seat.

"Yes. And no."

EIGHTEEN

JACOB TOLD PEPE HE'D NEED A PICK-UP AT 8 A.M. THE next morning. They agreed to meet at a tobacco kiosk about 700 yards from the hotel's main gate.

"You want me to grab you some cigars while I'm waiting?" Pepe asked casually.

Jacob nodded, handing him some cash. "Yeah, why not. Keep the change."

Pepe smiled. "You're too kind, Manny."

Jacob responded with a grunt, more out of habit than anything else. He wasn't in the mood for conversation. The adrenaline of the day was wearing off, leaving behind a numbing fatigue.

"I see you're exhausted," Pepe said, interpreting Jacob's silence. "I'll leave you to rest."

When they arrived back at the hotel, Jacob stepped out, paused for a second, and said, "Make sure your phone's charged tomorrow. I'm expecting a call on your number."

"*Por supuesto*. Of course. I'll be ready." Pepe grinned. "You are one mysterious hombre."

Jacob gave him a quick nod before heading into the hotel. It was 11:15 p.m., and the lobby was almost empty except for a few loud Canadian tourists nursing their last drinks. As he passed the reception desk, the woman from earlier, the one who had helped him check in, greeted him with a familiar smile.

"Did you enjoy your day gathering stories for your articles?" she asked, her tone playful.

Jacob smiled back, maintaining the persona of the friendly journalist. "It was enlightening," he said. "Havana hasn't disappointed."

Her cheeky wink told him he'd answered right. "Have a good night."

As he rode the elevator to his floor, Jacob's mind started to drift. The glossy, well-lit interior of the hotel felt like an entirely different world compared to the chaos outside. Havana's infrastructure had been failing for years: rolling blackouts, water shortages—yet here he was, in a place where everything worked efficiently.

The elevator doors opened with a soft ding, and Jacob stepped into the hallway. Motion-activated lights flickered on as he walked, illuminating his path in cool, white light. The setup seemed efficient, but he knew better—it was a sign of how tightly the government was rationing power.

Once inside his room, Jacob immediately went for the coffee machine, hesitated, then changed his mind. The day's events were still racing through his head, his nerves frayed, but the last thing he needed at this late hour was caffeine. His body was running on fumes as it was.

He had two tasks before he could rest: report to Fletcher and email Irina, find out if she was getting anywhere looking into Seb Goulding. But the beers from earlier had dulled his focus, and there was no avoiding the fact that Espinosa killing the Chinese spy had shaken him more than he'd like to admit. He was used to operating in gray areas, but this felt different. Even with Espinosa's reassurances, he couldn't stop thinking about whether they'd been spotted or if there was some detail they'd missed. Was anyone tracking their movements now?

The image of the dead man flashed in his mind again. Jacob wasn't naïve. Espinosa had been quick to eliminate the problem; however, that didn't mean they were in the clear. Tossing the man's phone had been a smart move, but it was just one small act that gave them a little breathing space.

He stepped into the bathroom and turned the shower to the coldest setting. The icy water hit his skin like a jolt. After drying off, Jacob's stomach growled, reminding him that he hadn't eaten in over eighteen hours. He picked up the phone and ordered room service—steak, salad, fries, and two bottles of cola.

He collapsed onto the bed, setting his alarm for a 30-minute power nap, and closed his eyes. The alarm screeched, jarring him back into consciousness, but the brief rest had done its job. When room service arrived with the meal, he ate slowly, savoring the juicy steak. Between bites, he opened his laptop and began drafting his report to Fletcher.

As he typed out the details of his meeting with Espinosa, his fingers moved almost automatically, recounting everything the Cuban had said. Even as he transcribed the conversation, part of him couldn't believe what Espinosa had told him. The scale of the plan—the military buildup, the looming event they were calling Operation Restore Dignity—it was all too big, too disastrous. What would Fletcher make of it?

After finishing the summary, Jacob recounted the incident with the Chinese operative and the moments leading up to the man's death. His mind kept circling back to one critical question: How was he supposed to get access to Domínguez? Espinosa's erratic behavior didn't inspire confidence, and Jacob couldn't shake the feeling that he might crack under pressure. The Cuban had been jumpy, flipping between confidence and uncertainty in a way that left Jacob unsettled.

Before signing off on the email, Jacob added a final note, asking Fletcher if it was worth considering bringing Espinosa to the US, giving him asylum in exchange for his testimony. With the scope of what they were up against, it seemed like the fastest way to expose the plan. Sure, it would be hearsay, but it might be enough to make Domínguez shelve his plans.

After hitting send, Jacob turned to his second task—an email to Irina. He asked her to look into the background of agent handler Wilfred Arnold, even though his gut told him the man was solid. This wasn't the time to cut corners: His gut had sometimes led him astray.

He put the laptop into sleep mode and opened the minibar, tempted by the row of tiny liquor bottles. A shot of something strong would take the edge off, help him get out of his own head for a bit. But he closed the fridge, knowing it wasn't worth the distraction.

Jacob lay back on the bed, prayed to his personal God, the one the official religions didn't know about, and asked him to lend a hand. This one was going to be too hard to do on his own. For once, he didn't feel in control.

A soft ping came from the laptop, cutting through his thoughts. He'd left it open, half-expecting an urgent response from Fletcher. Sure enough, there it was: a reply.

Yes, we can pull in Espinosa. But only after he gets the physical proof. No one will believe him without it. He'll just look like another defector trying to cash in. Get something solid first.

It wasn't what Jacob wanted to hear, but it was exactly what he expected. Without concrete evidence, Espinosa's words wouldn't be enough. The world needed more than speculation or suggestions of personal vendettas.

Jacob stared at the ceiling, thoughts lining up, one after the other. Sleep wasn't coming, not with all of this swirling in his head. He opened a blank spreadsheet on his laptop, trying to brainstorm ideas on how to get to Domínguez. He changed his mind about the booze and cracked a small bottle. Twenty minutes later, and with two shots of rum down, he'd scribbled out ten different plans, none of them viable. Each scenario felt more impractical than the last. He cursed under his breath.

Another email pinged. Irina. Her message was brief—she

hadn't found anything concrete yet but was digging deeper into Goulding and the Venezuelan connection; she would also look at Arnold. She promised to have something for him in a few hours, by the time he woke up.

Jacob stared at the screen, the weight of everything pressing down on him. Tomorrow, he'd meet Pepe, get the call from Espinosa—but what then? How was he supposed to break through the wall around Domínguez?

He closed the laptop with a sigh, feeling the uncertainty settle in. For the first time in a long time, Jacob had no idea how to proceed.

NINETEEN

The new Chinese restaurant in the Old Havava district drew lots of tourists eager to eat something different than Cuban food, but few locals visited. The prices, for one, were prohibitive. However, for elites like General Miguel Domínguez, cost was no barrier. Particularly today, with the genial and generous Mr. Zhou Jianyu, deputy director of cultural and strategic affairs from the People's Republic of China, picking up the tab for their late-night dinner.

"I know how busy you are, and I'm so glad you could find a spot for me in your schedule," said Zhou in fluent Spanish, his heavy accent a not-too-subtle clue as to his country of origin. His eyes were cast down in concentration as he helped himself to a large ladleful of steaming fried rice and transferred it to his own bowl. Next to his rice was a plate stacked high with a medley of green and leafy vegetables and all kinds of stewed, barbecued, and fried meats: beef, chicken, pork, and seafood. The man liked variety. Moreover, his bugling stomach bespoke a man who enjoyed food in large quantities. He offered his guest a warm smile. "Are you a fan of Chinese cuisine?"

"You want me to be completely honest with you?" said Domínguez, reaching for a small bottle of soy sauce. He drizzled a few drops on his lunch, which was a shrunk-down version of Zhou's massive helping. By contrast, it looked like a child's portion.

"Naturally." The diplomat smiled as he adjusted a pair of glasses that had slid down his small nose. The heavy black frames and thick lenses were straight out of a 1970s fashion magazine. "I wouldn't have it any other way."

"I'm not particularly keen on it."

"Oh," Zhou said, pursing his thin, purple lips. "I value honesty, but it's clear to me you could never become a real diplomat." He broke into a smile even broader than the first.

"How come?" Domínguez took a sip of red wine.

"Because a diplomat would have said yes. That he loved nothing more than Chinese food."

Domínguez smoothed the napkin in his lap. "And why would a diplomat do that? Lie just to be nice?"

"Not lie, exactly," countered Zhou. "Well, yes, strictly speaking. But it's a white lie. No harm meant, rather a way to flatter a host." He closed one eye and pointed a chopstick across the table. "I can see your mind ticking over. Of course, this type of behavior should only be condoned in the social setting. When discussing real matters of substance, of course, each party should speak their mind according to their actual position, or that of their government in my case. A diplomat often struggles with moral dilemmas, advocating an official line he may not be on board with a hundred percent." He laid his chopsticks down to refill his glass of red wine from the bottle.

"I have no moral dilemmas dealing with our cultural exchange program," said Domínguez. "It can only bring benefits to both of our countries."

"Will you be attending the musical soiree with me?"

Domínguez wiped his mouth with a cloth napkin. "Naturally. How could I refuse such a kind offer?"

"You know," Zhou said, looking at a couple of Chinese tourists paying for their meals at the counter. "It's pleasing to see how many of my countrymen are visiting this beautiful island these days. I bet you were getting sick of the Russians."

"Not at all. I welcome everyone to Cuba. Especially if they share our outlook on the world. And these days, that is more China than Russia."

"Excellent." Zhou stabbed a fat dumpling with a chopstick and bit a chunk off it. "Now enough of the small talk. Let's get down to business." He dropped his tone, even though no one was in earshot of them, positioned by a water feature in the garden section of the restaurant. "Has your niece been able to open an account on my behalf in Panama?"

A slow nod in reply. "For a diplomat, you don't beat around the bush."

Zhou gave a tinny laugh. "Not when it comes to my own personal affairs. I find being direct is the best way to get what you want."

Domínguez brought his own volume down to match that of his lunch partner. "She has done what you asked." He pushed a scrap of paper across the table and placed a salt shaker on top of it. "This is the account number, password, and name of the person managing your account in Panama City. Should you wish to travel to the bank in person, you also have a safe deposit box. Present your ID, and you will be given a key."

Zhou rubbed his hands together. "I believe that you and I have a long and mutually beneficial relationship ahead of us." He winked. "As long as my masters believe I'm doing a good job here."

"If you need a character reference, just ask me."

Both men grinned as a young male waiter refilled their empty glasses of water. He exchanged a couple of words in Chinese with Zhou, both of them laughing before the waiter shuffled away.

"The Cuban boy speaks very good Chinese. He's too good to be wasted in a menial job like this."

Domínguez blushed. Even for a highly qualified young person, finding a job to match that qualification wasn't easy in

Cuba. He tried to explain it away. "He's probably working part-time until he finishes his degree. Before we leave, I'll get his name. Perhaps a job in foreign affairs might appeal to him."

Zhou nodded, but Domínguez could see the man wasn't fooled. Their countries shared an ideological system. China was growing wealthier, Cuba was going backwards. That would soon end. "Once this operation is over and done with, everyone in Cuba will get the job they want. With your help, we will turn this basket-case of a nation back on course."

Zhou bowed his head. "China is ready to contribute in any way possible."

Domínguez had been delighted by the amount of assistance Zhou had already rendered for Operation Restore Dignity. Enhanced radar and sonar packages installed on the old Russian vessels, software for the MIG jets, surveillance and tracking expertise. He had hoped for more in the way of equipment, but it didn't matter. The entire operation was nothing but a show, just like the concert he'd be attending with Zhou.

"One final thing before I head back to my office," said Zhou. "When will the money be transferred into my new Panamanian account?"

This was a slightly sticky matter. The cash was coming in the form of a loan from Botvinnik, scheduled for transfer—via Lourdes—in 48 hours. Upon the successful conclusion of the operation, Botvinnik would get his money back plus some interest. No surprise the rate was 50 percent—Botvinnik the arms dealer was schooled as a gangster who learned his trade in the lawless 1990s in Moscow.

"You will receive the $5 million after three business days. You can call the bank in Panama Friday morning to confirm the transfer has been successful." He raised a glass. "A toast to your shiny new account."

Zhou's glass remained on the table. He whispered, "A day late with the money, and you know what happens."

Domínguez gulped and nodded at the same time. "It will not

be late. I promise. Everything has been planned perfectly." All support would be withdrawn if the money failed to materialize. Which would cripple his logistics, making the landing look hopelessly inadequate. Authenticity, buoyed by the Chinese psy-ops targeting world media on the day of the attack and the weeks following it, was crucial to pulling this thing off.

Then, once the general was installed as the new president, Botvinnik would get the loan money back. That was in addition to the massive profits he'd made already off the hardware he'd supplied. All in all, the investment with Vitaly would be worth it, and more.

"Good." Zhou finished his wine and cast his eyes about in search of the waiter. His phone buzzed on the table. He nodded an apology and picked up the device. "Excuse me while I take this call. If my people call me in the evening, I know it's important." The diplomat answered in Chinese, a language Domínguez wished he spoke but knew he'd never have a hope of grasping. What he could understand was how the silver cigarette case lying six inches in front of him worked. He picked up the case and extracted a cigarette, at the same time pressing a button on the side that turned on a discreet recording device.

"WHAT?" Zhou said in Mandarin. He wanted so much to shout into the phone. Ever the consummate diplomat, aware of his surroundings, he quelled the urge. "Did you say you lost him?"

"We were tracking his phone. When the signal showed that he was stationary for too long, we knew something was up." A breathy pause, as if the speaker was loath to continue. Then, the voice stuttered, "We recovered his cell in a ditch, five kilometers from the park he last reported from."

"Who was he following?"

"He said it was one of Domínguez's men."

"Which one?"

"A man called Raúl Espinosa."

"And why was Guo following him?"

"He said it was simply a hunch, sir. Nothing more. We know you've been having talks with Domínguez. Espinosa was in the navy with the general. We've observed him working at an appliance repair shop over the last week or so, and then visiting Domínguez at the Ministry. Seemed a little odd, and Guo thought to chase it up."

"I agree. But probably nothing in it."

"Perhaps not. But Guo thought there might be. And now he's missing."

"Send some guys to the park. See if...I don't know. Just find him."

"Yes, sir."

Zhou scratched his head. "Where did Guo pick up the trail?"

"A bar in Cayo Hueso. Guo tailed him from his apartment to there."

"So a Cuban goes to a bar. Hardly a surprise!"

"Guo phoned in, said he was getting fed up waiting, getting ready to leave, when Espinosa left, walking fast. A minute later another guy followed him, and the two of them got in a Lada, headed west, away from town and Espinosa's residence. For some reason, Guo's internal radar must have been going off. After that, no more reports from him."

"Who was the other man?"

"Don't know, sir."

"Dammit." He paused. "Did he at least get a picture of the guy?"

"No, sir. We've been through his cell, and there's nothing new on there since yesterday morning apart from a couple of phone calls. Last photos were from a week ago."

"Get out there and find him, dammit."

"We've had people at the park tonight, sir. It was swarming with police and now the place is sealed off under flood lights. What if Guo's dead and the cops found the body?"

"Don't panic." Zhou felt sweat beading in the wrinkles of his broad brow. "Officially, he's a lowly consular functionary." His heart thumped against his ribcage. "If he got into trouble, it will look like some kind of misadventure."

"Maybe the cops are there for a completely different reason." The statement sounded more like a question.

"Keep me informed. I expect to hear from you in the next hour." He disconnected the call. Tomorrow morning he'd ask for CCTV from any cameras stationed along the route Guo took from Espinosa's apartment to the park.

No sooner had he hung up than the phone rang again. He looked at Domínguez, puffed out his cheeks apologetically, then answered the call. "Yes?"

It was the ambassador of the People's Republic of China. The cops had called to ask if any their people were missing. "Well, are they?" he roared.

"I'll call you back in half an hour."

"You will—'

Zhou disconnected the call.

"Everything OK?" said Domínguez.

"Just an admin issue." He stood, gathered his things. "Let's go. I'm feeling a little tired."

The sweat dripping off Zhou's face told Domínguez the man was lying.

THE RECORDING HAD REVEALED ONLY HALF a conversation. He walked to the window and looked at the car park beneath, the rambling buildings stretching into the distance.

What was the other person saying on the other end?

He walked back to his desk, spun the chair around, and sat his ass in it. He reread the lines of conversation, translated into colloquial Spanish by an app, ironically, of Chinese origin. What the hell wasn't these days?

A consular employee was following a Cuban from a bar, then the shit hit the fan for the Chinese guy. Missing. A park was mentioned. What park?

He placed a call to the to the National Revolutionary Police Force, the PNR, and demanded to be put through to the director. He got a return call ten minutes later. "Has something happened in a park that I ought to know about? A murder, perhaps?"

"I'm afraid I can't say."

"Are you the director?" He already knew the answer to that.

"No."

"Then get me the fucking director!"

"Señor," said the sheepish voice, "it's very late. I cannot disturb the director at this hour. Beside, the information you are asking for is classified. I have had orders from the intelligence service to say nothing."

"Do you know who the fuck you're talking to, asshole?"

A sheepish voice said, "*Sí*. You introduced yourself."

"Then tell me about what happened in the goddamn park!"

"I'm sorry, that's classified. If you could call back tomorrow morning, I—"

"*Puta madre!* Motherfucker!" Domínguez slammed down the receiver.

He thumped his fist on the table. He'd find out who took his call just now and have them fired. Dammit, why didn't he simply ask Zhou outright? Because Zhou would have done what diplomats are trained so well to do—deflected, made up some bullshit.

Never mind. It was most likely a problem for the Chinese, nothing to do with him. If it had been, surely Zhou would have shared the information. Whatever, Domínguez would hit him up with direct questions about it later. After Operation Restore Dignity. He stood, lit one of his favorite short and stumpy cigars, and poured a shot of expensive scotch. Not usual—or advisable—for him to drink so late at night, but that casual brush off from the cops had rattled him a little. When he became president, no one would dare refuse to answer his questions.

As much as he tried to rationalize things, his thoughts drifted back to Zhou's reaction. The man was definitely rocked by whatever it was he'd heard on the other end of the line. Domínguez drained the shot glass. The alcohol burned his throat, then warmed his stomach. Two puffs on the cigar and he crushed it out in the ashtray. His nerves were ready to snap.

On the drive home, he called in at the residence of his young secretary.

"Sir?" The door opened, and a pair of tired eyes blinked hard under a yellow porch light.

"Juanita. Sorry to call so late." He decided to be direct. "I need one of your expert rubdowns."

"Excuse me?" she said, frowning. "At this time of night?" Her petite shoulders shook under a sheer blouse. Domínguez knew she hated having to service him physically, and he hadn't asked her to compromise her morals for at least six months. He was always gentle and considerate with her, but that hardly mattered.

"I'm wound up like a spring. Just a shoulder massage this time," he assured her. "Then I'll be on my way."

"You said that last time, Miguel." She sniffed dismissively. "You...forced me."

He could barely look her in the eye. He glanced over a steel railing toward the faint lights of neighboring buildings. She was standing with her hands on her hips, he knew, staring at him with condemnation in her eyes, jaw set hard. Her eyes were burning into him like lasers; he could feel it. Finally, he looked back and said, "You know what? Forget about it."

"Gracias." She disappeared like mist back into her apartment.

Fifteen minutes later, he was alone in his home office. Wife and two boys asleep. In the stillness, his mind would not relax as he contemplated the enormity of what he was about to set in motion. Tonight he wondered again, as he often did, if other historical figures had been as tense as he was ahead of a momentous occasion. One they knew was coming, that terrible event they had prepared for; that might cost many lives, their own life. How did Richard the Lionheart, Alexander the Great, Napoleon feel before leading their soldiers into the maelstrom? Were they nervous? Shit-scared, even? Or were they cold, without fear? Unlike those great men, Domínguez would not be on the front-lines. Why would he be? It was way back in 1743 that the English monarch George II had the honor of being the last king to lead his troops into battle. There had been no leader brave enough since then to risk his own life. Still, even as an armchair general with guaranteed physical safety, the tap of nervous energy, the constant flow of jitters, was hard to turn off.

Maybe some meditation would help. It was a technique he'd learned from a Tibetan monk some years ago on a tour of Asia. Tibet was China, he realized. May as well call him a Chinese monk. The irony.

He turned on soft, classical music, kicked off his shoes, and stripped to his underwear. An hour in transcendent peace flew by like it was nothing. The old Buddhist's techniques were almost magical.

He stood, calmly putting his clothes back on.

Now he knew when to launch the operation. Lourdes would confirm the transfer to Zhou and another to Ḅotvinnik on Thursday afternoon. The attack would commence on Sunday, 5 a.m., ninety minutes before dawn.

He picked up his cell and made the first of many calls to his loyal lieutenants.

"Hello. Raúl?"

"*Sí?*"

"Not too late to disturb you?"

A raspy chuckle came down the line. "Did that ever stop you before?"

Domínguez pretended he hadn't heard the remark. "Have you got somebody to feed your mangey cat over the next few days, maybe into the weekend?"

A long pause. "I have. The old lady in the flat above me."

"I wanted to give you plenty of warning. Come to my holiday

villa at Viñales on Friday morning. Bring several changes of clothes and your can-do attitude."

"You normally do this kind of thing via text message. What's changed?"

Domínguez detected a slight edge to the man's voice. Only natural for him to be nervous. "I'll admit it to you, compadre, but to no one else. Caution is always advisable. However, I've been a little too paranoid over the last few months. Good news—my head is now clear of distractions. I've surrounded myself with the best people. I see a clear path to success."

"Great to hear." A slight scratching sound as a match scraped on a matchbox. "Wait a second while I fetch my ashtray."

"Of course."

Twenty seconds later, Espinosa said, "I'm back." He inhaled deeply. "If I'm going to be totally honest, Miguel, I was starting to get worried about you. That you had bitten off more than you can chew."

Good old dependable Raúl. Always concerned about me. "No need to worry. If everyone focuses on their own role, it will run like clockwork." He paused for a second, then switched off his green banker's light, ready to head to bed. "Your new uniform is cleaned and pressed, by the way. Buttons shiny."

"Weapons?"

"You probably won't even have to get out of the boat, but I've got a cache of pistols for all the commanders. Brand-new Udavs courtesy of a good friend of mine. Just for waving around, you understand."

"Have you chosen the date for Operation Restore Dignity?"

"I have."

"When?"

"Nice try, *hermano*." He chuckled. "I will tell you when I tell the rest of the commanders. Be at my villa on Friday at 7 a.m. sharp."

TWENTY

Working from Fletcher's Tribeca office had distinct advantages. Access to databases most hackers and tech geeks could only dream about. A giant walk-in butler's pantry stocked with pre-prepared gourmet meals, snacks, and drinks. And if the selection wasn't quite to her liking, she had a blank check to order takeout.

Despite the perks, guilt gnawed at her.

Irina's heart sank as she read Vova's texts. He'd handled a bully before, but now the kid had backup. *I dealt with it, mom. But I'm sick of them.* Vova's tough tone didn't fool her; she saw through the bravado. Yakov's lessons had made him resilient, but the bullying—name-calling, jeers about his accent, and mockery of his black outfits and painted nails—was taking its toll. Despite her advice to tone it down, Vova insisted America was about freedom to express himself. She couldn't argue with that, but the guilt tightened. He needed her, and here she was, chasing a mission instead of being there. She vowed to wrap things up soon, call an Uber, and rush home to give him the comfort he needed. A hug, reassurance, and some home-cooked Russian food—just enough to help, even if only for a while.

She pushed the thoughts aside and turned her focus back to

the assignment. Her deep dive into the background of Sebastian Goulding—hoping to find some thread, some smoking gun—had come up dry. His record was flawless, almost unnervingly so. A valedictorian in college, an impeccable career in Alabama's Law Enforcement Agency, and a highly decorated CIA operative with commendations lining his jacket. During his time in Caracas, he had even helped local law enforcement dismantle two drug operations, resulting in the arrests of a number of Venezuelans and US citizens. Nothing out of place, nothing that stood out. It was as if the man's life had been polished to a sheen—spotless and untouchable. The search into Wilfred Arnold had delivered nothing incriminating either. The two men appeared to be paragons of virtue. She compiled all her findings into a separate file, encrypted it, and attached it to an email.

Frustration simmered as she dived into Lourdes Domínguez's profile—a social media darling and oil industry figurehead, praised as an environmentalist despite profiting from Venezuela's fossil fuel industry. Lourdes's striking looks made her a paparazzi favorite, but Irina needed more than surface-level charm. She needed a way into Lourdes's financial dealings. The public data—balance sheets, profit and loss statements—was squeaky clean. Irina had to find the backdoor, something concrete to crack open the carefully built façade.

The key piece of evidence would be hidden in her personal or business accounts, the ones tucked away in offshore tax havens. But Irina had no starting point, no breadcrumbs to follow. And the Venezuelan system was proving impenetrable. Irina had tried hacking into Caracas Station itself, hoping to gain access to Goulding's mailbox. Hopeless. Military-grade encryption, firewalls stacked upon firewalls, layers upon layers of security. She'd managed to evade the intrusion detection systems once. A couple more tries and they'd catch on.

Desperate, she'd tried Havana Station next. Even more hopeless. The system was air-gapped—completely isolated from the Internet. She leaned back in her chair, rubbing her temples, and decided it was time to pull in help. Fletcher had given her the green light to reach out to the US Treasury Office on Terrorism and Financial Intelligence (OTFI). She'd sent an encrypted email to their liaison office, disguised as a State Department message to avoid setting off alarms. Still, no response.

A thought sparked in her mind. Maybe the reply had landed in her Skia junk folder. There it was. A reply from a Laura Stapleton, asking for an urgent phone call. Irina skimmed the email and then composed one to Jacob.

"Yakov. Bad and good news. I've found nothing to help you with the money trail, but I'm talking with someone from the OTFI in the morning. I have also thought of a way for you to gain access to interview the Deputy Minister. See attached. Will update tomorrow."

On her way to the internal elevator, Irina saw Fletcher on his sofa, absorbed in a replay of a football game. She interrupted him, a sigh of disappointment in her voice. "Bad news. I couldn't find anything useful on the CIA men or the Venezuelan woman."

Fletcher paused the game and stood up, offering her his hand. "You've done your best."

An alert buzzed in her pocket. The second of two daily reports she received from a search engine she'd designed herself. Fletcher noticed the buzz and raised an eyebrow.

"Don't wanna get that?" he asked, nodding toward her handbag.

"It's not a phone message," Irina explained. "It's an alert from a custom search engine I set up. It trawls the Internet for keywords and phrases, scans images for facial recognition."

"Anything interesting come up?"

"Nothing much so far," Irina said. "Just a few red earrings."

Fletcher chuckled. "Red herrings, you mean."

Irina laughed, realizing her mistake. "Yeah, them. Unhelpful leads."

"Show me," Fletcher said, reaching out his hand. "You go home; I'll chase it up."

Irina frowned, curiosity tugging at her. She pulled out her phone, opened the app, and her eyes widened.

"Good news?" Fletcher asked hopefully. "It better be, because I've paused the game in the last quarter, and the score's tied."

Irina fumbled with the phone, excitement messing with her English grammar. "I think is good news," she said. "Wait a minute. I forward it to you and also Yakov."

Fletcher darted to the lounge and grabbed his phone off the coffee table. It dinged just as he opened the screen. "Looks like you've picked up a story from a newspaper. A candid shot of Lourdes Domínguez and her husband at a party. Champagne glasses and hors d'oeuvres in hand. It's all in goddamn Spanish, though."

Irina appeared by his side in an instant. She plucked the phone from his hand and pointed at the screen. "See the man in the background? The one with the trim beard and glassy eyes?"

"Yeah, I see him," Fletcher said, squinting at the image. "Barely."

"I am sure that is the man Yakov asked us to look into—Sebastian Goulding," Irina said with a faint smile. "The AI matched him to another photo we have."

Fletcher's face lit up. "Holy shit. But there's another guy there your software didn't pick up."

"Not surprising if he's not well known or if his online presence is minimal."

"No, it's totally understandable," Fletcher said. "You can only see a fraction of his head in the corner. But I recognize that salt-and-pepper curly hair and the diamond stud in the ear. It's Vitaly Botvinnik, goddammit."

"Give me one minute," Irina said, her fingers moving in a blur. She copied the URL of the page and ran it through a translation app. She handed the phone back to Fletcher. "You can read it now in English. It's late. My boy needs me. Good night."

Before Irina could head toward the elevator, Fletcher gripped her in a bear hug. "I swear one day I'm going to steal you from that bank to work for me full-time."

Irina smiled, slipping out of his embrace with ease. "We shall see," she said with a playful glint in her eye.

FLETCHER SPENT the next hour sitting in bed, rereading the translated webpage. The photograph had been taken during an event hosted by ALBA, the Bolivarian Alliance for the Peoples of Our America, at its headquarters in Caracas. The organization was founded in 2004, its initial members Cuba and Venezuela, and had grown to include ten members by 2023. Russia, now politically isolated, had even been invited to take part in the so-called ALBA games.

Fletcher shook his head in disbelief. He knew about the secret military agreements between Cuba and Venezuela, the ones that had propped up the Venezuelan government amid economic collapse and rampant crime. What shocked him wasn't the article's content—it was the fact that Goulding and Botvinnik were in the same room at the same event in Caracas.

Without wasting time, Fletcher fired off an email to Jacob. *Get hard evidence of Operation Restore Dignity, then get the hell out of there.*

Fletcher's eyes were heavy, his thoughts racing. In all the excitement, he realized he'd forgotten to catch the last moments of the football game.

TWENTY-ONE

A KNOCK. HE OPENED HIS HOTEL DOOR, AND A YOUNG man wheeled in a cart. Jacob tipped the kid generously. Two fried eggs with toast on the side, spicy mushrooms, a mound of sliced chorizo, and a pot of freshly brewed coffee.

He lifted a tray off the cart, placed it carefully on the table, then grabbed the newspaper that had been delivered to his door before the breakfast arrived. The name of the publication, *Granma*, brought a smile to his face. Nothing to do with anybody's grandmother; it was name of the yacht that transported Castro and 81 other rebels to the shores of Cuba to launch their revolution. A thin publication of only eight pages, it wouldn't take long to read it front to back.

He buttered a piece of brown toast and spooned sugar into the thick, rich coffee, stirring slowly. He flicked open the broadsheet. The propaganda machine in full swing. Headlines promised a brighter future for Cubans thanks to greater opportunities in tourism. Better relations with the United States and other countries were a positive sign for the country's future. Good news all around.

Yeah, sure, Jacob mused. *As long as Miguel Domínguez doesn't fuck it all up.*

On page two, he studied a large photo of a bloodied and battered boxer. A former Olympic gold medalist, this welter-weight champion was going to destroy all comers in next week's tournament. People were urged to attend the championship and support the country's fighters, with tickets reduced to a couple of pesos.

Then it caught his eye. A tiny article on the bottom of page 5.

Body of Asian tourist found in Parque Metropolitano de La Habana.

Havana detectives are investigating the unfortunate death of an Asian man found concealed in bushes. The man had been shot three times in the head. The police are calling for any witnesses to come forward. The mayor of Havana said, "This type of crime is an unusual event. People should not panic and should continue to visit the park as always. Have no doubt. The perpetrators will be found, tried, and punished to the full extent of the law. Cubans and visitors alike deserve to feel safe in our peaceful country."

Crime was rarely reported in Cuba, especially violent crime. Jacob's heart raced. His gut told him the article wasn't a genuine attempt to get help from the public, rather a public warning from the DI to whomever had slain the Chinese spook. *We're watching.*

They had left few clues at the murder scene. Espinosa was careful, but, as an ex-intelligence officer, his DNA was undoubtedly on record with the DI and other agencies. If he'd left behind any hairs or skin flakes, he'd be screwed. No one had been executed in Cuba since 2003—officially—but the death penalty was still on the books, and treason remained a capital offense. Jacob must proceed as if the crime would *not* be solved. He couldn't afford to let nerves distract him from the task at hand. Nevertheless, extra caution would have to be exercised now, a fact he would drive home to Espinosa.

He checked his watch. Still an hour to go before meeting up with Pepe. He retrieved his cell phone from a charger plugged into the wall, reflexively checking for messages and missed calls. None.

His laptop rendered more fruitful results. Three emails in his Skia inbox. Two from Irina, one from Fletcher.

He opened Irina's most recent email first. Inside, the article from the ALBA function. His pulse accelerated. The link was all but established. Goulding and Botvinnik, together with Lourdes Domínguez. He shook his head. Jacob guessed they must have had legitimate reasons to be there, otherwise why risk it with Operation Restore Dignity approaching? Getting snapped in the same photograph as Lourdes, even if they were unaware of it, reflected either arrogance or carelessness.

Next, Fletcher's message. It contained the same article Irina had sent, but with some context. Jacob replied: *Good idea re talking to Caracas Station chief before we make up our minds about Goulding. See if they're amenable to releasing email and phone logs. Communication between this trio would have been carried out very carefully, likely in code. If they're handed over, Irina could look at the logs. And as for me getting out of here, it's a priority, don't worry.*

Finally, Irina's first email, sent just after midnight. The OTFI had a reputation for finding needles in financial haystacks, and it made sense for them to assist. He looked at Laura Stapleton's profile online. Middle-aged and frumpy, the embodiment of an accountant. Perfect. The email included Irina's list of logical, official ways Jacob could score an interview with Domínguez. Some he'd thought of already, others not. Problem was, all of them required time he didn't have.

He dressed lightly for the warm weather, cotton jacket a necessary evil to conceal his S&W. Black cap and sunglasses were donned the minute he stepped out the door into a delightful, sunny Havana morning. The colorful old cars were cruising the streets, some with tourists, others empty but scouting for trade. Picture-postcard gorgeous.

Stepping onto the sidewalk, he retraced the memorized route in his mind. A couple minutes later, he saw Pepe in an animated conversation with the guy selling cigars. He guessed the subject matter was the upcoming boxing tournament. Pepe was even flailing his arms around, shadow boxing, showing the tobacconist moves Jacob knew would see the taxi driver knocked out in seconds by any opponent with half a clue about boxing tactics.

He coughed as he walked behind Pepe, continued to where *la mierda china* was parked, pulled on the handle, and sat in the passenger seat. He watched as Pepe extricated himself from the conversation, allowing another man to step up and purchase something. The bearing of the new customer caused Jacob to focus on the man. Nothing he could be specific about: the guy simply aroused suspicion like a neon sign. Like it often was, this assessment was based purely on gut instinct. As Pepe moved toward his taxi, the other man turned his head ever so slowly, almost nonchalantly, and followed Pepe's steps. A microsecond before the man could spot him, Jacob slid down below the level of the window. Despite his face being darkened by the sunglasses and hat, he was taking no chances. Paranoia? Perhaps. But as a crusty Russian spy once told him, even paranoid people have enemies.

Pepe slid in behind the wheel, peeked under the sun visor, then put it back. "Checking for spiders," he said. "Habit. One dropped into my lap a couple years ago, and I drove into the back of a bus. Cost me a fortune in repairs. Now I can't drive off without making sure."

His ramblings were cut short by the insistent ring of his phone in the console. Jacob snatched the vibrating Samsung before Pepe could reach it.

"Alcatraz," said Jacob. The odd greeting was met with raised eyebrows in the rearview mirror.

"San Francisco," said Espinosa without hesitation, establishing their bona fides.

"I need to meet you in a hurry." Jacob spoke in rapid English, maintaining the Argentinian accent, which elevated Pepe's eyebrows even farther. "Are you available?"

Espinosa understood Jacob perfectly but chose to reply in Spanish. "Sí. But not for long. I'll explain. Meet me at La Playa de

Cojímar. I'm there now. Your driver will know it. There's a rotten wooden hut set back from the rocky beach. Blue with a red roof. It's isolated, and we won't be disturbed. Make sure no one follows you."

Pepe nodded as Jacob told him their destination. "Fifteen minutes, tops."

The touristy part of the city was coming to life as they pulled away from the curb. Vendors were already setting up their stalls of tacky souvenirs, and early risers shuffled along the cracked and weed-infested sidewalks. People walked dogs. Pepe hummed softly to a tune on the radio as they rolled along. The breeze wafted inside the cab, bringing with it the tang of sea spray. Every thirty seconds or so, Jacob glanced behind him. No tail established.

As they drove farther east, buildings made of cinder blocks and bricks gave way to patches of green, the buildings becoming sparse and worn, their walls stained tan by decades of salt air and neglect. Cojímar loomed ahead, the village's coastline just visible in the distance, where the sea lapped against rocky shores under pastel morning light. The road soon narrowed, bordered by tall grass and palm trees.

Pepe eased the taxi to a stop just outside a weathered hut on the edge of the beach, rocky outcrops stretching toward the water only a few yards away. The structure looked abandoned, its roof slanting under the weight of dead palm fronds, with faded wooden planks barely clinging to the frame. A handful of small fishing boats bobbed on the horizon. Pepe cut the engine and turned to Jacob.

"I'll be nearby," he said, his voice low. "Call me when you're ready, and I'll come back."

"I could be going someplace else with my contact. I'll let you know."

"Understood."

Jacob stepped out of the car, the crunch of sand and gravel under his shoes and the murmur of traffic a few blocks away the only sounds as he approached the fishing hut. Espinosa said the place was isolated, that no one would stumble across them by accident. Jacob wasn't that confident. Pepe's taxi turned back toward the road, leaving Jacob alone with the wind and the whispering waves.

Wisps of silver-gray smoke leaked through the cracks in the planks. Jacob peeled away a makeshift door made of corrugated iron, then slid it back into place. Inside, Espinosa sucked hard on a cigarette, pacing back and forth. Rectangles of sunlight shining through the boards marked his face. Even from a distance of ten feet, Jacob could smell body odor. Men preoccupied with worry often neglected their own hygiene.

"I've got news," said Espinosa, not bothering with pleasantries.

"I like a man who gets straight to the point," said Jacob. Anything he himself had to say could wait a moment. "What is it?"

"Domínguez has summoned me to his villa. I've got a feeling this thing is about to kick off."

Not a good development. "You got a time?"

The color had drained from Espinosa's face. "No, but I don't need a specific time. The asshole told me he's got my uniform ready, even polished the buttons. Guns in a box to hand out to the commanders like fucking Christmas crackers. He's off his head." He flung the cigarette butt onto the rocky floor. "No more messing about. We have to inform the Western media of this now."

Jacob shook his head. "I've been instructed to hold off until we have the physical proof. I mean..."—he waved his hand in a meaningless gesture meant to calm—"with this massive boxing tournament about to start, international guests arriving in huge numbers, no one is going to believe you." He recalled Fletcher's words. "They'll think you're just another defector trying to cash in."

"But Cain, Passo's murder. Surely..."

"Stop!" Jacob hissed. "I told you, what happened to them is unprovable and irrelevant."

Tears welled in the corners of Espinosa's eyes, still encrusted with sleep dust. "I nearly had the prick, you know. I tried to record him when he rang me last night. The machine failed on me. Can you believe it, an appliance repairman, and his own tape-recorder doesn't even fucking work."

Jacob's fists bunched low by his sides. How he wanted to bash some sense into this guy. Pessimism is contagious, and he didn't want to catch it. "Never mind about that." Jacob crossed his arms over his chest. "Not your fault."

"Imagine, *argentino*," he continued to rail, "we live in a world full of fantastic sound recording devices, some so small and powerful you'd have no idea they were even there. And me?" He pointed at his chest. "A Sony piece of shit from the 1980s. It's like we're living on another planet here."

Sounds drifted in of a man and a woman laughing, a dog yapping.

"Are you sure we're safe in this location?" said Jacob.

A nod in the direction of the door. "*Sí*. No one would think of coming in here during the day." He gestured toward a corner, where a discarded condom lay next to an empty beer bottle. "Only at night."

Despite the bad body odor, Jacob risked standing closer to Espinosa, the sounds coming from outside eroding trust that the location was secure. He whispered, "We still have time for me to interview him."

"Not that again. I told you—"

Jacob held up a hand. "We've got a couple of days. There could be a way. Just hear me out."

TWENTY-TWO

"There must be someone close to him who doesn't like him." Jacob chewed furiously on a stick of gum. The connection of taste with scent helped fight off the sickly sweet scent wafting off Espinosa.

Teeth bared like a pissed-off hyena, Espinosa said, "Sure. Me. I can't stand the *pendejo*."

Jacob shook his head. "No. We agreed. You have no plausible reason to know me, so any introduction can't be through you." Jacob pointed his finger at Espinosa and began to pace. "And, you also said surveillance was so intense that you wouldn't be able to sneak a look at anything or steal from his office without being detected."

A light bulb flash briefly illuminated the darkness of his nervous anxiety. "*Momentito*. He's in a temporary office right now, while his usual one is being renovated. I haven't been inside it. Maybe there's no bugs or cameras in there?" His tone grew increasingly optimistic. "Money's tight in Cuba. Perhaps they decided not to install any."

"How would you even be able to tell if they had?"

A pair of pursed lips then a defeated shake of the head. "I wouldn't."

Jacob waited for a moment, then said, "Who else doesn't like him besides you? If he's the asshole you make him out to be, there must be quite a few."

Espinosa's hands went up in mock surrender. "Listen. I'd be surprised if anybody likes Domínguez. But whether the dislike is enough to get them to turn on him...I don't know. It would be a big risk."

More noises filtered in from outside. Flirtatious, youthful laughter; a boombox in the near distance playing reggae music heavy on thudding bass. The low-frequency boom-boom set Jacob's teeth on edge. He concentrated, blocking the sound from his thoughts. He'd been prepared for option one to fail. But he had two more cards to play. He aired the first one, watching Espinosa's expression closely.

"Good old-fashioned bribery. I like it in theory. How much are you prepared to pay?" said Espinosa when he'd heard out the first scenario.

"Whatever it takes. The old cliché is true: every man has his price."

"Who's close to him and who could do with some extra cash?" Espinosa sat on a large piece of driftwood, scratching behind his ear as he thought out loud. "There's his office secretary. She makes a sour face every time she enters his office. At least when I'm there visiting."

Jacob laughed. "Maybe she's making the sour face at you?" He held back the urge to remark on his foul body stench.

He nodded with a half smile. "Could be the case, *argentino*. But I'm pretty sure it's reserved for him. I picked up negative vibes from her when she looked at the bastard. Not surprising why. He talked down to her, like she was inferior, know what I mean?"

"You think he bullies her?"

"He's abusing his position to fuck the country, so..."

An idea occurred to Jacob. "He might be abusing his position to...fuck her? I mean, literally. The power imbalance would make it easy for him to use her and get away with it."

Espinosa lit a cigarette, then offered one to Jacob, who declined. "She dresses a little on the skimpy side for someone in such a serious position. Maybe at his insistence?" He rubbed his jaw. "What you say makes sense. Problem is, I've never exchanged a single word with her, so it's all just theories, isn't it?"

"Know her name?"

He took a deep breath. "Juanita."

Against all hope Jacob asked, "Last name?"

"*Lo siento.* Sorry. No idea."

"I think we should find out. And also where she lives." Jacob outlined his plan. A simple one. Espinosa would follow her home at the end of the work day. "You capable of that?"

He affected a look of being offended. "I'll be the shadow of a shadow."

"Can we take a walk outside?" said Jacob. "I'm feeling a little claustrophobic in this dirty old hut."

"Sure. We should stick close to the tree line."

The footpath was clear for fifty yards in either direction. "Which way?" said Jacob.

"Follow me." Espinosa headed north-east, away from the direction where Pepe had dropped them.

"What's the plan once we make contact with Juanita?" Espinosa stopped dead in his tracks. "And...what if it turns out my perceptions are wrong and she's loyal to the core? If so, offering up a bribe to her could backfire. She'll go squealing to him, and it's game over."

The Cuban had a fair point. How would Domínguez react to the news Espinosa was a rat? He could either pull the pin on the operation (good), or he could lose his cool and bring the whole shebang forward (bad). If that happened, his conscience wouldn't let him leave Espinosa dangling in the wind. Smuggling him into the embassy or Naval Station Guantanamo Bay wouldn't make him too many friends, but the man deserved protection.

"Here's another idea," said Jacob, picking up a flat rock and skimming it across the water. "We find her address and leave a note in her mailbox."

"What kind of a note?"

"A note from Manuel Vargas addressed to Domínguez. It would say something like, *I know there's a mole in your ranks. This person has leaked information to me that concerns you. Let me interview you for a story if you want to know who it is.*"

"That's ludicrous. He might think it's me!"

"Nonsense. If he grants me an audience, I'll tell him it's his own superior, the minister. He'll be powerless to act against him, maybe shelve his harebrained operation."

They stopped at a narrow section of the path to let an elderly cyclist ride past. She rang her bell in thanks, offering a grin with more gum than teeth. "And how do you know this fact?"

Jacob touched the side of his nose. "Anonymous source. Same thing all reporters say."

"I'm supposing it's the same anonymous source who told you where Juanita lives, right?"

"You're catching on, Raúl. One day you'll make a rather good spy."

Espinosa smiled as he flipped the bird. "Fuck you, *extranjero*."

"Now I'm 'foreigner,' huh? What happened to *argentino*?"

"You're starting to lose my respect." He lit the last of his cigarettes, crumpled the packet, and shoved it in his pocket.

The men resumed their leisurely walk.

"What's your plan for when you get inside?"

"I'd rather keep that to myself."

Espinosa tossed out the anchor and turned to Jacob. "No, no, no. That won't fly. You're asking me to tell you everything but you won't reciprocate." He turned, started to walk back in the direction of the fishing hut. "Sort this out yourself. I'm done."

Jacob ran a few steps and grabbed him by the shoulder. "Wait. You've stuck your neck out far enough already. I'm not telling you so I can protect you."

"From what?"

Jacob wasn't entirely sure himself. "From retribution. If I get caught and tortured, who knows what I might reveal about your involvement?"

Espinosa shook his head. "You're so full of shit. Whether I know a lot or a little is irrelevant. You only have to reveal my name for the world to come crashing down on my head."

"True. But if you get hauled in and can't offer up concrete details, they'll be more inclined to believe I was using you to get what I wanted. That you weren't mixed up in the plot to thwart his plan. He'll be more lenient."

"Leniency does not exist in Cuba." Espinosa pulled himself free of Jacob's grip, still being applied to his shoulder. "Tell me what you plan to do or I *will* walk away now. You'll be on your own with no other option but to alert the press about what you know. Proof or no proof. Which, in my opinion, is still the sensible way to go."

Hands on hips, exasperated, Jacob relented. Espinosa was his key. Pepe was a good driver, but he'd be no good in the trenches if things got tough. The local CIA operatives were also ruled out in his mind. Too attached to their posts to embark on a path of adventurism on the scale Jacob had planned.

"I'm going to pretend that I'm an ideological ally. That I want to interview him about the state of the country's military preparedness in the face of evil sanctions by hostile nations. He'll lap it up. In return, I'll divulge who the traitor is. Then I'm going to knock him the fuck out, copy everything on his computer—extract the hard drive and steal it if I have to—and get the hell out of there."

Espinosa's eyes widened like dinner plates. "That is the biggest load of shit I've heard since the last presidential address to the nation."

"Of course it won't be that simple."

"Damn straight it won't be," he shot back. "He'll have a top-level media adviser with him. Maybe a protective phalanx of goons. The adviser to make sure you don't ask questions that are too sensitive, but also to stop Domínguez from answering such questions. The goons to keep you on the straight and narrow. You can bet they'll be armed, and if they're not, highly trained in unarmed combat. You'll get yourself killed. The whole idea is preposterous."

Every point Espinosa made was like a low blow to the solar plexus.

"Not so easy, is it?"

Jacob shook his head as he realized his dour expression must be telling the story of what was in his mind. He swore under his breath.

"Now, if he was the minister of sports and you wanted to talk about the upcoming boxing tournament, that might...might..."

"Might what?" Jacob could imagine the cogs spinning furiously in Espinosa's brain. "Spit it out."

"You know, I'm sure he's intending to attend the championship next week. Only not as deputy minister of MINFAR, but as president of Cuba." He tilted his head back, hand shielding his eyes as he observed a line of clouds scudding across the sky directly overhead. He looked back to Jacob. "Perhaps a different approach would work, without involving poor Juanita or having to deal with Domínguez's advisers."

"How?"

"Chances are pretty remote."

"Just tell me, dammit!"

"I also have a boxing background. Got a few belts as a youngster. Even now, I hit the heavy bag when I can. Speed ball, too."

"Please, get to the point."

Espinosa held up his hand. "I'm getting there." He cleared his throat. "I sometimes go to a gymnasium not far from my home where some of the big-name fighters train. A relative of Domínguez is a retired boxing coach who used to operate out of that gym. He's an old man now. But back in the day he had some

Olympic champs in his stable. His portrait hangs in the gym. His heyday was a long time ago, early 1970s, I think. But that doesn't matter. Nostalgia pieces are very popular in our media." He jabbed a finger in Jacob's chest. "That's your angle!"

"I still don't get how that's my entrée to Domínguez."

"Do I have to spell everything out for you, *argentino*?" He paused, taking a mock-indignant deep breath. "You visit the gym while I'm training. You interview me, make sure people notice. You're looking to discover what the average person thinks about the tournament, what it means for Cuba, blah, blah, blah. I mention the photo of the old man on the wall, you ask the manager of the gym who he is. You say you heard a rumor he's related to an important government minister. He'll know for sure who that is. You say you'd like to speak to Domínguez—could he arrange it? This is where your 'checkbook journalism' comes into play. For a fee, he'll set the wheels in motion."

"And if he doesn't?"

"Then you'll have to think of something else or we target Juanita after all."

They stopped to nod a greeting at a young couple walking the path, hand in hand, smiling like new lovers do. The brief encounter made Jacob smile. And think of Irina. He glanced at his watch. 10:30 a.m. "When does this gymnasium open?"

"It's been open since 6 a.m. Doesn't close until later tonight." He gave the address.

Jacob called Pepe on Espinosa's cell and told him to pick him up at the fishing hut in ten minutes. Handing the phone back, he said, "Meet you at the gymnasium in two hours."

"*De acuerdo.* OK."

He couldn't resist giving some parting advice. "I saw you finished that pack of cigarettes. If you want to be a better athlete, don't buy any more."

The bird flipped again. "Want to try me in the ring?" Without warning, Espinosa unleashed a lightning four-part combination, each punch missing Jacob's face and body by a fraction of an inch. Jacob barely had time to blink before Espinosa's hands were again resting by his sides.

TWENTY-THREE

A LITTLE BELL ABOVE THE DOOR GAVE AN ECHOEY tinkle as he opened it. He entered a small reception area. A quick visual scan of the space—dark, dusty, old-school—told Jacob it was unlikely there were security cameras installed in the gym.

"*Buenos días*," said the woman working the front desk. He pegged her as late twenties to early thirties. She yawned, then sighed, then reapplied to paper the ballpoint pen she was using to doodle concentric circles. "How can I help you?" she said, paying scant attention to the visitor.

"My name is Manuel Vargas," said Jacob in a businesslike tone. "I'm a reporter looking for a man called Edmundo Casamayor. I've been told he's in charge of this gymnasium." He tapped a fingernail on the counter as she continued with her drawing.

The sound made her jump slightly. She looked up, sour face instantly turning sweet. The woman twirled a stray lock of straight black hair as she stood, eyed Jacob up and down with an almost lustful desire. Despite the lightest covering of acne and two wonky front teeth, she was built like a swimsuit model and exuded sensuality. "I can tell by your accent that you're not from Cuba. Maybe I can help you?" she said with a pout.

"Any other time, and I'd definitely say yes." He delivered a thin-lipped smile.

"What's wrong with this time?"

"A demanding boss and my tight schedule." He pointed at his watch. She stared at it for a moment, clearly not familiar with timepieces as ostentatious as Jacob's Breitling. "Tell you what," he relented. "Give me your name and number and perhaps I'll give you a call later this week for an interview?"

Her eyes lit up. "Really?"

"Absolutely." He let his eyes roam over her body in a feigned expression of sexual interest. "Looks like you work out, like to keep fit."

A light peach blush crept into her cheeks. "That's why I like working here. I can train at the end of my shift. Or before I start." She smiled. "I want to start boxing against other women. I'm not quite ready. Soon, though." She held up a hand with crossed fingers.

He leaned a little closer to her as he propped his elbows on the counter. She matched his movement, her mouth moving silently. "You know," he said in a hushed tone. "I wouldn't mind a date for the boxing championship. Are you planning to go?"

"Oh... wow. Yes!" The blush intensifying, she revealed her name was Lucinda, but she wasn't able to afford a cell phone that he could call her on. She'd only just started working here, and money was tight. "Can I have your number? I could call you from here."

"I'm using my Argentinian SIM on business here in Havana. It would be quite expensive to call me on it, I imagine." He nonetheless gave her a business card with his number on it.

"You can always ring the gym if you want to talk to me," Lucinda said hopefully, clutching the card close to her bosom.

Jacob touched the side of his nose. "Great thinking." The flirting with Lucinda was an enjoyable distraction, but he had a job to do, and he hadn't been kidding about the tight schedule. "You think you could take me to see Señor Casamayor now?"

"*Momentito.* I'll go check if he's here."

Three minutes later, a man in loose-fitting tracksuit pants and a net vest appeared through the fly curtain. Lucinda was a step behind. Casamayor's mahogany skin glistened with a sheen of light sweat. Flinging a white towel over his shoulder, he said, "Lucinda told me there was a journalist here wanting to talk to me. That you?" The man tried to play it nonchalant, but an underlying excitement shone through his dark-brown eyes.

"*Sí.* I'm looking to get some color—a little background for a piece I'm writing about Cuban tourism. The upcoming tournament has brought thousands of extra guests into the country." He paused for a second, manufacturing a look of confident optimism. "And with that in mind, I'd really like to talk to some of the customers here. Get a feel for what the man-in-the-street thinks about things."

Casamayor regarded Jacob with a slightly suspicious eye. "Why'd you pick this gym? We don't get too many outsiders poking their noses in here."

"I could say I chose it at random. But that's not quite true. I was looking for a bare-bones gym, a little out of the way, a grassroots place where real Cubans come to keep their fitness and skills up."

"There's plenty of places like that in Havana."

"Sure. But I also wanted to find a gym where a kid might rise from the streets, make a success of his life after starting off behind the eight-ball." He glanced at a glass cabinet housing trophies and medals in display cases. Casamayor's eyes followed Jacob's. "My research told me some top fighters have begun their climb to the top in this very gym. And that you"—he inclined his head toward Casamayor on a slight angle—"are responsible for nurturing a couple of them. That true?"

His chest puffed out. The ego stroking seemed to have cooled his suspicion. "*Sí.* It is true. I've coached a couple guys who made it to the national titles. One got selected for the Pan American games."

Jacob pursed his lips and nodded in admiration. "Mind if I take a look around inside? I can hear the sounds of people working hard back there." He gestured with his thumb to the fly curtain. Asking Casamayor too many questions straight up might rekindle the initial skepticism. "I won't annoy people if they want to be left alone, I promise."

Casamayor said, "I'm going to need permission to let you have access to the facility."

A wrinkle. But one easily ironed out.

"Let me save you the time and bother." Jacob pulled out his accredited media representative visa and a letter of introduction from the National Institute of Sports, Physical Education, and Recreation that looked authentic, right down to the ink-stamps.

Casamayor ran a hand through his frizzy hair as he scrutinized the document. "If it's from INDER, then I cannot possibly say no."

Perfect.

"Here's my passport, too, if you'd like to check that," said Jacob, holding the document in his extended hand.

"No, not necessary." He folded up the letter and handed it back. "All seems in order. Come with me."

At the entrance to the sprawling gym, Casamayor waved Jacob in. "Feel free to wander around." He flashed a smile, revealing a gleaming gold tooth, a relic from another era. "I'll be over there." He gestured toward a tall, lanky man in red trunks, pummeling a speedball with timed, precise flicks of his hand. The rhythmic patter filled the air. "That's Luís, my latest protégé. He's fighting next Wednesday, up against a tough Russian opponent." Casamayor's smile broadened. "Luís will destroy him."

Jacob raised an eyebrow, catching a hint of something darker than pride behind Casamayor's words. "You got something against Russians?"

"Who doesn't?" Casamayor shot back with a bitter laugh. "And the Chinese are worse." He leaned in, his voice dropping a notch, his eyes scanning the room as if spies lurked behind the weight racks. "But don't quote me on that."

Jacob grinned. "Strictly off the record."

Casamayor returned his attention to Luís, barking encouragement as the fighter intensified his attack on the speedball. Jacob took the opportunity to survey the gymnasium. The equipment was ancient. The walls, peeling and grimy, hadn't seen a coat of paint in years. The overwhelming stench of sweat hung in the air, thick and pungent.

There were no TikTok influencers or designer clothes here—just gritty, real people. Torn shorts, faded T-shirts, even jeans. Jacob watched a man in his fifties doing pull-ups in work gear, and no one cared. What struck him most was the lack of gym culture—no obsessive wiping of benches or focus on aesthetics. You lay on the sweat-soaked bench and kept going. No one disinfected anything; it was all part of the grind. Jacob shuddered at the thought of the showers, doubting hygiene was a priority.

He pulled out a small spiral notebook and scribbled a few quick notes, keeping up the façade. Then he made his way over to a tall, striking woman squatting under the weight of a loaded barbell. Her form was near perfect, and the veins in her neck bulged under the strain as she gritted her teeth. Jacob approached, explaining his 'job' as a journalist looking for a story on Cuban fitness culture. The woman immediately perked up, eager to pose for his camera. She managed to maintain a smile even as her muscles trembled under the weight, the sweat streaming down her arms. Jacob snapped a few photos, making sure to capture her effort. When she finally collapsed onto the bench, spent, he handed her a card and promised to include her in the story.

"Watch for it on the website," he said, flashing a practiced smile. The woman beamed.

Two younger men were less enthusiastic. When Jacob approached them, they quickly declined, refusing to be photographed or interviewed. Their refusal raised a small red flag, but Jacob didn't press the issue. Probably just shy. He nodded politely and moved on.

He descended two steps to a lower section of the gym. The sounds of grunts, clanking weights, and whizzing jump ropes filled the air. Pepe, his driver, had told him earlier that morning that boxing ranked as one of Cuba's top three sports, alongside baseball and soccer. Jacob hadn't believed it at first, but now, seeing the sheer number of people training here, he realized Pepe hadn't been exaggerating. The energy in the room was raw.

In the middle of the open space, a raised boxing ring stood a couple of feet off the ground. Inside, two Afro-Cuban kids were going at it, fists flying, under the stern gaze of a heavily tattooed trainer. Across the room, a man was viciously pounding a heavy bag. Jacob squinted, recognizing Espinosa.

Jacob pulled out his notebook again, pretending to jot down more notes, his eyes drifting in Espinosa's direction. When he was close enough, he called out, "Excuse me?"

Espinosa's hands shot up, stopping the heavy bag mid-swing. His expression darkened as he turned toward Jacob, his lips twisting into a half-sneer. "What do you want, *pendejo*? You've upset my rhythm."

"Didn't mean to interrupt your workout," Jacob said amicably. "But I'd like a word, if that's OK."

Espinosa's eyes flicked to the side, assessing the situation, then back to Jacob. "I haven't got all day. Make it quick."

They continued the charade, speaking in terse, businesslike tones for a few moments. Espinosa's mood quickly shifted from suspicious to cooperative. He became almost friendly, pretending to realize the journalist was doing the gym and the country a favor by coming here to research his 'feel-good' story. Jacob felt the weight of eyes and ears on them, but that was fine, as long as they stuck to their roles. Espinosa wiped the sweat from his brow with the back of his wrist, then leaned against the heavy bag, giving Jacob just enough time to drop the pretense and mutter a quiet phrase. "I'm going back to the gym manager. Let's execute what we discussed." He turned to walk away, then remembered something. Keeping the volume at minimum setting, he said, "I'm getting out of here once I'm done with Casamayor. Call me on Pepe's number in three hours. And have a shower. You stink like old road kill."

JACOB WAITED for Casamayor to give his boxer a break. As the exhausted kid leaned against the ropes sucking in big breaths, he approached with a friendly wave of the hand. "I'm nearly done collecting information."

"Anything else I can do to help you?"

"Maybe." Jacob explained how a client had mentioned that one of the coaches from yesteryear had trained an Olympic gold medalist.

A vigorous nod. "*Sí!* Agosto Domínguez was a master coach. Started his career here before moving to the boxing academy, the famous *Escuela de Boxeo*. We are very proud of him."

"Is he the man in the photo in the reception area?"

"*Sí.*" He frowned. "I hope you don't want to interview him. He's very old. Nearly 90. Got dementia, so they say."

"No. But I couldn't help noticing he resembles a well-known member of your government."

The man scowled. "Since you are a foreigner, I feel I can say this. It is not my government." He paused, nostrils flaring. "But you are right. His nephew is that asshole, Miguel Domínguez."

"I'd live with eternal regret if I didn't try to score an interview with the deputy minister."

"Whatever for?" He turned away and told the boxer he had three minutes of rest left before the real serious stuff started. Turning back to Jacob, he said, "The man is a pig. Don't waste your time."

Jacob gestured for the coach to come closer. Casamayor's

distaste for Domínguez could be a trump card. “Listen. I’ve also heard less than positive things about him. That he wants to...”—*careful what you say, Hunter*—“isolate Cuba after recent steps forward. If I can get to him through his ties with his old uncle, make him think I only want his views of the international boxing tournament, some nostalgia about Agosto, then I can flip the interview to expose his hostile political agenda.”

Casamayor made a “stop” gesture with his hands. “*Basta.* Enough. I don’t wanna get involved in politics.”

Jacob pursed his lips. “You wouldn’t be, I swear. Even as an accredited journalist, some officials in the country are out of reach unless I jump through a hundred hoops.” He tapped his notepad with a pen. “One reference from you might do the trick. Tell him...tell him I’m going to write a double-page spread for a bunch of syndicated publications, and his face will be in every lounge room from Buenos Aires to Madrid.”

“Forget it.” He gestured toward the door. “I wish you well, Señor Vargas, but it’s not worth it for me. Despite what you say, if you write one bad word about him after I make the introduction, he’ll think I set him up for a fall. Cuban politics is too dangerous to meddle in.”

Jacob gritted his teeth. He didn’t want to have to pull out the bribery card, but it was all he had left. “Your gym equipment could do with a serious upgrade.”

Casamayor blinked.

“A complete refit to bring it up to modern standards,” Jacob whispered. “Plus a tidy bonus for you.”

The wheels were turning, but the man wouldn’t bite. He shook his head. “I’m sorry, no.”

Jacob handed his card over. “In case you change your mind, call me anytime.” He looked around the gym. “I can imagine an ice bath over there, some of those great big fans...Anyway, think about it.”

As he walked back through the reception, Lucinda beamed at him. “Get what you wanted?”

He forced a smile in return. "Almost."

"What about our date?"

"I'll call you," he said at the door without turning around. He sensed the disappointment in her heavy sigh.

He walked three blocks to where Pepe was waiting. Sitting in the car, he placed his head in his hands. Using Juanita to access Domínguez was an option he did not want to exercise.

His cell buzzed. He glanced at the screen. A text from an unknown number. The content meant it could only be Casamayor. *I've changed my mind. Call me at 8 pm.*

TWENTY-FOUR

Zhou leaned back, enjoying a rare sense of satisfaction as he thought about his new Panamanian account. The tangible piece of paper detailing it felt reassuring—discreet and far from the prying eyes of regulators or cyber sleuths. No risky online logins or traceable IP addresses, just a traditional setup. Intermediaries handling details, no need to constantly monitor balances online. Zhou liked the simplicity and control, finding comfort in knowing this part of his empire remained hidden, disconnected from the digital world.

Sometimes, the old ways were still the best.

This was no gift, though. He had earned every dollar. Supplied what the idiot Cuban wanted, even exceeded expectations.

The money would definitely come. He knew it. Not because he trusted Domínguez. Precisely the opposite. Zhou understood perfectly why the man was so widely disliked. And like a true narcissist, he was blissfully unaware of it.

Domínguez, however, was a very useful vehicle for China to not only become a strong influence in Cuba but to completely dominate it—economically, militarily, and even culturally. The island state had been a joke since that fool Castro and his minions wrested control. They weren't even communists to begin with. Only aligned with the ideology later, when it became convenient. And they were still bumbling along. Not like China, whose leaders had quickly learned the need to be flexible, pragmatic.

Zhou grinned as he reread the email. The words felt good. His embassy counterpart in Venezuela, also due a windfall for his close liaison with Lourdes Domínguez, assured Zhou that her uncle wasn't lying. The promise that all transfers would be made on Thursday and those who were due payment into their new Panamanian accounts would see the sums by Friday morning would be kept.

That was the good news out of the way. Now the not-so-good news.

He picked up the newspaper and re-read the small article about his agent. Feared missing, then confirmed dead. Not via official channels, but in the damned press. Zhou's jaw clenched. It was a body blow. He'd been counting on Guo. The agent had been too useful to lose. But it wasn't just the loss of a trusted operative that bothered him—it was the utter lack of control. The fact that this had been reported before they'd even confirmed the details was a vulnerability he couldn't ignore.

Zhou reached for a small bottle of heart pills, his hands steady despite the knot of anxiety tightening in his chest. He threw a couple down his gullet and washed them down with cold green tea.

This dilemma needed resolution. Now.

He dialed the number, his fingers tapping rhythmically against the desk. When the line connected, he put the call on speaker, his frustration almost palpable. The cool, calm voice of the ambassador on the other end did nothing to soothe his growing irritation. "Yes? I hope you're calling me for a good reason. I'm rather busy right now."

"Sir, as you know, Guo has been missing since Sunday afternoon." Zhou's voice quickly rose in pitch. "Now I'm reading a story in the paper about—"

"Please, do not shout when you are speaking to me." The ambassador's words were an order, but the tone was measured, unflappable. The kind of calm Zhou had always admired but found increasingly grating in moments like this.

Zhou gritted his teeth as he glared at the phone. "Sorry, sir."

"I have also read the newspaper report." The ambassador's voice remained steady, almost detached. "Prior to that, as you requested yesterday morning, I had reached out to the Cuban Ministry of the Interior. Let them know one of our employees is missing. The minister himself called me back and vowed to contact the police and get to the bottom of this."

"More than 24 hours have passed. You should have heard from him by now," Zhou snapped, pacing the thick carpet that covered his office floor.

"Well, I haven't." A short pause. "He'll get to me soon enough. Remember, the newspaper report says the victim is Asian. You know how broad the term 'Asian' is to Westerners. It could be a bloody Pakistani for all we know."

"It's Guo, sir. I know it." Zhou turned abruptly, his hands balling into fists. He stalked across the room to the window and twisted the venetian blinds open with an angry snap. Outside, the lush green gardens stretched out in tranquil contrast to his inner turmoil. "We supplied photographs of him, didn't we? The police can identify him, or confirm it's someone else, based on that alone. We should demand a viewing at the morgue or wherever the hell they're keeping the body!"

"Again, I'd advise you to lower your tone. Do you think we can't easily find a replacement deputy director of cultural and strategic affairs? Not exactly the most qualified role in the embassy."

Zhou froze at the comment, feeling the sting of the words even though he knew it was just the ambassador's way of reminding him of the bigger picture. It wasn't just about Guo. It was about how Zhou, as head of MSS in Havana, had to maintain control over his agents and his operations.

"You know that's not my real job." Zhou's voice was low, composed now, though the anger seethed beneath the surface.

A muffled cough came down the line, followed by another sound that made Zhou's ears prick. The ambassador had company. Zhou's irritation flared. He hoped he wasn't on loudspeaker on the other end but didn't dare ask.

"Indeed. And one which you are supposed to be qualified in. As the boss of MSS in Havana, you are not supposed to lose agents in the field. Especially ones keeping an eye on Cuba's critical personnel."

"This one went rogue, sir. He wasn't acting under my instructions, believe me." Zhou clenched his jaw, not wanting to go into too many details. Guo had somehow transformed from top asset to liability. His instincts had led him into dangerous territory, when Zhou had authorized only minimal surveillance, nothing more. "He was supposed to be keeping tabs on local developments—not... getting involved in things he had no business being involved in. He—"

"Irrelevant," the ambassador interjected. "Yes, we want to build and strengthen our influence in Cuba, but we can't run around demanding the local power structures bend to our will. This is still a sovereign country, and we must respect that."

Zhou's nostrils flared.

"I appreciate your concern for the fate of Guo," the ambassador continued. "Touching. If I were you, I'd pray it wasn't Guo. If it turns out to be him, I may put in a request to have you replaced. You may think being MSS chief means that you're top dog. You are not. Do not call me again about this matter until we have more facts to hand."

The ambassador exchanged a few words with someone; they spoke so quietly Zhou had no hope of making it out. Zhou's fingers tightened around the rolled-up newspaper in his hand, but he remained silent, waiting.

"Have you understood me correctly?" the ambassador said curtly.

"Yes, sir." A pause to draw breath. "Again, I apologize. As you said, my main concern is Guo's well-being." He faked a laugh. "He's got a reputation for liking the local ladies. Let's hope he's simply met up with a hooker, went on a drinking binge. He resurfaces, all sheepish, then we send him home."

"A minute ago you were positive the dead man was Guo. Now you're not so sure?"

"Your words have made me rethink matters, sir. Let's look at all options before rushing to judgment." Zhou exhaled slowly, forcing himself to calm down. Technically, the ambassador wasn't wrong. It was smarter to wait. But he knew in his heart Guo was dead. He'd been on to something. It was possible, Zhou thought, that Guo had simply been unprepared when the hunted became the hunter.

He paced again, his brain kicking around possibilities. He needed to stay ahead of this. He couldn't afford to let a minor setback derail the larger plan.

A deep breath, another heart pill before he logged on to send a message.

No calls to Domínguez about this. If his hunch was wrong and he pissed the man off, Operation Restore Dignity could backfire. It was too risky. No, Zhou had a better idea.

He picked up his phone and sent an encrypted email to MSS headquarters Beijing.

Send Chen Wei immediately. Have him contact me the minute he arrives.

Desperate times called for desperate measures.

TWENTY-FIVE

He glanced at the clock on his laptop. The time switched from 7:59 to 8 p.m. Casamayor picked up after the third ring.

"What made you change your mind?" Jacob asked.

"Your offer to help with the gym upgrades," Casamayor said. "No one else is offering us a leg up."

Jacob waited for more, but nothing came. He had to prompt, "So what's next? Have you set up the meeting?"

"Are you serious? It's not that simple. Tomorrow, I'll head over to MINFAR, see if I can get a meeting with Domínguez."

Jacob felt the weight of frustration falling on his head. Did Casamayor really think he could just waltz into the Ministry of the Revolutionary Armed Forces and ask to meet General Deputy Minister Domínguez? "Why are you confident you can pull this off? You don't have any connections higher up that could get you in the front door?"

Casamayor gave a raspy laugh. "*No, hermano*. In Cuba, sometimes you just have to take the bull by the horns."

Jacob suppressed a groan. The coach was naïve, thinking he could break through the bureaucratic wall simply by asking to be admitted. "Perhaps we should hold off for now. I can try another angle—maybe see if the Ministry of Foreign Affairs can get me an introduction at a more official level through INDER." He wasn't sure how much sway that would have, and it would take too much time. He might need to loop in Juanita, see if she could help. Not a preferred option. "In fact, I'll make some calls myself."

"No need for that," Casamayor said, his tone suddenly firm. "I've got your business card, haven't I? That's more than enough for those *pendejos*." His earlier reluctance had given way to resolve—the lure of Jacob's money doing its job. "I know there'll be gatekeepers, but I've been in Cuba long enough to know how to get through them."

Jacob hesitated. "Even at the Ministry of the Revolutionary Army? They don't mess around."

Casamayor snorted. "My wife with a rolling pin is scarier than those guys."

Jacob allowed himself a small grin. Maybe the old coach wasn't as naïve as he seemed. Casamayor had a streak of boldness, a willingness to push when others would hold back.

"I'll call you when I'm there," Casamayor continued. "And after that, the next call you get will be from Domínguez himself."

"*Buena suerte*," Jacob said. Good luck.

The line clicked dead. Jacob set his phone down and leaned back in his chair. Casamayor's confidence was surprising, but Jacob knew better than to get his hopes up. Cuba was a different beast—especially when it came to someone like Domínguez. Too many gatekeepers, too many eyes watching every move.

Casamayor was no pussy, that much was clear. But Jacob wasn't banking on that alone. He needed a contingency plan, something to fall back on if Casamayor's bold approach failed. As he stared at the ceiling, grim reality hit home. The bag of good ideas was just about empty.

Jacob wiped the sweat from his brow, toweling off as he moved across the room. He tossed the towel over a chair and slipped into the luxurious hotel robe, the soft fabric clinging to his still-warm skin. Two hours in the gym, pounding away at the heavy bag like a man with a score to settle, and yet the frustration still gnawed at him. His knuckles ached, raw from the force he'd put behind each blow. He flexed his fingers, wincing slightly, then cracked a half-smile as he thought of Espinosa.

The Cuban had speed. More than Jacob had anticipated. If it came down to a real fight, Espinosa would probably take him down. He hated to admit that. Maybe, just maybe, Jacob could outthink him in a brawl, use experience over raw power. But that was a consolation he wasn't in the mood for right now. He stretched his shoulders, muscles tight and sore, and slumped onto the couch.

The television remote lay within reach, but he hesitated. A flicker of static, then the blue screen, his finger poised over the button to search for a news bulletin. He scanned the handful of state-run channels. He was hoping for something, anything, about the Chinese operative Espinosa had killed. Nothing.

Not surprising, Jacob thought with a bitter twist to his lips. There had been the tiny obscure article in the paper, but Cuba's state-run media would never go in-depth on an incident like that. Certainly not broadcast it on television. He leaned back, the sterile comfort of the hotel room enveloping him. The high thread-count sheets, the polished wood, the muted tones—nothing about the space felt real, not with everything that was happening outside in the real Cuba.

He grabbed his laptop and checked the local news again, though he already knew it was pointless. Frustrated, he closed the lid, rubbing his temples.

He pushed himself up from the couch and wandered over to the minibar. The tiny bottles of rum and whiskey caught his eye, but he shut the door before temptation took root again. Booze wasn't the answer. Not now. Not when he was this close to blowing a fuse.

Instead, he picked up the phone and dialed room service. Twenty minutes later, a knock on the door signaled the arrival of lunch. He'd ordered a local favorite, *ropa vieja*—shredded beef in a rich tomato sauce, served with rice and flatbread. The smell alone was enough to make him realize how hungry he was. He tucked in, savoring the new flavors. For a moment, the act of eating gave him something else to focus on, a brief escape. But as soon as the plate was empty, frustration crept back in.

He needed more options. Despite his bravado, Casamayor was at long odds to come good. Juanita was the next-best route to the deputy minister, but in this case, next-best was still a poor option. And after that...nada.

He moved back to the couch, pausing his hyperactive brain long enough to read an email from Irina that had arrived in the last 20 minutes. She had established contact with Laura Stapleton from the OTFI. The woman was eager to assist but had to follow certain protocols when dealing with other agencies. OTFI's investigations were, of necessity, thorough and complex, but Stapleton hoped (emphasis on hoped) to have something concrete in a couple of days. Encouraging, thought Jacob, but too damned slow.

He began drafting an email to Irina.

Subject: Progress Report

Body:

I've got a local working on securing a meeting with Domínguez. The odds are slim, but if it works, we'll need to dip into the funds again. I promised a big payout if he can get me inside the Ministry. The guy's got chutzpah, so his bluff might be our best shot to avoid the bureaucratic maze that I'd have to crack to get in officially. We don't have time for that. Espinosa is convinced D-Day is coming fast —days away. I've attached my report. Sending vibes that Stapleton can find the concrete proof we need. Tseluyu. *Kisses.*

He hesitated, then deleted the final line before copying the email to Fletcher. Jacob stared at the blank screen for a few seconds longer, fighting the urge to call Irina. If the room was bugged—and there was no way to know for sure—calling her could be suicide. Even having someone sweep the room for bugs could raise suspicion. His hands itched to pick up the phone anyway, but the risk was too great. He needed a detector, or at the very least a signal jammer. Dundas could arrange something at the embassy.

He fired off another email, this time to Dundas, requesting a secure route to the embassy. He had questions that needed answers, and a face-to-face meeting was the only way to satisfy them. Without Irina's calm, guiding voice, the tension clawing at him was getting worse.

To pass the time, Jacob plugged in the pack-of-gum USB, the encrypted files unfolding on his laptop screen. He dived into the history of the original Bay of Pigs invasion, shaking his head as he absorbed the incredible details. It had been a disaster from the start. Jacob clicked through the documents, dissecting the dumb decisions that had led to the catastrophe, piecing together how it was all playing out again—this time in a more dangerous and more heavily armed world.

Jacob sat back, rubbing his eyes. A small envelope icon blinked in the corner of his screen—Dundas had replied.

Meet at Calle 21 between Calles L and M. White truck. 16:47.

There was enough time to make it to the rendezvous without rushing. He shaved slowly and methodically, the blade gliding smoothly over his cheeks and scalp. He dressed, again unhurriedly, tucked the S&W under his belt, and grabbed his jacket.

Jacob stepped out of the hotel room, closing the door quietly behind him. His heart beat a little faster as he made his way down the broad corridor. The luxury hotel was an oddly inconspicuous place in the shabby city, perfect for blending in with foreigners, but it was also a potential trap. More places for tech to be hiding—watchers, too. He couldn't afford to be complacent, couldn't afford to seem too predictable. Every corner, every street in

Havana was a potential threat. He was slipping into the habit of looking over his shoulder constantly, his mind picking apart the faces in the crowd, looking for signs of anyone who might be following him. Chinese faces were now the subject of closer scrutiny.

He made his way across the hotel lobby and stepped out into the warm afternoon air. He kept his pace steady but purposeful, moving through the crowd like a shadow, the peak of his cap tugged down.

After a few minutes of weaving through a maze of narrow streets, he found the payphone he'd been looking for—tucked away in a dingy alley, barely noticeable amid the dumpsters and debris. He dropped a coin into the slot, punching in Pepe's number with a steady finger.

"Pepe," Jacob murmured as the line crackled to life.

"Manny," came the reply, though the static made it hard to hear. "You ready for a pickup?"

"Be quick." He glanced around. "It's scorching out here."

"You're off the beaten path again, huh? Why not call from your hotel?"

A legitimate question, one that caught Jacob off guard. He hadn't even realized it—his paranoia had become second nature. Pepe was a safe contact. He could've called from the hotel without an issue like he had already done before. But walking the streets had felt necessary, a way to shake off the nerves.

"I'll tell you when you get here," Jacob replied, dodging the question.

The ride to the nominated rendezvous point took fifteen minutes. Too fast. They were early, so Jacob told Pepe to drive around for a while. The detour brought them past several historical sites, including the hotel where Ernest Hemingway had once lived. Pepe grew animated, pointing out the landmarks with pride. Jacob played along, though his thoughts were elsewhere, already focusing on the rendezvous.

Jacob asked Pepe to drop him off a block from where the

white truck was waiting for him. As he climbed out of the car, he said, "I'll be in touch when I need another ride."

Pepe grinned. "You know where to find me."

When he got to Calle 21, he saw three trucks parked along the street. Jacob easily spotted Dundas's five-ton van—it was the same one from before. Probably the only one they had, he mused with a half-smile.

Jacob approached the truck and tapped lightly on the rear door. The driver jumped out, opened the back, and ushered him inside. Linens, freshly pressed and stacked neatly in baskets, lined the walls. It was the kind of detail that reminded Jacob of how thin his cover really was behind the façade.

As the door shut behind him, sealing him inside with the scent of clean sheets and the rumble of the truck's engine, Jacob's mind churned.

TWENTY-SIX

"You look tense, Señor Vargas," Dundas said, leaning back in his chair, folding his hands across his chest. "Havana's left a mark on you after only a couple of days. What's going on? Any closer to finding the evidence we need to determine whether this thing's the real deal or not?"

"It's the real deal, all right. And the proof is..."—he held his thumb and index finger a millimeter apart—"this close." Jacob's ears caught a scurrying sound, like mice behind the drywall. His eyes shifted to the door, as though expecting someone to come barging in. He shook his head almost imperceptibly, trying to bring himself to his senses. "I need backup, Señor Dundas," Jacob said, his voice rougher than he intended. "It's too hard operating in this backward country."

Dundas arched an eyebrow. "Backup? Last I checked, you said you wanted to handle things yourself."

"That was before I had the pleasure of experiencing the reality of Cuba." Jacob rubbed the back of his neck. "Things are escalating. I need more in my arsenal."

Dundas edged forward, eyes narrowing. "Sounds cryptic, Vargas. Are you worried about something?"

Jacob didn't answer immediately. He wanted to lie, to deny it, to pretend this was just another job in a long line of dangerous missions. But what was the point?

"Yes," Jacob finally admitted, his voice barely a whisper. "I'm worried. I feel like I'm swimming in quicksand."

Dundas leaned back again. "Need backup in the field?"

"No," Jacob replied firmly. "I need more resources, but not the human kind."

Dundas chuckled dryly. "You already wormed a pistol out of us. First foreigner to ever do it. Congratulations." He took a deep breath. "What else do you want?"

Jacob blinked a couple of times. "First, a bug detector. One of those multifunction ones that finds every damned thing no matter how it runs." He sensed the steady rise and fall of his chest as he began reciting his shopping list. "I'm hamstrung in terms of comms. Having to send emails back to the State Department all the time, then wait for a reply, is slowing me down. Things are heating up now, and I need to be able to communicate immediately if necessary. Which means I might have to make a phone call from my hotel room. So I'd like a signal jammer too."

Dundas tilted his head, his lips halfway between a smile and a sneer. He jotted the items down on a sticky note. "Anything else?"

"Yes." Jacob leaned forward, locking eyes with Dundas, whose blink rate increased. "Knuckle dusters. Maybe a garotte. Whatever you've got that I can carry in a bag back into the hotel without raising suspicion."

Dundas's eyebrows shot up. "Jesus, Vargas. If you didn't have the State Department backing you, I'd tell you to go jump off a bridge."

"I've been followed, and it nearly ended badly for me." He'd leave it at that. No mention of Espinosa, especially the fact it was the Cuban who executed the tail.

Dundas tugged on his black-and-yellow necktie. "This doesn't have anything to do with a dead Chinese man in a park, does it?"

"You read about that, huh?"

He nodded. "Read about it. Heard rumors in the lunchroom. Everyone's got a theory. You got one?"

"I'm pleading the fifth." He quickly added, "As you Americans say."

"I won't press you on it." Dundas allowed himself a smirk. "Just be damned careful." He leaned over and opened a drawer, pulling out a small package. "As it happens, the State Department must've been thinking along the same lines as you."

Jacob raised an eyebrow. "What's this?"

Dundas slid the package across the desk toward him. "Open it up and see for yourself."

Jacob eyed the package warily, suspicion swirling in his gut. "I'd rather do that in private."

Dundas laughed, unbothered. "No need, amigo. State gave me the heads up about it. If you hadn't checked in today, I'd have had someone deliver it straight to your hotel. Discreetly, of course."

Jacob's hands shook slightly as he ripped open the package, like a kid at Christmas anticipating the latest PlayStation. Inside was a black box about seven inches long, four inches wide, and three inches deep. It looked for all the world like an ordinary smartphone—nothing special about it. His heart skipped a beat.

"You're kidding me," Jacob muttered, staring at the device in disbelief.

"Make sure you don't get caught with it," Dundas said with a hint of amusement. "You're not allowed to import satellite phones into Cuba without the government knowing. It's considered an extremely serious offense with stiff penalties."

Jacob cradled the device in his hands, feeling the cool plastic on his skin. Fletcher had mentioned a low earth orbit satellite network being set up by Skia, separate from the CIA's operations but patched in to the wider National Reconnaissance Office (NRO) network. It was in its final stages of procurement, and this phone was the first of its kind. A game changer. No intercepts possible. He could call whomever he liked on this phone. With the frustrating exception of Espinosa. His phone would be monitored for sure.

He tore through the pamphlet and handwritten note tucked inside, speed-reading the essential details. The satellite functionality was as secure as you can get. The phone was a sophisticated piece of equipment, capable of everything from encrypted calls to high-level data transfers.

While he was reading, Jacob hadn't noticed Dundas had been on the phone. Only when Dundas's voice cut through the quiet did Jacob realize it. "I'll make sure it gets delivered to the safehouse discreetly," Dundas said, hanging up the phone. He switched focus to his computer monitor, quickly typed something, and clicked his mouse a couple of times. He smiled for a second then looked up at Jacob with a deadpan expression.

"What was all that about?" said Jacob.

"The call was a totally unrelated case. The details would bore the socks off you."

"How long before—"

Just then, there was a knock on the door. A woman entered, carrying a black zip-up sports bag. She set it down next to Jacob, not speaking a word, and left just as quickly as she had come.

Dundas didn't seem at all fazed by the intrusion. "Your order," he said dryly. "One radio frequency scanner disguised as a ballpoint pen, a signal jammer hidden inside a phone charger, and a pair of brass knuckles. Couldn't get the garotte, though. Maybe you can stop by the local Home Depot and get the parts for a DIY job."

Jacob took the bag, not bothering to hide the relief on his face. Throwing off the shackles of limited communications was a massive fillip to the mission. "Thanks. Although I think the Home Depot part went over my head," he lied, although it was a fair statement: an Argentinian would likely not have heard of the chain of stores.

"No matter. I'm done for the day. Need a ride somewhere?"

Jacob nodded. "Do I need to get in the trunk?"

Dundas snorted, shaking his head. "No, the back seat. But I'll put a blanket over you for five minutes or so. You cool with that?"

Jacob's mouth quirked upward slightly, a rare moment of levity breaking through. "It would be a nice change from the laundry truck." He threw the bag over his shoulder and followed Dundas out the door. "Take me back to Calle 21. I'll call my man to fetch me."

"Your man?"

Jacob explained how he had a local cab driver on the hook.

"Is he trustworthy?" said Dundas.

"I'd almost stake my life on it."

"Perhaps I could offer him a job once you're gone. Trustworthy folks are thin on the ground in Havana."

The car ride was uneventful—apart from three minutes under a blanket—the low hum of the engine a welcome distraction as Jacob's mind churned over the new equipment he'd just received. The satellite phone, the bug sweeper, the jammer, the brass knuckles—everything had a purpose, although he hoped the last item would not have to make an appearance.

When the car pulled up at the designated spot, Dundas glanced over at Jacob, again reading through the specs of his new satellite phone. "Good luck, Vargas. Watch your back. If you need anything more, give me a call on that bad boy."

Jacob nodded curtly, appreciating the sentiment but not needing the reminder. His negative assessment of Dundas was on hold for now. The guy seemed to be inclined to help, no matter the way he initially bristled at having Jacob give orders. He stepped out of the vehicle, his mind already shifting back to the mission. Pepe's taxi waited under a jacaranda tree, the owner smoking a leisurely cigarette in the afternoon shade.

TWENTY-SEVEN

AFTER THE MEETING WITH DUNDAS, JACOB WAS READY to turn his hotel room into a safe place to conduct communications. Pen tucked into his top pocket, sound function set to silent, he walked the entire floor area. Not all at once, and not in a hurry. Over the course of two hours, he watched snatches of local TV, made himself a coffee, visited the bathroom, and sat on the balcony, admiring the view. He'd covered every inch. Not a single vibration was felt against his skin under the shirt. No microphones. At least none that were detectable by this device.

Then he pretended to be engaged in an animated phone conversation with his imaginary Argentinian girlfriend. As he performed the charade, he casually pointed the pen at various points around the room where he believed a passive camera might be secreted. After 15 minutes of talking to no one, he ended the 'call.' No reflections of camera lenses had been detected.

Next, Jacob reached into the black bag and pulled out the fake phone charger. He plugged it into the outlet by the nightstand, still moving like he didn't have a care in the world. The small device hummed quietly, a hidden signal jammer now blocking any transmissions in or out of the room. No bugs would work now—at least for the time being.

He leaned back in the soft recliner, stretched his legs out, and flexed his fingers, arms extended behind his head. His lips drew upwards into a smile. He would call room service, enjoy the most expensive meal on the menu—lobster thermidor— then take a stroll along the seafront and call Irina on the satellite phone. No one could touch him now.

GULLS KEENING, the sun's rays softening as it took one last look over the city of Havana, he strolled the Malecón. Hands pushed deep into his pockets, a cool breeze on his face after the hot day, he fought an urge to smile at the throngs of people sitting on the low stone-and-concrete wall. But he kept his head straight, eyes down, a nondescript man in the crowd. If not for the thoughts swirling around in his brain, this would be a perfect evening to simply relax and forget about the mission.

He imagined a line of military boats thundering toward the harbor, people running and screaming as the invaders launched rockets. Men leaping from the vessels onto the dock, armed to the teeth and ready to die. In response, guerilla forces, overwhelming in number and firepower, emerging from the dawn shadows between the decaying buildings. Fighting would ensue in the urban landscape for a couple of hours until the landing forces were crushed. In the meantime, casualties—of combatants and civilians, up and about early and caught in the crossfire, or shelled in their homes and hotels near the shore—would climb astronomically.

And from the smoking rubble, General Miguel Domínguez would emerge. The savior of the Cuban people, foiling the Americans.

A terrible thought occurred to Jacob.

For Domínguez to win, the invasion would be just the beginning. He would lock the country down while he launched the next phase—his mass psychosis psy-op. Repressions, arrests, media blackouts. Maybe he would let stranded foreigners go. Maybe not. Every distasteful ingredient imaginable would be included. Operation Restore Dignity could drag on for some time.

He found a quiet section of the wall, well to the west of where he started his walk, pulled out the satellite phone, and dialed Irina's number. There were no contacts stored on the device, but it didn't matter. He had memorized close to a thousand phone numbers, some essential, others in the 'you never know' category. Every new one he collected was added to that archive.

Irina answered on the fifth ring. No warm greeting. Instead, "Yakov. What the hell are you doing calling me? I told you not to do that. Is there an emergency?"

"How did you know it was me?" He stopped to let a woman pushing a child in a stroller go around him. "You would have seen 'unknown number' on your screen."

"It was a guess. It's nine o'clock at night. Who else would call?"

"Telemarketers?"

A sigh. "They never call this late. I think it's illegal." She paused then said, "You didn't answer me. Is there an emergency?"

The conversation had started in Russian, and he aimed to keep it that way, even when out of earshot of passersby.

"There is an ongoing emergency. One I'm trying me damndest to avert." He dropped his voice. "They've given me a satellite phone that looks like an everyday iPhone. No one can detect this call."

"You sure?"

"That's the claim." He wasn't totally sure, but research told him the risk was virtually zero. Unless they'd been tracking him from the start, which he doubted was the case. "Even so, let's not talk for more than a couple of minutes."

"I miss you, *zaichik*." He heard some old-school 1990s grunge in the background. Vova's pick. Irina hated that style of music. "The sooner you get home to me, the better."

He closed his eyes, letting the sound of her voice wash over him. "I miss you too." She had brought new meaning into his life. Before Irina, he'd approached everything with a high degree of recklessness. It was corny, but she kept him grounded when all around him was turning to shit.

"How's Vova?" Jacob asked. It wasn't a change of subject: He was genuinely concerned about the kid. "I bet that's him listening to Pearl Jam, right?"

"It's definitely not me," Irina said with a laugh. She paused a beat, then in a more serious tone said, "He's a lot better. I called the school, threatened to make a fuss if they didn't take him seriously."

"I can imagine you making a scene."

"Nothing over the top. No throwing objects, just a lot of shouting and waving my arms about. The principal is working with him now, not against him. I've got a feeling one of the bullies will be expelled."

Jacob smiled at the thought of Irina taking matters into her own hands. She was as fierce as she was beautiful, and hearing about her standing up for the kid made him feel like everything might be okay.

"I'm glad," he said softly. "And you?"

"I'm good," she replied. "But I'm more worried about you."

He hesitated, the weight of everything pressing in on him. "Don't worry. I'm fine. Just...trying to keep my head in the game."

"Are you taking extra precautions?"

"Of course." He resisted the temptation to laugh. She sounded like his mother when he was a younger man, making sure he had condoms in his wallet. Time to steer the conversation back to the nuts and bolts of the mission. "How are you going with the financial investigation? Something—anything—to tie in Domínguez, Lourdes and Botvinnik will be enough to blow the whistle on this madness."

"You read my email?"

"Yes. The OTFI promised to get back to you soon."

"Not very specific, I know. But I got good vibes from Laura Stapleton. I think she's gonna do everything she can to help."

"But what can they really do? Can they x-ray the bank accounts of every tax haven on the planet?"

A heavy sigh. "I don't know, Yakov. But I'm assuming they have serious capabilities. They get plenty of funding from the government."

"Did she sound confident?"

"Hmmm. I'd say she was non-committal."

Jacob gritted his teeth. He had to be realistic. OTFI finding evidence would be the icing on the cake, but he doubted it could seal the deal. In any case, it would probably come well after Operation Restore Dignity was either crushed or, heaven forbid, triumphant. Domínguez himself, that was the key. "I appreciate everything you're doing. And I hope Fletcher does, too."

"He keeps offering me a full-time job, so I think he does." Irina's voice softened further. "Be careful, Jacob. Please. Whatever's happening out there, don't take unnecessary risks."

"I won't," he vowed. A part of him wondered if he would ever be able to keep that promise.

TWENTY-EIGHT

THE MINFAR HEADQUARTERS BUILDING, TALL AND blocky and austere, loomed over Edmundo Casamayor like a fortress. It didn't exactly invite feelings of warmth and friendliness. Quite the opposite—it made his heart pound like a freight train. The gym manager stood beneath the giant Cuban flag fluttering in the breeze and muttered a quick, silent prayer to the Lord above. In a country that prided itself on its atheism, Casamayor remained an ardent Catholic. For him, prayers were a test of faith. When they were answered, it was proof of God's intervention. When they weren't, it was simply God's will, and he could accept that too.

Today, he hoped God was in a good mood.

The young soldier at the gate, a corporal who didn't look old enough to shave, scrutinized him with a suspicious gaze. When he spoke, his voice was surprisingly deep, making Casamayor take half a step back.

"You cannot come in here without an appointment. The rules are black and white."

Casamayor, accustomed to navigating stubborn gatekeepers, flexed every muscle in his face and stretched his eyebrows as high as they would go, giving the corporal his best 'you've made a mistake' expression. "*Hostia!* I have one. It must be in the book. Check again."

The soldier manning the sentry booth pushed his military hat up with the flat of his hand, sighed, and flipped through the appointment book again. His eyes skimmed the pages with boredom. He then pressed buttons on a keyboard and stared at a rolling screen on a computer monitor, shaking his head. He turned back to the strange man. "What did you say your name was?"

Casamayor puffed out his chest, as if preparing for a medal to be pinned to it. "Edmundo Casamayor." He craned his neck to peer at the book. "May I have a quick look?"

The corporal shrugged and gestured with open palms, his indifference unbroken. "Sure, I could do with a laugh."

Casamayor leaned in, scanning the list for a name that wasn't there. He scratched his head, trying to give the impression of a man supremely frustrated, not comprehending how his meticulously planned journey had gone off the rails. "I don't get it. I was told to come here at 10 a.m., and someone would escort me to the deputy minister's office."

Or escort me the hell out of here, he thought grimly.

The soldier closed the book and sighed again, clearly uninterested in Casamayor's predicament. "Sorry, there's nothing I can do. Your name's not in the computer or the visitor register. I kindly ask you to turn around and go back to wherever you came from."

Casamayor's mind whirred. He couldn't just leave. This meeting was too important to give up on. There was big money at stake. But he was ready for this turn of events. In fact, he had anticipated that it would go exactly like it had. With the confidence of a Shakespearean actor, he busted out the lines he had rehearsed in his head on the bus ride over.

"*Escuchame, hermano*. Listen to me, brother," he said, leaning in conspiratorially. "Could you make one call for me? Just one. Please tell the esteemed General Domínguez that Señor Edmundo

Casamayor has something very important to discuss with him. It's an extremely personal matter about his poor uncle Agosto. The kind of thing people don't discuss over the phone."

The soldier's posture shifted slightly at the mention of the name. His blinked a couple of times as he processed the information. "You mean the famous boxing coach?"

"The very same." Casamayor touched his bent nose—a badge of honor from his teenage years in the ring. The disfigurement, earned from a right hook, seemed to convince the soldier that Casamayor was the real deal. He watched the corporal size him up.

"Okay," the soldier relented, his tone softening. "One phone call. But if it turns out you're full of shit, I'll personally march you out of here at the end of my rifle. *Entiendes?*"

Casamayor grinned. "*Entiendo, hermano.* I got it, brother. No need for the Kalashnikov."

The corporal disappeared back into the booth, leaving Casamayor to fidget nervously. He stared up at the building, imagining the conversations happening inside. Deputy Minister General Miguel Domínguez was no small fish, and Casamayor wasn't naïve about the challenge ahead. Getting Domínguez to agree to an interview with the Argentinian, Vargas—especially an interview centered around the international boxing tournament—was a long shot. But if he could find the right leverage, he had a chance.

The door opened again, and the corporal stepped out, holding the phone slightly away from his ear. He glanced at Casamayor, then back at the phone.

"Okay, Señor Casamayor. I can't believe it, but you're in luck. General Domínguez said he's prepared to give you a couple of minutes. Come with me."

Casamayor let out a breath he didn't realize he was holding. "*Muchas gracias.*"

After a lengthy security check—passing through an x-ray machine, frisking, and fingerprint and facial recognition scanning

—he was given the all clear to proceed farther into the labyrinth. They took an elevator. How many floors, he had no idea. He only comprehended that it went up. He was concentrating on his breathing and trying to stop his legs from buckling under him. The doors opened, and they walked in silence down a sterile hallway. The air was thick with authority, the kind that made your skin prickle. Casamayor noticed cameras in every corner, following their movements. Even his footsteps seemed louder than usual on the marble floor.

The young secretary jerked a thumb toward the door. The corporal knocked twice, waited for the word, then opened it.

"General Domínguez, Señor Casamayor is here to see you."

The general sat behind a small pine desk that occupied a large portion of the floor space. A computer monitor sat in the middle of the desk, a mountain of paperwork to his right threatening to become an avalanche, and there was a stained coffee mug to his left. The room was warm and stuffy, filled with faint traces of cigar smoke. Domínguez looked up, his eyes sharp and observant. A civilian now, he wore no uniform. His muscular chest filled out a crisp white guayabera that contrasted against his tanned skin.

"Señor Casamayor," Domínguez said, leaning back in his chair. His arm made a sweeping motion. "Apologies for the surroundings. Renovations that are taking longer than I had hoped." He rose, extending a large hand with tufts of black hair on the knuckles. "A pleasure to meet you. I hear you've got some talent under your wing."

The coach was genuinely astonished. "You have?"

A slow nod. "I've got my finger on the pulse in the boxing world." He extended a box of cigars to his visitor. Soon, the air in the cramped space was thick with pungent tobacco smoke. Domínguez cracked open a window, clearing the air somewhat, but the haze remained. Back in his chair, he quirked an eyebrow and said, "What brings you to my office? The corporal said you mentioned my uncle Agosto." He rested his glowing cigar in an ashtray and ran a hand through his hair. "I've got a very busy schedule today. I can give you 10 minutes. Enough?" The last word was a question, but the tone made it clear there was only one way to answer it.

"*Sí, gracias.*" Casamayor forced a smile, trying to quell his jangling nerves, which were close to snapping. "I have to admit, your uncle's name was the key I needed to get in to speak with you. Agosto's portrait hangs proudly in my gym. We respect him very much."

"You've got some kind of a nerve," said Domínguez with a shake of the head. "But I have to admire your courage and initiative."

Casamayor sighed with relief. "I've got something important to talk about, Señor General. And it's not just about boxing—although I know you're a big fan."

Domínguez grinned. "You've got me there. Boxing runs in the blood. Uncle Agosto always said it was a sport that teaches you more about life than any other. What about your gym? Tell me, who's the most promising fighter in your stable?"

Casamayor nodded, grateful for the opening. "There are a few, actually. The best of them is an exciting young fighter called Jorge Martínez. He's got talent, speed, good technique."

Domínguez's eyes flickered with interest. "Jorge Martínez, huh? I've heard of him. Light heavyweight. Quick on his feet, good with the left cross. What's his record now?"

He did have his finger on the pulse. "Eight and one," Casamayor replied, pride seeping into his voice. "That one loss was close, could've gone either way. Kid's only getting better."

Domínguez nodded approvingly. "That's what I like to hear. We need more fighters like that to show the world what Cuba's made of."

Casamayor leaned forward, sensing the moment. "That's exactly why I'm here, Señor General. I've been approached by a journalist—Manuel Vargas. He's a very nice man, from Argentina. You wouldn't believe it. He dropped into my gym, saw the portrait of your uncle Agosto and noticed the close resemblance."

"The prominent chin, I imagine?" said Domínguez, rubbing the feature he'd just referred to.

"Indeed." Casamayor could barely conceal his excitement now. "Vargas is well known in Argentina. Around the world, actually. He's come here to do a story about tourism, but he's also covering the international boxing tournament. He'd like to feature the top Cuban fighters, with a tribute to the legacy of your Uncle Agosto."

Domínguez's expression shifted slightly. "I don't trust the Western media."

"Rightly so." Casamayor coughed into his fist. "I've got a good feeling about this man, though. He's not a Yankee."

"That's something in his favor, at least." Domínguez glanced at his watch, lips twisting to one side.

"Yes it is," Casamayor said quickly, knowing he'd have to make his case soon or Domínguez would show him the door. "And I get the sense Vargas is a fair and objective person. He's got a lot of respect for the sport, understands the importance of its history for Cuba."

Domínguez donned a pair of glasses and typed something on a keyboard. "What's Vargas's first name again?"

"Manuel."

A couple of mouse clicks. "I see he's written many syndicated stories. A variety of topics. Published in a number of Latin-American countries." He pushed his keyboard to one side and fixed Casamayor with a look that dared him to break contact. "Why are you doing his bidding for him?"

Casamayor was ready for this one. "He's tried to call but..."—a fatalistic shrug—"he ran headlong into our bureaucracy. Couldn't get past the gatekeepers. He says he called the Ministry of Foreign Affairs Office and ran into a brick wall. Got handed from one section to another before he gave up."

Domínguez nodded. "MINREX isn't famous for being cooperative with foreigners."

"Exactly." Casamayor focused on a point just above the window behind Domínguez. "I'm sure Vargas is not some tabloid writer looking for scandal. He wants to tell the world what your family has done for Cuban boxing."

Domínguez leaned back in his chair, fingers tapping rhythmically on the desk. He wasn't convinced yet. "My uncle," he said slowly, "is no longer in a position to be interviewed. He's in his nineties. He doesn't remember much these days, let alone boxing."

Casamayor nodded empathetically. "I understand, Señor General. And that's why Vargas wants to talk to you. You've been carrying on your uncle's legacy for years. You're the one who knows what he stood for, what he fought for. Vargas wants to capture that—through your eyes."

Domínguez was silent for a moment, as if weighing the risks versus the reward. "You're asking me to trust this Vargas. You know how these things go. The media can twist words, make stories out of nothing. I have to protect my family's name."

Casamayor saw his chance. "That's exactly why *you* should talk to him. If you don't, someone else will, and they might get it wrong. But if you're the one telling the story, you can control how it's told."

Domínguez exhaled slowly, still tapping his fingers. "You're a damned good talker, Casamayor. I'll give you that."

Casamayor grinned, though he could feel the sweat beading at his temples. "I'm never short of a word, that's true. You gotta know how to motivate your boxers when they feel like throwing in the towel."

A few moments of tense silence passed, and then Domínguez gave a half-smile. "All right. I'll think about it. But I'm not making any promises."

"That's all I'm asking for." Casamayor reached into his jacket pocket, pulled out a small card, and placed it on Domínguez's desk, relief washing over him. "If you decide you're ready, here's Vargas' card. You can call him directly."

Domínguez glanced at the card but didn't pick it up. "We'll see," he said, his tone noncommittal. "But you better make sure that kid Martínez is ready for the fight. We don't want him embarrassing us on the international stage."

Casamayor chuckled, sensing the shift in tone. "Don't worry, he won't lose. Martínez is going to make us proud. Just like your uncle would've wanted."

Domínguez gave a curt nod, and Casamayor took his leave, walking out of the office with a mix of relief and uncertainty. Back on the bus, he sent a short text message to Manuel Vargas. *I think you might be in luck.*

TWENTY-NINE

LEFT ALONE, MIGUEL DOMÍNGUEZ SMILED TO HIMSELF. He picked up the receiver, called the sentry box, and identified himself by barking his own name.

The reply was measured and polite. "*En qué puedo servirle?* How can I help you?"

"Has that fellow left the facility yet?"

"What fellow?" Genuine confusion on the other end.

A mental head slap. This might not be the same soldier who brought Casamayor to his office. He briefly described the short-statured boxing coach.

"Gotcha. I see him. He's about 30 meters away, heading toward the bus stop."

"Is he in a hurry?"

"No."

"Does he appear flustered?"

"I'm no body language expert, Señor General, and I can only see him from behind, but judging by his gait, I'd say he looks pretty relaxed. Want someone to go and get him for you?"

"No, it's fine." He hung up the phone, satisfied there was no need to investigate Casamayor any further. At least not today. With no one picking him up and him heading back on public transportation, it seemed likely that Casamayor was being genuine.

He chewed the end of a half-smoked cigar. It was certainly a coincidence, Vargas turning up like that on Casamayor's doorstep. And the fact that Uncle Agosto's photo happened to be on display.

Didn't mean there was anything sinister in it.

On the plus side, Vargas providing positive publicity about Domínguez, showing his 'human' face in the Western media, would go a long way toward securing the legitimacy of his rule once he was installed as the new president. He anticipated a shit-storm of condemnation against the United States for attempting a Bay of Pigs II, but doubters would emerge. Lots of them. All accusing Cuba—*him*—of a massive false-flag operation. They'd be correct—and the truth might even come out eventually—but the longer the gap stretched between the actual attack and any revelations, the better. And one of the best ways to shore up international support was positive PR.

There were no guarantees in life, however. Vargas could well be a phony. Good old Ponzoa would settle it for him. A call to MINREX, where Ponzoa was the boss of the visa section, would remove any lingering doubts.

"Miguel? I haven't heard from you in a while. To what do I owe the pleasure?" The man's voice was congenial and light. He always seemed to be in a good mood, no matter what was happening.

And it was true; it had been a while. He hadn't spoken to Osvaldo Ponzoa for months. Perhaps it was as long as a year. And before that, the last time they spoke, in person at least, was back in December 2016. Castro's funeral. To Domínguez's chagrin at the time, Ponzoa had been closer to Castro than he was. In fact, the MINREX heavyweight was considered by many to be a close confidant of the leader of the Revolution. After Castro's death, Ponzoa's influence waned, but he still managed to retain power in a key ministry, a role he had clung on to tightly for nearly 20 years. He showed no signs of wanting to give it up. After Operation Restore Dignity, Domínguez would keep Ponzoa in his position, a reward for unstinting loyalty to his country. A rare gem.

"Osvaldo. Please don't think ill of me, calling to ask for a favor when we've barely exchanged words for so long."

Ponzoa laughed merrily. "Not a problem. We've all got our jobs to do. You know I don't take anything personally."

A couple more minutes of small talk ensued before Domínguez pulled the trigger. "I want to avoid going through the DI. Can you look into a person for me?"

"Certainly. Who?"

"An Argentinian journalist called Manuel Vargas." Domínguez explained the approach by Casamayor. "He said this Vargas told him your Ministry stuck a spoke in the wheel, throttled his attempts to contact me. Because of that he had to use a middle man to get to me."

Again, Ponzoa laughed. "Yes, it's quite possible. If there were no records of representations at governmental level, one of my employees may have decided to brush the guy off." He paused, and Domínguez heard the sound of a drink being swallowed. "Let me look into it for you. Give me 30 minutes?"

The man was too obliging. "Take as long as you need. It's not urgent. I'm still tossing up whether or not to do an interview at all."

With Ponzoa on the case, Domínguez resumed his own Internet searches on Vargas. Page after page of results. Photos, a couple of videos. He watched a two-minute clip of the man called Vargas attending a press conference with the Argentinian national football coach. About to switch off his computer and head to the cafeteria for a pastry and a coffee, he had an idea. He isolated a photo of Vargas, downloaded it, and sent an MMS to Ponzoa asking him to get his people to double check that the photo on the visa application matched the one he'd just sent. After pressing send, he gave himself another mental head slap. His identity would have been verified forensically by MINREX already, photos and all.

Back in his office after the short trip to the cafeteria, he stared blankly at the pile of unfinished paperwork before deciding to leave it all until tomorrow. Mostly, they were procurement contracts requiring his signature. They'd been vetted and approved by his Department head, but he never signed a document without thoroughly reading through it first. An ingrained habit after his first wife had swindled him in a divorce settlement.

Still buzzing from the sugar rush of a guava and cream cheese pastelito washed down with an extra-strong, extra-sweet café cubano, he noticed his cell blinking at him. He'd deliberately left it on his desk to get some peace and quiet. Some members of the cabinet had been dogging him over the last couple of weeks to support a social reform bill that he totally disagreed with. The lot of them would be tossed out of the government in less than a week. He plucked the half-cigar from the ashtray, lit it, and took three puffs before stubbing it out violently. Jitters. Pre-match jitters. That's all it was. He lit it again, determined not to let nerves ruin his frame of mind.

He checked the notification on his cell phone. MINREX extension. Osvaldo answered on the second ring.

"Thanks for calling back."

"Find anything?" Domínguez brushed away a light coating of pastry flakes that had settled on his shirt.

"Didn't take long. The guy's clean as a whistle. Press visa issued in Buenos Aires about a week ago, all screening procedures carried out to the letter. On the form he stated he was coming to learn and report on the growth in Cuban tourism." He chuckled. "Our checks tell us he's a well-regarded journalist. If I were you, I'd be getting in touch with the man and lining up that interview now. His wide reach could be a massive boon to our country's reputation. I think we need it right now."

Ponzoa was right. The economy was tanking big time. Domínguez knew it wasn't all down to the Americans and the evil

West. Gross incompetence, laziness, and corruption were as much —if not more—responsible for the mess Cuba found itself in. The boxing tournament was a side show, a distraction, but also an opportunity.

"You know if the DI has been watching him?"

A cough. "Not that I'm aware of. I do know he checked into his hotel and is still residing there."

"Will you keep an eye out for any irregularities with his stay here?"

"No problem." A slight pause. "He's got a full 30-day press visa, and he's stated he'll be staying at the Meliá Cohiba for the duration with a flight booked back to...ah...Buenos Aires. That tell you anything?"

"Not really." Rubbing his eyes, Domínguez thanked Ponzoa, promising not to let time drag until their next conversation. After hanging up, be made a special note in his diary, a month from today, to reward Ponzoa generously for his efforts. He also thought about swallowing his pride and calling the DI to ask them to put a tail on Vargas.

THIRTY

He snuffed out the cigar, for good this time, and ground it into the ashtray. His trusted 2IC, Colonel Rafael Varona, Chief of Operations, MINFAR, would be along shortly. He hated short waiting periods like this: not enough time to tackle any demanding tasks, not enough time to relax.

His thoughts drifted to the boxing tournament, though it wasn't the spectacle that occupied his mind. It was everything the event represented—Cuba's strength, its resilience, and his own family's legacy. Something he'd be willing to discuss in an interview with Vargas. Uncle Agosto had played a pivotal role in building that legacy with his bare hands, training champions who were more than fighters—they were symbols of Cuban endurance.

Boxing, even in Cuba, wasn't pure anymore. It had become just another tool for politics, for making fortunes and doing deals behind closed doors. Domínguez knew his uncle, if not lost to dementia, would have hated that.

Those days of idealism were long gone. Now every move Domínguez made was calculated. Especially now, with Operation Restore Dignity just days away. The mock invasion was set to begin, and Cuba's military would crush a fabricated enemy for the world to see. And America would get the blame. For it to succeed, everything needed to go off perfectly. No mistakes.

Juanita's voice came through the intercom. "Señor Varona is here."

Domínguez barely glanced up as Rafael Varona stepped inside. He gestured to a chair as Varona placed a thick folder on the desk.

"Everything's in place," Varona began without preamble, flipping open the folder. "We need to review the final tactical details. There's no room for error."

Domínguez scanned the map Varona spread across the desk. His eyes locked on to Havana Harbor, where the bulk of the audacious operation would play out. "Talk me through it," he said.

Varona tapped the map. "The invaders will land in the harbor—a massive amphibious assault. Four battalions spread across the northern coastline from Punta Sotavento to Punta Guayacanes, nearly 4,000 soldiers. The numbers will make the show look real.

"They'll come in fast, overwhelming the docks and pushing toward the center of the city. We expect them to reach the outskirts of Plaza de la Revolución by 0600 hours. From there, they'll move toward the Ministry of the Interior, as if forcing our hand." His face grew somber. "Some shelling will take place from the old Osa-class boats in the harbor. All precautions will be taken to minimize loss of life. There will be deaths, Miguel—civilians, invaders, even among our defenders. Unavoidable, I'm afraid."

"I understand," he said, tracing the route with his finger as if the topic of collateral damage hadn't even arisen. Overall, the optics of such an assault were perfect. A bold, dramatic attack right at the heart of Havana, in full view of the international press. "And the response is the same as we had planned from the start?"

"*Por supuesto*. Of course." Varona's lips curled into a thin smile. "You'll lead the counterforce. We'll mobilize the 3rd Armored Division and elite commando units stationed just outside the city. The idea is for the invaders to breach the outer defenses but be crushed before they can make it far. The T-62 tanks will roll in from the east, cutting off their escape routes. Mi-17 helicopters will provide air support, creating a chaotic battlefield. The invaders will be funneled toward Malecón, where the final stand will be staged. That's where you'll personally oversee the 'victory.'"

Domínguez leaned back, his jaw tight. "How soon until the press gets involved?"

"They'll be fed edited footage, also fake video made by our Chinese colleagues showing our forces overpowering the invaders. No live coverage, of course. Too dangerous to let the press get close." He looked up. "There *will* be footage taken from nearby hotels. That's unavoidable. Internet services will be cut for a number of hours, which means any citizen journalists' videos won't see the light of day until the event is over and done with. Any reporters—civilians in general—venturing onto the streets will be detained."

"Sounds like you've thought of everything."

He nodded. "We'll control the narrative entirely. By the time the media publishes or broadcasts anything, the story will already be written."

Domínguez grunted, satisfied. "And the air support? I want those planes in the sky by the time the first shots are fired."

Varona nodded. "The MiG-29s will be in the air before dawn, conducting simulated airstrikes over Havana Harbor. They'll fly low enough to make an impact on the visuals. We'll also have helicopter gunships strafing the beaches, making it look like a real firefight."

Domínguez stared at the map, feeling the weight of what they were about to stage. "And the invaders? They're equipped with basic arms, right?"

"Yes," Varona confirmed. "Light infantry weapons. Mostly AK-47s and a few RPGs for effect. They're not meant to put up serious resistance, just enough to make it believable."

Domínguez nodded, his mind already moving to the next step. The whole world would see Cuba's strength on display, and he would be the man leading the charge. But the operation's success hinged on precision. Even a single misstep could unravel everything. "What about our contingency plans? If any of the invaders goes rogue and manages to slip past our forces?"

Varona's eyes darkened. "We will station elite units at all key checkpoints across the city. If anyone tries to go off-script, they'll be neutralized before they can cause any real damage."

Domínguez gripped the edge of the desk, his mind momentarily drifting to Espinosa. The man had been dependable once, but lately, Domínguez sensed cracks in his resolve. Espinosa knew too much about the operation and had started asking too many questions. His nerves were fraying, and that made him a liability. "What about my pal, Raúl?" Domínguez asked, voice low, almost afraid of the answer he might get.

Varona stiffened. "To be honest, he's been a little erratic at our pep talks. If you ask me, he's close to breaking. We know he's not been the same man since he left the DI. You want me to handle it?"

Domínguez considered it for a moment. "He's been a lifelong friend. I know deep in his heart he wants to be in the middle of the action. Keep an eye on him during the operation, will you?" It pained him to utter the next words. "If he becomes a problem, have his second-in-command on the boat take him out of the equation—quietly."

Varona nodded without hesitation. "Understood."

The room fell silent for a moment, the weight of their plans hanging between them. Domínguez's mind flicked to the journalist, Manuel Vargas. He made a snap decision to share with Varona the information about the Argentinian's overtures.

Varona shrugged. "If MINREX say he checks out, then my inclination would be to play this card that's fallen into your lap. Take up the offer. He's entered through Havana's airport with clean papers. Come to cover tourism, write a legit story about the boxing tournament. There must be dozens of such journalists in the country right now."

"True," Domínguez conceded.

"Just make sure to keep your guard up, if I may employ a boxing analogy. A journalist poking around this close to the operation? Could be trouble if you let him sneak a tricky question or two through your defenses. If we use him to our advantage, it can only be a plus."

Domínguez grunted. "I've got Ponzoa keeping an eye on him. His credentials may be legitimate, but I want to make sure he doesn't have a broader agenda."

Varona smirked. "You think he's got other plans?"

"Journalists like Vargas are always looking for a bigger story," Domínguez said, his voice hardening. "If he starts digging where he shouldn't, I want him dealt with."

"You got the DI involved?"

Domínguez frowned and squinted at the same time. "You know I don't trust them. Once I've got control, there'll be a broom going through that agency. It will be one of the first things I'm going to do."

"I've got people under my command who can watch discretely for you." Varona's smile faded, his tone serious. "I'll make sure Vargas doesn't become an issue."

"Would you do that for me? The last guy I used, someone I thought I could trust, fucked up big time." He shuddered. "Nearly cost us the game."

"Don't worry. My people are the best." He pursed his lips for a second. "I can get a guy to follow Espinosa, too, if you'd like."

"Do it. Absolute discretion is a must." Domínguez stood, walked to the window overlooking the Havana skyline. "The whole world will be watching," he said quietly. "We can't afford any mistakes."

Varona stood beside him. "There won't be. This operation will go off like clockwork. The world will see Cuban resolve, crushing the Americans, and you'll be the one leading the charge.

After that, our nation will only bargain with others from a position of strength."

Domínguez stared out over the harbor, imagining the chaos that would soon erupt—the gunfire, the smoke, the staged victory. He could already hear the cheers as his forces crushed the fake invaders, restoring Cuba's dignity for all to see.

He turned back to Varona. "Finalize everything. I want the commanders briefed by tomorrow morning. No loose ends."

Varona saluted, his face a mask of steely resolve. "It'll be done."

As Varona left the room, Domínguez returned to his desk, his gaze falling on the card Casamayor had left. Manuel Vargas. He picked it up, turning it over in his hands. Vargas might say he wanted to talk about boxing, but Domínguez knew better than to trust a foreign journalist—especially one with such convenient timing. He would meet with him, but only on his terms.

No one, especially not a nosy reporter, would jeopardize what was about to happen.

He tapped in the number and listened to the dial tone.

THIRTY-ONE

Irina checked her iPhone again. She was ten minutes late now, and it wasn't just the slow traffic fraying her nerves. The meeting had taken some slick maneuvering to set up, and now she was slipping. Sleet pelted the streets, slushing underfoot and turning the sidewalks into a grim ballet of people dodging puddles, collars turned up against the biting wind.

The cabbie glanced in the rearview mirror, offering an apologetic shrug, as though his helplessness could absolve the gridlocked streets. "Just another two blocks, miss. Fifteen minutes, maybe? This crazy weather's got everyone stuck."

Irina didn't have fifteen minutes. "I'll walk," she said abruptly, throwing some bills into the front seat. She stepped out, clutching her coat tighter as she braced against the wind and darted into the thick of the city. Wet hair clung to her cheeks as she picked up the pace, boots splashing through shallow pools.

The Green Slate Café was nestled on the Lower East Side, the kind of place that was nondescript if you didn't know what you were looking for. Irina pushed through the door, welcomed by the thick aroma of rich espresso, the clanking of spoons on crockery, and the hum of conversation. The warm air hit her all at once, and for a moment, she just stood there, allowing the heat to thaw her damp limbs. It wasn't busy; the afternoon sleet had kept most people in their apartments and offices. The few patrons who sat scattered at tables were absorbed in their own worlds.

Her eyes found Laura Stapleton easily. The woman matched her description: middle-aged, portly, her body language speaking of someone used to blending into the background. She had a matronly air, like someone you'd expect to host tea parties with freshly baked scones. But Irina knew better than to judge by appearances.

She approached, giving a quick nod.

Laura glanced up from her cup of coffee with a knowing smile. "Bit wet out there."

"Sorry I'm late," Irina muttered, shaking droplets from her coat and tossing it over the back of the chair. "Traffic."

"Don't worry about it. The weather's caught everyone on the hop today." Laura's voice had a lilting cadence, but there was steel underneath. She leaned in slightly. "You ready for this?"

Irina cut to the chase. "I wouldn't have come in this mess if I wasn't. What have you got?"

Laura folded her napkin, setting it neatly beside her bagel with cream cheese, lox and a sprinkling of capers. "Let me make this clear: none of what I'm about to tell you exists on paper. It's all unofficial. In fact, officially, this conversation didn't happen."

"Good." Irina leaned in, mirroring Laura's posture. "But I need more than just words."

"You'll get what you need," Laura said, her voice dropping just above a whisper, "but you won't get it in writing. Not yet. It's too sensitive."

Irina frowned. "Why the cloak and dagger? It would have been just as easy to send me the information in an encrypted email; you could've dropped it on a private cloud server, given me a one-off code to get the information, then blocked me."

"You impress with your knowledge." Laura tapped her fingers on the edge of the table. "But none of that would fly. We didn't follow the usual channels to get the information. And neither should you." She glanced around, her eyes darting to the door and then the counter where a lone barista wiped down an espresso machine. "Look, you asked me to get you something concrete on Domínguez and his niece. I got it. But we had to...improvise."

Irina's curiosity was piqued. "Improvise how?"

Laura sighed, stirring her coffee as if weighing how much of her organization's methods to give away. "Let's just say we bypassed the formal route. Treasury's tools are good, but they're restricted by layers of bureaucracy and red tape. We don't have the luxury of waiting for subpoenas or warrants to dig into offshore accounts. So we worked around it."

Irina's brow furrowed. "Meaning?"

Laura leaned in, her voice a low murmur. "Meaning we hunted around some Caribbean tax havens, then struck gold. Or maybe oil is a better analogy in this case."

"You hinting at the Venezuelan connection?"

Laura grinned. "Correct. More of that in a minute." She took a breath. "We homed in on Panama, cracked into a couple of Panamanian banks without official permission. No warrants, no requests. Just backdoors. Those systems are supposed to be airtight, right? But they aren't. Nothing is. You know the old adage—every lock has a key."

Irina's eyes widened slightly, but she kept her composure. "And you found the key?"

Laura smirked. "More like we made one. We used a tool we've been developing off the books—AI-driven, no fingerprints, no trail. As your bosses in State requested, we traced the money flows from Miguel Domínguez to his niece Lourdes, from Venezuela to Panama and back again. And then we dug deeper."

Irina crossed her arms, intrigued. "What exactly did you dig up?"

"Lourdes Domínguez has been funneling money through Panamanian shell companies for years, under the guise of her legitimate business operations. But here's the kicker: we tracked payments to a Russian front, one connected to Vitaly Botvinnik, from a Cuban government-linked account via one of her business accounts in Venezuela. The same Cuban account is linked to a series of shipments—supposedly humanitarian aid—moving through Caribbean ports."

"Russian weapons," Irina said, not even phrasing it as a question.

"Maybe." Laura shrugged. "We just trace the money. Unfortunately, my section doesn't have x-ray vision and can't see inside steel shipping containers. Our terrorism specialists do believe, like you do, that it's mainly for Russian weapons, funded through Domínguez's access to his country's limited cash reserves. Although I have noted other activity. Bank accounts opened for other people, including a Chinese diplomat based in Havana. Suspicious payments, substantial enough to raise eyebrows but not big enough to pay for weaponry." She paused for breath. "This money is probably for 'services rendered.' In other words, kickbacks, bribes for looking the other way." She offered an amiable smile. "All cleverly hidden behind his niece's logistics company. It's clean on the surface, but once you start following the paper trail—or in this case, the digital trail—it falls apart."

Irina processed this for a moment. "And you got all of this without triggering any alarms? Without them knowing?"

Laura grinned. "That's the beauty of it. They have no idea. We didn't break through their defenses—we slipped under them. We tracked patterns, identified slight discrepancies in transaction timings, metadata mismatches. It was enough to give us a roadmap."

"And the Panamanian bank? They're not aware you've been in their systems?"

Laura shook her head. "They're as clueless as ever. We were in and out, clean. Even if they did catch on, it would take them months to figure out how we got in, and by then, it won't even matter. The principal players will be either arrested or otherwise dealt with."

Irina's mind raced. The implications of what Laura had just

said were massive. If they had indeed cracked the accounts of the Cuban Deputy Minister of MINFAR and transactions involving a Russian arms dealer, made using Lourdes as a proxy, the entire operation could be blown wide open before it even began. If Jacob could confront Domínguez with the evidence in his hand, the Cuban madman might cancel his operation altogether. Would he punish Jacob for delivering the news? She shuddered as the expression 'kill the messenger' flashed in her mind.

"I'm so grateful you were able to fast-track this job," she said as Laura accepted a coffee refill from a waitress. "I know you've probably got a lot on your plate." Irina filled a glass of water from a carafe when the waitress was gone.

"What are you implying?" Laura chuckled, glancing at her own plate, covered in nothing but crumbs after the bagel had disappeared almost unnoticed during their conversation.

"Nothing...I...ah," Irina stammered. "I was thinking of Ukraine, Palestine, and all the other flashpoints around the world you've no doubt got your eyes on."

"Don't worry." She winked. "It's just my folksy humor coming out."

"Ah ha," said Irina, not having a clue what 'folksy' meant.

"Seriously, though," Laura continued. "You need to get this information to your man on the ground as soon as possible. Our department's not privy to all the details State has—we just carry out orders—but we're not stupid. We understand something massive could be brewing in Cuba. It's why I stopped all my other work to assist with this."

Irina nodded. "There are people handling it. I can't confirm or deny anything, but it would be..."—she searched for the word in her language brain-archive and finally latched on to it—"... disingenuous of me to think you guys can't make educated guesses. Especially when you already know the names and roles of the key players."

"That's one of the reasons we didn't apply for international warrants and all that shit..." She gave an apologetic grimace. "Forgive my profanity."

Irina laughed. "I hear a lot worse from my son every day."

"Of course." Laura dabbed the side of her mouth with a napkin. "Like I said, if we'd done this by the book, Domínguez would've gotten wind of it long before we made any progress. And with time a critical factor, we'd still be twiddling our thumbs waiting for the Panamanian government to come to the party." She glanced out the window, following the path of a pigeon zeroing in on a scrap of food on the sidewalk. Looking back at Irina, she said, "The niece could be a vulnerable link in the chain." She blushed slightly. "That's just my opinion. Formulated from reading too many thriller novels, perhaps. It's clichéd but true. Where there's a beautiful woman in a position of wealth and power, there are usually men lined up to do her bidding and...I'm rambling now."

"No, no," Irina countered. "Tell me what you think."

"Lourdes is the key to whatever door it is you're trying to open. Or keep closed. She's been making transactions for her uncle, that much is obvious. Our analysts think she's just a pawn in Domínguez's overall plan. She might be thinking she's just helping him move money around to avoid the gaze of the Cuban treasury—business as usual. She grew up in Cuba, as far as I know, so she knows the lay of the land there. But if she were to find out he's involved in moving weapons rather than the humanitarian cargo she thinks is being transported across the Caribbean, it could be enough to turn her against him."

Irina raised an eyebrow. "You think she'd turn against her own uncle?"

"If she knew what was at stake, yes," Laura said. "She's in deep, but I'd say she's not stupid. If someone can make her see that Domínguez is dragging her down with him, she might flip. And if she flips, you'd have everything you need to...do whatever it is you have to do."

Irina exhaled slowly, the weight and complexity of the situation pressing down on her like a heavy stone. She knew Jacob was good at his job—the best—but this was different. He was dealing with high-level Cuban officials in a totalitarian country harder to navigate than most, a Russian arms dealer who cut his teeth in Moscow's brutal gang world, and an enigmatic Venezuelan-Cuban businesswoman with deep pockets and a direct line to her adoptive country's president. One wrong move, and it could all unravel, with fatal consequences for Jacob.

She reached into her pocket, pulled out a small notepad, and scribbled a few quick notes. "You said you found a connection between Lourdes and Botvinnik. How solid is it?"

"Solid enough," Laura said. "There are several transactions between her Panamanian accounts and a shell company linked to Botvinnik. The dates match the dates of weapons shipments flagged by international arms inspectors, the amounts commensurate with large cargoes of weapons. We also intercepted messages between Botvinnik and Domínguez, discussing 'shipment coordination' and 'final payments.' It's all there, Irina. The only thing left is to confront Domínguez with it."

Irina tapped the notepad with her pen, deep in thought. "If we confront him too soon, he'll cover his tracks. Maybe act too soon for us to counter. We need to make sure our man has enough leverage before he makes his move."

Laura nodded. "That's why you need to get this information to your agent now. Like you said, if Domínguez gets a whiff, he'll be angry as a hornet."

Irina glanced up, meeting Laura's gaze. "You said this isn't in writing. But you've got more than just the trail, don't you?"

Laura's eyes gleamed. "Of course I do." She reached into her handbag, pulled out a USB drive. "Everything you need is on here —transaction logs, intercepted communications, account numbers. It's all there." She inhaled deeply. "You need a password to open the drive. It's the address of this café including the zip code. All uppercase, no spaces. Got it?"

"Yes." Irina hesitated for a moment, then reached out and

took the drive, slipping it into her coat pocket. "What if somebody mugs me on the subway and steals the flash drive?"

Laura gave a small, humorless smile. "Nobody mugged me. And I got it all the way here from DC."

"DC is safer. I need an alternative."

"Memorize this. Do not write it down." She recited a series of eight characters and then a URL. "I will activate the one-time code from my cell. It'll be valid for three hours only. If you lose the drive, everything on it is mirrored on our private cloud."

"But you said before that option wouldn't fly."

"Never mind what I said." Her jaw tightened. "This is a backup I didn't want to resort to. Recite the details back to me."

Irina did so, struggling with the last two characters of the code. Laura corrected her, then made her recite it again. This time, no mistakes.

Laura nodded. "Good. Repeat that over and over in your head until you get home. Under no circumstances will you stop and write it down. I could lose my job for granting you access to that. If you forget it, don't bother asking me to tell you again. Understood?"

"Got it." Irina stood, pulling her coat back on. "I'll get what's on the USB drive to our man, don't worry. Once again, Laura, thank you."

"I've enjoyed being part of this. A diversion from my usually sedate desk job." Laura's smile slowly faded, replaced by a hard edge. "Now it's up to you to do what you can with what I've delivered."

Irina held up a finger. "One more thing. I almost forgot. You didn't mention Sebastian Goulding from the US embassy in Caracas. Did you find anything connecting him with Domínguez, his niece and Botvinnik?"

"You bet." She pushed her empty coffee cup to the side. "It's on the USB in his own separate folder. Remember what I said about men lining up to get access to rich and powerful women? He's a guy cut from that cloth. Goulding looks to be getting a share from all of this. How he's involved, I can't even begin to guess. He's not being paid millions like Botvinnik is, but it's probably enough to see him marched out of his job and straight into the waiting arms of a grand jury."

Irina nodded, giving Laura one last look before turning toward the door. The cold air hit her as soon as she stepped outside, but she didn't care. Her mind was already racing ahead, thinking about how Jacob would use the precious intel, how he would corner Domínguez and shut down the entire operation before it was too late.

As she turned the corner and headed for the subway station, a large man bumped into her, grabbing her by the shoulders as his feet slipped in the slush. The two of them crashed to the ground. He lumbered back to his feet and hauled Irina up like she was made of balsa wood. The man smiled, big white teeth behind full purple lips. "Sorry, ma'am. I feel like such a fool, not watching where I'm going."

"It's fine," said Irina, catching her breath.

As the man walked off in the opposite direction, she reached into her pocket, terrified she'd just been the victim of a clever pickpocket. A huge sigh escaped her lips as her fingers brushed the USB drive then clutched firmly around it. She had to guard the damned thing with her life; there was no other option. The code she'd been so diligently reciting over and over in her head—something Jacob could commit to memory as easily as brushing his teeth—was now completely forgotten.

THIRTY-TWO

THE INSISTENT RINGING OF HIS CELL PHONE JARRED Jacob from his focus. The mantra shattered. He cursed softly, his attempt at meditation rudely interrupted. He untangled his legs from the lotus position and bolted toward the kitchen where his phone lay charging on the counter. Unknown number—no surprise there. He hesitated for a beat before pressing the green button and holding the phone to his ear.

"*Hola?*" If his tone was a color it would have been beige.

"Is that Manuel Vargas?" The voice on the other end was deep, authoritative, with a dark undercurrent Jacob couldn't quite place. It wasn't just commanding—it had a weight, a sinister edge. He tightened his grip on the phone.

"*Sí*. Who's asking?"

The reply came in the form of a low, rumbling laugh. "Don't sound so surprised, Señor Vargas. Your friend Edmundo Casamayor left me a business card and some...compelling reasons to give you a call."

Jacob's mind snapped into gear, slipping fully into the role of Manuel Vargas, South American journalist. His demeanor shifted, his voice sliding effortlessly into the accent and persona of the Argentinian reporter. "Ah, the ever-obliging Señor Casamayor.

He did mention you might reach out. Seems he wasn't exaggerating."

There was a brief pause on the other end, a cough that sounded impatient. "Don't get ahead of yourself. I'm not agreeing to anything yet. Tell me—why should I, Deputy Minister General Miguel Domínguez, interrupt my busy schedule to talk to you?"

Jacob felt a cold trickle of anxiety. This was the moment. If he misstepped, everything would be over before it began. He took a breath and leaned into the faux charm that had pulled him out of sticky situations before. "Minister, with all due respect, it's not just about me getting paid for a story—it's about the future of Cuba. This interview can only do your country good. I've been tracking the numbers, the projections—Cuba's economy is in a precarious position. Sanctions and trade embargos are still in place. Tourism, the new backbone of recovery, hasn't picked up as fast as everyone hoped. I can help turn the world's attention to more positive things."

Domínguez snorted. "And what's that got to do with me? I'm the Deputy Minister of the Revolutionary Armed Forces, not some flunky in the Ministry of Tourism. You want to talk about hotels and beaches? Wrong department."

Jacob expected the pushback. He took the rebuke in his stride, lowering his voice to a tone of empathy, as if speaking as one professional to another. "I know, and that's exactly why I'm calling you. Look, I've been trying to get through the bureaucracy to tee-up meetings with important people like you, but I'm hitting roadblocks at every turn. The ministries? They won't talk. Which is a shame. Because what I'm proposing to write about in my articles is more than just tourism—it's a story about Cuba's resilience, its fight for a better future. Boxing is a wonderful...analogy...for that struggle. And there's no one better suited to talk about that than you."

There was silence on the other end. Jacob's heart pounded in his chest. He could almost hear the gears turning in Domínguez's mind, weighing the merits of the proposition. Domínguez might have already decided whether to accept or reject the offer of an interview and was now simply toying with Jacob. If the answer was 'reject,' he had to change the man's mind. Fast. He pressed on with the confidence of a pushy foot-in-the-door reporter. "Your uncle, Agosto Domínguez—he's a legend, a hero in Cuba. I saw the portrait on the wall in the gym. Even though I'm not a Cuban myself, I felt something...deep...in Agosto's eyes. Everyone knows his name. This isn't just about tourism; it's about legacy. Your family's legacy."

Domínguez's attitude shifted, ever so slightly. "Agosto..." There was a pause, and when he spoke again, his tone had softened, though not without wariness. "My uncle's time has passed. He's an old man now. He'll be lucky to see out another year."

"Exactly," Jacob said, seizing the opening. "But his legacy will continue to live on. The boxing tournament next week? It's the perfect opportunity to highlight that. I want to talk about him, the fighters he trained to Olympic glory. How his work represents the strength of the Cuban people—especially in hard times like these." He had a thought, icing on the cake that was Domínguez's ego. "And how a man like Agosto could inspire the armed forces you are in charge of today."

Domínguez's continued silence was telling. Jacob could sense his interest building, the flattery working its magic, though he knew Domínguez wouldn't acquiesce easily. He had to keep pushing, but oh, so carefully. "Look, I get it. You're busy, and this may seem trivial. But people outside Cuba—they don't understand what you're building here. They only see the negative headlines. This interview could show the world a different side of Cuba, a different side of you. Not just as a military leader, but as someone connected to a national hero. A man carrying forward the ideals his uncle stood for."

"Publicity isn't my concern, Vargas," Domínguez replied gruffly, but Jacob could hear the crack in his armor. The repeated mentioning of his uncle had stirred something. "Agosto is in a nursing home, being fed through a tube. He doesn't even remember half the things he accomplished."

Jacob let the moment breathe, then carefully offered a final nudge. "Maybe not, but the people remember. And the world audience will lap it up. And they'll listen when you speak about it." Now for a whopper. "I've interviewed international athletes, trainers—they all revere him for his never-say-die philosophy. This isn't just about the past; it's about the future of Cuba. A story like this—it helps." He paused. "And I'm not looking to trap you. If you don't like where the interview goes, we'll drop it. I'll even let you vet the draft." There would be no vetting because there would be no draft.

Domínguez grunted, clearly still weighing his options. A hard nut to crack. Jacob stayed silent, waiting. He knew better than to push any harder.

After what felt like an eternity, the dam wall broke. "I'll think about it. If you want an interview, meet me at the Chinese Cultural Evening tonight."

Jacob felt an adrenaline surge, his throat constricting slightly. "That's rather short notice."

"I told you, I'm a busy man. If you want to see me as badly as you say you do, then I'd say three hours is plenty of notice. If a bomb went off downtown, would you rush to the scene or stay put because you didn't have enough notice?"

In a scenario where every minute counted, Domínguez was right. Three hours was an eternity. "OK, I'll be there. What is it and where?"

"It's an event for dignitaries hosted by our friends from the Chinese embassy. Costumes, music, dancing, that kind of thing. At the Gran Teatro de La Habana."

"Got it." Jacob pictured red and yellow dragons, screeching stringed instruments, fire crackers.

"I can give you fifteen minutes in the interval. To get a feel for you...as a person. Talking on the phone is one thing, face to face is the clincher. After that, if I don't like you, no interview." The sound of a match striking, the inhalation of smoke. "My assistant will call you with details about the time and the venue. She will organize a VIP pass for you to pick up at the door."

Jacob's pulse quickened. Deep down, he'd been cold on this move. He hadn't thought Domínguez would roll over. In the end, ego won out over caution. He kept his voice steady and said, "Thank you, Deputy Minister. I'll be there." Before Domínguez could hang up, Jacob added, "One last thing. I'd love to do the interview at your uncle's gym, where he trained his champions. It would give my story more depth, more connection to the people."

"No. I have a better idea. If I agree—which I haven't—you will come to my office at a time of my choosing." Domínguez waited a moment. "I feel more comfortable there with strangers."

I bet you do, thought Jacob. The prospect was terrifying and mouth-watering at the same time. Access to MINFAR, where so many secrets might lay buried, was a gift. "Less than ideal," said Jacob, hoping his disingenuousness didn't come across as obvious. "But it's better than nothing." More flattery: "To be totally honest, I'd be happy to talk to you anywhere."

"Don't get ahead of yourself. You have to get through tonight's cultural event." He laughed. "Drink a strong coffee before you come. It's bound to be a snooze fest."

Jacob offered a polite laugh. "Understood. I'll see you soon."

The call ended, leaving Jacob standing in the quiet of the hotel room. He was too pumped up to resume his yoga session. Against his expectations, Casamayor had come through. A solid workout in the ground-floor gym would help clear his head, prepare mentally for tonight's meeting with Domínguez. He glanced out the window at the bustling street. So much potential in this city—in this country. Every small step forward would be erased by that man if his wild scheme succeeded.

It must not.

He exhaled slowly, letting the tension drain from his body. The hardest part of the plan had just fallen into place.

His phone rang. Unknown number again. *Shit, he's changed*

his mind. He answered, steadying himself for the let-down. Instead, a robotic female voice spoke to him. "You can pick up your pass at the entrance on Paseo del Prado at 7 p.m."

Jacob thanked her.

"*De nada,*" she said. "Don't mention it." No emotion, no joy, nothing. Espinosa had nailed it. Juanita was being bullied.

Jacob's heart pounded. Take a chance or not? The line had to be monitored.

"The number you just called me on came up as unknown. Can you give it to me in case I need to call back and ask the Deputy Minister something?"

"*No es posible.* Not possible."

He waited for an explanation, an excuse. Nothing was forthcoming. What happened to that famous Cuban friendliness?

"Make sure you don't lose my number then," he said, feigning joviality. "In case the Deputy Minister loses it...Juanita."

A pause. "How did you...know my name? I didn't introduce myself."

"The Deputy Minister told me," he lied. He decided to lay it on thick, so she knew he had an idea of her predicament. "Señor General Domínguez told me how much he appreciated you, that he couldn't do his job properly without you by his side."

She stammered something that sounded like "*Bullshit.*"

"Anyway, keep my number. Ciao!" He hung up before she could say anything else. If she got desperate enough and—more importantly—if she could read between the lines, there was a remote chance she would contact him. She'd certainly have a trailer-load of dirt on Domínguez, perhaps know a way to get into places prying eyes were meant to be kept away from.

He pulled on loose shorts and a T-shirt, green tracksuit on top of that. Small sports bags with personal items tucked over his shoulder, he headed for the door. Turning the handle, his cell buzzed in his pocket. *Will I ever get peace?* he thought.

An email from Irina, cc'd to Fletcher. Subject line: URGENT.

He dropped the bag, sat at the desk, and flipped open his laptop. His eyes bulged as he scanned the brief message. At the bottom: a link to Skia's cloud server. Fingers trembling, he clicked the mouse, and a number of folders appeared.

The digital trail showing the financials behind Operation Restore Dignity.

He absorbed every detail, every transaction and communication intercepted by the OTFI. It was a puzzle that the average person would have no hope of putting together. For Jacob, it was like a jigsaw for four-year-olds.

But was it sufficient proof?

Technically, no. Shady payments, messages mentioning 'shipment coordination' and 'final payments' were highly suspicious. The timing of these payments sometimes matched arms shipments flagged by weapons inspectors; however, no actual inspections had taken place. The vessels could be carrying anything. If the details were brought up in a court of law, much of the evidence would be classified circumstantial at best, maybe even inadmissible.

Still, he could confront Domínguez with the digital trail, bluffing him into either confessing or shelving the project. But doing so meant risking his life. Jacob knew he could convince Domínguez he had enough evidence to stop the operation, but it wasn't enough on its own. He needed more concrete proof from the inside. His mind raced with options, knowing many decisions would be made on the fly.

The only detail in the package that could lead to immediate concrete action was the payment to agent Seb Goulding. Using it now would be a mistake. He hit forward, told Fletcher to sit on the information about Goulding for now, clicked send. Once the case was wrapped up tight, *then* they could rat him out to Caracas Station. Now his arrest could only escalate matters.

A TEN-MINUTE SESSION of stretching exercises, a cold shower, back to his desk. To forestall any awkwardness, he composed a list of subjects to broach at the cultural event. A series of 'warm up' questions to break the ice with Domínguez. Satisfied, he memorized the list and deleted it.

He slowly dressed for an evening of cultural enlightenment, called Pepe, and headed for the elevator.

THIRTY-THREE

Espinosa gripped the steering wheel hard. His eyes locked on the road ahead as the clapped-out Lada jostled over the uneven dirt track that led to the property on the outskirts of Bauta. The ashtray overflowed with butts, a half-bottle of beer sat in the console, trumpet-heavy music blared out of the stereo.

A chug from the bottle, another drag on the cigarette. His mind was a tangled mess of uncertainty, a knot of nerves tightening with every kilometer traveled. The old house had always been the perfect hideaway for secret meetings, a place for making people disappear. This time, it was none of those things. It was a psych ward, a refuge, a place for the noise in his head to settle the fuck down.

The confrontation with Domínguez was approaching fast. He'd hoped for a last-gasp solution from Vargas—an idea, anything—but the Argentinian had come up empty. No contact since their meeting yesterday morning. He'd rung the taxi driver's number from a payphone two blocks from his apartment; old Pepe was waiting for the next call-up and had no idea where Vargas was. Tempting as it was to give the cabbie his own cell number, ask for a callback should Vargas surface, he wouldn't risk it. Espinosa had hung up in frustration.

There would be no salvation from Vargas. As if there ever could have been. He was naïve to think a lone stranger like that would come to the rescue like Superman.

Maybe, when it came down to it, Espinosa wouldn't have the balls to defy Domínguez, to take him on. Instead, there was every chance he would simply capitulate to the crazy bastard. Drive the boat, fire shells at buildings, take part in the grand deception, cheer Domínguez on when he was installed as the new president.

That option, the coward's way, was definitely on the table. After all, he'd meekly gathered his modest gear and thrown it into a clutch bag, ready to travel to Viñales, to unquestioningly do the Deputy Minister's bidding. And maybe hitching his wagon to Domínguez *was* the sensible route. What future would he have if the asshole was victorious and he had been stupid enough to stand in his way?

The answer was obvious.

A damned short one.

And so, as commanded, on Friday before first light, he'd rock up to Domínguez's villa together with the other commanders. Bloodthirsty, the lot of them. There would be others there, too—advisers, strategists. He despised them. Above all, he didn't trust that son-of-a-bitch bootlicker, Rafael Varona. Too quick to agree to whatever Domínguez wanted. Varona had butted heads with Espinosa a number of times over the years. That prick was capable of anything.

Espinosa slowed down a fraction as the cratered road got even worse. Nudging the car forward in third gear, bumping and grinding over ruts, he thought about the stupid name Domínguez had dreamed up: Operation Restore Dignity. What a sick joke. There was no dignity in manipulating innocent people, in them dying under the guise of defending Cuba. No dignity in serving a megalomaniac like Domínguez, whose only goal was power at any cost.

Espinosa had known the price of insubordination, of betrayal, his entire life. Seen men die for daring to defy orders. He'd executed men himself. In dank dungeons and even here, at the old house. Always believing his actions were justified.

That was until Domínguez shattered Espinosa's illusions with his ridiculous plan. The fragility of that plan was exposed with the public and brutal murder of Passo, the attempt on Cain's life. The damned Chinese spy trailing him, maybe Vargas too. It was only by a miracle he'd managed so far to keep his own nose clean. He suspected Varona had sniffed him out, but so far he'd delayed playing his hand. Why? Was he waiting to do something nasty at the villa?

He swallowed hard as the thought occurred to him that Domínguez was now fully aware of his betrayal. The choice of assembling at dawn—was it symbolic? Executions often happened at dawn. He dragged hard on the remains of the fifth cigarette since leaving his home, then flicked it out the window.

From out of nowhere, a dog darted in front of the car. He yanked the steering wheel to the right, nearly skidding off the road. Or was it his imagination? He stopped, pushed open the door, and vomited onto the dirt. He wiped his mouth with a rag he found in the glove compartment and took a slug of beer. *Damn it. Calm down. Just get to the house. Your head will be clearer there, as will the path forward you need to take.*

He crossed himself three times, looked up at the sky, asked for divine guidance, and drove on.

THE SUN DIPPED low on the horizon, casting long shadows over the road as Espinosa neared the house. He glanced at the rearview mirror, half-expecting to see headlights far in the distance, someone following him up the steep incline. But there was nothing.

Espinosa pulled the car to a stop in the gravel driveway, killed the engine, and sat there for a moment, the silence pressing in on him. He took a deep breath, willing his frayed nerves to settle. No more vomiting would be a good start to a long and arduous night ahead.

Stepping out of the car, he stretched his legs and surveyed the area. The building stood in the fading light, its roof sagging, the walls weathered and cracked from years of neglect. He approached cautiously, avoiding the most rotten parts of the steps onto the porch.

He opened the front door and stepped inside, the air thick with dust. It was warm inside; even with its abundance of cracks, the building trapped heat. The interior was just as he and Vargas had left it. The hideaway wasn't much, but it would do.

Espinosa moved with the slow, languorous movements of a man whose mojo had gone AWOL. He placed his bag on the makeshift bed he'd cobbled together from packing crates, an old mattress, and hessian bags. Next, he made sure the windows were shut tight, gave them a good rattle in their frames, and closed the front and back doors on slide bolts. Securing the place like this was largely symbolic—a good kick could smash open either door, the glass in the windows was thin and would shatter easily with the tap of a pistol butt. Still, it was better than leaving everything wide open like an invitation—*please come in and kill me.*

He dropped onto the worn couch in the corner, leaning forward with his hands pressed against his cheeks. When he pulled his hands away, he saw the black crescents of grime beneath his fingernails. No shower in days, even after the workout at the gym—he stank like a dead rat. Vargas had had no hesitation calling him out on his lack of hygiene. It wasn't like Espinosa at all. It was disgusting, and he knew it. There was no plumbed water on the property, but a small stream ran a hundred meters from the back door, carrying with it crystal-clear water. He'd take a dip in the morning if he remembered.

A soft rustling sound from outside broke through his thoughts, jolting him upright. A feral cat, maybe? They were plentiful out here. Then another sound, a hollow knocking.

Espinosa froze; his heart thundered, a lump forming in his

throat like a wedge. Fear climbing, he tiptoed to the battered table in the middle of the room and pulled his cell phone and loaded Makarov from his bag. He gripped the gun hard, his free hand gently turning down the kerosene in the lamp until he had the barest minimum amount of light to see. His eyes darted to the window; the light outside was almost gone, and he couldn't see anything through the dirty glass.

He'd been ultra-careful when he left his home, double-checking the car for electronic trackers. He was sure no one had followed him.

So who the hell was out there? Vargas? Surely not.

The rustling came again, shuffling sounds, louder this time, followed by the faintest crunch of what sounded like footsteps on dirt. His senses dialed up to eleven, and he listened as hard as he could.

Someone was definitely out there.

THIRTY-FOUR

CHEN WEI CROUCHED LOW, WATCHING THE SHACK from the cover of a sprawling jatropha bush. His eyes were trained on the dilapidated structure where his target, Raúl Espinosa, had holed himself up. A tracking device, attached magnetically to the underside of the Lada's wheel well, was all it had taken to find him. Ninety minutes earlier, he'd watched from a safe distance as Espinosa thoroughly checked his vehicle before leaving his home. The sophisticated tracker Chen had attached was so small as to be virtually undetectable to the naked eye, even to the touch. A hand running over the metal lining of a wheel well might feel it. Espinosa's hand did not. The coordinates provided by the tracker meant Chen didn't have to follow too closely behind in the Jeep.

As the sun finally disappeared below the horizon and darkness descended, he donned a pair of wraparound night-vision glasses. This model was virtually indistinguishable from ordinary sunglasses. The Havana tech team had provided him with everything he needed. *More* than he needed to terminate one man. If forced to choose, he'd always prefer to kill a target with a garrote or a knife. Nice to exercise a bit of skill when ending a person's life. Guns were too easy. If he was very lucky, Espinosa would be asleep, and he'd be able to cut the man's throat with no resistance, enjoy the gurgling sounds as the blood bubbled in the gouge in his neck. Then he'd snap off a couple of pictures for Zhou and get the hell out of there.

That was purely conjecture at this point. Probably wishful thinking, too. He had to assume the man would resist. He was a trained intelligence officer and a boxer into the bargain. And boxers were used to fighting their way out of corners.

After observing for twenty-five minutes, Chen had detected no motion inside the building. Then, as he was about to reassess his options...a body walked slowly past the window. Espinosa. The body disappeared. A few minutes later, he still hadn't crossed back past the window. Chen gritted his teeth. He could set up his sniper rifle and pick him off the next time he walked by the window. Or wait until Espinosa came outside—to fetch something from his car, to get better reception on his phone, to take a piss over the porch. Either way, Chen could be in for a very long wait. Sensing a cramp starting in his right foot, he made the decision.

Time to move.

He screwed the suppressor onto his pistol. His backpack, slung over his shoulder, contained all his other favorite killing toys. Whatever confronted Chen inside that building, he would be ready for it.

Small, careful steps. Each stride required absolute focus. The ground was not only uneven, it was strewn with rocks, bushes, weeds, ant mounds, all kinds of debris that had accumulated around the property over many years. A rusted can lay directly in his path. He made a slight adjustment, his foot hitting the ground millimeters from the can.

Stooped like a soldier creeping up on an enemy encampment, he was now twenty meters from the back door as he approached from the western side. He'd have liked to move faster, but that was a no-go. The rough terrain meant he couldn't solely focus on the building as he walked; he had to keep glancing down to make sure he didn't trip over an obstacle.

A slight breeze ruffled his hair. Blowing in his face, away from the shack, hopefully carrying sound out of Espinosa's earshot. Suddenly that was a bonus, as he stepped on a twig which snapped dryly under his boot.

Ten meters away.

Through his night-vision glasses, he now saw Espinosa's shadow moving around inside the building. His jerky body language indicated a tired man, lacking confidence. Perhaps under the influence of alcohol or drugs. He blundered to the other side of the shack, checked a window, and gave it a shake. Then he pressed his hands against the bottom of the window frame and seemed to freeze. Espinosa was a sitting duck.

Chen calibrated the distance with a LiDAR app on his cell phone. Seven meters. He could shoot the foreskin off a fly at this distance with his eyes closed. He took three deep breaths, raised the barrel of the pistol to eye level, aimed for a point directly in the middle of Espinosa's skull. On the count of three. One... two...

An insane pain ran through his calf. An injection of fire directly into the muscle. Then an even more intense sensation, like someone had applied a blowtorch to his skin. He muffled a cry, glancing down. A line of ants were crawling beside him, some on his boot. One of the fuckers must have sneaked in under his trousers. He stepped out of the way of the marching line; thankfully, the ants weren't interested in him, just on getting to wherever the hell they were going. The pain from the bite reached its peak and began just as quickly to subside.

He looked up.

Espinosa had moved.

Chen swore under his breath as he leaned down and rubbed the spot, itchiness now replacing pain. He knew certain species of ants with vicious bites could send some people into anaphylactic shock. As sweat pooled under his clothes, inside his glasses, he thanked his lucky stars he wasn't one of those people.

The question arose in his mind. Had he cried out when the ant bit him? He was positive he hadn't, but in the moment...

Damn it. There was no time to waste now. It was all or nothing.

Still in stealth mode, he padded his way to the back door, placed his hand on the loose handle, and pushed it downward. He felt something give. A shoulder pressed against the old wooden planks, he gave it a fair nudge. The door rattled slightly in the frame but went nowhere. There must be a slide bolt on the inside.

He waited a minute, weighing up whether to try the door on the other side of the shack. Most likely it, too, would be bolted from the inside. This door would have to be it. Chen rolled his broad shoulders, took one stride backward, and blew a massive hole where he assumed the bolt was. He kicked as hard as he could, and the door swung open. He took a step into the darkness, pistol at eye level, scanning the walls, the floor. He had the advantage. He had night-vision glasses. Espinosa was lucky he even had that pathetic kerosene lantern, its wick barely a glimmer in the blackness.

And there, hiding in plain sight in the corner, was Espinosa.

Ramón Melo shifted in the passenger seat of the dark-green Skoda, looking through tinted windows, his hands fidgeting with the frayed edge of the seat. His eyes darted from side to side, scanning the empty streets as they passed through Bauta. He had been on edge ever since Colonel Varona had given him the assignment. Tracking down Espinosa, one of their own? That didn't sit right with him. But Varona had made it clear—Espinosa was a problem, and problems didn't last long in MINFAR. Now, out in the countryside, his nerves were as taut as guitar strings.

The phone call had come as he was peeling potatoes, helping his wife prepare a modest meal for the family. "Sorry to do this,

Ramón, but you're the best man I've got free right now. And don't worry, you'll get paid well for this job."

"What's up?"

Varona explained there was a potential rat in the ranks—a threat to national security—and he wanted eyes on him. "I can't say too much, but Espinosa poses an existential danger to the nation," Varona had said, his voice cold. "For now, just keep a close eye on him. Set up a post near his house."

"Where's he live?"

Varona reeled off the address like he recited it every day. "You know how to fly under the radar, Ramón. If he goes anywhere, follow him. If he does anything weird, get rid of him. We've got no time for subtleties."

Melo and his driver, Pancho Quintero, had thought they'd be in for a boring night, telling each other bawdy jokes to stay awake. A parabolic microphone was pointed at the glass balcony of Espinosa's apartment, but all they were hearing was music from a radio. The occupant was alone and not making phone calls.

An hour before sunset, Espinosa appeared by his car with a small travel bag. He checked under each wheel well, jumped in the driver's seat and...sat there. Two cigarettes later, he drove off slowly. Before Quintero could engage first gear, a sleek Jeep cruised into view, a Chinese man behind the wheel. It stopped in front of the entrance to Espinosa's apartment block.

"Wait a second." Melo held up a hand.

The driver, a tall athletic man with slicked-down black hair, wearing jeans and an olive-green button-down shirt, emerged from the Jeep. He began to pace the sidewalk, speaking into a cell phone.

"Espinosa's getting away!" Quintero growled.

"Too late. He's already out of sight. Something's going on. I've got a strange feeling about this. Follow the Jeep instead." Melo could get his butt kicked, but often his intuition proved correct.

Quintero tilted his head to the side and pushed in the clutch. "Your funeral, amigo."

Forty-five minutes later, after driving through sleepy Bauta, the Jeep took a left onto a minor road. Melo had no doubt his initial hunch had been correct. *El chino* was heading for the infamous abandoned house, where he suspected Espinosa was already located. "Stop here," said Melo outside a cantina at the city limits.

"What for? I thought you wanted to follow the Jeep."

"I know exactly where he's going. Let's have a coffee first. I need to think."

"You sure?"

A nod. "Technically, we're only on a watching brief." He pulled out a cell phone and rang Varona. Maybe he'd have a clue about the identity of the man they were following. No answer. He cursed as he put the phone away. "He's at that Chinese cultural event with the Deputy Minister. The fucking irony."

"Indeed," Quintero said, wincing as he sipped his coffee.

With two bland, lukewarm beverages and a couple of stale pastries under their belts, Melo made the decision to head to the old house. "You been there before, Pancho?"

"Never really knew much about it." The driver shook his head as he moved around the front of the car. "Above my pay grade."

"I didn't think anyone went there much these days," Melo said with the rising inflection of a question. "Used to be a training ground for the special forces until a new one was built. Been derelict for at least fifteen years, maybe more. I suspect it's overrun with rats and vegetation. The perfect place to hide."

"Fifteen years, you say? You sure you remember the way from here?"

Melo puffed out his cheeks, looked up at the darkening sky with hands on hips. "I reckon we'll be OK. As far as I remember, there were only two roads off this one, forking about a kilometer or so from here. We need to take a left when we hit that fork."

"I'm worried the Skoda's not going to handle the rough conditions too well."

Melo laughed. "If Espinosa's Lada can get there, we'll be fine."

Melo had worked off the books for Varona for five years, long enough to know that when the colonel issued an order like this, there were no questions, only action. Still, Melo couldn't shake the feeling of unease grabbing at his gut. Espinosa had been a respected officer, a man many in the ranks had admired. Out of action for a couple of years, he was now a simple appliance repairman with no ax to grind. To turn on him now felt...wrong.

The fork in the road loomed, just as Melo's fading memory had suggested. They took the left and immediately felt the change in terrain through the struggling suspension. Deep ruts tossed the men around in the car like they were riding at a rodeo. Quintero swore loudly as the chassis repeatedly banged hard against the ground.

"Up there." Melo pointed. "Slow down, dammit." Headlights picked up the Jeep, fifty meters ahead. "Kill the engine, *hermano*. You wait here while I go and check things out. If I'm not back in 30 minutes, come looking."

"Be careful," whispered Quintero. "You've got your city shoes on." He paused for breath. "And so have I."

Melo's fear level rose as he realized how unprepared he was for going bush. He closed the car door gently behind him and lit up the way with his cell flashlight in his left hand, right hand firmly clutching a loaded Makarov. The last time he'd used a gun was six months ago on the range. His aim had been off. Fuck this, he thought as his ankle twisted slightly in a hole. He stopped and assessed. No physical damage.

Slowly, slowly, he crept along in the gloomy hellscape. He choked off a scream in his throat as a fern frond flicked his face in the darkness. He disliked forests at the best of times; at night that became a deep loathing. With each stride, he could feel sharp rocks and snapped-off branches under his cheap shoes. Broken bottles could mean deep cuts, tetanus. Dammit, he had to stop the negativity or it would be his undoing.

The Jeep was only a couple of meters away; he approached in

a low crouch, listening for any sounds of life. He stood ever so slowly, trying to look inside the rear section of the vehicle. Black as coal.

Then, a little farther ahead, he could just make out the faint outline of Espinosa's dirty white Lada. The tumbledown shack looked like something from a horror movie. His heart thudded as he weighed up the options. Hang back and wait, or sneak up closer and observe? Espinosa was a tough hombre, capable of anything. Cornered and startled, he'd be more dangerous than ever.

He took a deep breath that expanded his chest to the point of snapping a shirt button or two, then told himself to calm down. He had a job to do, so just do it. Logically, the fear he was experiencing was generated by his own need to stay unexposed, not by any imminent danger or threat. Perhaps the Chinese stranger had been sent to talk some sense into Espinosa. Melo knew how pally Domínguez was with the Chinese movers and shakers in Cuba. He'd heard rumors of their role in some upcoming big maneuvers, how they couldn't go ahead without their technical input. That was easy to believe, considering how backward his own country was. He shook his head as he compared the Lada and the 10-year-old Skoda they had arrived in with the gleaming new Jeep at the Chinese guy's disposal.

Melo double-checked the pistol and tucked it into his pants. As he stared through the gloom at the shack, which looked as though it could collapse like a house of cards at any moment, his instincts flared. Something didn't feel right. The night was too quiet, the air too still. There were no birds, no crickets, nothing but the soft rustle of the wind through the trees.

He glanced back at the Skoda. Perhaps discretion was the better part of valor tonight. A look back at the shack's side window. The faintest of light flickered inside, but there was no movement—no sign of Espinosa or the Chinese man.

Melo crouched down farther, biting his bottom lip. The scent of the earth at his feet made him think of soil piled up beside an open grave. His mind spun like a clothes dryer on high. Sensory overload.

Espinosa had to be in there somewhere. Was the Chinese guy in there with him, or was he... shit, where was *he*?

Then he heard it. The muffled sound of a suppressed pistol firing. One round. Then the crack of wood breaking, splintering. Blood rushed in his ears as his military training kicked in. Fear evaporated as pure adrenaline took over.

He hunched as low to the ground as he could and made for the eastern side of the shack. His inner voice said: *Save Espinosa*.

ESPINOSA FROZE. The doorhandle turned slowly again. Vargas would have announced himself, from a distance. This was foe, not friend. The sneaking-up bullshit meant only one thing. Despite his initial confidence that he'd been free of a tail, someone had followed him. With one aim—to kill him.

He might die here tonight, or he might miraculously survive. Current odds favored the former. There could be other men out there as backup. If Domínguez had smelled a rat, he wouldn't hesitate sending an entire squad of goons to make sure the job got done properly. Espinosa clenched his jaw. If he went down, it would be in a blaze of glory.

A survival plan formed in his brain. He hit the deck, scurrying on hands and knees to the makeshift bed. Squatting low, he pulled his shirt over his head and wrapped it around a dirty pillow that was nearly as old as he was. Next, trousers and another pillow, even filthier and older than the first. Shoes at one end, a baseball cap at the other. A terrible effort, but to someone bursting into the room, over a split second, the ruse might be just convincing enough.

He crawled back in the opposite direction, like a reticulated lizard, squatting in front of the rusted-out stove two meters to the right of the back door. His heart hammered in his chest so hard he thought it might crack ribs from the inside. Adrenaline pumped through his veins, making everything a blur before his eyes. Yes, he was terrified, but oddly thrilled at the same time. A rush like he had never experienced in his life. He gripped the Makarov tight in his right hand, knuckles turning white. The trophy Chinese pistol he'd souvenired from the spook was held fast in his left duke. He could shoot left-handed with marginal accuracy, amplifying the output of the Russian weapon.

Espinosa held his breath, waiting. Seconds passed like hours, the silence thick and suffocating. Then, without warning, the door handle rattled a second time.

He readjusted his body in the uncomfortable sitting position, pushing his back harder into the metal stove. He retightened his grip on the Makarov, his finger hovering over the trigger. The trigger on the Norinco felt short and stumpy by comparison, but he could still use the Chinese weapon to good effect.

Then the *thwup* of a shot from a silenced gun. The slide bolt mechanism broke away, clanging against the floor.

Espinosa's heart rate spiked. This was it. He shifted again, wriggling his ass onto the floor as if that would give him better purchase. The Norinco got discarded as a bad idea. Two hands gripped the Makarov in outstretched arms. He stared, unblinking, at the door, willing whoever was outside to come in and show his damned face.

Splinters and chunks of wood flew everywhere as the door caved in. A blood-curdling scream echoed in the small space.

The door frame remained empty, the assassin too smart to barge right in. Three shots spat from the muzzle of the intruder's weapon, finding a home in the pillow effigy. Espinosa mimicked a cry of pain.

The idiot swallowed the ruse and marched toward the scarecrow on the bed.

Espinosa smiled as he took aim at the proudly striding figure. *Te pillé, hijo de puta!* Gotcha, you son of a bitch!

THIRTY-FIVE

Jacob's eyes swept the vast lobby: marble pillars reaching high up to a vaulted dome, gleaming polished floors, broad staircases leading to galleries on five levels. Opulent and magnificent, the Gran Teatro de la Habana was as imposing and beautiful as any building Jacob had ever been in. The men in tuxedoes and women in cocktail dresses, tiaras, and stilettos were as elegant as any he had ever seen. He felt underdressed in his lightweight cotton suit. The decision to add a tie—even a garish yellow one—now seemed inspired.

There was no line at the open ticket counter. His heart started to race. Was this a set-up? Why would the window be open just to serve him? He approached with a sinking feeling in his stomach, which quickly gave way to relief. He gave his name and showed his Argentinian passport to the bespectacled woman at the window. She ran her eyes over him. "Here is your ticket, Señor Vargas." She inclined her head to the left. "Take the second set of stairs. An usher will show you to your seat."

The usher, an obsequious Afro-Cuban man in a smart gray suit, greeted Jacob at the top of the stairs at the fourth tier. "Come this way, sir."

After they had traversed a semicircular corridor lined with

purple brocade drapes, the usher stopped abruptly, pulled aside a curtain, and gestured with an extended white-gloved palm. "Your party awaits."

Jacob slipped the guy twenty dollars, bringing a humble bow and a whispered gracias. With the usher retreating, Jacob sucked in a big breath. There would be two theatrical shows taking place tonight, and he prayed he didn't fluff his lines.

Inside the gallery box sat Domínguez, whom he recognized immediately, a Chinese man with a pot belly and a serious face, and two women Jacob suspected were the men's respective spouses. The resemblance of Domínguez to his Uncle Agosto was truly uncanny. The deputy minister stood, smiling at Jacob like he was his long-lost son. He made the introductions: first his wife Helena, a demure, birdlike woman; then their host, Zhou Jianyu, deputy director of cultural and strategic affairs of the People's Republic of China; finally the diplomat's wife, Ying. There was no time for more than three minutes of small talk as the show soon got underway with a tremendous fanfare.

By intermission, Jacob's ears ached. The traditional music and dance show was playing out at the maximum level of decibels allowed anywhere apart from an airport runway. Still, he smiled politely when Zhou asked him his opinion of the performance.

"Fantastic," said Jacob. "Makes me want to visit China for the next lunar New Year festival."

The comment seemed to affect Zhou, his bottom lip quivering slightly as he nodded. "We are very proud of our cultural traditions."

"And rightly so," said Domínguez. "As are we Cubans." He looked at Jacob; they all looked at Jacob. He squirmed in his seat under their intense scrutiny. "Señor Vargas wants to write an article on tourism in our country for... which newspaper was it, again?"

Was this a trap? He answered the question in a measured tone. "Magazines, actually. Plural. I'm syndicated to a number of popular publications across South and Central America." He laughed. "Although if newspapers are interested in buying my work, I won't say no." He blinked like an innocent lamb, hoping the vague response was satisfactory. Judging by the quartet of nodding heads, it was. They all laughed, except for Ying. Did she not understand Spanish? Her husband whispered something in her ear, and she giggled, too.

"I'm yet to decide whether to agree," said Domínguez, rising to his feet. "We've got twenty minutes of the interval left. Let's retire to the bar and relax for a while."

The five privileged theatergoers were treated like royalty in the bar, with the staff deferring to Domínguez's every wish. The only thing missing was forelock-tugging. If Jacob didn't know the evil plan the man was hatching, he would have believed Domínguez was one of the most charming, urbane, and gracious politicians he had ever met. He insisted on paying for all the drinks, gifted Jacob a box of Montecristo Shorts cigars, let Zhou rave about his country's culture, and flattered the ladies about their appearance. On the way back to the loge, Domínguez walked part of the way up the stairs with the palm of his hand in the small of Jacob's back. If, after all of that familiarity, he knocked back the interview request, Jacob would swan-dive from the fourth tier into the stalls below.

The five resumed their seats. An almighty gong rattled Jacob's back teeth. It seemed the first stanza was just the warm-up.

Jacob took a settling breath as he watched the unfolding spectacle. Below him, the performers, dressed in intricate silks of crimson, gold and emerald, glided across the stage, every step choreographed precisely. Costumed dancers moved in unison, their fans snapped open like knife blades flashing, silk fabrics whooshing through the air in silent arcs. From Chinese instruments poured haunting music, to Jacob's ear discordant, yet Zhou and his wife nodded along like it was the sweetest sound imaginable. Jacob gritted his teeth as a bow dragged across an elongated two-stringed instrument—called an erhu in the program. Thankfully, it was over quickly, the remainder of the spectacle taken up with less painful melodies. The finale, a dragon dance, featuring sinuous movements by lithe men and women wearing dazzling outfits, brought the crowd to its feet. Jacob joined in the thunderous applause, the squeaky-gate tunes all but forgotten. Zhou's eyes were glistening at the end, his inscrutable expression transformed into a gleeful grin. His wife wore an equally radiant smile. The Deputy Minister and his wife, more restrained in their emotions, clapped along rhythmically with the entire crowd.

"Let's wait until most of the people have gone," said Domínguez. "We shall end the evening's entertainment with a nightcap at one of my favorite jazz clubs."

The crowd began to mill out slowly; looking down, the scene in the auditorium was like liquid pouring through tubes, escaping via the fastest routes.

Back outside, at close to 11:30 p.m., the air had grown slightly chilly. Domínguez and Zhou smoked; Jacob engaged in small talk with Helena, who, to Jacob's surprise, translated their words into English for Ying. He immediately switched to his accented English, bringing a clap of delight from the Chinese woman.

A shiny black Hyundai eight-seater van, a rare sight on Havana's streets, pulled up as if by magic as Domínguez and Zhou finished their cigarettes. As the vehicle glided to a stop, in the corner of his eye, Jacob caught a glint—something metallic—across the street. He shifted his position slightly, ready to leap into the back seat of the van. He knew it was nothing, just paranoia sticking its head up again. He willed himself to stay calm. Play along, enjoy the night, keep charming the devil.

"Everyone in," commanded a smiling Domínguez, combining bossy with jovial.

Outside the pulsating nightclub, people of all ages milled beside velvet ropes looped through brass stanchions, waiting for the bouncers to let them inside. No waiting for Jacob and his party of VIPs: a man with an earpiece, who looked more like a CIA operative than anyone he'd seen at the US embassy, led them past the gazes of unhappy folks in the line. Fearing the noise inside the jazz club would be even louder than at the concert, Jacob fired from the hip. He cleared his throat, turned to Domínguez, and said, "So. Have you made a decision?"

"*Sí.*" He nodded. "We stay for an hour at the club, maximum, then home. Helena is feeling tired."

The volume of the music increased as they reached the club's main entrance. "I meant about the interview."

"I know what you meant." Domínguez winked, plucked a card from his wallet, and handed it to Jacob. "This is the address of my family villa at Viñales. The phone number is on there, too, in case you get lost." He smiled thinly. "Please come tomorrow evening at around... shall we say 8 p.m.? It's about a three-hour drive. If you like, I can send a driver for you."

"Ah..." Jacob stammered, not believing how forthcoming the man was being, at the same time wondering if there was some other agenda behind this generosity. It was all too easy. "Thanks for the kind offer, but I've got my own driver who's been looking after me since I arrived in Havana."

"As you please. But if you change your mind, let me know."

"Would you also have a cell phone number for me?" Jacob ventured.

Domínguez's expression darkened a fraction. "I'm sorry. It's a policy of mine to only give out my private number to those closest to me. For a man in my position, you can imagine that's not many people."

"Of course," Jacob agreed. And it did make sense.

"I'll be at the villa from about lunchtime. If you need to talk to me before that, call via my assistant at the office."

Jacob was just about to explain that she'd refused to give him the office number when Domínguez preempted it. "She did the right thing by not telling you. Put it in your contacts now." He reeled off the number, and Jacob logged it.

"Thanks." He gestured toward Helena. "To be honest, I'm feeling a little worn out, like your good lady."

"That was the least subtle hint I've ever heard," Domínguez laughed. "If you want to take off, go back to your hotel, I won't force you to stick around. I'm sure you've plenty of other things to do. Preparing questions for me, for example."

Jacob's plan to hit the man up with some gentle warm-up questions tonight had failed to come off. He didn't care one whit —he'd scored an invite to the family villa. After shaking Domínguez's hand, he bade the others goodnight, Helena appearing envious that he was able to bail while duty kept her there.

He walked halfway around the block and called Pepe, who arrived twelve minutes later. "Haven't you got a life?" said Jacob, clambering into the back seat.

"Not as exciting as yours." He jerked his head back toward the theater as they drove toward the Meliá Cohiba hotel. "I've never been in that fancy theater in my life, and I'm a goddamn habanero." A shake of the head. "Ordinary plebs are allowed to go." He turned and grinned. "But only to the shittiest of events."

A block from the hotel, Pepe announced, "A guy called earlier. He asked about you, but I was careful."

"Did you get a number? A name?" said Jacob. He knew it could only be one person. Espinosa. The person whose number he didn't have but now wished Pepe did. Maybe he'd called because he was in trouble, needed help.

"No. He just hung up on me."

Jacob recalled the address that Arnold had written down for him and recited it to Pepe.

"If I may say so, Manny," said Pepe, "you sound a little rattled. Did I do something wrong?"

"No. All good. The guy who called might've been a contact I've been chasing for my story."

"Why'd he ring me, then?"

"Too complicated to explain. Just take me there now. And hurry."

The apartment sat on the second floor. From the street, no

lights glowed inside. Not surprising, considering the late hour. Jacob had no idea where the man parked the Lada, but a drive around the block and two adjoining ones failed to locate the vehicle. A quick reconnaissance of La Taberna del Marinero was also a failure. The bar was closed up tight. There was only one more place he could think of where Espinosa could be.

"Pepe," said Jacob, mentally giving himself an uppercut for not thinking of it before, "did the guy who called you have caller ID switched off?"

"I can't remember. I think...wait." He pulled over, scrolled for a couple seconds, turned to Jacob, and pointed at the screen. "There's his number, right there."

"Mind if I..."

"Take it. I can see you desperately want to contact this man."

It was now 12:14 a.m. The call rang out, but he left a message. "Raúl. Where the hell are you?"

THIRTY-SIX

The tall Chinese man advanced like an automaton, long strides, his upper body rigid and controlled. He fired off another five shots into the pillows. Espinosa silently leapt to his feet in one swift motion, hands not even touching the floor, as the attacker froze in his tracks. The light mounted on the intruder's pistol was now illuminating feathers flying from the bullet-ridden pillows. His brain was registering the deception, but with his back turned to Espinosa, it was too late for him to do anything about it.

"*Que te jodan*. Fuck you," hissed Espinosa. He squeezed the trigger, launching three 9x18mm cartridges into the back of the assassin's skull, bits of brain, blood, and bone spraying everywhere. He dropped like a stone, collapsing onto the scarecrow, pistol clattering on the floor. Espinosa grinned—a second Norinco pistol to add to his collection of Chinese weapons. He dodged the gore, picked up the gun, and turned off the mounted light. Darkness was his best friend right now. He patted the body, finding a phone and wallet, and retrieved both.

Unlike the dead agent, Espinosa would not waste bullets when the job had been done. It was still unclear if there were more of them. His gut said no: another agent, communicating via earpiece with the first, would have crashed the front door at the same time in a shock-and-awe move. And Espinosa would have been dead by now.

But there were other plausible scenarios involving multiple assassins outside: late arrivals, broken comms, tactical ploys. The best thing he could do now was to sit it out until morning, prepared to repel as required. He was hungry, thirsty, and tired. Keeping his eyes open would be a challenge; survival instinct would override that.

Crunch.

Hostia! What was that? A tree branch snapping off in the stiffening breeze? Or more members of the Chinese death squad?

Espinosa gripped his Makarov tighter than ever, every muscle in his body tensing. There were more of the fuckers out there, dammit. He swiveled on his ass to face the door frame, now void of a door. Just fragments of wood and rusted hinges. In the darkness, he made out the faint outline of a round object sailing through the doorway, striking the ground with a clacking sound, like stone-on-stone. It bounced into the center of the room before coming to rest against the left hip of the corpse.

It wasn't a flash-bang, that was certain. No smoke, no deafening bang. *Oh shit... not a grenade. Please, not that.* He closed his eyes and gritted his teeth, waiting for the explosion that would tear his arms, legs, and head from his body. Ten seconds passed. Not a grenade either. Just a rock, lobbed in to get his attention.

A faint voice calling out. He couldn't make out the words, but it was in Spanish, not Chinese. Again, louder this time. "Raúl!"

Didn't sound like Vargas.

Again, very insistent: "Raúl! Are you in there, *coño*?"

The voice was unknown to him, yet addressing him with crude familiarity. Another asshole sent to kill him. Had Domínguez finally found out what Espinosa was up to? Sent someone as backup in case his Chinese flunky failed?

"I'm not here to hurt you," said the voice. "Please. I heard shots. Come out of the house. If you're hurt, we can take you to the hospital."

Espinosa checked the magazine. Plenty of rounds left. He wouldn't reply; wouldn't fall into the trap. Let the bastard come in here.

"Look. I understand you're scared. Who wouldn't be?" A short pause. "Is the Chinese guy in there with you?"

The more he spoke, the more something twigged in the back of Espinosa's brain. He couldn't be sure. If the man said a few more words...

"Come on, Raúl. There's no point in you sitting in that hovel all night."

Melo! Ramón fucking Melo. One of Varona's stooges. Not the brightest soldier, if he remembered correctly. One to blindly follow orders, no matter how stupid or dangerous they were. Espinosa crawled to the table, reached up, and turned the kerosene lamp up a fraction. He called out, surprised to hear the croakiness in his own voice. "Is that you, Ramón?"

"*Sí, soy yo*. Yes, it's me."

"Am I glad you turned up! I need your help. The back door's been blown off. Come through it."

He stood, moving to the wall beside the empty door frame. The wind stilled for a minute; Espinosa strained with all his might to hear. Soft, tentative footsteps. Then the tip of a pistol pointing through the door. Another step, and Melo was inside. Espinosa smashed the man's wrist with the butt of his Makarov, drawing a yelp of pain.

Before Melo could react, a strong right forearm snaked around his neck. An equally strong left forearm pushed Melo's head forward. Espinosa applied pressure to the sides of Melo's neck, cutting off blood flow. The struggling soon stopped; Espinosa released the pressure and eased the man to the ground.

Seven words rang out in Espinosa's head. *We can take you to the hospital*. We, plural. That meant there was at least one other person outside waiting. He changed his mind: he wouldn't sit it out; he would be proactive.

Espinosa rolled the sleeping man onto his back, unbuttoned his red-and-black checked shirt, and removed his shoes and trousers. He switched off his cell and removed the SIM and battery. Already stripped down to his underwear after making the scarecrow, he donned Melo's gear.

Outside, after tip-toeing about in the darkness for a minute, in the faint starlight he made out the outlines of two vehicles in addition to his own. *El chino* would have come in the new Jeep. Alone, it seemed clear now. Espinosa commando-crawled to the Jeep and tapped a fingernail on the bottom of the front passenger door. If anyone was inside, they would have heard the pings.

Nothing.

He changed direction, crawling toward the Skoda. He stood at the driver's side, head facing away. The window wound down. "What's going on in there, Ramón?"

Espinosa turned and punched the driver in the face with three right jabs. He said a mental apology to the guy. Face bathed in blood, the man lost consciousness. His head fell squarely onto the middle of the steering wheel, setting off a raucous honk. Pulse beating wildly, Espinosa grabbed the unconscious man by the hair, yanking his head back to stop the wailing of the car horn.

If there were others in the vicinity, they'd be swarming him in no time. He stood, chest heaving, and calmed himself for a minute.

Silence reigned in the forest.

He breathed in and out slowly, trying to figure out what the hell to do next. Vitals more or less normal now, he yanked open the car door, grabbed the unconscious driver under the arms, and dragged him out. Grunting and swearing, walking backwards, he hauled the limp body across the uneven ground toward the shack. Sweat trickled down his spine as he neared the door, stepping over the shattered wood. With a groan, he pulled the man inside, dumping him beside the lifeless body of the failed Chinese assassin.

Espinosa turned up the kerosene lamp to high. He crouched and hooked his arms under Melo, dragging him toward the cellar door located directly under the kitchen table. The cellar had been used to store root vegetables and spare ammo back in the day but was now an empty cave. He flipped open the creaky wooden hatch and rolled Melo into the dank pit, his body thudding softly as it hit the dirt below. Espinosa climbed in and pulled Melo to one side to make room for the next deposit. The driver was next. This one took more effort, his flabby limbs hanging like a ragdoll as Espinosa deposited him in the same unceremonious fashion. Down the ladder, libertate the asshole's cell phone, up again. Finally, he grabbed the Chinese agent, dragging the cadaver by the ankles before dropping it into the hole with a satisfying thud.

Espinosa crouched at the edge, shining his cell flashlight into the hole. He peered down at the two unconscious men and the dead one beside them. Melo groaned, stirring awake. His eyes fluttered, widening in terror as he realized where he was. "What the hell are you doing, Raúl? I came to save you."

"Bullshit, Ramón," Espinosa said, his voice calm but firm. "You were sent on a similar mission to the Chinese bastard. I oughta finish you off for your treachery. Fat boy there, too. Lucky for you, I'm tired. Tired of killing."

"You can't leave us down here." He moaned as he rolled onto his side and saw the wide-eyed stare of the dead operative. "Is he... Oh, my God!"

"Shut up. You're going to be fine. I've got a few things to work out. When I do, you'll be released. Hopefully not too long."

"Raúl!"

"Stop whining." A thought occurred to him. "Who sent you?"

Silence.

"I said, who sent you? If you don't answer truthfully, your driver there will be the only one they find alive."

"Varona." No hesitation.

"I knew it." Espinosa reinserted the SIM back into Melo's cell and jumped back into the pit. Aiming his pistol at Melo's head, he made the shivering man send a text to Varona. "Tell the fucker I'm tucked up in bed, nothing to report. Show me the text when you're done."

Melo's shaking fingers tapped on the screen. He handed the device over, and Espinosa read it, nodded, then pressed send. "Now shut the hell up. If you don't keep quiet while I get some rest, I will end you. Not a fucking peep!" Espinosa shut the cellar door and latched it.

He collapsed onto a wooden chair, took a long drink of water from the canteen he'd brought along. His eyes began to close involuntarily. He stumbled to the bed and fell onto it, feathers flying in all directions. He quickly fell into a deep, dreamless sleep.

The shrill ring of his cell phone startled him awake. Espinosa only got two lousy bars of reception out here, but it was sometimes enough. His head snapped toward the table, heart pounding. He crawled on all fours, muscles aching, and grabbed the phone. It was the cabbie. Maybe he'd located Vargas.

"Raúl!" Jacob's voice crackled on the other end. "Where the hell are you? I've been trying to call you all night. Are you OK?"

"Barely." Espinosa wiped the sweat from his brow. "You're not going to fucking believe this."

THIRTY-SEVEN

"Get your driver to drop you at the corner of Avenida Primera and Calle 60." Elijah Dundas couldn't hide the urgency in his voice. "Near the National Aquarium. We need to move quickly on this."

"No, not there," said Jacob, pressing the sat phone to his ear. He watched a black woman in a tight-fitting swimsuit do a tumble turn at the end of the pool area. "Regla district." He recited the address of the abandoned dry dock Pepe had taken him to four days ago. He knew he could get to it from the hotel undetected.

"Why there?" Dundas said impatiently.

"Too many people at the Aquarium. If Domínguez is watching me closely and one of his men sees CIA spooks picking me up..." Jacob left the sentence hanging.

A frustrated sigh. "Your call, Vargas."

Lying on a banana lounge, Jacob took a long, slow sip of his iced tea. The woman had managed another lap in the blink of an eye. He could watch her all day, admiring her athleticism and grace.

The hastily called meeting at Havana Station in an hour's time was going to be intense and unpleasant; he felt it in his marrow. It shouldn't even be going ahead. He cursed Fletcher for his impetuousness, for ignoring his advice. Tipping off Caracas Station and Dundas about Goulding was a big mistake. If Domínguez or one of his coterie found out the agent had been rumbled...Christ knew what steps the madman would take next.

As he gathered his things, the woman slowed to a stop at the diving block a couple of yards from where Jacob stood. She sprang out of the water and walked toward a cane chair, hips gyrating and wet feet slapping on the concrete. She took off her bathing cap, shook out long black hair, laid a towel on the chair, and sat. A man in a white linen suit sat in another chair next to her, back toward Jacob and partly shielded by a beach umbrella. The woman leaned over and kissed the man on the lips, a lingering kiss. She whispered something in his ear and sat down, both of them laughing. He reached for a cocktail and saluted her with his glass. Jacob strolled past and heard a brief snatch of their conversation. They spoke Russian. Unusual, because the woman was Black, and her speech was unaccented and flawless.

He walked another ten yards to the gate leading out of the pool, then turned around to get a better look at the pair. From his memory banks, he remembered the photographs he'd seen. The man was Vitaly Botvinnik.

THE SMALL, featureless room was the same one in which Jacob had spoken with Wilfred Arnold just two days prior. The walls were painted graphite gray, the space illuminated by fluorescent lights. There were no windows, no decorations, no clocks. Most striking for an 'interview,' no recording devices. The only furnishings in the room were a simple steel table and two matching chairs. In one corner was a checker-plate aluminum toolbox, a bucket containing water and a washcloth, and a pile of towels on the floor.

At the center of it all was the guest of honor—Sebastian

Goulding. Recalled from Caracas, he'd been told his replacement needed to speak with him about the management of human assets in Cuba. From the airport, he'd been brought straight to Havana Station and, unsuspecting, straight into the interrogation room. Not Gitmo, famous for 'enhanced' interrogation techniques, but, Jacob was sure, winding up here at the US embassy wasn't much better. According to Dundas, he'd been stewing alone in the interrogation room for several hours before Jacob arrived. Goulding's arms and legs were bound to the steel chair with thick leather straps. Another strap was wound around his broad chest. He was going nowhere.

Sweat dripped from his brow, soaking into his white T-shirt. His gray boxer shorts clung to his skin; there was a dark wet patch on the crotch where he'd pissed himself. His feet were bare. His head hung forward, eyes shut, breathing labored, as if he knew what was coming next. Jacob, Elijah Dundas, and the interrogator, Spencer Briggs, stood in a semicircle around him.

"Señores, you people aren't the Gestapo," Jacob said, inclining his head toward Goulding, who was breathing like a worn-out compressor. "I'm not sure I approve of this scenario. Señor Goulding shouldn't be immobilized like this." He stared at Dundas. "The man should have legal representation in an interview of this nature, no?" Jacob was deliberately playing the 'good guy' for Goulding. To give the captive man a crumb of hope, something to cling to while the interrogator did his thing.

"Interview?" laughed Dundas. "This is what we call an interrogation. Young Seb here"—he flicked the prisoner under the chin—"has carried out plenty of them himself, never was inclined to show a lot of mercy. He knows what to expect."

"That's right," scoffed Briggs, his voice rough and dismissive. Briggs had the build of an NFL linebacker and a sadistic face that would frighten off a rabid guard dog. He cracked his knuckles and donned a pair of black leather gloves. "The man told me he was good, didn't want any representation." He leaned down, face inches away from Goulding's. "Ain't that right, Sebbie boy?"

“Fuck you,” Goulding snarled, then spat squarely in Briggs’s face. The reflexive punch to the face came like lightning, landing flush on the prisoner’s nose, the sound like a piece of 2x4 lumber smacking concrete. Briggs retracted his fist, gave it a shake, and wiped his face with the back of his wrist. Blood poured in two streams from Goulding’s nostrils, the nose twisted and clearly broken. To his credit, he did not cry out in pain.

Dundas reached into the toolbox, pulling out a pack of cotton balls. He roughly inserted one into each of Goulding’s nostrils. The wads immediately turned crimson, but the blood flow stopped.

Jacob’s stomach churned. He had seen a lot of rough stuff in his years, but this room, this situation—it felt different. He knew the punch to the face was only the start of what was to come. Goulding was stoic—the CIA didn’t employ shrinking violets—but Briggs exuded a special kind of brutality. How long would Goulding hold out? Jacob shot a glance at Dundas, who stood silently, then aimed a cold gaze at Goulding.

Dundas tut-tutted, then said, “I’m very disappointed in you, Seb. You were such a...”—his fingers circled in the air as he searched for the word—“*diligent* agent here in Havana. Your assets seemed to work well with you. The intel they brought in was useful. We were sorry to see you go. And now...” He sighed. “Such a disappointment.” He paced back and forth for a moment.

Briggs, waiting to be let off the leash, looked on wide-eyed as the station chief spoke.

“Lucky for us here in Havana,” Dundas continued, “Your successor, Arnold, turned out to be much more trustworthy than you.” He half-winked at Briggs, who unleashed a bitch-slap. The unsuspecting Goulding grunted as his head rocked to the side. “Now,” Dundas said as if the slap hadn’t happened, “before Spencer can have his wicked way with you, Señor Vargas would like to ask you a couple of questions. If you answer truthfully, Spencer will not touch you again, and you can have a shower and a hot meal. In a few hours, you’ll be on a plane to Florida.”

Getting this wrapped up quickly was a priority for Jacob. Not only did he want to spare Goulding from the worst of the interrogator's depravity, if he didn't confess, Jacob would need to get to Bauta, pick up Espinosa, and haul ass to Domínguez's villa in time for his 2 p.m. meeting with the deputy minister. A long interrogation would compromise that. A witnessed, signed confession from Goulding was all they needed to end Domínguez's plans. Whatever it took to get that signature on paper—considering what was at stake—was justified.

"I've got all the evidence, Señor Goulding," said Jacob. "Everything linking Miguel Domínguez, his niece, your friend Botvinnik...and you. Got anything to say?"

"I've got no idea what you're talking about," said Goulding, eyes forward, not an ounce of emotion in his voice.

"Come on. Lying now does not help your cause." He pulled out a copy of the photograph showing him in the same room with Botvinnik, Lourdes Domínguez, and her husband. "This, together with the payment to you from Lourdes's shell company, which was found by the OTFI, is all the evidence needed to lock you away for a long time."

"He's right," said Dundas. "You've still got time to cut a deal. There's a confession all prepared; it just needs your signature."

"I ain't signing nothing," hissed Goulding. "Not under duress like this, and not without a lawyer."

"So," said Jacob, trying hard to conceal the rising excitement he was feeling, "...you would be willing to confess if certain conditions were met? I think—"

"No!" roared Dundas. "This treasonous motherfucker doesn't get to dictate the conditions to us. He either signs it now, or there's no deal."

Jacob cradled his chin between thumb and forefinger. This belligerent side of Dundas surprised him. He side-eyed Briggs and saw him blinking hard, fingers twitching, clearly anxious to get physical again.

“Ready to start talking, dipshit?” Briggs said, eyes blazing. “Or do you want me to show you what I’m really capable of?”

“I want a lawyer. Now.”

“Where am I going to find a lawyer at such short notice?” said Dundas. “I can’t just ask one of the embassy guys, now can I? I’d have to send for one from Langley, and that would take too long. Señor Vargas tells me Domínguez is ready to move with his plan, could be as soon as tomorrow. You confess to being part of Operation Restore Dignity, you get to go home. You don’t...I can’t promise Spencer here will listen to me when I tell him to stop.”

“Yeah,” Briggs growled softly. “Sometimes I don’t hear so good.”

Goulding’s lips gave a tiny quiver, but he remained silent, his eyes darting around the room, looking for an escape that wasn’t there.

“If that’s how you wanna play, I’m happy to oblige.” Briggs fetched the metal bucket from the corner, sloshing the water around. He slowly wrung out the washcloth, droplets splattering on the floor. Then he dunked it in again, getting it soaking wet. “Just confess to your crimes like these nice gentlemen asked you to, and I put the rag back in the bucket.”

Goulding’s breath hitched, but he remained silent. Jacob felt the bile rise in his throat.

“Or,” Briggs drawled, slowly walking behind Goulding with deliberate steps, “we can go about this the hard way. I’ll count to three. One...”

Jacob wanted to look away, but his eyes remained glued to Goulding.

“Two...”

“Come on, Sebastian,” said Dundas. “Do the right thing.”

“Three!” Briggs slapped the cloth over Goulding’s mouth and broken nose, pressing down hard with the flat of his hand. Goulding thrashed in the chair like a fish on a hook. Muffled cries filled the room. Briggs stood on tiptoes and pushed down harder, his tongue working out of the side of his mouth as he concentrated on his work.

"That's it, asswipe," Dundas said through clenched teeth. "Think hard about Domínguez. About Lourdes. Cain, the journalist. Passo, our murdered asset. He died because you ratted him out, you son of a bitch. Sign the fucking confession, and I'll make sure you're spared the death sentence."

Dundas nodded at Briggs, who removed the rag. Goulding shook his head. "No lawyer, no deal. I know my rights."

"Listen, Sebastian," said Jacob, an idea flashing in his mind. "I saw that friend of yours, Vitaly Botvinnik, in town this morning. Relaxing by a pool, enjoying cocktails. Kissing a lady. *Muy atractiva.* Very hot. Imagine that bastard enjoying himself while you go down in flames, hey? You'll never get close to a pair of tits again."

Briggs re-soaked the rag and placed it on Goulding's face. With one of his massive hands, he pushed down on the forehead; with the other, he tipped water from the bucket over the cloth.

Goulding's body jerked like he was being electrocuted, his wrists and ankles straining against the leather straps as he choked. The tendons in his neck stood out as he tried to get air into his lungs but was only sucking in water.

"Briggs..." Jacob's voice came out weak. He cleared his throat. "Spencer, I—this... I don't think this is necessary."

Briggs didn't glance at him. "I haven't even started on him yet, Vargas." He nodded at the toolbox. "I've got things in there that can take a toe off easier than slicing butter."

Goulding's thrashing grew weaker. His eyes bulged, the veins in his neck pulsing as his face turned purple.

Briggs finally let up, pulling the cloth away. Goulding gulped in air, gasping and heaving, then his head lolled forward. The interrogator stomped to the toolbox, flipped open the lid, and took out a rolled-up felt pouch. Once flat on the table, Jacob could see it contained a range of shining metal implements—surgical and gardening tools. Briggs took out a pair of pruning shears, holding them up to the light. "I'm tired of messing around, Goulding."

Jacob's teeth clenched. He turned and stumbled toward the door, throwing it open. He pretended to vomit in the hallway.

"Get it together, Vargas," Dundas said coolly from behind him. "This is what we do."

Goulding, head resting on his shoulder, muttered incomprehensibly.

"He's going to crack soon, I can feel it," Briggs said, wiping his hands on a towel like a barber about to give a customer a shave. "Just a little more time. I snip off the little toe on his..." He turned to Goulding. "Which is your dominant foot?"

Goulding's chest heaved as he gasped for breath, his voice weak, trembling. "Lourdes..." he whispered.

Dundas stepped closer, leaning in. "What about her?"

"She knows nothing about what Domínguez is up to... thinks he's... shipping humanitarian aid to Haiti." Goulding laughed, then coughed drily. "Imagine, a country even shittier than... Cuba or Venezuela. Lourdes..."

"You got a soft spot for her, that's clear," said Dundas. "But I think she's been leading you up the garden path. The woman is complicit."

"That's right," said Jacob. "We've got evidence she opened a bank account in Panama for..."

"Zhou." Goulding finished the sentence. "I know about that. Her uncle got her to do lots of shit, but she's ignorant of his... big plan."

Jacob narrowed his eyes as he stepped close enough to Goulding to smell the blood, the ammonia from the stale urine in his shorts. "Speaking of Chinese, there was a tail on Espinosa, your former asset. Maybe on me too."

Goulding nodded slowly. "Guo."

"Did you have anything to do with that?"

"Take these fucking cotton balls out of my nose. I can't... breathe properly."

Jacob ripped them out, tossing them to the floor.

"Did you?"

"Yes!" he barked. "I set Guo on to Espinosa. Not you. I don't even know who the fuck you are. Espinosa's a... liability. You can't trust him. *I* couldn't trust him. He was gonna confirm everything about Domínguez to Cain." He leaned his head back and gave a hysterical laugh. "Passo thought I was gonna pay him a fortune for denouncing Domínguez."

Jacob's eyes narrowed. "Guo's dead. You picked the wrong guy to take on Espinosa."

"What about your buddy, Botvinnik?"

"He loaned money to... Domínguez...to pay Zhou for...expertise." Goulding's head lolled, his newfound energy fading fast, eyes half-closed.

"Excellent, Sebastian," said Dundas, stroking the captive lightly on the shoulder. "I needed to know you were speaking of your own free will before you signed the document."

Muscles twitched in Briggs's jaw. He turned to Jacob. "Is that it? I was hoping to do a little pruning."

Jacob nodded numbly. "That's it. Time to clean him up, get him to sign the confession."

A moment of silence settled in the room, broken only by Goulding's ragged breathing. Then Jacob's sat phone buzzed in his pocket. He pulled it out, his hands trembling. Espinosa, wanting to know Jacob's ETA. His fingers began to type the message.

"What the fuck!" cried Briggs.

Jacob froze and looked at the interrogator, who was holding a finger on Goulding's wrist.

"No pulse!"

Twenty minutes of frantic CPR failed to revive Goulding.

Jacob would be heading to Bauta after all.

THIRTY-EIGHT

Domínguez, medals polished and gleaming, shirt collar starched to maximum stiffness, sat in a comfortable antique wooden chair on the back deck of his two-floor villa in the rural town of Viñales. Vargas would take him more seriously in uniform. The rolling hills and fields of Viñales Valley sprawled before him, dotted with farms and plantations producing some of the best tobacco in the world. Tourism had been growing here too, the town being a gateway to the picturesque Sierra de los Órganos mountains. But it was still a rather sleepy place, and that's the way he liked it.

He also liked to imagine his villa as a kind of fortress, a place separate from Havana, where he could find time to take a breath, to focus on what really mattered rather than the minutiae of his job—the administration that he hated with a passion. He was a 'big picture' guy. Yes, there were fancier places in Cuba for the elite to have their holiday homes—the resorts of Varadero, the island of Cayo Coco. But Domínguez preferred it this way: understated, private, protected.

Across the table, Rafael Varona eyed the breakfast spread, his hands hovering over the cold meats and cheeses.

"Having trouble deciding?" Domínguez asked.

"Choice overload," Varona replied, adjusting his sunglasses as the morning clouds began to disperse. "I can understand why the dirty capitalists suffer so much from neurosis."

"I agree," said Domínguez, pouting as he picked up a dainty teacup. "Just take a bit of everything, and if there's something you don't like, leave it. My wife's Chihuahua would be grateful for the leftovers."

Varona, also in dress uniform, glanced off into the distance. A black hawk circled high in the sky, then dived swiftly, moments later taking off with a small animal in its beak. He turned back to Domínguez, a smirk forming.

"Just like us, eh? Silent, focused, efficient."

Domínguez chuckled softly but didn't reply. His mind had been elsewhere this morning, thoughts swirling around the upcoming meeting with Vargas, but more so, on the Chinese involvement in Operation Restore Dignity. What had Zhou been up to? He had been amicable at the end of the cultural evening, even had good things to say about Vargas. Domínguez sensed it had something to do with the Argentinian sharing his charm with the man's wife, Ying. He reached for a cigar in the box on the table, rolling it around between thumb and forefinger. Despite the urge to light up the first smoke of the day gnawing insistently, he'd wait until Varona finished eating.

Varona cleared his throat, sensing the tension beneath Domínguez's calm exterior. "We're safe here, you know, Miguel. Your best handpicked elite soldiers are stationed all around the estate. You made sure everything is locked down tight. No one's getting within a kilometer of this place without us knowing. I can see the worry etched in your face, but you need to let the stress go. Everything's in place."

Domínguez nodded, though his brow furrowed slightly. "I know, I know. It's just—I've got this nagging feeling. I can't shake it, Rafa." He pursed his full lips. "When you plan something as monumental as we have..."

"What's got you worried?"

"It's the Chinese. They're our allies, I get that. But damn, they are so hard to read. Zhou seems to embody that...inscrutability." He paused. When Varona wiped his lips with a napkin, Domínguez couldn't get the flame to the end of the cigar fast enough. Plumes of smoke rose into the air as he drummed the fingers of his left hand on the arm of the chair. "I recorded a call Zhou made but only got his end of it. From what I could gather, one of their agents went missing. I'm presuming dead. But who would have killed him?"

Varona shrugged. "CIA?"

"That would be the ideal scenario. Nothing to do with us. But Zhou's offered no formal acknowledgment. I get the feeling he's taking some independent actions I can't control."

"What kind of independent action?" Varona raised an eyebrow.

"Maybe tailing our people."

"You don't think...Espinosa?"

A tilt of the head. "He's efficient, that's without question. One of the best. If anyone could eliminate a tail and get away with it, he could."

"Have you asked him directly?"

Domínguez took a long puff on his cigar. "No. But I think I will when he arrives tomorrow morning with the other commanders. Did you set a tail on him like you said you would?"

A nod. "Yes, and I think it was a complete waste of time. My man texted late last night confirming Raúl was in his apartment, asleep."

"You said you'd watch Vargas, too. Anything?"

"He's a lot harder to keep tabs on. There are several ways in and out of the hotel and..."

"In other words, you don't know where he is."

"My bet is he's in his hotel, getting ready to make the drive down here to interview you. How about we get a driver to follow him once he leaves the villa?"

"No, Rafa." Domínguez shook his head. "He's just a reporter, for heaven's sake. You aren't the DI with a staff of spooks at your beck and call." He took a sip of coffee and leaned back, fingers laced behind his head. "Paranoia is a crippling force."

"Indeed it is." Varona raised his eyebrows as he reached for a cigar. Domínguez nodded his permission.

Domínguez plucked grapes from a bunch and chewed them, relishing the sweetness. "Paranoia is one thing, insubordination quite another. Can you believe the police gave me the brush-off when I asked about that missing Chinese agent? Refused to confirm or deny anything. The impudence!"

"You will have them all dancing to your tune in just a couple of days' time, Miguel." He grinned. "And I can't wait to see it."

"Damn straight." He gazed over the railing. "Some will find themselves in jail for the way they've sent our beautiful country down the toilet." He tapped a collar of ash into the ashtray. "But that Zhou, I tell you, he's not his usual self. Something's got him rattled, and I don't like it."

"Seriously, don't sweat it." Varona leaned back in his chair, resting his elbows on the armrests. "Zhou's an ally; they've supplied so much tech support for the operation, and at a reasonable price. But we both know the Chinese don't play by anyone else's rules. They have their own methods. Maybe he's cleaning up some loose ends on his side before we make our move?"

"True," Domínguez agreed. "He's playing his own game, outside the parameters of his role. His ambassador is clueless about what he's up to. In fact, Zhou's taking one hell of a risk. His regime is ruthless when it comes to rogue elements."

Varona shrugged. "I've had a lot to do with Zhou's people in coordinating the weapons systems. My feeling—he's dependable. Like you said, he's got a lot riding on this coming together. I assume you've made certain guarantees for him once you are in total control?"

A slow nod. "His family runs a cell phone company in China. We'll open new factories here. And that will just be the start. Cuba will become the economic powerhouse of the Caribbean.

Old factories that have been abandoned for years will be refurbished, start up again. The Americans can keep their sanctions going forever for all I care. It won't matter."

"Whatever comes up, we'll handle it," he said, smiling. "I've got your back. The operation's still under control, and you hold the upper hand. If Zhou tries anything, it won't derail the plan—it's not in his interest. Passo, Cain, Simón—all that's behind us now."

Domínguez patted the table twice, his shoulders loosening. "You're right. But let's not get too comfortable at the eleventh hour. There's still Vargas to deal with."

"You think he'll probe deeper than just the boxing tournament?" Varona's facial muscles tightened a fraction.

"Oh, I'm almost sure of it. He's too smart not to notice the cracks in the façade. He'll be well aware that not all Cubans live in poverty; once he claps eyes on this place, he won't be able to help himself with the questions. The luxury of the villa, the soldiers looking after me—he'll see the hypocrisy of our utopian socialist narrative."

Varona smirked. "I'm sure you'll be able to handle whatever he throws your way,"

Domínguez laughed. "I'll tell him Cuba plans to make true equality a reality someday. But in our version, everyone will be wealthy. After all, wealth is a sign of success, isn't it?"

"Not the only sign," said Varona with a slight frown.

"Sure. But it's the most obvious one. I'm reminded of a story a dignitary from the Emirates once told me. When a sheikh was questioned by an Englishman why he flaunted his wealth while the majority of his countrymen remained poor, he said his own good fortune was a sign that God can be generous to those who believe. Why should I hide my good fortune, Rafa? It's also a blessing from God, no?" He finished his coffee, now cold. "I'll tell Vargas that our government plans for everyone in Cuba to have the opportunity to achieve this...and more."

"Just don't let Vargas get too close. Some of these journalists are amateur psychologists. We don't want him tricking you into revealing the whole picture."

Domínguez frowned. "I'm not that stupid, Rafa."

"Of course not, Miguel. Far from it. You are the genius about to transform our country into something the rest of the world will envy."

"What would I do without you?" Domínguez tipped his 2IC a finger salute. "Just hearing your reassurances calms me, gives me strength. Come on, let's take a stroll around the gardens. I want to show you some new flowerbeds that have just gone in. Butterfly jasmine, ixora, and some other varieties whose names escape me for the moment."

The two men rose from the table, cigars in hand. As they walked the gardens, soldiers armed with automatic rifles greeted them with salutes. As they passed a pair of soldiers standing guard near the front entrance, Varona said, "See?" He gestured toward the men, standing to attention. "We're surrounded by the best. There's no way anyone can get to you here. We greet the commanders tomorrow and prepare over the next two days. Then it's battle stations on Sunday morning."

Domínguez nodded, his thoughts switching to the control-room bunker beneath the villa, from where he, Varona, and a team of communications and weapons technicians would oversee Operation Restore Dignity. Zhou's men had done a magnificent job of outfitting the bunker to a standard NASA would envy. All doubt must be cast aside. The plan would succeed.

They continued their leisurely walk, passing a gazebo where two more soldiers stood, chatting amiably with each other. Domínguez gave them a curt nod as he and Varona meandered along a twisting path leading to separate guest quarters.

"You know, Rafa," Domínguez said after a long pause, "in those moments when paranoia's not messing with my head, I ponder how lucky I've been to be able to put this all together. The plans, the alliances..."

"No luck involved." Varona exhaled a cloud of smoke. "It

came together thanks to strong will, brains, and good judgment. We've come a long way since you first hinted to me what was possible."

Domínguez glanced at him. "And what about after? When we've achieved what we want—what then?"

"Then," Varona replied, "your first task will be to consolidate your power, keep the right people in line. Purges, as unpleasant as that sounds, will be necessary in order to move forward smoothly. You have the vision to take Cuba into a prosperous future."

The two men climbed the stairs back to the veranda. The sun was beginning to rise higher in the azure sky, casting a golden glow across the landscape.

"I know you're right," Domínguez said quietly. He placed an arm around Varona's shoulder and pulled him in tight.

Footsteps came from behind. They turned to see a middle-aged woman in a maid's uniform standing in the opening of the French doors that led inside the main house. "Señor General Domínguez, there is a Señor Vargas on the landline. He wants to speak with you."

Domínguez's lips formed a knowing smile. "Well," he said, turning to Varona. "Speak of the devil."

THIRTY-NINE

"Want me to hang around, Manny?" said Pepe. He pulled up twenty yards behind the Skoda and killed the engine.

"No." Jacob shook his head. "Best if you turn around and head back to Havana."

The cabbie's eyes swept the scene: three vehicles parked in front of the tumbledown shack. "You sure? What if you get into trouble? This place looks creepy."

Jacob grinned. "I'm able to look after myself. A friend of mine's waiting for me inside. He's going to show me the tourism gems of the Viñales Valley, then bring me home."

"You already thinking of Havana as your home?" He smirked. "It's a shit-hole, but it tugs at your heart strings, no?"

"Something like that." There was an undefinable charm about the city, Jacob couldn't deny it, but the instinct to get the hell out of it ASAP was powerful.

Pepe gestured at the parked cars up ahead. "Hope you're not traveling in that clapped-out Lada." He tapped the dashboard three times. "Even *la mierda china* is a better automobile."

Jacob grunted. "I'd say it's an even-money bet on which is better." He lugged his bag off the back seat, trudged up the worn-out stairs, and turned to wave to Pepe. Too late; all he could see were the brake lights blinking as Pepe negotiated the tough drive back to the highway.

He turned the handle of the front door. Locked. Around the back—no door. Inside, he saw the curled-up figure of Raúl Espinosa on a bed made from what looked like old pallets. He lay in the fetal position, often a subconscious reaction to stress. Judging by the chaotic mess and the debris scattered around the room, the stress endured inside this shack had been monumental.

Espinosa's soft snoring and the chirping of insects were the only sounds breaking the silence of the late morning. Jacob decided to leave the man sleeping while he double-checked his own supplies for the next phase. Weapons: loaded S&W with two extra clips, knuckle dusters. Not much, and even they would be ditched before entering the villa. Journalist paraphernalia: legal pad and a couple of pens, miniature recording device, digital camera, extra batteries. Cell phone for backup. The satellite phone would stay in the vehicle with the gun and ammo until the task had been completed. Last but not least: salted peanuts, a can of soda, and a couple candy bars to revitalize Espinosa. Without him on board, in the best shape he could possibly be, Jacob's plan to take down Domínguez was a total hail Mary.

The snoring in the corner turned into a gurgling cough. Jacob looked on as Espinosa stirred, opened his eyes, and gave a wistful smile. He swung around to a sitting position, placing his hands on his knees. Lean, muscled, mean as the proverbial junkyard dog. Dressed only in his underwear, the man looked like he was three hot meals away from returning to prime condition. "Open the trap door and let 'em out," he croaked. "I've barely got the energy."

"What trap door?" said Jacob. *Had he lost his shit completely?* "And let who out?"

Espinosa stood on wobbly legs, opened his mouth to say something, and plopped straight back down onto the bed. Jacob was beside him in a flash, arm around his shoulder. The man reeked like an open sewer, but it barely registered.

"What trap door?" Jacob repeated.

"Under the table. There's a couple of guys in the cellar."

"You didn't tell me that when I called you." He fought the temptation to shout. "You said you'd...what was the word... immobilized them. Not thrown them in a fucking cellar."

"The dead *chino*, too."

"*Hostia!*" Jacob strode to the table, flipped it on its side, and pulled up the latch. Two pairs of eyes blinked back at him. Beside them was the stretched-out corpse. The stench from the pit was even worse than Espinosa's ripe body odor.

"Let us out," begged a man with a buzz cut, longish nose, and a porn-star mustache. "*Por favor.*" Melo pressed his palms together in a prayer gesture.

Jacob glanced back at Espinosa, his face a question mark.

"They're unarmed and not even slightly dangerous." He gave a mocking laugh.

Five minutes later, after Melo was allowed to put on the clothes Espinosa had 'borrowed' from him, the four men huddled around the kitchen table. Jacob quickly introduced himself as Vargas, an Argentinian operative working for the US State Department. The claim left Melo and Quintero with their mouths hanging open in shock. He broadly explained the situation with Domínguez.

"You know a man called Seb Goulding?" he asked both.

They vehemently denied any knowledge of the America traitor; Jacob believed them. He told them how Goulding had been about to provide the key confession to blowing the operation to smithereens but had 'mysteriously' died under interrogation. Other damning proof had been found that confirmed the plot, but, for reasons Jacob didn't agree with, that evidence wasn't enough. Now the only way to derail the operation that would destroy Cuba instead of serving its interests was to stop Domínguez. Capture him, kill him if that was the only way. Whatever it took.

Melo and Quintero affected attitudes of disbelief as Jacob

spoke, color draining from their faces, heads shaking, fingers twitching. Melo insisted Varona had sent them to keep an eye on Espinosa because *he* was involved in a plot to overthrow the government.

"They're full of shit," Espinosa scoffed. He pointed an accusatory finger at Melo. "You've known that asshole Varona for years. Done his dirty work for money when he couldn't get the DI to help him out."

Melo's mouth opened and closed like a fish, his face turning red; Quintero could only hunch his shoulders and stare at the back of his own hands. Melo finally found his voice. "I swear, Raúl! I was told to watch you—nothing more. Yes, I've been on Varona's payroll. Money's tight." He shrugged in a half apology. "You know how it is."

"I'm not convinced you aren't part of Operation Restore Dignity yourself." He banged a fist in front of Quintero's hands. "You, too, *pendejo!*" he roared. Quintero's ass lifted a couple inches off his seat.

"After I...heard...the first shot," stammered Melo, "my instincts took over. I came to make sure you were OK."

"I don't trust these *cabrónes*," said Espinosa. "They came here to kill me, just like the Chinese bastard did."

"No, no, no." Melo's head shook so hard sweat flew from his temples. "Just to watch you. I was going to save you, not kill you!" He looked pleadingly at Jacob. "I know you believe me."

Jacob looked at Espinosa. "Something tells me this guy's speaking the truth."

"What do you base that on?" Espinosa's voice trilled with disbelief. "Of course he's not going to admit he was sent to terminate me. Who would admit to that?"

Jacob thought quietly for a moment. Espinosa had a fair point. But at this stage in the game, having them on board would increase the odds of success by an order of magnitude. "They come with us but with strict conditions. Either one of us on our own could take both of these guys out. They're gonna be useful as lookouts. Provide cover if needed." He glared at Melo. "You even think about fucking us over, Havana Station will put out a hit contract on you and your family, immediate and extended. This is a small island, and I'm sure there aren't many people here prepared to risk their lives to save yours." He gave the men an ultimatum—help him and Espinosa take down Domínguez or get back down in the pit to keep the dead guy company until they came back to deal later. They agreed to the first option with the most vigorous nods Jacob had ever seen.

INSIDE THE VEHICLE was an imposing treasure trove of tech. Two QCQ-171 submachine guns in hard-shell carry cases, clips to feed it when it got hungry. There were other esoteric items Espinosa, a former military officer, had more of a handle on than Jacob did. Tools for knocking out communications: a portable drone jammer gun effective up to 2 km; a 1-km-range palm-sized signal tracker to locate enemy communications or hidden cameras; and a 500-800-meter-range tactical jammer, perfect for disabling radios and cell phones.

"Why has he got all this shit?" Jacob asked as they trawled through the gear. "Someone's clearly overestimated your capabilities."

"Or decided to be prepared. Which is more than I can say for you."

Jacob raised an eyebrow. "You know how to operate these things?'

A shake of the head. "*Tú de poca fe*. Oh ye of little faith."

An hour of head-scratching, trial-and-erroring later, and the rag-tag team more or less understood how the Chinese tech worked, aided by Espinosa's intuition as a self-proclaimed 'device whisperer.'

Four car doors clunked shut, and they were away.

FORTY

Jacob parked the Jeep on the crest of a small hill, the villa just under a half a mile in the distance. He and Quintero got out and stretched their legs, Quintero enjoying a small cigar. Moments later, the Skoda appeared, Melo at the wheel. He and Espinosa moved to meet the others under the shade of a spreading jacaranda.

They had an almost uninterrupted view, fractionally obscured by a couple of oleander bushes. "I'll drive the Jeep to the gate." Jacob held up a hand to silence the others and placed a call to the landline number provided by Domínguez. A man answered with a gruff '*Sí?*' Jacob gave the name Manuel Vargas and announced his imminent arrival. No need to call the deputy minister to the phone. *Please let him know I'll be there in about half an hour or so. Forty-five minutes max.*

"When do we move in?" said Quintero, a slight quaver in his voice. His eyes hovered in their sockets, nostrils flexed almost imperceptibly.

Jacob realized Quintero was the weak link in the group, a potential liability. However, he couldn't be totally useless; otherwise he wouldn't have been assigned to be Melo's driver. Jacob clapped him on the shoulder and said, "You wanna stay here,

Pancho? Out of harm's way?" He paused as the man remained silent. "I won't think any less of you. We could do with a pair of eyes watching the big picture." He opened the cargo door of the Jeep and pulled out a pair of binoculars. And his sat phone. "I'm taking a risk giving you this, *hermano*. Can I trust you?"

A rapid nod as he accepted the phone.

"*Bueno*." He touched the side of his nose. "Just remember, you fuck up or run away, abandon us, CIA spooks will hunt you down." He had pretended to be communicating on his cell while Pancho was driving to Viñales. "I'm sure you noticed me tapping away on my phone. That was an email to Havana Station. I named you and your amigo here." He placed his hands on his hips. "Here's the deal. If we somehow pull this off, there could be a big reward in it for you."

"What kind of reward?" Quintero's rapid eye movements intensified.

"US citizenship," Jacob lied. He turned to Melo. "You, too." Melo pouted and nodded, as if such a reward was only fair. Jacob didn't make the same promise to Espinosa, who he knew would never accept.

"Before you go anywhere in that Jeep, we've gotta do something about the tags," said Espinosa. "The vehicle belongs to the Chinese embassy; it's got diplomatic plates. I wouldn't put it past Domínguez to have his own LPR cameras set up at the entrance gate."

Jacob swore under his breath. "I was planning on telling him I rented it if he asked me."

A head shake. "Bad idea. Rental car plates start with a T, for *turismo*."

"Where the hell do we get a set of those?"

"I'll get them," said Melo. "The main part of town is over there." He extended his arm to the east. "There's bound to be some tourists checking out the tobacco farms in the area. There's a tool box in the Skoda."

Twenty-six minutes later, Melo was back, grinning like a kid who'd stolen a cookie from his mom's jar. He screwed on the stolen plates, stood back, and made a show of dusting off his hands. Jacob prayed the ruse would give them time before the owners of the switched plates reported it.

The men stood in a ring and put their hands out, laying one on top of the other. "We do this because we must," said Jacob. "Everybody ready?"

A chorus rang out by the side of the dusty road. "Sí!"

THE JEEP'S tires crunched gravel as he steered down the meandering 200-yard driveway. Unarmed and with only his wits as weapons, Jacob's heart thundered inside his chest with each yard traversed. The gates opened automatically when he was a couple of car lengths away. An unsmiling uniformed guard appeared, semi-automatic slung across his shoulder. He stopped Jacob going any farther with the show of a palm. His granite face was anything but welcoming.

"Papers!" he barked.

"*Por supuesto.* Of course." A passport changed hands; the guard looked at it for nearly a minute, switching his gaze back and forth between the photo and the man behind the wheel.

"Step out of the car, please, Señor Vargas."

A pat-down, then a pass through a metal detector. No alarms triggered, except for the careening heartbeat Jacob felt under his shirt. On the other side of the detector, another guard placed Jacob's bag on a desk, pulled out every item, held it up to the light, and placed it to one side. Once examined, everything was placed back in the bag. No words were spoken during the entire performance.

With the bag back over his shoulder, Jacob walked up a set of sweeping spiral stairs in the company of the second guard, loose-limbed and slightly more relaxed than his partner. Along a broad corridor to a pair of double doors. The guard executed a rapid quadruple finger tap on the wood, then two slow taps. A code?

"Come in!" A booming baritone.

Jacob recognized the voice.

Domínguez.

The guard ushered Jacob inside and took up a position by the door. The grand drawing room was striking in its opulence. Beside a pair of French doors looking out onto a balcony, Domínguez sat in a high-backed rattan armchair, resplendent in his military dress uniform. Next to him sat another man in uniform, sharp-featured with a pencil mustache. Domínguez rose to his full height, which Jacob guessed to be about 6'3". He introduced the other man as his adviser, Colonel Rafael Varona. The walls were lined with bookshelves, jam-packed with leather-bound tomes. A grand piano, a credenza supporting a box of cigars and numerous decanters, and a couple of chesterfield sofas rounded off the furnishings. On the brilliant-white walls hung a number of surrealist oil paintings.

"Would you like a drink before we start?" said Domínguez, gesturing to a third rattan chair, then glancing at the rum bottles on the credenza.

Alcohol-inspired courage was tempting. "No thanks."

"A coffee then?"

"Why not?"

"Me too," said Varona in the firm tone of a man who didn't enjoy being told what to do.

Ten minutes after the middle-aged maid brought fresh coffee, genuflecting when she withdrew, Domínguez smoothed the tops of his trousers and said, "Please, Señor Vargas, let's commence. I have rather pressing matters to attend to this afternoon."

"Of course," said Jacob. "Mind if I take some photos first? Naturally, you get to approve or reject them."

Domínguez waved—*go ahead.* He jutted out his chin and puffed out his chest as Jacob stalked around the room, snapping off photo after photo. Domínguez was happy with half of the images but demanded the others be deleted. He had no objections to the recording device being used—after Varona gave it the once-over. Jacob swallowed hard when the 2IC told him he was a gadget freak with a degree in electronic engineering. Thank God Jacob had only brought devices that did what they were designed to do and no more.

"Tell me about what Cuba means to you, Deputy Minister," said Jacob, pen poised. "I like to start with a broad brush."

"Cuba is the pearl of the Caribbean. Yes, she has lost some of her luster, but we in the government are working hard to restore our proud nation to her former grandeur."

Jacob scratched his nose and waved his pen around. "Like this magnificent villa?"

He nodded. "Exactly. Do not think this has been staged for you. It is like the beautiful theater we attended together. A reminder of what we once had, and what we will *all* have again."

Jacob glanced at Varona quickly, who was smiling beatifically as his boss waxed lyrical.

"Excellent," said Jacob. He jotted down some meaningless words, then looked up at Domínguez. "Very quotable. I can see you are used to giving speeches and the like."

"Part of the job." He sipped dark rum from a fine crystal glass. "Another part of my job is the important meeting I told you about. Time is marching on. Perhaps you can get to some specific questions?"

Jacob blew out his cheeks and checked his watch. Hopefully the group could get close enough for Espinosa to engage the comms jammers before they were spotted. He'd seen no drones on the drive to the villa, and his gut told him there were none. Domínguez was walking a tightrope: he needed to be secure at the villa, but he was operating on the margins without the blessing of his government. Drones constantly buzzing around in the sky near his country retreat could trigger alarm bells.

"Tell me what the upcoming international boxing tournament means for Cuba, but on a more personal level, for you and your family's legacy. What would your Uncle Agosto think about the way things are opening up?"

Domínguez began to relax, to ramble, as if there was no important meeting scheduled in his diary. He spoke for five minutes straight, barely drawing breath. If there had been a genuine article to go with the exaggerated bullshit Domínguez was spinning, it would probably have interested a lot of readers around the world. Real articles about the man, when they did come out, would be scathing. Jacob realized he had to strike soon, while Domínguez was showing trust.

"And so," concluded Domínguez, "I'm sure the positive effects of the tournament will be felt long into the future."

"Excellent, excellent," Jacob mumbled as he wrote more notes. He looked up, squinting. "Is there a bathroom I can use? The coffee's gone straight through me."

The guard escorted him to a cavernous bathroom with gold faucet fittings, marble benchtops, even an air-blower to dry his hands. A quick search of the vanity unit came up with some spare toilet paper, air freshener, liquid soap and...a toiletries bag. Inside the bag—a nail trimming kit. In that kit—a nail file with a sharp hook on the end. Not essential to pull it off, but the dramatic effect would be perfect.

Back in the drawing room, Domínguez and Varona were on their feet, talking at close quarters. The atmosphere was one of finality. The interview was done.

But not for Jacob.

"Thanks for coming," said Domínguez, tossing down the remainder of his shot of rum. "Esteban will see you back to your vehicle. Would you email me a draft of the article before it's published?"

"Of course." Jacob smiled, then bent to gather his things into his bag. He stood up and said, "You know, I forgot to ask you something."

"What was that?"

"Were you a boxer yourself?" Jacob's voice held just the right amount of curiosity. "You've got the build of a heavyweight."

"Cruiserweight, actually. And yes, I did some boxing back in the day." Domínguez grinned. "I even competed nationally."

"I was just thinking," Jacob said, chuckling nervously, "you probably have some brilliant moves. I'm so uncoordinated, it's embarrassing."

Domínguez's grin widened. "It's never too late to learn, Señor Vargas. I've got a couple of minutes up my sleeve. Let me show you some techniques."

The man's ego simply could not let the opportunity slip. "Really?" Jacob put down the bag. "I'd be honored."

Domínguez rolled his shoulders and flexed his fingers. He beckoned to Jacob, motioning for him to move closer. "Let me show you some jabs and blocks. Basic stuff."

Jacob stepped forward, heart thundering, affecting an awkward laugh. He let Domínguez flick out a couple of light jabs that stopped just short of his nose. "You need to try and block my shots. I could have knocked you out just now. Keep your hands up, like this."

Jacob took a half step back, nodding. "Gotcha." Domínguez threw out more left jabs, and Jacob held up his hands and half ducked his head at the same time, eyes directed at the floor. He even gave a girlish squeal for good measure.

"No!" bellowed Domínguez. "Looking away is asking for trouble."

"I'm very sorry," Jacob said, blinking rapidly. "I'm hopeless at this."

Domínguez sighed. "Pay close attention. I'm only going to show you this once." He took Jacob's wrists in a firm but controlled grip, putting them in a staggered defensive position. "Make strong fists, Vargas. Left hand out front, right tucked just behind. You block like this, then counter with—"

Jacob struck like lightning. His hands slipped free of

Domínguez's grip like he was covered in Vaseline. In one swift move, he was behind Domínguez, trapping him in a fierce headlock with his left arm. With his right, he pressed the nail file against the man's neck. He dug it into the skin a millimeter or two, dragging the tool until a trickle of blood appeared. He heard Varona gasp.

Domínguez struggled, but his resistance was only met with a tightening of the headlock. He gurgled and spluttered, his legs buckling as reality set in. The worst thing now would be for Domínguez to faint, so Jacob eased up a tad on the pressure.

"Don't fight me, or I'll stick you like a pig," Jacob hissed. He reached down quickly, slipped the nailfile into his pocket, and snatched the pistol from Domínguez's holster. Military men often wear an unloaded weapon for ceremonial purposes, but Jacob guessed this one was loaded with a full clip. He flicked the safety up with his thumb and pushed the end of the barrel into his captive's temple.

"It's not loaded," said Varona, leveling his own gun in Jacob's general direction. The guard, Esteban, also had his weapon trained on Jacob.

Jacob laughed sarcastically. "You reckon his isn't loaded, and you're aiming at me like yours is. You must think I'm the biggest idiot ever born." He moved the weapon down an inch. With the muzzle tucked behind Domínguez's fleshy earlobe, Jacob shielded his own head behind the Deputy Minister's and squeezed the trigger. The noise was deafening—he wouldn't have been surprised if Domínguez had just sustained a perforated eardrum. In a split-second, Jacob again pressed the muzzle against Domínguez's temple. The general groaned as blood drizzled onto the floor. "You're a dead man, Vargas."

Jacob tightened his grip on Domínguez, watching an antsy Varona out of the corner of his eye. The guard's extended arms holding his gun were shaking, the man clearly awaiting instructions. Jacob would be the one to give those instructions. "You two gentleman, sit down on the ground, toss your weapons over here, then flip onto your stomachs," Jacob commanded.

"Rafa...Esteban...do what he says." Their boss's voice shook.

The men slid their guns across the floor, adopting a prone position. "Lace your fingers behind your heads."

Again, instant compliance.

"He won't get far with five other soldiers on the grounds," grunted Domínguez. "They would have heard the shot."

"Esteban!" Jacob could feel Domínguez's sweat and blood on his forearm. "On second thoughts, go and tell your amigos that the deputy minister and Señor Varona have been arrested for treason. The other guards are to wait in the front garden, unarmed. The police will be here in the next hour. Once you've addressed the men, come back here. Bring some rope or whatever you can find so I can tie up these treasonous swine until the police arrive. If everyone cooperates, the punishment will be a lot more lenient."

Esteban leapt to his feet. Frozen by fear and indecision, his chest heaved as he contemplated the surreal situation he found himself in.

"Do it!" Jacob hissed. "Or both of these men die and you go to prison for the rest of your life."

Esteban fumbled with the door handle, backed out, and disappeared. Footsteps thundered down the corridor, grew faint, then faded out.

Jacob pushed Domínguez to his knees, blood continuing to drip from his wound. "Hands behind your head. Don't make a sound, do not move."

"Señor Vargas, I don't know why—"

"*Silencio!*" The butt of the Makarov connected hard with the top of Domínguez's skull, drawing a yelp. "It must be embarrassing getting pistol whipped with your own gun," Jacob mocked. "Now shut up unless you want your other ear shot off. Only speak if I ask you a question."

The same knock came on the door that Esteban used when he had admitted Jacob around 30 minutes ago. Four fast taps, two slow. Esteban entered, brandishing a coil of rope. As he took it Jacob said, "What's happening downstairs?"

"The men will return their weapons to the armory and assemble in the front garden as you asked."

"Got something to cut this with?" said Jacob, glaring at Domínguez. "Is there a knife in here somewhere?"

Domínguez shook his head.

Didn't matter; he'd tie them all up like prisoners on a chain gang. He began with Domínguez, looping the rope around his wrists and tying them tightly behind his back, then wrapping the length around his chest and arms, pinning them to his sides in a figure-eight pattern. Without stopping, he dragged the rope to Varona, securing his wrists the same way before binding his arms to his torso, threading the rope through the looped sections to ensure it stayed tight. The guard came next, his wrists tied behind him and his body wrapped tightly, just like the others. With all three now bound, Jacob used what was left of the rope to tie their ankles together in a daisy chain. He finished with a hitch knot.

Jacob stepped back, taking a moment to assess the situation. He'd pulled it off. Domínguez, Varona, and the guard, all trussed up and quiet. Hopefully, the guards downstairs had been convinced by Esteban. He couldn't assume it, though. Or even that he'd passed the message on at all. If the other soldiers decided to fight back, using Domínguez as a human shield should be enough to get them clear.

Jacob pulled out his phone and snapped a few photos of the scene. He called Espinosa. "It's nearly done. I've got them tied up. Get the others ready and walk to the gates now. Is Pancho still observing from the car?"

"*Sí.*"

"*Bueno*. There are at least five guards remaining on the property. They should surrender when you arrive, but be prepared for resistance."

FORTY-ONE

Esteban's pulse pounded as he felt the strain of the rope against his chest. This slick interloper had tricked his bosses. He wasn't who he claimed to be, that was certain. Who knew what he had planned next? One thing was certain: Argentinian journalists did not arrest Cubans, especially not patriotic ones like the general and the colonel. If he was legit, Vargas would have produced ID showing he had authority to make the arrest. The man was a liar and God knew what else. Esteban had told his comrades the sound of the gun firing was an accident, that they should go about their duties as usual. This foreigner scum wouldn't get away with whatever he was playing at.

The restraint technique training kicked in. Slowly, he began flexing his wrists, feeling the rough rope shift ever so slightly. *Keep calm*, he told himself. *Make no sound*. The knot around his wrists was good and would have kept most people immobilized. But it wasn't perfect—Vargas had tied it too quickly, not taken enough care. Millimeter by millimeter, Esteban's hands found more freedom, his fingers growing numb from the strain. Sweat beading on his forehead, he felt the rope give... just enough to wriggle one hand free. With Vargas busy talking to someone on his phone—watching his captives but not *seeing*—Esteban waited. Then

Vargas turned his back, speaking with more urgency. Esteban had to act now, or the chance would be lost. He flexed his pectoral muscles, relaxed them again, and the rope went slack. He shot a glance at Domínguez, a kind of paternal love emanating from the boss's eyes. Esteban blinked at Varona, whose eyes glowed like embers. The man was clearly ready for retribution. First things first. He reached for the knots around his ankles and quietly freed his legs. He paused, looking for the moment when he could take Vargas down.

OUT OF THE corner of his eye, a blurry motion. A hand reaching for one of the pistols on the floor.

"*Mierda!*" Jacob yelled, diving for cover as the guard fired a shot. The bullet fizzed, slamming into the wall behind him.

Jacob rolled to the side, never taking his eyes off Esteban. A second guard barged into the room, gun drawn. Guard two fired another shot as Jacob rolled again. As he rolled, more bullets sailed by, shattering glass and thudding into walls. One connected, found the meaty part of his calf; an agonizing pain arced up his leg.

He found cover behind an oversized ottoman and let fly with two shots of his own from Domínguez's gun. The guards ducked, giving Jacob the fraction of a second he needed to shoulder his way through the French doors. Limping along the balcony, blocked off by walls at either end, the only escape route was over the edge. With the angry voices of Esteban and his comrade screaming at him, he clambered over the concrete railing and fell ten feet to the cushioning foliage of a hibiscus hedge. Grimacing in pain, he dismounted onto the lawn, gripping the pistol like it was glued to his hand.

He stood, assessing his surroundings for the best way out. The villa was surrounded by a high, green metal wall; the only way in and out was through the front gate, on the opposite side of the property. From his position, he could make out an automatic back gate 60 yards away, but it was shut tight.

He scrambled to the nearest corner of the building. Bullets sprayed all around him as Esteban and his friend let fly from the balcony. He sheltered behind a column and peered around a corner. A lone guard had his semi-automatic rifle raised as he marched toward Jacob's position. Jacob tensed behind the brickwork as the guard squeezed off shots. Mortar and brick fragments flew before Jacob's eyes. He had to take the guy out, or he was one hundred percent dead. He dropped and rolled again, gripped the Makarov in two hands, and fired mid-roll while the guard was refocusing. Three shots, one bullet catching the man squarely in the left eye.

Jacob crawled to the fallen guard and relieved him of his AK-12 rifle. One dead, five to go. And maybe Domínguez and Varona were re-armed by now. He hobble-sprinted to a large concrete fountain, its ornate bowl held up by figures of six naked women. Under its cover, he called Espinosa.

"Where are you?"

"We're almost there," Espinosa barked. "Hold on."

Jacob regretted making Quintero stay at the observation post. An extra hand at the villa would have come in handy. He pressed his back against the cool stone of the fountain, the ringing in his ears from the gunfire still acute. His leg throbbed with pain where the bullet had gone through the flesh. It hurt like a motherfucker, but he didn't have time to think about it. His focus was on surviving the next few minutes, making sure Domínguez and Varona didn't slip away.

He crouched low, trying to get a sense of the guards' positions. They'd be coming soon from all directions, sweeping the gardens, figuring out where he was. His only hope was if Espinosa and Melo arrived soon and neutralized the soldiers before they had a chance to flank him. Not easy with the numbers stacked against them.

"Things have escalated," Jacob hissed. "No time for comms

jammers or any of that shit. It's turned into a fucking gunfight, and my team is short a couple of players. They're coming for me. What's your ETA?"

"We're minutes away," Espinosa responded. "Sit tight."

"Easy for you to say. Just hurry up!"

Another loud voice. Jacob glanced around the edge of the fountain and spotted movement by the side balcony. A guard was yelling as he sprinted along the length of the building, his rifle raised and ready. Jacob took a deep breath, leveled the AK-12, squeezed the trigger, and held it.

Barking shots echoed, and the guard dropped. Two soldiers down: four and the two plotters to go. The rest of the soldiers would be converging on his position any second now. He thought of Irina, how he would never see her again. It was only a matter of time: he was outmanned and outgunned. But he wouldn't go down easily.

Jacob crawled to the other side of the fountain, scanning the area again. Out of the corner of his eye, he caught sight of a silver flash. He turned his head: a Toyota Land Cruiser heading for the shut back gate. Then the deputy minister, a bandage wrapped around his head, moving quickly, hurrying toward the vehicle. Esteban was walking in reverse with his back to Domínguez, waving his rifle from side to side.

Jacob lined up Esteban in his sights, ready to squeeze the trigger. *Down the bodyguard, then the main target.* The metal gate began to roll on a track. Jacob held his breath, about to fire, when a motorcycle zoomed in front of his quarry. The dress uniform—Varona. Jacob pressed the trigger, but the bike was already out the gate in a cloud of dust. His bullets flew wide, allowing Domínguez and Esteban time to clamber inside the vehicle. Jacob kept firing, but it was too late.

"Raúl!" Jacob roared into his phone. "They're making a break for it. They've gone out the back gate."

He pushed himself up, ignoring the pain in his leg, and darted toward the driveway. As he sprinted—as best as he could holding a cell phone, hampered by a gunshot wound and toting a rifle—a sharp double crack split the air. The shots came from the second-story balcony. Jacob dived instinctively, rolling across the lawn as a second burst rang out. He got up and zig-zagged to get behind a cedar tree that stood close to the back gate.

Jacob gritted his teeth in frustration. He toyed with the idea of giving chase on foot; maybe he could shoot out the tires from a distance. But leaving the cover of the tree was certain death.

The sound of the Jeep's roaring engine mingled with bursts of gunfire. Jacob turned to see Espinosa, grinning maniacally behind the wheel, and Melo leaning out of the passenger side, the barrel of the Norinco automatic rifle pointing out the window. Melo fired off a couple of rounds as the car skidded to a stop near Jacob. The guards ducked for cover, the sudden assault putting them on the defensive. Espinosa leapt out of the driver's seat, spraying bullets at the balcony. Together with the fusillade coming from Melo's gun, it was enough to ensure the guards kept their heads down.

Espinosa reached Jacob, grabbing him by the shirt collar. "Come on!" He looked down and saw the bloodied trousers. "You hit?"

Jacob shook his head. "It's nothing. More important, did you see the Land Cruiser on your way here?"

"*Sí.*"

"Why didn't you chase it?" Jacob bellowed.

"We had to get the Jeep from round the front, didn't we? The we had to get you, *hermano*." He thumped Jacob on the shoulder. "But don't worry. Pancho called me, told me he could see where they're heading. There's only one place they could be going on that road. Puerto Esperanza."

Jacob didn't need to be told twice. He hauled himself into the back seat, his breath coming in short gasps. Espinosa slammed the accelerator to the floor, and the Jeep tore off, kicking up gravel as it sped after the fleeing SUV.

Espinosa's facial muscles twisted as he concentrated on the

uneven road, dodging potholes but not always successfully. "We'll catch them before they make it to the port. It's not a big facility, but he must have a boat there. We can't let him get on it."

"You've got that right," Jacob muttered, glancing over his shoulder to make sure they weren't being followed. Clear. Perhaps the guards now realized they'd been played for fools?

"How many soldiers were left back at the villa?" said Melo, caressing the barrel of the Chinese weapon.

"As far as I know two dead, four still alive," Jacob said. He added with a wry grin, "And a frumpy maid. Varona got away on a motorbike. But none of them are our problem anymore. Domínguez is."

The Jeep swerved; everyone was thrown to the left as Espinosa took a sharp corner at breakneck speed. Jacob spied the dust cloud from the Land Cruiser up ahead. The rough terrain was slowing it down. If they could close the distance, they might have a shot at stopping them before they reached the port.

"We can't let them get to the boat," Jacob said.

"We won't let that happen," Espinosa growled.

They crested a small hill, the vista of the coastline opening up. The sparkling blue waters of the Caribbean, and beyond that, a long pier that looked like it had only recently been constructed. Jacob's heart sank when he saw the boat. It was sleek and looked fast. He zoomed in on the satellite phone camera, snapping a picture. An Internet search told him it was a Princess V78. Capable of traveling at high speeds and long distances before having to refuel. Worth a shitload of money.

Domínguez wasn't just fleeing—he was escaping.

"Raúl," Jacob said, his voice tight with urgency. "If we don't stop them before they get to that boat, we lose them."

Espinosa's jaw muscles compressed. "We'll stop them."

The Jeep approached dangerous speeds that didn't match the appalling condition of the road. They were closing the gap—bouncing like an airplane in high turbulence—pulling within a few dozen meters of the Toyota. Melo leaned out of the window again, lining up the Land Cruiser. He fired on full automatic mode, bullets hitting the back of the SUV, shattering glass but missing the tires. Jacob tried with the stolen AK-12, unable to aim properly with the Jeep jumping all over the place.

"They're too close to the pier," Melo muttered, frustration evident in his voice. "If we all get out, it's a gunfight at close quarters. Who knows what weapons they have with them."

Jacob glanced at the boat again, then back at the SUV. A barrel emerged from the back passenger seat. The Jeep's windshield exploded, shattering into tiny glass squares. Espinosa screamed but with anger, not fear. "*Puta madre!*" He accelerated hard, and everybody's heads jerked back. Jacob placed both hands on the headrest in front of him and closed his eyes as the car tore along the road. He opened his eyes again; they'd managed to catch up. Espinosa jerked the steering wheel hard to the left, ramming into the side of the Land Cruiser. Jacob braced as his ribs felt the bone-jarring impact. The sound of metal scraping metal set his teeth on edge. Espinosa rammed them again, harder this time.

Jacob looked on wide-eyed as the silver SUV veered off the road and plowed through a wire fence. At the same time, the Jeep was tilting onto its side at an alarming speed. Another roll, and they finished up with the roof on the ground, all three of them dangling by their seatbelts. Even from an upside-down perspective, it was clear Espinosa was unconscious. Melo, his greasy hair hanging down in front of Jacob like a curtain, groaned in pain.

So close, Jacob thought. His stomach heaved.

A voice. "Señor Vargas?"

Jacob glanced to the right. He saw a man leaning down on his haunches, staring at him. The perspective of the angle made him want to throw up—or maybe it was the muzzle of the rifle three inches from his nose. The voice belonged to Domínguez.

"You blew off my ear, *cabrón*. What do you think I should do to you in return?"

"Hurry up," pleaded another voice, one Jacob didn't recognize. It must have been the driver of the Toyota. "We need to get out of here."

"Where are you going?" said Jacob. The end had come, but he wouldn't go out without a parting sarcastic comment. "Running to seek asylum somewhere? Venezuela, perhaps?"

"Señor!" This time it was Esteban. "Please, the captain is right. We must hurry. Finish them all off and let's be on our way."

Jacob blinked, looking at his comrades, hanging like carcasses on butchers' hooks. They had done all they could and come up short. He then closed his eyes for one last prayer.

Bang!

His eyes sprang open, expecting to see Melo or Espinosa with half a head missing. No, still intact.

A split second later came two more shots. Then a peaceful silence that lasted maybe five seconds but seemed like five minutes.

"*Hola, muchachos!* Hey, guys! You OK?"

Jacob could barely keep himself from crying.

"Over here, Pancho!"

FORTY-TWO

Like in a corny movie, one of the wheels of the upturned Jeep was still spinning slowly. He stood next to Espinosa, watching as Quintero assisted Melo out of the front passenger seat. Melo had sustained minor cuts and abrasions from the shattered windscreen. Espinosa, still reeking like a skunk, had taken a head knock but otherwise appeared uninjured.

"Let's check the damage," said Jacob once they were all out. "Then we decide what to do next."

"I can tell you already," said Quintero, a look of satisfaction on his chubby face. "Two are definitely dead." He pointed at the bodies of Esteban and another man, wearing a naval uniform, both taken out by clean shots to the head. "And one is playing possum. Follow me."

They walked over stony ground to where the still figure of Domínguez lay face down. Quintero rolled up his sleeves and spat in the dirt. He pulled his leg back and gave the deputy minister an almighty kick in the region of the kidneys. A scream of utter agony followed, a hand darting to the spot where the pointy end of Quintero's boot had connected.

Jacob exchanged a nod with Espinosa, and the two hoisted Domínguez to his feet. They removed his belt to secure his wrists behind his back. Then a look of horror as he realized one of his captors was his supposed ally. "You have helped this... whoever he is... ruin Cuba's last chance for greatness!" Finally, a head shake and a frown of dismayed understanding. "Rafa warned me..." He shook his head. "But I didn't take him seriously enough."

"Varona is a coward. Deserted you when the shit hit the fan." Espinosa tilted his head back and roared with laughter. "The only thing you take seriously enough, *cabrón*, is yourself. The president is going to be very annoyed with you, Miguel. I predict you will be the first Cubano to face the firing squad in a long time."

Jacob absorbed the calming sounds of the sea as he watched the superyacht bobbing at the end of the pier. He looked at Espinosa with a quirked eyebrow. "Raúl, you were going to drive a military boat for this asshole." He nodded toward the vessel. "Do you think you could drive that thing?"

"Without a doubt, *hermano*. What are you thinking?"

"I'm thinking it will be a lot more comfortable going back to Havana in style than the five of us squeezing into that shitty Skoda. Or, as my taxi driver might call it, *la mierda checa*."

"Hey!" protested Melo. "It's not that bad." Despite his words, he was grinning like a loon.

Espinosa needed no coaxing: he was already wheeling around in the direction of the pier, pulling Domínguez and Jacob with him in an arc. "Just let me frisk the body of the dead captain for the keys."

Twenty minutes from Havana, after enjoying a hot shower on the boat and a change of clothes selected from somebody's wardrobe, a refreshed Raúl Espinosa placed a call to the Port Authority of Cuba. He informed the man on the other end of their imminent arrival. He then called the director of the National Revolutionary Police, to whom he had a direct number from his days in the DI. He calmly relayed what had happened at Viñales and the dock, what Domínguez had been planning. The PNR should dispatch detectives and a military escort to the villa. There, they would find evidence of Domínguez's plan, as well as evidence to put away his co-plotter Rafael Varona, whereabouts unknown. There could be resistance from loyal fanatics, but he doubted it.

At 14:56 p.m., an officer tied off the *Destino Oscuro* to cleats at the Port of Havana. A group of senior detectives and a raft of representatives from other government departments greeted the arrival party and took them away for questioning.

Jacob's heart pounded as he sat in the back of a government vehicle. Would his cover hold under the intense scrutiny of the Cuban government? At face value, his identity as Argentinian journalist Manuel Vargas was believed.

In a large, sparsely furnished interview room, three police officers took notes as Jacob recounted his role in the showdown. The men had rehearsed their answers on the boat, each agreeing to tell the same story. Jacob waived the offer to have a representative from the Argentinian embassy present at the interview.

"Quite a terrifying experience for you," said Detective Lieutenant Colonel Hugo Delgado. "Getting your story when, all of a sudden, you find yourself in the middle of a rebellion?"

Jacob shook his head. "You're telling me." He leaned forward and said conspiratorially, "Although, from what the men told me on the boat, they had planned on taking Domínguez out a long time ago. They despised him and Varona."

Outside, three grueling hours later, Espinosa sucked a cigarette like it was connected to an oxygen tank.

Espinosa said, "While they were talking to me, word came through from Viñales. The place had been deserted; however, the bunker contained enough evidence of the plot to officially arrest Domínguez. Strangely, there had been no recorded security camera footage; the concealed cameras only worked in live mode. Which"—he pointed his cigarette at Jacob—"is very lucky for you!"

Jacob nodded. Had there been footage of him taking Domínguez hostage, bigger questions would have been raised, his cover almost certainly blown. "They would have dug deeper, found out I'm not just a journalist."

Melo said, "They *will* dig deeper. This was only a preliminary interview."

"The entire investigation will be very thorough," added Espinosa. "They will connect the dots. Lourdes Domingues and Botvinnik. Casamayor. The death of the two Chinese spies, Passo, your countryman, Cain, all of it. Evidence will emerge of your involvement in a bigger action. Many questions will be asked. Meaning—"

"Meaning," Jacob interjected, "I better get the hell out of Havana."

The men embraced. Jacob turned to Melo and Quintero. "If you are interested in speaking with a man called Wilfred Arnold from the US embassy, give me your phone numbers."

The men handed over cards willingly. He looked at Espinosa with a raised eyebrow. "You?"

"This is my home, *hermano*. I cannot leave."

Jacob walked away smiling, hands thrust deep in his pockets. There were good and honest men everywhere. He used the satellite phone to call Elijah Dundas. "It's over."

"What do you mean?"

"Operation Restore Dignity is finished. Have someone pick me up at the dry dock in an hour. I need to leave Cuba. Fast."

"We might have to fly you out via Gitmo."

"You think I care at this point? Just take me home."

He hung up and took a deep breath. He was getting so used to the smell of decay in this city that it was beginning to take on a quality of familiarity. He called Pepe. "One last job for you, amigo."

"Coming right away, Manny."

FORTY-THREE

The snow outside the Barclay Street pub was pelting down. You could barely see a yard beyond the windows as the whiteout intensified. Inside, Jacob stared at the red and brown exposed bricks of the wall behind the bar. Comforting, somehow. A far cry from the dilapidated Taberna del Marinero. He absorbed the hum of people chatting, the snatches of laughter. On various screens, sports played out: entertainment for the people. He nestled his lower back into the leather barstool, letting the rum warm him as he grabbed a handful of pistachios from a bowl. Next to him, Grant Fletcher sipped a pint of craft beer, the kind that Jacob thought tasted like garden compost. To each their own, he mused.

"I'm glad we're in here," Jacob said, nodding toward the window. "We might have to make camp for the night if it doesn't let up."

Fletcher smirked, took a sip, and wiped a sheen of froth from his trim mustache. He gestured toward the glass shelves behind the bar. "Thank God they've got a decent range of booze. Nearly as good as my own private collection."

Jacob's eyes followed the slender-shouldered bartender, who sported painted fingernails and a manbun. The man switched the channel on the biggest screen to a news broadcast and turned up the volume. A couple of drunk men objected. "Shut up!" the bartender yelled, his attitude belying his flamboyant appearance. "The football's still on the other screens, just without the sound."

Patrons laughed as the objectors slunk back into their seats.

The news anchor's deep voice announced: "In breaking news, celebrity Venezuelan oil and transportation billionairess Lourdes Domínguez has been arrested in Chicago on charges of violating international arms embargoes. She is also rumored to be wanted by the Cuban government for treason. Although she has lived in Venezuela for many years, she was born in Cuba and has dual nationality. Her uncle, Cuban Deputy Minister of the Armed Forces General Miguel Domínguez, has been arrested in Havana, charged with treason and a host of other offenses."

The bar went quiet as a handcuffed Lourdes Domínguez, head bent low, was escorted through a crowd by a couple of federal agents.

"Damn," Jacob muttered. "Goulding claimed she knew nothing, said she thought the payments were for humanitarian aid."

"You think she's a scapegoat?"

"No." Jacob ran a finger around the rim of his glass. "There's no way she didn't know." He fixed Fletcher with a narrow-eyed stare. "She helped set up accounts for a Chinese diplomat who was backing her uncle to the hilt. She's too rich and powerful to be that naïve."

"Pity," said Fletcher with a lascivious look in his eye. "She's a total babe."

The screen cut to a recorded press conference. The newly elected president of the United States, Hannah McIvor, stood outside a Washington, DC, tobacconist store, rebuilt after a fire.

"In the wake of the scandal with the Domínguez family and discussions with my counterpart in Cuba, who has assured me that at the end of his term, there will be free democratic elections in that country, I am delighted to make the following announcement. Effective from February 1 next year, we are lifting all sanctions and trade restrictions on Cuba. The embargo is history," she said. McIvor then reached into her coat pocket, pulling out a fat cigar. She nodded to an aide, who produced a Zippo lighter and lit the stogie. She blew out a cloud of smoke and said, "I mean, why shouldn't Americans have the best the world has to offer?"

The crowd in the bar exploded in cheers, whistles, and foot stomping. It was as if she'd just scored the winning touchdown for the Jets.

Jacob shook his head, grinning. "She takes populism to the next level. We haven't seen a president like this since Kennedy."

"She's certainly got balls—I mean guts," Fletcher laughed. "Ironic you mentioned JFK, since we've just prevented a repeat of the Bay of Pigs."

Jacob leaned over, flicked his fingers to get the bartender's attention, then turned to Fletcher. With mock annoyance, he said, "Hey, what happened to the 'and by we, I mean you' line? For once, it would be appropriate."

"Sorry. I meant you."

Jacob pushed cash toward Manbun as he deposited two drinks and asked him to close off the tab. "Apology accepted, Fletch. But I gotta say, a couple of local Havana boys helped me out big time. They'll all get honorable mentions in my final report."

Fletcher raised his pint of pale ale. "To Hannah McIvor, for ending a long and senseless embargo."

The men clinked glasses. "Those sanctions certainly hurt the average Cuban," said Jacob. "The poverty there is off the scale. They could have so much." He savored the oaky notes of the dark rum. "But the privileged—they're not affected at all."

Fletcher set his glass down. "Joel McDonald called this morning. Passed on some updates he'd gotten from Elijah Dundas."

Jacob raised an eyebrow. "What did he have to say?"

"The Chinese diplomat Zhou's been sent back to China in disgrace. Dundas reckons he's facing a firing squad when he gets to Beijing."

Jacob winced as he nodded. "The Chinese don't do things by halves. He was operating without his masters' blessing." He toyed with a beer coaster. "What about my main man, Raúl?"

Fletcher took a deep pull on his beer. "Espinosa's wiped his hands of Havana Station. Seems the National Police were impressed with his efforts. Made him a job offer, and he's accepting."

"How does Dundas know this if Espinosa's cut ties with the spooks?"

"Because the other two operatives, Melo and Quintero, have listened to you and agreed to be handled by Agent Arnold. And for now, Espinosa is happy to communicate with Havana Station via those two guys."

"So they didn't take up the offer of immigration to the USA?"

"Yup," Fletcher confirmed. "Not interested."

"Patriots to the core." Jacob gave a mental fist-pump, even felt a sense of pride that he knew principled men like that.

"Or maybe they anticipated McIvor would ease the sanctions and Cuba wouldn't be such a shithole to live in anymore."

Jacob smiled and shook his head. "Weren't you listening, Fletch? She's dropping them completely."

"Oh, yeah." He scratched a cheek. "It's such a dramatic shift in policy, I can't get my head around it."

The men stopped talking for a moment to watch the replay of a spectacular 100-yard touchdown from a game taking place on the other side of the country.

"Oh," said Fletcher when the replay had finished. "You're gonna love this—Varona? Dundas says the guy offed himself. Preferred to throw himself off a bridge rather than face the music."

Jacob remained impassive. "I'm not surprised. He was a coward." He stared at his rum, then looked back at Fletcher. "No one will miss him. One less asshole for the world to deal with." He paused for a moment, then said, "My prediction—Domínguez will be tried and executed as an example to others."

Fletcher nodded but said nothing.

New images filled one of the screens. The international boxing tournament in Havana. The camera panned over the cheering crowd, zooming in on a ringside reporter. He roared words into the microphone.

"What did he say?" asked Fletcher. "You're the language expert."

"He said the trophy for best boxer will go to Jorge Martínez, protégé of the legendary coach Edmundo Casamayor."

"That the same Casamayor that got you inside the palace?"

Jacob nodded. "Sure is. The one I promised money to."

"You and your generosity with the government's money..."

"It's for a good cause. A refit of his shitty gym."

Fletcher side-eyed him. "You gotta be kidding me..."

"Never been more serious."

They watched for a moment, the camera focusing on the youthful face of Jorge Martínez in the ring, beaming with pride as the trophy was handed to him. Then a shot of Casamayor next to him, smiling just as brightly.

"So," Fletcher said after a beat, "another round?"

"No thanks. I'm done."

They shook hands firmly, then quickly embraced in a man hug.

"Catch you later," Fletcher whispered. "Take a long break. You deserve it."

"Until the next emergency, you mean."

"Something like that."

The bell over the door rang as Jacob stepped out into the swirling snow, the cold nipping his face as he flagged down a cab. As the car cruised by the frozen Hudson River, he took a deep breath. He typed out a quick message to the only person in the world he wanted to be with right now: Irina.

Don't miss THE AMSTERDAM FILE. The riveting sequel in the Jacob Hunter Thriller series.

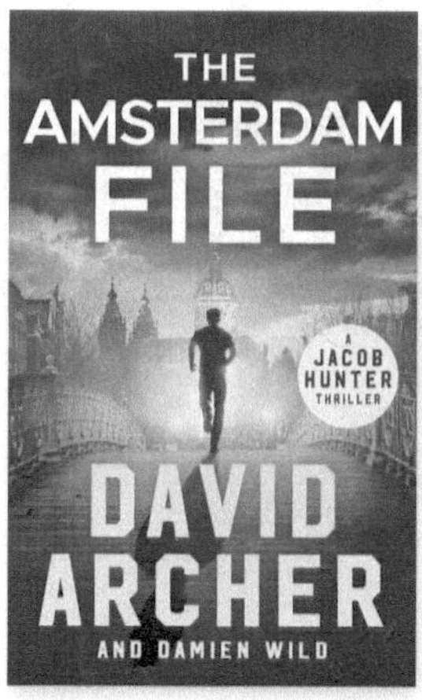

As rival factions clash and danger closes in, Jacob must pull off the impossible to rescue Irina.

Jacob Hunter's European getaway with his partner, Irina, was supposed to be a relaxing break from the spy life. But when Irina is abducted in broad daylight, Jacob's world turns upside down.

Refusing to let her slip away, Jacob defies his boss's orders to return to the U.S. and hunts for her in the criminal labyrinth of Amsterdam. A notorious syndicate forces Jacob into a high-stakes art heist, pushing him to the edge.

As rival factions clash and danger closes in, Jacob must pull off the impossible to rescue Irina.

Scan the QR code below to purchase THE AMSTERDAM FILE.

Or go to: righthouse.com/the-amsterdam-file

NOTE: Flip to the end for an exclusive sneak peek!

DON'T MISS ANYTHING!

If you want to stay up to date on all new releases in this series, with this author, or with any of our new deals, you can do so by joining our newsletters below.

In addition, you will immediately gain access to our entire *Right House VIP Library,* which includes many riveting Mystery and Thriller novels for your enjoyment. Including a prequel novella to this series!

righthouse.com/email

(Easy to unsubscribe. No spam. Ever.)

ALSO BY DAVID ARCHER

Up to date books can be found at:
www.righthouse.com/david-archer

ROGUE THRILLERS

Gates of Hell (Book 1)
Hell's Fury (Book 2)
Ice Burn (Book 3)
Judgement by Fire (Book 4)

JACOB HUNTER THRILLERS

The Kyiv File (Book 1)
The Bogota File (Book 2)
The Havana File (Book 3)
The Amsterdam File (Book 4)
The Saint Petersburg File (Book 5)

PETER BLACK THRILLERS

Burden of the Assassin (Book 1)
The Man Without A Face (Book 2)
Unpunished Deeds (Book 3)
Hunter Killer (Book 4)
Silent Shadows (Book 5)
The Last Run (Book 6)
Dark Corners (Book 7)
Ghost Operative (Book 8)
A Fire Burning (Book 9)
Dawnlight (Book 10)
Dead Ice (Book 11)
No Loose Ends (Book 12)

ALEX MASON THRILLERS

Odin (Book 1)
Ice Cold Spy (Book 2)
Mason's Law (Book 3)
Assets and Liabilities (Book 4)
Russian Roulette (Book 5)
Executive Order (Book 6)
Dead Man Talking (Book 7)
All The King's Men (Book 8)
Flashpoint (Book 9)
Brotherhood of the Goat (Book 10)
Dead Hot (Book 11)
Blood on Megiddo (Book 12)
Son of Hell (Book 13)
Merchant of Death (Book 14)
Extinction C-14 (Book 15)
A Vengeful God (Book 16)

NOAH WOLF THRILLERS

Code Name Camelot (Book 1)
Lone Wolf (Book 2)
In Sheep's Clothing (Book 3)
Hit for Hire (Book 4)
The Wolf's Bite (Book 5)
Black Sheep (Book 6)
Balance of Power (Book 7)
Time to Hunt (Book 8)
Red Square (Book 9)
Highest Order (Book 10)
Edge of Anarchy (Book 11)
Unknown Evil (Book 12)
Black Harvest (Book 13)
World Order (Book 14)
Caged Animal (Book 15)
Deep Allegiance (Book 16)

Pack Leader (Book 17)
High Treason (Book 18)
A Wolf Among Men (Book 19)
Rogue Intelligence (Book 20)
Alpha (Book 21)
Rogue Wolf (Book 22)
Shadows of Allegiance (Book 23)
In the Grip of Darkness (Book 24)
Wolves in the Dark (Book 25)
Olympus Must Fall (Book 26)
Children of the Empire (Book 27)
Wolf at the Gates (Book 28)

SAM PRICHARD MYSTERIES

The Grave Man (Book 1)
Death Sung Softly (Book 2)
Love and War (Book 3)
Framed (Book 4)
The Kill List (Book 5)
Drifter: Part One (Book 6)
Drifter: Part Two (Book 7)
Drifter: Part Three (Book 8)
The Last Song (Book 9)
Ghost (Book 10)
Hidden Agenda (Book 11)

SAM AND INDIE MYSTERIES

Aces and Eights (Book 1)
Fact or Fiction (Book 2)
Close to Home (Book 3)
Brave New World (Book 4)
Innocent Conspiracy (Book 5)
Unfinished Business (Book 6)
Live Bait (Book 7)
Alter Ego (Book 8)

More Than It Seems (Book 9)
Moving On (Book 10)
Worst Nightmare (Book 11)
Chasing Ghosts (Book 12)
Serial Superstition (Book 13)

CHANCE REDDICK THRILLERS

Innocent Injustice (Book 1)
Angel of Justice (Book 2)
High Stakes Hunting (Book 3)
Personal Asset (Book 4)

CASSIE MCGRAW MYSTERIES

What Lies Beneath (Book 1)
Can't Fight Fate (Book 2)
One Last Game (Book 3)
Never Really Gone (Book 4)

ABOUT US

Right House is an independent publisher created by authors for readers. We specialize in Action, Thriller, Mystery, and Crime novels.

If you enjoyed this novel, then there is a good chance you will like what else we have to offer! Please stay up to date by using any of the links below.

Join our mailing lists to stay up to date -->
righthouse.com/email
Visit our website --> righthouse.com
Contact us --> contact@righthouse.com

facebook.com/righthousebooks
x.com/righthousebooks
instagram.com/righthousebooks

EXCLUSIVE SNEAK PEEK OF...

THE AMSTERDAM FILE

PROLOGUE

THE MOURNERS CLUSTERED TOGETHER, HEADS BOWED as a cold drizzle fell like icy needles from a sky of tarnished metal. They gathered in a desolate corner of a forgotten Queens cemetery —a fittingly bleak resting place for the woman in the plain pine box. Sturdy spruce trees battled the rising wind, their branches lashing yet unbroken. The scene was grim, a day that gnawed at your bones.

Jacob Hunter tightened his grip on Irina's hand as she stood silently beside him. He rolled his shoulders, battling the tension creeping up his neck as his breath clouded in the cold air. He wanted it over—longing to return to his apartment, bury himself in blankets with Irina, and forget this godforsaken winter day. But for now, he remained impassive, eyes fixed on the casket, willing himself to endure.

Inside lay Zerina Mills, once a brilliant field agent, now just another casualty. Not taken down by a bullet or a knife in a dangerous operation but stolen by a far crueler enemy: motor neurone disease. Twenty-six and gone with only a few mourners marking her passing. No family, no friends—just Jacob, Irina, and a handful of Skia operatives. She deserved better.

Grant Fletcher, the director of Skia, a clandestine security organization named after the Greek word for shadow, stood at the edge of the grave. His voice carried over the wind, low and measured, as he began the eulogy. "Zerina came to us like a gift from heaven, one we cherished and will miss greatly." His gaze flicked to Jacob and Irina, their eyes darkening with sadness as Fletcher continued. "She was rescued from an orphanage in Tirana, Albania, minutes before she and other girls were about to be sold into a sex-slave ring destined for the Middle East."

Fletcher's words cut through the rain-soaked gloom. He spent five minutes outlining the highlights of her short, brutal life—a girl who bounced through European foster homes until an American family took her in. She never really fit in—too fierce, too rebellious. Intelligence agencies eyed her even before she graduated high school; her physical and mental talents were impossible to ignore. Skia recruited her immediately after graduation, offering a new identity, a fresh start—but at the devastating cost of severing all ties with her adoptive family. It broke her heart, yet she accepted the sacrifice, her hatred for the criminals who tormented her burning fiercely. She returned to Albania, determined to crush the kidnapping rings that had once tried to steal her life.

And she had. Last year, with assistance from Jacob, Zerina had led an operation dismantling the region's largest trafficking ring. Gang leaders now rotted in Burrel Prison—the worst hellhole on the planet. Zerina had done it—she'd won. But fate had other plans.

"Two weeks after that mission, it was clear something was wrong," Fletcher said, his voice tightening. "Several months later, she was dead."

The silence that followed was suffocating as the drizzle turned into a steady downpour. Jacob closed his eyes, the weight of the moment pressing down on him. Zerina had been a warrior—she deserved to go out fighting. Instead, something that no bulletproof vest or combat training could stop took her.

When his number came up, how would he go? Ultimately, did it matter? Dead was dead.

The service ended, and the mourners bade their good-byes and got into a line of waiting vehicles. Jacob clicked his seatbelt, melted into the leather seat, and felt himself drifting off to sleep.

A nudge in the ribs and a soft Russian voice woke him. "*Zaichik. Ty spish? Priekhali.* Darling. Are you awake? We're home already."

He turned and smiled at Irina, her angelic smile banishing his morbid thoughts.

"Nightcap before bed?"

She nodded. "*Da*. But only one drink—we've got a red-eye flight to Amsterdam, remember?"

A smile creased Jacob's lips. "My first real vacation in years. I'll be so glad to visit a foreign country and actually get to enjoy it!"

"Did you not enjoy your visit to Moscow when you met me?"

He roared with laughter. "Apart from nearly getting killed a couple of times, that was the only part I enjoyed."

"Worth it, though, wasn't it?"

He leaned over and kissed her on the cheek. "And then some."

Despite the day's sorrow, tomorrow promised the gift of a new dawn.

"But why Europe in the winter, Yakov? We could go anywhere in the world, somewhere warm? Australia, for example."

He sighed. "I suffered enough in the heat and humidity of South and Central America to last a lifetime." He pulled her closer, whispering in her ear. "Cozy nights by a fire in the Dutch countryside, eating Edam cheese and drinking Heineken beer. Doesn't that sound romantic?"

She twisted her lips and shook her head. "You are a cunning devil. Yes, that does sound romantic. I can't wait to get there."

CHAPTER 1

A LIGHT DRIZZLE FELL UPON THE PAVERS, TURNING them slick and slippery. Laughter bounced off the walls of tightly packed slanting buildings, pressed close together in the narrow street. Tourists ogled a seemingly unending row of casement windows. Behind the glass, scantily clad women of all colors and ethnicities—but predominantly young and white—their faces covered in garish makeup gyrated, twisted, and twirled their bodies, running their tongues around their lips alluringly.

The majority of people strolling the red light district tonight—and every night—were merely curious, eager to see how the reality of Amsterdam's nightlife tallied with its famous reputation for unfettered freedom. To them, the women behind the glass were little different from the art hanging in the Rijksmuseum. The tourists grinned at them, shook their heads as they laughed at the prostitutes on display. Occasionally a man, or even couples of various gender combinations, might negotiate with the woman, hand signals and gestures on either side of the glass. A price agreed, they'd enter the inner sanctum to engage in sexual acts with strangers as other strangers ambled past only a few feet away.

"This is disgusting, Yakov. Can we go somewhere else?"

"I thought you'd be interested to see the red light district. It's a tourist mecca." His surprise was genuine; she was no prude, in fact the opposite in their intimate life. Irina did things no other woman he'd been with had been interested in.

She stopped, tugged on his hand, and looked up into his eyes. "Zerina's barely cold in her grave, and you..."

A mental head slap. How could he have been so stupid? The Albanian woman they'd mourned only days before had fought human sex trafficking with every fiber of her being. Still, he found himself justifying his choice to come to the district. "These girls are here of their own free will. The industry is properly regulated in the Netherlands."

"Yeah, right," she scoffed, shaking her head. "And you believe that, do you?"

Jacob fell silent for a moment as an alcohol-fueled female voice shrieked with laughter. He turned to see a couple in their early twenties making faces at a leggy blonde in red suspenders inside one of the booths. "Yes," he said finally but without a lot of conviction. "Of course, some might fall through the cracks. But on the whole—"

"On the whole!" she barked. "Even if one of them is being held captive by some pimp, a gang of criminals? If the government knows nothing about her? What then, huh? Does that justify"—her hand made a sweeping gesture, encompassing a half dozen booths—"letting this filth trade flourish?"

He squeezed her hand, encased in a woolen glove. "Sure, babe. You've got a good point." He hadn't suspected his own feelings would also tend toward disgust, but it was also tempered by pity, even for the women who were renting out their bodies voluntarily. "Let's get some of that apple pie I was telling you about."

"Anything to get out of this place." They picked up the pace, navigating the rabbit warren that was known as De Wallen, one of three red light districts in Amsterdam. Irina kept her eyes down as they squeezed between the throngs of people. "You know some of those women are in the cabins against their will, don't you?"

"Could be," he conceded. Jacob could have argued that the

Dutch authorities were all over the flesh-trade, keeping an eye on things. The women had regular health checks, their welfare was a priority, and everything was hunky-dory. But that would be a lie. Wherever there were drugs and prostitution—even in a legalized and regulated form—crime flourished. As much as Irina might want to liberate them all, set them on the straight and narrow, there was nothing either of them could do. "Let's get moving."

They traversed the relatively uncrowded Oudekennissteeg, a narrow alleyway bisecting densely packed brown-brick buildings. Jacob's eyes subconsciously scanned his surroundings. He wasn't expecting trouble—he'd been to the Netherlands before but never on assignment. In theory, he hadn't had the opportunity to piss off any local bad guys. In practice, he may have. Which was unfortunate, since the gangsters here were renowned for their brutality.

The underworld in the Netherlands, known as the *penoze*, had a reputation for ruthlessness the equal of any of the better-known mafias from Italy, Russia, or Albania. In recent years, a new brand of criminal gangs had emerged in the Netherlands—the Mocro mafia. Ostensibly headed up by Dutchmen of Moroccan heritage, it also included West Indian, South American, and Balkan criminals. Thanks to these dark and violent organizations, the Netherlands, together with Belgium, had become the European hub for the importation and distribution of cocaine and other illicit drugs through the giant ports of Rotterdam and Antwerp. On the surface, Amsterdam portrayed itself as a peaceful, happy city, where everyone had the freedom to do as they pleased. And to visitors like Jacob and Irina, there was no reason to be worried. The Mocro mafia wasn't interested in the average man and woman on the street.

The red-lit windows behind them faded into the shadows as they quickened their pace, shoes echoing off the damp cobblestones. Ahead, the narrow street opened onto the Oudezijds Achterburgwal canal, the water below an inky-black mirror reflecting the lights cast from street lamps, souvenir shops, and noisy bars. They crossed a small bridge, heads bent low as a frigid breeze picked up from the north, its bite amplified as it whipped off the surface of the canal.

"Is it far to this place?" Irina asked. "I'm gonna freeze to death if we don't get there soon."

He could sense her body shivering under her winter coat. Was it just the temperature making her body react, or had the sight of the hookers in their glass cages contributed to her agitation? "You're a Muscovite," Jacob chided, one eyebrow raised. "You can't be feeling cold. It's at least 50 degrees."

"That tells me nothing," she groaned. "What is it in normal units, meaning Celsius?"

Jacob grinned. It would take her a while to get used to Fahrenheit, the system he'd grown up with. As far as he remembered, it was just the United States and a handful of small nations sticking to the antiquated imperial scale. He did a quick mental conversion. "Ten Celsius."

"This is a different kind of cold, *zaichik*. It doesn't have to be subzero to be uncomfortable."

He nodded. The humidity and the wind certainly added to the level of chill. Besides, they weren't wearing the multiple layers you'd have on in the middle of a bitter Moscow or New York winter. He was about to respond when two large males in hooded sweaters rounded a corner and ascended the short bridge behind them. He tracked them in his peripherals as they got closer. There was no one else around. It was getting on for 9:30 p.m. on a Sunday. Understandably, the crowds had thinned out with the weather not helping the tourist trade tonight.

Jacob wrapped an arm around Irina. It seemed as if the men were standing farther apart than you would expect a couple of friends to be. His senses were going off like a fire alarm. Were they shepherding him and Irina, planning a mugging on two flanks? He turned, squared his shoulders, and glared at them. Only ten feet away now, and they were moving faster.

His fingers flexed, fists balling as a reflex action. A wispy fog descended over the shoulders of the approaching pair.

The two men had barrel chests and were almost as tall as Jacob, who stood at 6'2". Now their faces were visible. Both had dark brown eyes and sported trim beards, their complexion hinting at Middle Eastern or North African extraction.

The taller of the two stepped forward, his gait unhurried yet purposeful. He stopped a few paces from the couple, his hands tucked loosely in his pockets. A packet of Marlboros appeared in his meaty hand; he plucked out a cigarette and waved it like an orchestra conductor. "Hey, friend. You got a light for me?" He spoke in accented English, his tone not exactly friendly yet lacking the menace you might expect judging by his threatening appearance. Jacob's acute ear picked the man's first language as Dutch but with the influence of his own culture, the phonetic patterns of Arabic, affecting the accent.

Jacob's eyes narrowed as he assessed the situation, sensing Irina's growing disquiet as she gripped his hand tightly. The muscles in his neck tensed and bunched, his breathing quickening. Of course, this could be a perfectly normal interaction, the men genuinely lacking a lighter or matches. His gut told him otherwise, but there was nothing to base it on except raw suspicion. The man's companion, a couple inches shorter but still a big guy, sniffed as he nodded, eyes fixed on Jacob for a moment before flicking to Irina. The lustful glint in his eye sent a message to Jacob's brain: Toss the creep into the canal. He bit down on the impulse.

There was a brief pause, an eternity compressed into seconds. The chill of the night seemed to deepen, the quiet murmur of people in adjacent streets fading into the background. Jacob's eyes looked from one man to the other, watching for a knife or a gun. If they chose to attack, there were no witnesses, no one to come to their aid. He would have to call on every ounce of his training to deal with the two brutes. Irina had improved her martial arts skills, but the odds were still stacked against them. Finally he spoke.

"I'm sorry." Jacob felt the flaring of his nostrils. "I don't have one." It was a lie. A non-smoker with a cigar excuse, he carried a Zippo in his pocket most of the time. But the real reason for keeping a lighter was utility. It was a damned handy piece of kit. You could use one in all kinds of applications: to ignite flammable items as a distraction, as a signaling device if your phone flashlight failed, or hold it in your fist to magnify the power of a punch.

"What about the nice lady?" said the second man, a slight lisp affecting his speech. "You got a light, baby?"

It took every bit of willpower Jacob could muster not to lash out at the man with his fists. He set his jaw and said, "Disrespect her one more time, asshole, and you and your friend will both be taking a late-night swim in the canal."

The man raised his hands in a surrender gesture. "OK. Don't lose your shit, man."

"I don't have one either, I'm afraid." Irina shrugged apologetically, the 'baby' slur apparently making no impact on her. "But if you head back the other way, there's a couple of coffee shops full of people smoking their heads off. You'll find a hundred lighters there, I'm sure. It's less than a minute away." She pointed a finger toward the other side of the bridge.

Jacob, blood still boiling as the second man ogled his woman, nevertheless grinned. Irina's reply was beyond perfect.

The two men exchanged a couple of gruff words in guttural Dutch, then, without a backward glance, turned and melted back into the night, their departure as sudden and quiet as their arrival.

Irina's hand tightened around Jacob's. "That felt weird," she whispered, her voice trembling slightly. "Did it feel weird to you?"

Jacob rubbed his chin thoughtfully as their footsteps faded into silence. "Sometimes low-lifes like them get a buzz out of intimidating people. Nothing to stress over."

She chuckled in the back of her throat. "*Da.* You get assholes like them everywhere. There was no shortage of that kind of thug in the Moscow neighborhood I grew up in. Probably worse than those two."

He took both her hands in his. "Statistically, we are safer in Amsterdam than we are at home in New York."

She swept a loose lock of hair from her face. "I guess so." A bright smile stretched her cheeks, rosy from the cold. "He sure backed down when you told him you'd throw them off the bridge!"

"Like all bullies do when you stand up to them. The main thing to worry about here are professional pickpockets, not muggers." A broad smile from Jacob was enough; the furrows on her brow smoothed as her stress melted away. "Still," he added, "no need to tempt fate. Let's keep moving."

They resumed their walk, conversation put on hold for now. Despite his words of reassurance, there was something in the eyes of the two men that sat uneasy in his mind. He hadn't told Irina what he'd heard one of them say before they scrammed. *That's enough for now, Hassan.* Hassan was a common enough name these days, even in the Netherlands, and alone, that fact should mean nothing. Yet his thoughts drifted back to a mission he'd carried out seven years ago. One of his first operations as a Skia operative, in neighboring Belgium. One of the key figures they'd arrested back then had tried to dump the blame on a man called Khasan—a variant of Hassan—Kadyrov. Logic told him this could not be the same Hassan. The guy on the bridge would be thirty years old, maximum. Kadyrov would be pushing sixty by now. Still, it set off a train of thought he couldn't switch off.

His brain went into hyperdrive as he recalled the details of the case. It had been a long and sensitive mission. Foiling the multimillion euro drugs shipment had required detailed planning, lots of waiting around and observing from a distance, and meetings with shadowy and dangerous types. They had failed to pin the leader, a Belgian national called Valentijn de Vries, who was slipperier than a bucket of eels. His legal representative had somehow managed to get all charges against the man dropped. There were whispers of bribes and corruption in the Belgian legal sphere.

Something Jacob and his collaborators couldn't influence. Last time he checked, de Vries was still at liberty.

Jacob's nerves had been on edge a month before the Belgian sting, the biggest to date of his burgeoning career with Skia. Working under the alias David Reeve, he'd chewed his fingernails in the lead-up, lost twenty pounds in the heat of the case, and by the end of it, he thought his hair was starting to fall out. Sleep deprivation due to extended surveillance shifts had contributed to him crashing a vehicle in a high-speed chase. The accident had left a man—a local facilitator for the crime syndicate and close friend of de Vries—paralyzed from the waist down. With the Belgian police covering his tracks, Jacob had managed to dodge the blame for the accident. Rumors soon reached Jacob's ears that de Vries, the man at the top of the syndicate whom the authorities were unable to lay a finger on, was incensed about what happened to his loyal soldier and was hell-bent on revenge.

Jacob took a deep breath as they neared the bistro. Was he wise in choosing Amsterdam as a destination, so close to Belgium? He wanted to explain all of this to Irina, but she'd panic, for sure. The men on the bridge probably were just a pair of innocents. But why push your luck? Tomorrow they would cram in a day of sightseeing, then he'd book the next available flight to Tahiti. Irina was right—they should have gone somewhere warm for their vacation.

The route to the bistro was short—a direct path through another quiet side street that led into a small, well-lit square. The square was dotted with a few late-night cafés and a bench where a teenager in a bright-red quilted parka, arms ablur, thrashed drumsticks against a row of upturned plastic buckets. His skill and charm were such that the hat on the ground bulged with coins, even a few notes poking out here and there.

Jacob, never able to completely switch off from work mode, kept his eyes alert, scanning the crowd. Irina, as if reading his mind, reached out and squeezed his hand. "You're not still thinking about those two men, are you, Yakov?"

"No," he said curtly. "Well, maybe just a little."

"You've had a rough couple of months. Nearly getting killed in Havana, then Zerina dying so suddenly. It's just paranoia affecting you, *zaichik*." She wrapped an arm around his waist and snuggled into his chest. "You said before we were safe here. Have you had a change of heart?"

Jacob managed a small, reassuring smile. "We're fine, Irina. But it never hurts to be cautious." He shared his idea of cramming in the sights tomorrow and then jetting off to Tahiti.

She let go of him and stood back a pace. A radiant smile stretched across her face. "This is a beautiful city, you were right about that. But let's come back in the spring, shall we? I need sunshine."

He nodded. "I should have listened to you. We'll return when the tulips and crocuses are in bloom and we can sit at an outdoor café drinking pints of lager and gorging on cheese."

"Sounds perfect."

Finally, the red brick monolith—the Beurs van Berlage—loomed ahead. Once the beating heart of commerce as a stock exchange, it stood transformed, hosting conferences and exhibitions like a modern-day agora. At its far end, they entered the attached bistro, a quiet haven of rustic charm shielding them from the noise of the outside world. The wooden floors creaked softly underfoot, and the gentle murmur of conversation mixed with the clink of cutlery and the occasional burst of laughter. The aroma of cinnamon and baked apples filled the air. They found a free table near a window where they could watch pedestrians, cyclists, and trams rattling along the Damrak thoroughfare.

Jacob ordered two slices of apple pie, each generously dusted in a light mantle of powdered sugar, alongside steaming cups of strong brewed coffee. As they waited for the waitress to bring their order, Jacob steered the conversation to domestic matters.

Irina's parents had finally settled in a gated community in Florida, new identities arranged by Fletcher and a peaceful life stretching out in front of them. After running from the Russian

SVR, hiding out in Latvia for months on end in fear for their lives, it was a dream come true for the old couple. The house they'd scored was big enough for Irina's son, Vova, to stay with them until she returned from Europe.

"Are you sure he was happy to go to Orlando?" said Jacob, smiling at the waitress as she placed plates and cups on the table.

Irina shook out a napkin and placed it beside her slice of pie. "Are you kidding? He hated the idea. But it will teach him a lesson in not being selfish."

"Cut him some slack." Jacob rested his fork on the plate. "The kid is still adjusting to life in a strange country. He's been bullied for being different, wearing eye makeup and dressing like an emo."

"Goth," Irina corrected. She smiled wanly. "I think that's it."

"Whatever," Jacob said with a shrug. "And on top of all that, he's got teenage hormones raging inside him; his body's changing by the month. The last thing he wants to do is spend his winter break with a couple of oldies."

Irina shook her head. "They adore him, despite Vova being 'non-traditional,' as it's popular to call non-conformers in Russia these days. He actually sent me a text. Wanna read it?"

Before Jacob could answer, she was already scrolling through her phone to find the message. She flipped the device around; Jacob read the Russian text. Handing it back, he said, "He sure went from hating the idea to loving being there in a hurry."

"It's amazing how a trip to Disney World can change someone's mind." She laughed infectiously, eyes shining in the softly lit café.

Jacob joined in the laughter, holding her hand across the table. They must have looked like a couple of love-struck teenagers.

As they finished their dessert and prepared to leave the bistro, Jacob took a final, lingering look at the cityscape outside the window. The night was still relatively young, and Amsterdam's secrets were labyrinthine and mysterious. But they wouldn't be discovering them tonight. Irina had a twinkle in her eye, and he knew very well what that meant.

They stepped back into the cold night, their path illuminated by the soft glow of streetlights and headlights of cars, trams and bicycles.

"Sorry for the tour through the sleazy part of town," said Jacob. "I should have known better."

She tugged on his hand. "It's not your fault. I might have overreacted, to be honest."

"No, I—"

She shushed him with a finger placed to his lips. "It's a legitimate tourist attraction in this city. Everyone knows that. It's just... you know...Zerina's story kind of impacted my thinking."

"Quite natural," Jacob agreed. Zerina had hated the sex industry in all its forms, and to wander the streets of de Wallen so soon after her funeral was the height of bad taste.

"However," she whispered, making Jacob jump as she squeezed his crotch, "you know I'm no prude, don't you?"

His smile was so wide his facial muscles hurt. "I know it only too well."

CHAPTER 2

They were the only tourists on board, so they sat right up front behind the captain. The sky was china-blue perfect after days of drizzle, but the temperatures had plummeted. The man at the wheel, a smooth-talking native of Amsterdam not far off retirement age, had assured them the canals would freeze over in the next week. "You timed it right," he said with a lopsided smile. "Soon the waterways will be full of ice skaters. There hasn't been a total freeze of the canals since I was a boy, back in 1963."

Ten minutes into the tour, the long, narrow boat seemed to be on a collision course with the looming stone bridge. Irina gripped Jacob's hand tightly. He grinned as she clamped her teeth. A few seconds later, the vessel slipped through the gap in the centuries-old tunnel, the underside a patchwork of moss and lichen. Mere inches separated the boat's sides and glass roof from the stones.

"*Gospodi!* My God, that was close," Irina whispered when the boat emerged on the other side into bright sunshine and a cloud of squawking seagulls.

Jacob laughed as he pulled her close to his side. "They'd never even attempt it if there was a risk of not getting through safely."

"I know that." She slapped his wrist playfully. "Still, it's a close-run thing, and you can't blame me for flinching."

"You're very safe in my hands." The captain, wearing a badge that said *Dirk*, turned around, rubbing his neatly trimmed white beard. "I've only had one accident on the canals."

Jacob took the bait. "What happened? Anyone get hurt?"

"No injuries." His large belly wobbled as he chuckled. "Only my pride was wounded. A little kid escaped from her parents, came running up the aisle, and crashed into my legs. I lost balance, yanked down on the wheel, and steered the boat into the canal wall before I could make a correction. Minimal damage, but luckily the parents signed a letter to prove I wasn't at fault." He swung around and adjusted course as another tourist boat came at them from the opposite direction. "So I got to keep my job, which I've had for...lemme see...thirty-four years."

"Congratulations," said Jacob, musing that he had thirteen years left of his unbreakable contract. The end of his spy career seemed as far away as New York. He had a love-hate relationship with his job. He loved sticking it to the bad guys; he hated putting his life in danger every time Fletcher handed him a damned file.

They cruised the famous Prinsengracht, admiring the colorful canal houses with their crow-stepped and neck gables. Most had hooks attached at the top for hoisting loads directly from the water. The boat slowed for yet another bridge tunnel. Popping out the other side, they were confronted with a long yellow vessel, this one full of tourists who could care less about the weather.

"Oh, no!" cried Irina. The hulls of the two passing boats crunched together at their widest points. The sound was like giant fingernails raking down a chalkboard. Jacob and Irina exchanged a glance of disbelief. Dirk, hardly fazed, gripped the wheel firmly and wiggled his hips. He must have heard the loud noise and felt the contact, but he made no mention of it, keeping his eyes firmly toward the front.

At the end of the tour, they shook hands with the skipper, wondering if his assertion that he'd only had one accident might not be the gospel truth. On the other hand, maybe the other skipper had been at fault. "I'm glad we did that," said Irina as they jumped on a tram for the next stop of the tour. "But I wouldn't be in a hurry to go out with old Dirk again."

"Me either," said Jacob. "His retirement might be closer than he thinks."

THE LINE at Anne Frank's house was mercifully short. The winter season had its benefits after all. As they shuffled along, waiting to be admitted, Jacob felt a sense of pride that Irina had agreed to come. She had needed some serious convincing when it came to this one. She feared she would break down in tears, embarrassing herself. Jacob had encouraged her to read the girl's famous diary before arriving in the Netherlands, and her emotions were already dialed in. The museum, dedicated to the heroic girl who'd hidden with her family from the Nazis in a secret annex behind a bookcase, was a must-see attraction. Jacob said she'd regret it later if she bailed on this opportunity. And so she'd relented.

Inside, Irina's worry that she would lose her shit came true. Her eyes were brimming with tears minutes after ascending the steep stairs to the secret rooms. Only she wasn't embarrassed at all. She was in good company. Among the handful of others in their small tour group, all of the women and one old man could not control the flood of tears. Although also moved by what he heard through his earpiece and what he saw in the cramped space, Jacob held his emotions in check. He knew Anne Frank's story backwards, having read the famous diary a couple of times, plus a lot of other material on the Holocaust. Under the protection of patriarch Otto, the Franks and four other refugees had hidden in a tiny space, surviving off rotten potatoes and scraps. Most important, they had to keep absolutely quiet when outsiders came to the premises. Virtual house arrest for two long years. As the wooden floors creaked under his boots, Jacob could only imagine the terror they felt on the other side of the partition every time they heard strange noises and voices. Jacob had seen the horrors of Auschwitz in Poland, walked the vast empty fields, seen the suitcases and shoes of the dead, their bunks, the crematoria, the gas chambers. And yet, somehow the intimacy of the tiny house on the canal made the plight of these victims even more profound.

Outside on the street an hour later, Irina's eyes were red and spider-veined from constant crying. "I'm sorry, Yakov. I..."

He wrapped his arms around her as she buried her damp cheeks in his overcoat. "Nothing to apologize for. A couple of years ago, before I got inured to man's capacity for cruelty, I would have reacted exactly the same way."

She pushed herself away half a pace, staring up at him with incredulous eyes. "Bullshit. I have *never* seen you cry. Even when you speak about Sally-Anne Vincent, you only have determination on your face. Never grief."

He pursed his lips hard. She was right. "That happened over twenty years ago. The pain fades over time. Now it's just a dullness in my heart."

"*Nyet*, Yakov. That's also not true. In case you'd forgotten, I've spent dozens of hours—I wouldn't be surprised if it was over a hundred—trawling through databases for you, digging into archives, looking for that clue that will find whoever killed her." She jabbed a finger at his chest. "So I know exactly how obsessed you are with her."

He swallowed hard, then cleared his throat. "Come on. That's not fair. I simply want justice for Sally-Anne."

"Yes. And you vowed to never stop looking for the killer." She smiled warmly. "I'm not jealous of a dead girl from your past. But you know, I'm now as determined as you are to find the answer; then at least I know you'll be focused a hundred percent on me."

Every fiber of his being ached for Irina, but he wouldn't ever shed tears in her presence. Was he physically incapable? he wondered. Her ability to push jealousy aside, to understand his need to see this through to the end, melted his heart. "For the rest of this trip—and after we leave for Tahiti tomorrow—you will be my total focus. I love you, and that's all there is to it." He looked around to get his bearings. He'd memorized the map of greater Amsterdam, brought to mind the grid of the streets and walkways they needed to take to get to their next destination. "One more sight for the day, and then we're done, OK? Like I said, we'll come back another time. In my humble opinion, Amsterdam is the most beautiful capital in Europe, and you deserve to see it in its full glory."

Irina fished out a flyer from her jacket pocket and rested her finger on an attraction that she'd circled with black ink. "I want to go here."

He took the pamphlet, folded it up and handed it back. "The Heineken brewery?"

She nodded enthusiastically. "Why not? You get a free beer as part of the tour."

He frowned. "I was hoping to take you to the Rijksmuseum. Aren't you interested in seeing famous paintings by the Dutch masters? Rembrandt, Vermeer?"

She shook her head. "I know you value honesty, *zaichik*." She sighed and exhaled, sending out a cone of steam in the cold air. "After that harrowing experience at the Anne Frank house, I'd like a pint or two of lager followed by a sauna back at the hotel. Then you can rub my back, get me nice and relaxed. Then I'll take off your—"

"Heineken it is!" Jacob exclaimed, already recalibrating the route.

THE IMPOSING Rijksmuseum with its red brick and white stone façade stood before them like an ancient sentinel as they crossed the short Museumbrug bridge. Turrets climbed skyward, gables crowning its steep roof lines. The early sunshine was long gone, replaced by cement-gray clouds. Fluffy snowflakes began to fall obliquely in a gently rising breeze, lending the scene a fairytale quality. Despite the afternoon freeze, the line to the front door extended almost all the way back to the bridge.

"I thought we weren't coming here?" said Irina with a note of impetuousness. The timeless beauty of the Dutch neoclassical building with a hint of Gothic did nothing to entice her inside its walls.

"Don't stress," Jacob reassured. "It just happens to be on the way." He gave her a sideways look. "But since we're here, maybe you'd like to take a peek...?"

She stamped her foot in an exaggerated fashion. "You promised beer! I'm too tired to be traipsing around a building as big as that. We've got some massive museums in Russia, in case you've forgotten. The Hermitage, for example. Buildings like that can be like rabbit warrens; you're looking for the nearest exit five minutes after you enter."

He tugged her along as they made a left turn onto Stadhouderskade, leaving the lovers of culture to enjoy the museum's treasures without them. Jacob noted that, even in the miserable cold, Amsterdammers on bicycles were out in force. The clanging of the bike bells was as constant as the honking of car horns in Manhattan. You almost had to have eyes in the back of your head to avoid getting hit. Their journey took them through a linear park that hugged the southern bank of the Singelgracht canal. Naked tree branches waved eerily in the breeze, ruffled wavelets appearing on the surface of the canal. They hurried the one-third mile, eyes closed tight against the stinging snow, now more like icy pellets of sleet.

As they stood before the red-brick behemoth that was the old brewery, Jacob ventured that Irina might prefer the warmth of the cozy pub right across the street. A firm shake of the head. "*Nyet*. I want a beer from in there."

Inside, they were greeted in the foyer with interactive light displays, posters, all kinds of memorabilia. Jacob arranged for them to take a guided tour with a bunch of other tourists. Tickets and, more importantly, beer vouchers firmly in hand, he marched back to Irina, waiting patiently by a wall. As he took a seat next to her, he sensed his phone vibrating in his pocket. Then the ring tone started to play. A corny song from an old James Bond film. The melody could only mean one thing. Fletcher was calling. He knew Jacob was on vacation and wouldn't call unless it was of the utmost urgency. Irina, eyes wide, shook her head.

"Don't answer him, Yakov," she implored. "Please."

He looked at the screen of his cell and pressed the red button to reject the call. "Come on, let's go wait over there." He pointed at an unoccupied sofa twenty feet from the entry. "The tour's starting in ten minutes."

The phone rang again. The ambient noise in the foyer was growing louder, the volume of the electro-funk background music higher than it needed to be. It reminded him of the thumping music clothing stores like to play to draw in a younger crowd. More people were starting to gather near the tour starting point, their conversations ratcheting up to compete with the music. Jacob flashed Irina a look of apology. "I'm sorry, honey. If he calls twice without leaving a message, it must be important."

"More important than me?" she said with a pout of her full lips.

He furrowed his brow. "You know that's not fair."

She gave a nod of understanding. "I'm sorry. Find out what he wants. But be quick."

He stood, gesturing toward the exit. "It's too noisy in here. I'll take it outside. Wait for me and don't move. I won't be more than a couple of minutes."

www.ingramcontent.com/pod-product-compliance
Lightning Source LLC
LaVergne TN
LVHW041114080826
845145LV00007B/1810

9781636964690